TOLSTOY LIED

A Love Story

Rachel Kadish

A MARINER BOOK
Houghton Mifflin Company
BOSTON • NEW YORK

for Michael

First Mariner Books edition 2007

Copyright © 2006 by Rachel Kadish

ALL RIGHTS RESERVED

For information about permission to reproduce selections from this book, write to Permissions, Houghton Mifflin Company, 215 Park Avenue South, New York, New York 10003.

www.houghtonmifflinbooks.com

Library of Congress Cataloging-in-Publication Data
Kadish, Rachel.
  Tolstoy lied: a love story / Rachel Kadish.
      p. cm.
  ISBN-13: 978-0-618-54669-5
  ISBN-10: 0-618-54669-3
  I. Title.
  PS3561.A358T65 2006
  813'.54—dc22   2006000476

  ISBN-13: 978-0-618-91983-3 (pbk.)
  ISBN-10: 0-618-91983-x (pbk.)

Book design by Melissa Lotfy

PRINTED IN THE UNITED STATES OF AMERICA

QUM 10 9 8 7 6 5 4 3 2 1

I am indebted to Assia Gutmann's translation of Yehuda Amichai's poem "Quick and Bitter" (reprinted in the bilingual edition of *Love Poems,* Schocken Publishing House, 1986), which I consulted as I translated the poem; and to Andrew Carroll's *Letters of a Nation: A Collection of Extraordinary American Letters* (Broadway Books, 1999), where I discovered the November 1851 letter from Herman Melville to Nathaniel Hawthorne.

"This is my letter to the world," "After great pain a formal feeling comes," "Struck was I not yet by lightning," and "Did our best moment last": Reprinted by permission of the publishers and the Trustees of Amherst College from *The Poems of Emily Dickinson,* Thomas H. Johnson, ed., Cambridge, Mass.: The Belknap Press of Harvard University Press, Copyright © 1951, 1955, 1979, 1983 by the President and Fellows of Harvard College.

"Wedlock Is a Padlock" by Angelo Bond, General N. Johnson © 1980 by Gold Forever Music. All rights administered by Songs of Universal / BMI. Used By Permission. All Rights Reserved.

Acknowledgments

In the process of researching this novel I was fortunate to encounter many people who gave generously of their expertise and time. To Pat Chu, Daniel Donoghue, Laura Harrington, Alison Hickey, Jonathan Kay, Daniel Kim, Laura Kolbe, Frances Lippmann, Dara Musher-Eizenman, Rachel Riedner, Jock Russell, and Helen Vendler, my heartfelt thanks. Special thanks to Ravit Reichman.

Many friends and family extended themselves to offer support. I would particularly like to thank Susan Power, Brian Morton, J. B. Zimmerman, Michael Lowenthal, Doug Stone, Alan Burdick, and Wayne Brown; Sharon Musher and Daniel Eisenstadt, Danya Handelsman and Jed Shugerman, Ellen Grant, Orran Krieger, Tom and Holly Scott, Shannon Olin, Michelle Silberman, Laurel Chiten, and Lilly Singer. Ashley Fuller, Sarah Wally, Sandra Morgan, and Abby Brown allowed me to settle at my desk with peace of mind. To the families Brown, Sodickson, Rosenn, Harlow and Zacker, Sherman and Sherman-Kadish, Kadish and Rivkin, my gratitude . . . and a very special thanks to Anna and Larry Kadish: Grandma and Grandpa Ex Machina.

Sarah Burnes believed in this book when it needed a champion. And Jane Rosenman helped it become its best self. To them, to Chris Lamb, along with Libby Edelson and Jayne Yaffe Kemp and the whole team at Houghton Mifflin, my unending thanks.

From early on, two people saw clearly the book I was writing; to them, my thanks for being both indefatigable friends and literary conscience. This novel and its author are better for Kim Garcia's gentle questioning and pitch-perfect advice. And Carol Gilligan's wisdom, unerring ear, and deep honesty made, over and again, all the difference.

I could not have written this book without the sustaining support of the National Endowment for the Arts, the Massachusetts Cultural Council, the MacDowell Colony, and the Virginia Center for the Creative Arts. To these organizations and the wonderful people who staff them, my resounding appreciation. To Steven Zipperstein, Stephanie Singer, and everyone at the Koret Foundation: the months I spent in residence at Stanford University were a writer's idea of heaven.

Finally, to my daughter, Talia, and now my son, Jacob, my dazzled gratitude for your joyous company. And my deepest thanks, for the audacious notion of happiness, to Michael.

PART I

THERE IT IS. Right there on the novel's first page. Right there in the first line, staring the reader in the face. A lie.

Nothing against Tolstoy. I'm an admirer. I simply happen to believe he's responsible for the most widely quoted whopper in world literature.

Happy families are all alike; every unhappy family is unhappy in its own way.

Literary types swoon over that line, which opens *Anna Karenina*. But have they considered the philosophy they're embracing?

If Tolstoy is to be taken at his word, a person must be unhappy in order to be interesting. If this is true, then certain other things follow. Happy people have no stories you might possibly want to hear. In order to be happy, you must whitewash your personality; steamroll your curiosities, your irritations, your honesty and indignation. You must shed idiosyncratic dreams and march in lockstep with the hordes of the content. Happiness, according to this witticism of Tolstoy's, is not a plant with spikes and gnarled roots; it is a daisy in a field of a thousand daisies. It is for lovers of kitsch and those with subpar intelligence.

Yolanda would say I'm taking this far too personally. Yolanda thinks any idea that keeps a person home working on a Saturday night is hideous. Also, that I need to start wearing tighter clothing if I want my weekends to headline something more exciting than collating.

3

But even she would get riled if she realized what Tolstoy fans are swallowing whole — there's nothing more likely to enrage Yolanda than the topic of happiness.

For people who claim to want happiness, we Americans spend a lot of time spinning yarns about its opposite. Even the optimistic novels end the minute the good times get rolling. Once characters enter the black box of happiness, no one wants to hear a peep out of them. I've learned exactly how hard it is to find a good nontragic American novel on academia's approved-reading list. I struggle every semester to design my Modern American Lit syllabus with just one plotline that doesn't make you want to jump off a bridge. Paine's wish that "the New World regenerate the Old" notwithstanding, the tragic European tradition was hardly o'erthrown on our shores. Hester Prynne doesn't make out too well in the end, does she? Ethan Frome and poor Billy Budd and just about everyone Faulkner or O'Connor or Porter ever met are doomed. Even sensuous Janie in *Their Eyes Were Watching God* goes through three husbands and then has to shoot the best one of the lot. Moral of the story? Never trust joy. (Do not ever say this aloud on a conference panel. Literature professors don't, ever, call books depressing. The correct word is "disquieting.")

Let me be clear: some of my best friends are tragic novels. But someone's got to call it like it is: Why the taboo? What's so unspeakable about happiness?

I think people are terrified of happiness. I don't mean just Americans; this goes for everybody. And that's why Tolstoy's gotten away with that cheap shot all these years. But he's got to be wrong. If happiness — let's say, for hypothetical example, an honest, requited, passionate love — is really the death of individuality, why would anyone want it?

What I want to know is this: Can the American story have an ending that's both honest and happy? Can we ditch the venerable idea that life is meaningless without tragedy — that every one of us has a choice between numbed-out conformity or noble suffering, with no option to check the box marked "other"? Or are the doom-mongers right?

I say there's hope. And I don't just mean early Mark Twain. Look for the subversive plot twist, the wink at the bottom of the page, the sly, stubborn sidestepping of doom. I want to write about what Washington Irving implies about happiness; and Thoreau and Whitman, Eaton and Welty, Paley, Bambara, even Vonnegut. There's a trail of bread crumbs to follow. There are American writers who dare venture into the treacherous waters of fulfillment. Most of them do it stealthily, as though it's imperative not to get caught talking about joy.

I'm saving this, of course, for my post-tenure book. I'm not naive. Talking about happiness is career suicide. I'll be accused of championing pap — of responding to a book not as a critic, whose role is to dissect, but from my kishkas. Add to my crime the sin of trespassing the boundaries of several specialties. Academics today aren't supposed to address overarching concepts. We're supposed to locate within context, place within tradition, and say as little as possible along the way about the original texts. One is not to cut a skylight in the intellectual house; one is to rearrange a few sticks of furniture in the basement. Do more, and you're accused of trying to be a public intellectual. When I first understood how mincing the academic conversation could be, how capable of silencing a novel's heartbeat, I nearly turned tail. For three weeks I sat in a graduate school seminar on *Moby Dick;* no one mentioned the whale. I circled job listings. But I didn't leave school. I became, somehow, more determined to become a professor — a tenured one, able to forge my own path. I learned, when the occasion absolutely demanded it, to keep my own counsel, to stay mum about the leviathan lurking beneath the refracting surface of every line. I even developed a grudging respect for the basic academic vocabulary. It may be pretentious, but it serves a function. It's the antiseptic garb a surgeon dons before she cuts, for the life-and-death drama of the operating room demands that she be utterly dispassionate — her keen eyes and masked face inspiring our trust in the sureness of her hands, their innocence of the germs of easy emotionality. Still.

Upon accepting my faculty appointment, I made a private vow never to say "simulacrum" if "cheap imitation" will suffice. Never to decry the dumbing down of American culture while smarting up my own ideas with showy verbiage. Never to say "debative quality" when I mean "argument," or hedge with "it might be said" when what I mean is, I believe.

Each morning I wake to the blandishments of my clock radio,

set to a pop station I'd never tolerate in anything but semiconsciousness. I dress, stuff my briefcase with the papers stacked on my bedside table, and walk twenty blocks to the building the English Department shares with Classics, Sociology, and — improbably — Architecture. This is home: its peculiar scrollwork and mustard yellow façade a thumb in the eye of the stately street; its narrow elevator jammed with both faculty and students, mocking the professorial discomfort with intimacy. Anticipating the elevator's closing doors, I quickstep into the building, but not before I'm handed a flash of myself in the half-dome security mirror over the door: a somewhat lanky figure in muted professional attire; pale curls restrained in a ponytail; an unadorned, up-peering face that startles me with its gameness.

I sit among books all day, lecture from them, underline their pages emphatically. Between classes I comb the library for a spark of insight left buried in the stacks by a thinker I'll never meet. You get used to it: a life mining the ore of literature. It's not as airless as it sounds. Anyone who thinks books are sterile objects hasn't really drawn breath in a library. The older volumes are autumnal, evocative of smoke and decayed leaves. The newer ones smell like glue and vanilla and import. Books have a sound, too — turn their pages for enough hours and years and you start to rely on it, just as people who live by the shore assimilate the rhythm of the waves: the sweep and ripple marking the end of a page, a sound that seems to be made by the turning of your thoughts rather than the movement of your hand.

Evenings find me at home on my sofa in sweatpants and threadbare socks, nursing a soda and doling out advice. Yolanda, my old Seattle high school classmate, now fellow New Yorker, phones with bulletins from the field: tales of relationships gone bust. It's my job to be shocked. I'm careful to share her outrage as long as she needs before helping her sift the love-wreck for salvage. Later at night my cousin Gabby phones from California to ask whether I think it's okay to date a guy thirteen years older; six inches shorter; without job or hair or visa; with accent, or wife, or laboratory results marked INCONCLUSIVE. Phone pressed to my ear, surveying my toes through fabric worn to cheesecloth, I opine. Through relinquishing desire, say the Buddhists, one attains understanding. And through having no romantic life of my own, I've discovered my calling. Tracy Farber: lit critic by day; by night dispenser of romantic advice.

How did this befall our dashing heroine?

There was Jason. He was — still is — dependable, kind, smart, prudent. Perfect. I kept tilting my head to make the picture hang straight. Walking down the street, he'd notice the signs and the shops, the grinding gears of the city. The considered pace of his observations, not to mention his unremitting practicality, made me want to run laps around the block. I could hardly explain it to myself, let alone to him. How do you tell a man you've been desperate for him to say something startling, make you laugh, even prove you wrong? That at the beginning of an argument, you don't want to know you're going to win? I kept hoping for the hesitation to evaporate so I could do the sensible thing and adore Jason back. But even in Wharton novels you can't argue with *almost but not quite.* All I could do in the end was ask him, didn't he think we might be a horse and a llama? Similar enough to like and respect each other, but still . . . a horse and a llama. That was the first and only time Jason got angry. He thought being cautious about making a commitment, when we so obviously cared for each other, was absurd. I replied that when you're an only child and you've spent years cracking jokes to cheer up your relentlessly quiet parents . . . and you've seen your father sipping a cup of tea with that expression that says *no way out,* and your mother once let drop like it was nothing that she'd given up her dream of a graduate degree in physics when she had you; and you once found a blank piece of paper on which she'd scribbled *was it worth it;* and your father sat you down at age ten to ask what you wanted to do when you grew up and then addressed you with awkward unprecedented seriousness about *fulfilling yourself* and *following your dreams,* and when one day you add up the dates and realize they got married because you decided to spring yourself on them, and your parents sometimes do seem happy but how happy, is this the love they wanted, is this — honestly? — who they wanted to be?

Then caution starts to look like the pinnacle of good sense. That is, unless both sides feel truly inspired.

I hurt him.

After Jason, there were a couple of short-lived flings. Then a flurry of dates, most awful. I got set up with New Age musicians;

solid burghers; brilliant, hilarious computer programmers who found eye contact painful. A few of the dates were promising, but only to one party. I obsessed. I was obsessed over. Bad feelings were had; let's leave it at that. I made the requisite efforts to give love a chance, along the way braving the thousand psychic shocks a single woman is heir to. At a friend's engagement party I noticed the caterer, a sweating man in a starchy black suit, checking my hand for a ring. *Don't prejudge,* I admonished myself as he approached. "Soon also for you it should be this happy," the guy lilted, his scalp shiny under thinning hair. "And when it is, you should know who to call." The business card he slipped intimately into my palm read MR. OMELETTE — KOSHER CATERING FOR ALL OCCASIONS.

My dating slowed to a trickle a few years ago, mostly because I didn't cultivate it. I decided I didn't want to be a collector of people or of grudges. I didn't want to be like Marcia, the pretty library assistant who sits in the park every day at noon fishing gourmet leftovers out of another styrofoam container: *Lousy guy, good restaurant.* I didn't want to be like my grad school classmate Trina, who, upon clearing out her computer hard drive shortly after her wedding, ran across three files titled "asshole" and had no idea which nearly forgotten ex had inspired each.

Dating emptied me out. One evening, returning from a tepid dinner with a perfectly nice man ("perfectly": adverb of dating doom), I turned on my TV and stared bleary-eyed at a nature special about the tropical rainforest. There, amid platter-sized dasheen leaves and aerial roots, cinnamon laurels and primeval ferns, were the hunter vines: stout branches that sprouted from the forest floor, hitched onto the nearest tree, spiraled halfway up its trunk, then — a dozen feet up — groped out into open air to find another, likelier trunk, around which they grew for a dozen months or years until switching to another tree and then, finally, up in the canopy, leafing out into golden sunlight. I thought: I know people like that. That evening I opted for early retirement. I told my friends thanks, but no more blind dates.

Now, at thirty-three, I'm well past the stage of being ticked off at married women who have that well-fed, big-eyed, satisfied look. Past feeling irked by the Marriage Mafia, those concerned citizens who recite dire matrimony statistics to single women over thirty, as prelude to an offer (bachelor cousin, formerly gay colleague, themselves) we can't refuse. I'm past being annoyed at married girl-friends over a crummy pronoun. ("How are you?" "*We're* fine.") And I no longer rant to my silent living room because Hannah, with whom I hadn't spoken in three weeks, told me over the line: "Ed is home, I should get off the phone" — as though she didn't see Ed every day, as though there could be no value in spending a few minutes on the phone with her once best friend. I've accepted reality: Hannah's priority is Ed, and together they form an iron-clad front. I've accepted that my single friends call because they want to be in touch; my married friends call because not being in touch makes them feel confused about their lives; and my friends with kids call hoping to get my answering machine, so they can discharge their friendship obligation and still have time for a nap. I'm past worrying over just whose world is shrinking — my married friends' or mine. And even past the ache I felt when I learned Jason was getting married. Her name is Julie; she's very nice, and rather quiet; and she has absolutely no sense of humor. Or at least, she doesn't get my jokes. But Jason is happy, and I can feel genuinely glad about that. And when that fails, I remind myself: I was the one who said I couldn't marry him, because — though I may be, as he put it, the *world's most unlikely romantic* — after two years I still, inexplicably, couldn't coax my sensible, pragmatic self to say yes to a man with whom I wasn't in complete utter total witless love.

Long ago I came to the conclusion that all married people are with the CIA. Once they were truthful women and men; friends I understood and knew intimately; people like me, whose every up and down was acknowledged and evaluated in the company of confidants. Then came the wedding. That old saying is nonsense: a wedding never made an honest woman or made an honest man out of anyone. During the ceremony brides and grooms take a vow of secrecy. Afterward, they could tell you what makes their marriage tick; they could explain how they manage day to day without throttling one another; whether they have regrets; and why, in fact, the institution of marriage is desirable in the first place. But then they'd have to kill you.

I'm retired now. My role in life: to supply patience and reason to all comers. Long after Yolanda's other friends refuse to come to the phone, I listen to her jeremiad of flopped romance. Knowing my own pessimism wouldn't be livable for her, I urge her to persevere toward her ideal of happiness — which is, after all, the purpose of friendship. And when my cousin Gabby phones from California to complain about her mother, who recently presented Gabby with four enormous boxes of dishes (Aunt Rona bought the set on sale years ago, planning to give them to Gabby for a wedding gift, "But," she told Gabby with stoic sadness, "it looks like maybe that's not going to be. So take. Use them in good health." Gabby took. She has been driving around with a trunk full of dishes for weeks, unable to bring the boxes into her apartment because of the unshakable sense that the act will curse her to eternal singlehood), I tell my cousin to put the dishes in basement storage and use the story as a joke — and if that doesn't help, she might casually inform Rona she's considering buying her a walker; of course it's premature but they're on sale.

When I can't sleep I take a book to the all-night café on Sixth Avenue. I sip seltzer alongside the giddy and the drowsy-eyed and those quarreling in foreign languages. In the tight quarters of Manhattan cafés, it's polite to feign deafness, but of course everyone listens. This is the intimacy of New Yorkers, unmatched anywhere in the world. Night after night, I listen to people talk about love. Midnight, two A.M., three: New Yorkers cluster in cafés, the daytime's distractions at last shed.

Where love is concerned, there are two kinds of people: those who think a relationship with a decent, devoted person is a keeper unless there's a resounding minus; and those who think a relationship with a decent, devoted person is a starting point. New York City, being populated by eight million opportunities for trading up, is peopled primarily by the more exacting variety of romantics. They settle on hard plastic chairs, order coffee or herbal tea, and speculate about the one they'd like to know, used to know, hope to meet: his moods, her intelligence, her breasts. The person like no other. Sometimes my students come in, and after a cautious wave pick a table far from their professor. I do them the courtesy of burying my nose deeper in my book, and send them a silent wish for luck. College students are specialists in love and its many homonyms, and can't fathom a life without them. Male and female, they spend hours in fierce debate: *Would you give up a job, a friendship, a religion, for someone you loved? Would you rather a spouse with whom you could have great sex, or one who gives great back rubs?* The café on my block harbors abiding concern over Deepsters — white guys who take a woman to a drum circle for a first date, throwing themselves into the fray of African dancing, and they're good at it, flapping their arms as convincingly as any eagle in midtown Manhattan. Men with wingspan. Men pious about their politics. Then there are the whisper-voiced women who insist you remove your shoes in their apartments. A man can never be vegetarian enough for such a woman. There are the men who fall in love instantly and woo hard, poeticizing their own abasement, proud of the psychic bruises they incur in their desperate pursuit . . . then when the woman agrees to start a relationship, they run away so fast you hear the thunderclap: sonic boomers. There are the women who worry aloud about hurting their dates, women so unsure of what they want in a relationship that they're torn in half; they really care for you, they've never met anyone quite like you, but they're so busy with their own struggle to find themselves they can't be with you right now, though perhaps in the future, it's nothing personal, we are sorry, your call is important to us please hold.

People look alike when they cry. Faces naked, thrust forward, each ragged breath a question. The younger women give in most easily to the messiness of the production, honking their noses and letting out peals of anguish. When the worst is past they blink at the bright café with puffy eyes. To watch them come back to themselves — to hear that first muffled giggle — is to witness the return of expectation. Sometimes the men cry too, their heads absolutely still — a discipline requiring untold effort. They don't use tissues, only the backs of their hands, and they never look in the café's many mirrors when they're done: if you don't acknowledge tears, they aren't real.

Night after night, book and tea mug in hand, I hear men groaning under the weight of their girlfriends' ticking clocks. I hear women sighing to one another over the stupidities of their boyfriends, cementing late-night womanly bonds of exquisite martyrdom. *Well,* they pronounce with heavy shrugs, *we've got to live with it.*

And I want to say: *No one's forcing you.*

One night I will do it. I will stand up on my table, clink spoon against glass, and give my blessing to the crowd. *Don't settle,* I will say. *And don't pursue love against the interest of your own health, like an addict in need of a fix. And don't give up hope, if you think there's something out there worth waiting for. When you meet that person, you don't just want to be kind of happy. You want to be preposterous-happy.*

I miss sex. That's a vertiginous, aching fact. But my fascination with love goes deeper than sex. Love is the channel of mysteries. The unlocker of secrets, decoder ring of souls. People are ciphers until you love them. The prosecutor whose underlings tremble at his command? Love this man and he will show you his Giant Killer Gecko imitation. His hidden fear of drowning. His single child-hood memory of his grandfather. Love is a window, and in this city of façades we lone pedestrians can't help trying to warm ourselves by its light.

At home I watch figure skating on television with the sound off: couples slipping across the ice with exuberant ease. I'm not sure whether to believe their high-wattage smiles. Most of the time, I think of love the way I think of literature. It moves me; I study it; my study helps me understand the world around me. But although I believe in the epic power of Hamlet's struggles, I don't expect to run into him walking down the street. Some days my life feels muffled, not fully lived, because it's conducted alone. I think: if a concrete block fell through my ceiling tonight and I choked on a muffin and drowned in the sink, just how long would it take until someone realized I was missing? Other days singleness is euphoria. I am a meteor passing through this city, showering sparks.

I'm happy in my own way. Maybe scorning happy people — making them sound uninventive and stupid — comforted Tolstoy during his own unhappy life. But deep contentment is as individ-ual as a footprint. For example:

Sitting at my desk the morning of February 15, watching the florist's truck pull up across the street and a delivery boy emerge with a bouquet of red roses. Those heavy crimson heads whip in the wind as he searches for the right buzzer. I imagine the argu-ment that must have ensued the previous night when someone's valentine fell asleep on the job. And I lean back and munch car-rot sticks and consider the satisfying hours I spent reading Welty on the evening of February 14, arguing and agreeing in blue ink in the margins; prodding the limits of my understanding; reveling in the intimate, exacting company of my own mind. Then calling a friend and, later, watching a favorite *L.A. Law* rerun. And how I probably had a better time than the woman across the street whose boyfriend has dispatched this delivery boy. One hurt and shaken woman, and two men desperate: the boyfriend for forgiveness, the delivery boy for the right doorbell as the wind nearly spins the roses out of their vase. You tell me who had a better Valentine's Day.

Like that. That's how I, Tracy Farber, am happy.

There's a knock on my office door. Four o'clock on the dot. Entering, Elizabeth practically genuflects. "Is this a good time?"

"Of course." I wave her to a chair. "I was expecting you."

Seated, Elizabeth rummages in her backpack for a notebook, which she opens primly on her lap. "Here's what I'm thinking of saying," she begins in a wobbly voice.

I settle back in my seat. Elizabeth is in her mid-twenties, petite, Midwestern, with straight, dark hair pulled back in a loose knot and pale skin that only amplifies the darkness of her eyes — a doll's large black-button eyes. If this were the 1600s, someone would write a sonnet to her ebony gaze and high, flawless brow. Listening to her outline an analysis of Dickinson's romance motifs, I have little to say but *terrific observation* and *nice framing*. After a few minutes I interject: "Elizabeth, I just want to make certain that you're comfortable with December."

Reluctantly she raises her eyes from her notes.

"We can always schedule a later date for your defense. There's no need for you to overextend yourself."

"No, no, I'll be fine."

She looks baffled by my smile — reminding me that graduate students never understand how invested their advisers are in their progress.

We in the English Department are odd birds. My colleagues stride the corridors chasing the flapping tail of the next thought, getting exercised about the misinterpretation of a chiasmus, pausing to scan conference flyers that woo participants by describing the host city's sky as "pellucid." But Elizabeth's oddness is more apparent than most. She treads the corridors like a prairie dog just popped up from a tunnel, blinking at the light. Unlike the average jaded graduate student, Elizabeth still treats faculty like demigods. Without my repeated invitation she wouldn't have presumed to schedule this meeting to discuss her introductory remarks for her dissertation committee. Though technically she ought to be dissatisfied — the unexpected retirement of our Dickinson specialist two years ago denied her the chance for a long-tenured, politically powerful adviser — she's embraced my predissertation background as a nineteenth-century specialist, never mind my subsequent switch to the twentieth century. And Elizabeth acting as though she's won the jackpot, adviser-wise, makes me forget that the time I sink into her thesis doesn't help a whit toward my tenure. I see it, instead, as a chance to watch a brilliant mind at work. When Elizabeth talks, it's as if literature is one of those antique glass clocks: all the minute, miraculous workings suddenly apparent. Muddy texts emerge from her hands clear and shedding light. Elizabeth is not only the youngest grad student in her cohort, but also, due to her habit of hatching an idea and drafting a searing chapter the same day, the closest to completion. The only drag on her dissertation process has been her tendency to indulge side projects, producing an impressive output of papers only peripherally related to her specialty. And even that idiosyncrasy, while it's slowed her otherwise lightning progress, will pay off prodigiously when she goes on the job market. She's already getting a reputation as one of the sharpest scholars in departmental memory. Rumor has it she started college at sixteen.

"I have a few questions." Elizabeth opens her notebook to a finely printed list and concentrates for a moment. "Do you think I ought to shore up my analysis with more responses from British critics?"

Two years of Elizabeth's lists have taught me that my job as her adviser is to keep her from obsessing over minutiae. "If you find a useful reference," I say, "it's worth anecdotal mention. Nothing more. Your argument is original, and it stands."

She takes a moment to write this down — presumably verbatim. Even I don't think my every utterance worth immortalizing, but I've learned to hold my laughter. Teasing only embarrasses her. I wait as she scribbles, fingers clamped around a visibly tooth-marked pen. I like Elizabeth. It's not only that she reminds me of my own grad school years (I, too, was the youngest student, and — while not so intellectually capricious as to be the subject of mythmaking by my fellow students — gave it my all, zipping through my dissertation in the time it took some of my fellow students to refine their topics). Elizabeth's off-kilter earnestness makes me feel hopeful, and more at ease in a not entirely hospitable department.

"Which poem do you plan to lead with?" Not that I need to know — I just enjoy Elizabeth's recitations, and she doesn't disappoint me.

"This is my letter to the World / That never wrote to Me." Her voice is soft, her face rapt as a child's.

It takes twenty minutes to make our way through the rest of her questions. As soon as we're done she shuts her notebook, jimmies it into her crammed backpack, and makes the usual polite inquiry. "How is work going on your tenure packet?"

"Coming along."

"That's good, good, I'm glad." In her rush to clarify that she wasn't prying, Elizabeth dons her jacket and leaves without thanking me for my time. By day's end, I know, I will find in the dim cavity of my departmental mailbox an utterly unnecessary thank-you note.

In fact my tenure packet is coming together more easily than I'd expected. My *Literature of the American City* anthology will be published this month, and, together with my first book and other publications and record of university service, this ought to put me in good stead. Seated at my desk, I tinker with tomorrow's lecture, a consideration of American poetry's relationship to interwar social change. For an opener, I've chosen Edwin Arlington Robinson: dark, but reliable bait for the depressive elements among my sophomores. Once I've gotten the skeptics' attention, I can talk frankly about our contemporary indifference to poetry. Why else be a Ph.D., if not to stand as a lion at the gate of our cultural heritage? I'll remind my audience that the most well known four words by an American poet were penned by beatnik Lew Welch, who supported himself with a day job in advertising. "Raid Kills Bugs Dead." This ought to worry all of us. Hence my admittedly unfashionable course requirement. My undergraduates must memorize a poem, which they recite in the privacy of my office before the end of term. Their choice. *The Cat in the Hat* will do.

Jeff gives a lazy thump on my office door. Pushing it open with his foot, he indicates the clock without a word. Four-thirty: the Bitching Hour. I leave my desk and join him in the hall.

"How goes?"

He shrugs. "Another day dredging the sewers of Brit lit." With his narrow face, blue eyes, black hair, and the long, square sideburns accentuating his pale skin, Jeff is at once handsome and stern. For such a rail-thin man, he has a startlingly deep, gravelly voice. It commands respect, both in the classroom and out. Jeff was hired as junior faculty the year before I finished my dissertation. Back then I helped him learn the ropes; he's been guiding me since. He's the closest thing I have to a friend in the department.

"Paper's going that well?" I say, locking my office door behind me.

He feels his shave. "It'll work out."

Of course it will; Jeff's papers always land in top-notch publications.

We proceed in silence down the corridor, past colleagues' doors — mostly closed — featuring bulletins advertising favored campus groups; cartoons that make arcane literary references and cartoons that mock them; brief poems; and, on the doors of two Romanticism profs, gravestone etchings. The department, occupying the whole of the building's ninth floor, is laid out in a perfect square. Its circulatory system — this windowless hallway obviously designed for the comfort of submariners — holds the outside-facing offices of senior faculty and the inside offices of us junior folk, our walls brightened by posters. At one end of each corridor is a bulletin board crowded with undergraduate announcements and study-abroad notices — barely glanced at by the handful of students hunching through these halls, each in an apparent rush to get someplace else: a burly redhead whose wary expression implies the English Department is trying to kill him; a lank-haired junior (one of my brightest twentieth-century students — we exchange waves) with a grim set to her face and a fluorescent T-shirt she wears at least once a week: STOP VIOLENCE AGAINST WOMEN. Near the end of the corridor we pass the chairman: round-faced, balding, smelling of tobacco. "Nice tie," says Jeff solemnly.

Patting the green pinstriped bow tie at his throat, the chairman nods his thanks.

When we've rounded the corner, Jeff leans close. "Makes you feel sorry for the man."

"Because?"

"Because anyone who wears a bow tie is confessing more than he ought. Neckties are just cloth arrows pointing to a man's prized possession."

I match his conspiratorial murmur. "You think?"

"Come, girl. Don't be naive. Observe the cut of the cloth. Follow the arrow." With a flourish he indicates his own tie, running down the navy plane of his shirt and terminating in a sharp V an inch above his belt. "Men who wear bow ties have, I'm sorry to say, no penis."

"And guys who wear bolo ties?"

"Have hardly any penis at all."

I indicate the subtle design on Jeff's tie. "Don't think I want to know what the pattern means."

He smirks.

"Why so dressed up?"

With a look that says *I'll tell you inside,* Jeff reaches for the door of the faculty lounge. By now the lounge is empty and nearly clear of pipe smoke, the departmental aristocracy—two professors who drift, high-minded, above the fray—having retired from taking their tea. Neither of these gentlemen has published a paper in at least as long as I've been here; neither bothers to attend conferences; both have been known to nod off during colleagues' lectures. *Le premier état:* Professors Grub and Paleozoic.

Names have been changed.

Grub, our bow-tied, middle-aged chairman, always votes yes on tenure (all his faculty candidates are, naturally, above average), never asks questions at dissertation defenses, and promptly delegates all new initiatives to exploratory committees. His office door stays shut. I've seen the room's interior only once, when I was summoned for a brief hail-fellow chat shortly after my hiring. Grub cares about the department in the manner of a ship's captain secluded in his cabin, a military-style chart on the wall marked with colored pins for the faculty's formidable list of publications and professional honors. The galley slaves row, the stewards shovel coal into the flames, and Grub emerges now and again to give a pep talk. He manages the department with a strategy I'm convinced he picked up from Dickens's Inspector Bucket, though I suspect the *Bleak House* character used it with more charm: when conflicts erupt or persuasion is necessary, Grub tells his faculty about themselves.

"You're the kind who stays on course," he'll say to a disgruntled professor, buttonholing her in the corridor. "You're the sort who would never let a small matter derail her."

People love to hear about themselves. They blush under the assault: *Is that how I come across? Un-derail-able?*

I shouldn't criticize; the strategy seems to work. Faculty eat out of his hand.

Paleozoic, seventy-something and perpetually rumpled, was chairman for two decades before Grub and he's sticking around to make sure it all works out. Paleozoic sheds his outdoor shoes the moment he enters the department at eight A.M. and dons the felt slippers in which he pads about the department for the remainder of the day. You'd never know he was coming if not for the pipe smoke that permeates his clothing. He abstains from all departmental votes (reportedly he's leery of throwing around his chairman-emeritus weight, lest he unfairly influence the weak-minded). He is a decent man: decent in his 1950s sense of humor, his sexism, and his incomprehension of the new subspecialized courses (African American Lit, Homosexuality and Text, Women and the Novel); decent, too, in his disapproval of anything written after 1700 (which is, and I quote, "so much gah-gah"). These days he teaches only one seminar, thinly attended by undergraduates who emerge from the three-hour sessions glassy-eyed. Conversation with Paleozoic has a surreal quality. Learning I've just come from the library, he'll begin with a reference to the stacks, segue to Dante's circles of hell, and somehow, several minutes later, alight on Hemingway. Regarding Hemingway (good bloke, shame the way it ended), he will become animated. "Have you ever been to Morocco?" His shaggy eyebrows rise and stay aloft, awaiting my reply.

I have not.

The eyebrows drop. He struggles for another metaphor to illustrate his sentiment about Hemingway. "Have you ever been sailing?" Up with the brows. "On a blustery day?"

"Yes."

A smile expands across his face. "Enough said." Patting me on the shoulder, he departs with hushed tread.

At three P.M. our two senior gentlemen take their tea. Whichever is last to reach the faculty lounge discovers his waiting companion with a cry of "Aha!"; the one already seated in the lounge replies in kind, and once this attendance has been taken they settle down to business in earnest. In the sanctum of the lounge, beneath a large NO SMOKING sign (relic of the days before smoking was prohibited in all university buildings), Paleozoic strikes a match and lights his pipe, and the two commence a tranquil hour's throat clearing while the rest of us make ourselves scarce.

The Bitching Hour now convened, Jeff opens the lounge's single window. I flap a manila folder to clear the remaining smoke.

"Word is Dean Hopkins has a crush on Faulkner," says Jeff. "He's hinting about pushing for a more contemporary curriculum, presumably expanding our twentieth century offerings. Look who's going to win the tenure jackpot."

"Wouldn't it be nice. But I'm not counting on it."

Jeff is my "tenure-shepherd." It's his job to advise me on tenure-packet preparation. It's my job to fish for reassurance.

"Of course you're not," he says approvingly. "Still, it looks good for you. Despite your rosy youth."

"Ha."

"Well you have to admit it's not every day profs come up for tenure at twelve."

"I'm thirty-three. And—"

"What I'm saying"—he cuts me off—"is that beside your standout record, you've got a bulletproof specialty. I expect to see you crowned in the next few months. Then maybe once your job is secure you'll admit how much you despise undergrads."

I grin. "You're projecting."

"You hate teaching too, you just can't admit it because you're still an idealist. At least I'm honest about the spoiled buggers. Once you're tenured you'll tell the truth too."

I try again. Maintaining my students' posture in their creaky wooden seats is an unsung art, one I undertake with zest. "I like my students," I say. Even if the endearing thing about them is how dumb they think we are. Even if they toss thin excuses at our feet: lazy dares. Undergraduates find their professors' infatuations unfathomable . . . except when a book has gotten to them. Then they queue up cross-legged on the speckled floor outside my office, radiant with the need to have a thorny passage explained, or some bracing moral challenge resolved. The trust they're willing to place in my hands, then, is stunning.

Jeff smiles with one corner of his mouth, telling me no argument I can summon will be worth the effort. "Why the tie?" I ask instead. "Black turtlenecks not good enough for you anymore?"

"The Emory chairman's in town. I'm going to attend his lecture on the fascinations of *Beowulf*." He takes a mug from the cabinet and looks inside dubiously, then rinses it in the mini-sink. "Continuing the profound and brilliant impression I've been making on him. And letting it be known, parenthetically, that I might be persuaded to alter my present circumstances. For the right offer."

"Why would you want a job at Emory? This is a much better department."

"Upward mobility," he says tartly, setting the mug down.

"No way you're going to leave Manhattan for Atlanta. Even for love. I know you. Can you really see yourself in the land of seven-lane superhighways? Where everything in town is sponsored by Coca-Cola?"

Saying nothing, he empties the coffeepot and sets it up for another round. I watch his profile. Jeff has known he was gay since he was seven, and he claims this early intimacy with what W.E.B. Du Bois called "double-consciousness" (living by one set of societal rules, all the while experiencing a different, unvoiced identity) trained him well for the path he's chosen. Life is about strict separations, and Jeff's boundaries are concrete: British Drama by day, Chelsea dance clubs by night; never the twain shall meet. In any other line of work Jeff's dress would mark him as obviously, stereotypically gay, but here in the world of lit he slips under the gaydar. He's routinely mistaken for just another straight Europhile liberal arts professor in tight black jeans, synthetic black shirts, and chunky black belts — one of dozens of boy-men stamped with the standard academic-chic pallor. Guys who dance with their eyes half closed and break the hearts of female grad students with their eternal, eloquent, tormented ambivalence. Who have, where romance is concerned, more second thoughts than is mathematically possible.

In fact Jeff is anything but ambivalent. He knows exactly whom he loves (Richard) and what he wants (an apartment together with a spare room so they can share a home office). They've agreed to cheat on each other freely until they can figure out a way to be together for more than just vacations. At that point neither of them will have wild oats left to sow, and they'll buy a place in whatever city will offer stable attractive positions for two British lit specialists, one (Richard) with a subspecialty in queer theory. The fact that such opportunities are supremely rare has not escaped Jeff's notice, and although he is usually closed about his personal life, the relationship's glum prospects have fueled an occasional gripe session. Jeff, to his own surprise, is a lousy cheater. And Richard doesn't seem to have more success down at Emory. Despite all efforts, they're engaged in what is, according to Jeff, one of the colossal stupidities of the universe: a monogamous long-distance relationship. The prospect of spending three solid months together this spring — Jeff having at last succeeded in arranging a semester's leave — seems only to have sharpened Jeff's frustration.

Other than this inexplicable indiscretion of his loyalty to Richard, nothing fazes Jeff. He can read a department's politics like a page of Shaw, analyze, deconstruct, and tell you what's going to happen in the next scene. He's witty enough that conversation with him is intellectually seductive — there's a buzz I get from staying on my toes with him — and also fatiguing. I don't let my guard down entirely, because he doesn't. We watch each other's backs, but it's clear who's got the keener eye. Jeff lives and breathes cynicism. To talk to him is to measure the volume and density of my own naiveté. And though I know I'm his favorite in the department — I am, as far as I can tell, the only one who knows about Richard — there's something about his unshakable control that makes me uncomfortable. After Jeff's tenure was approved two years ago, he announced to me that the time had arrived for him to come out to his students. Now that he wasn't at risk, he didn't mind being a role model on campus. He dropped a couple of hints during lectures, the faculty got wind rapidly, and now almost everyone seems clued in, with the exception of Paleozoic.

As Jeff pours a first cup of coffee, the lounge's door swings open: Grub, returning for a misplaced volume. Watching Grub search the haphazard towers of books on the end table, Jeff is the picture of solemnity.

"*Ve-ry* nice tie," says Jeff.

Volume in hand, Grub straightens, smiles, and claps Jeff on the shoulder.

I like Jeff, and I find him scary.

I meet Hannah at the front of the reception hall. She looks composed, as always: brown hair tucked behind her ears; slender silver pendant resting above a not too deep V-neck; competent, calm, cheery. She's already filled a paper plate with hors d'oeuvres and is bolting them with the prayerful concentration of the pregnant.

As we hug, her considerable belly bumps me, and we smile.

"What's new in the hallowed halls?" she asks.

"Too many papers to grade. Otherwise it's a good semester so far. Just a couple problem students. How are you?"

"We're all fine — tell me more about you."

In someone else it might be a power play, this habit of deflecting questions, drawing me out while revealing almost nothing of herself. With Hannah it's modesty, and a genuine love I've never taken for granted. Through college and after, Hannah and I were nearly inseparable. But in the years since we last shared an apartment, work and marriage and then motherhood have laid claim to her schedule. Now a coffee date requires three weeks' advance planning. In a rare show of exasperation last week, Hannah suggested a quick meeting at this reception to celebrate her office's new collaborative project with city charities. She's here for only twenty minutes, then off to pick up her three-year-old, Elijah, from preschool; but the reception is right around the corner from my department, and at least it's a place where she has a chance of conducting an adult conversation.

"Tell me about your problem students," she says.

"One of them called last night to ask whether he could skip class to get tickets for a Tragically Hip concert. He said he's a poet and the concert would really *inspire* him."

"What did you say?"

"Exactly what he expected: I gave him a lecture about the concertgoing habits of Emily Dickinson. Part of my job is managing undergrads' limits-testing."

"Sounds like parenthood." Hannah nabs a pig in blanket from my plate. She rolls her eyes in ecstasy, then bites into it. I trade my full plate for her empty one.

"You're sure?" She eyes my mushroom puffs.

"Eat. What's new in your world?"

"Ed is good. He likes the new job."

"Hey, I saw George recently."

"Oh, thanks." She prods upward with her tongue, then ducks her head and daintily removes the piece of food that had lodged between her upper canine and its neighbor. "He still around?"

"Nope, he's vanished."

Hannah flashes me a big, George-less grin. "Yet again you've saved me from social catastrophe."

George is the code name not only for a piece of crud that gets stuck between your teeth, but for a wandering bra strap, an undone zipper, a piece of toilet paper stuck to your shoe. The guy helped Hannah and me alert each other to potentially embarrassing social situations through college and beyond, including the time I overslept the arrival of the first guests for predinner drinks, woke to the sound of the doorbell, and dressed from the top of my clean laundry pile — neglecting to notice, as I greeted our guests, the pair of underwear static-clinging for dear life to the back of my blouse. Bless Hannah, who came into the living room as I was greeting our guests, put an arm around me, and casually asked me whether it had come to my attention that George, who had previously left town, was *back*.

As I watch Hannah bite into a mushroom puff, it strikes me how far we've traveled, my college friends and I, since those giddy years before careers, spouses, and dignity installed themselves in our lives. It takes an old friend now — one grandfathered in from my twenties or earlier — to bring out the goofiness in me. As Hannah chews, I rue the sobriety of the thirties: all life choices and strategy, no slapstick.

And even with Hannah, dignity needs its due. "Tell me about Ed's job," I say.

"Oh, it's *fantastic!*" It's clear that the promotion is a source of pride not only for Ed but for Hannah, who details the changes in Ed's responsibilities with relish. Beneath her excitement I hear relief. Hannah's job has always been more prestigious than Ed's. And while she's never made mention of a certain sulkiness from Ed where her work is concerned, it hasn't escaped my notice.

"Oh, and big news from Adam," Hannah says.

"He's joined a luge team in Finland?"

"I wouldn't have been surprised." Adam, Hannah's younger brother, hung up his teaching shingle a couple of years ago in Prague, then moved on to Rome and Parma, taught English in the countryside in Holland until he and his Dutch girlfriend split, then bartended in Gorky *to get a little Russia in.* "But he's done with his travels," says Hannah, "and he's moving back to New York. My mother just told me last night." She licks her fingers discreetly. "He called her from Moscow."

"Adam in New York?" I say. "Poor Elijah will have to adjust to an uncle who thinks eggs are for juggling. I give it a week before Adam teaches him to shoot spitballs."

"Adam's grown up a bit, you know."

"*Adam?*" I say. "I know the rest of the human race grows up. But *Adam?*"

Our laughter attracts the gaze of Hannah's boss. Hannah flashes him a disarming smile. "I need to be a little social," she whispers to me. "Can you stand two minutes of networking?" She leads me to the center of the room and into a conversation with one of the charity administrators, a fifty-something-year-old woman named Nancy whose husband, Victor, has the decency to ask me about my teaching style, and the pros and cons of a classical education for students of literature. As I summarize the canon wars for Victor's benefit, Hannah stands beside me in her dark jacket and black slacks, waistline thickened, eyes sparkling with freedom. I can't remember the last time she and I were in a social situation without Ed or Elijah clinging to her, Elijah with earnestly lisped requests, Ed with an expression of faint bewilderment that hasn't gone away in three years of fatherhood. I know women who would run for the hills at her responsibilities. But motherhood suits Hannah. She's among those luckiest of souls — people who like being needed.

Hannah tips the contents of her plate onto mine. "Here," she whispers. "Now I'm too full to eat." With a quick apology for not having more time, she hugs me goodbye, plans a business call with Nancy, and leaves with a promise to let me know the minute Adam shows up.

Victor alights on his passion for archaeology and his stints volunteering at digs. I check in often enough to agree at the appropriate moments, but I'm not listening. Instead, I continue to indulge a rare hit of nostalgia for those postcollege years when Hannah and Adam and I all lived together. We argued over the remote control, the telephone line, the grocery list. We consoled one another, roughly or with delicacy, for personal idiocies. We made important decisions in one another's company: lying on our backs, staring at the ceiling, making dust angels on the floor.

"What was fascinating," Victor continues, "was how much the dig's yield varied from day to day."

Nancy and I listen with such strained attention it's obvious we're both bored. Victor, I realize, is bored too, reciting a story he's told before out of some well-bred impulse to keep conversation flowing. I try to focus, and fail. When a child is named Victor, does some other set of parents somewhere have to name their child Loser? Turning away to mask a smile, I notice an angular blondish man a few feet away in a dark sweater sipping from a cup of seltzer. He's looking at the crowd a bit stiffly, like someone who's opened a box of pastries only to find them stale. His features are regular, his hair straight. Other than the expression of distaste, nothing stands out except his height, which invites me to imagine his view of Manhattan: a city of combed crowns and dandruff, cramped restaurant seating, hazardous doorways. He turns his head and, without meaning to, I catch his eye.

He steps toward us. *Not my type,* I think reflexively. Though in truth, he's not bad-looking; he's got a pleasantly lean face and, now that he's engaged, a comfortable, lived-in smile. He looks as if he's just woken up, and glad of it.

"Hey there, Nance," he says. Nancy kisses him hello, and Victor thumps him on the back, positively grateful to be interrupted.

He turns to me. "Hi," he says. Then, before I have a chance to respond, he gives me a look that catches me off-guard. It's a look of quiet mischief, as though reminding me of a subversive joke we share. It's also unmistakably, gently sexy . . . right here in the heart of a professional reception.

"This is Tracy," says Nancy.

"Hi, Tracy." He inclines his head. "I'm George."

Without warning the plate in my hands, already soggy from Hannah's food and mine, buckles. Grabbing absurdly at the flying mushroom caps, I fail to keep the food from sailing or a short bark of hilarity from escaping me. The hors d'oeuvres splash my blouse and make a dramatic mess on the carpet, which has been, until this moment, beige. Conversation between Nancy and Victor stops.

George looks solemnly into my eyes, which, to my surprise, have gone watery with embarrassment. Then he lofts his own paper plate like a coat-and-tails waiter, tosses it into the air, and lets it spin to the ground, scattering tabouli.

"Happens to the best of us," he says.

I look at the mess. I look at him. For an impish, stunning instant I imagine grabbing his hand and whispering *Let's go*. Then Nancy hands me a wad of napkins. And we are down on our hands and knees, cleaning.

"Thanks," I say.

He doesn't answer, only laughs and accepts the napkins I proffer.

"Nice move," I say.

We work the mess out of the carpet.

"Didn't cover the area I'd hoped for." He has a nice voice — low and friendly. "I'll have to practice my throw." He stops cleaning for a second. "I don't often get that response when I introduce myself to women. It's very flattering."

"Well." Surveying the remaining crumbs, I consider explaining that the plate was soaked, but decide that's protesting too much. Is he going to leave me out on a limb, playing this as though he wasn't flirting? "Nice move," I repeat, but with less warmth. His angular frame looks suddenly less sexy. Attraction de-soufflé. Blinking, I turn my attention to the carpet.

"You work here?" he says.

"No, just visiting."

"Same." He surveys the room. "I didn't think a nonprofit could be so stiff. I would have worn my clown nose and fright wig."

I can't help chuckling. I glance at him. "You should see the people I work with."

"Stiff?"

"Embalmed."

"I'm sorry to hear that."

"It's not all bad." I apply myself once more to the carpet, which is almost clean. "In fact I love it most days. I'm an English professor. But academics aren't the most easygoing crowd."

"So I hear." George sits back and settles his arms loosely around his knees as he watches me. His eyes are a bright brown and wonderfully still. It's perhaps the most open gaze I've ever seen on an adult: taking in every detail, interrogating the world thoughtfully and without cynicism.

Above and around us the reception buzzes. A waiter sidesteps George with a worried cluck. George doesn't budge.

Unsure how to respond to his silence, I gesture at the crowd. "At least these folks aren't all flagrant egotists. Some of them ask a question with the intent to actually listen to the answer."

He considers this.

I work a piece of tabouli out of the rug with my fingernails. Almost without meaning to, I continue: "I've always thought you can diagnose a workplace the minute people open their mouths."

"How?" he says.

Resting on his forearms, his hands are wide and strong-looking. Knobby in the right places. What hands ought to look like. Along the back of one is a faint scar.

A red-business-suited woman utters an irritable "Oh!" as she nearly walks into George. He gives her a genial salute, then turns his focus back to me.

"Just listen for the verbal tics." I pick several flakes of pastry off the carpet, delay meeting his gaze. He waits, attentive. My eyes drop to my blouse, which is splashed with tabouli and dressing. Rising, I indicate the kitchenette at the rear of the reception hall. Without a word he stands and follows me.

"Verbal tics," he says.

At the sink, I wet a paper towel and attend to the dark fabric of my blouse. He settles opposite me, one hip against the counter. I give my blouse more attention than it requires. When I speak it's with a sense of unplanned acceleration: an uncontrolled surge like a car shifting into higher gear than expected. "Did you ever notice," I say, "the people who start every sentence with *No* — even when they're agreeing with you? You say, 'Seems like the Yankees are having a bad streak,' and they say, 'No, it's just that they can't get together a game strategy.'" I wipe my fingers on the damp towel. "Which I've always thought tells you you're dealing with a critical person. Somebody who's going to be unhappy with himself and — by extension — with you."

He's silent for a moment. "Interesting," he says. "I've met a few of those."

I wet and wring a fresh set of paper towels, for the carpet. "We've got a heaping serving of them in my department. Which makes for a hard-driven lot."

"Who else have you got," he says, "in that department of yours?" As he speaks he extends his hand.

I stare at it, my own hand poised indecisively; did he read my mind earlier? Then, understanding, I quickly hand him what he's asking for: a damp paper towel. I say, "The Look-Listeners."

He folds the paper towel.

"You know, the ones who start every statement with a directive. 'Look, the Yankees aren't always strong at the season's start. Listen, they just need a better coach.' These are the people who consider themselves weary bearers of unpopular truths." I'm not sure what I'm doing. Daring him, perhaps, to lose interest? "Cassandras . . ." I glance. He's listening. ". . . who speak their consciences though they expect to be ignored. They're more pleasant than the No types. But prone to lecturing." He follows me out of the kitchenette, back to where we started. "Then you've got the armies of Yes-ers: 'Yes, though I think the Yankees have maybe done better than people realize, but, yes, you're right.'" Stopping, I enunciate in my most professorial voice. "Sycophants. So conflict-averse they feel compelled to sneak their opinions under the radar."

He's smiling softly.

Trouble. Delight.

I crouch down on the carpet, then look at it dumbly. There's nothing left to clear. "Add the slight British lilt among the graduate students," I say. "And the all-black wardrobes. And that's my department in a nutshell."

He doesn't say anything.

"Which makes us, I guess . . ." my voice drifting to a lame finish, "typical."

Beside me he surveys the carpet, no trace remaining of the reckless mess we made together.

"And you?" he says. I can't read his face.

"Where do I fit in?" I echo.

A man with a heaped plate of hors d'oeuvres almost stumbles as he comes upon us. As he pivots he lets out a disapproving grunt that unaccountably emboldens me.

"Into the Look-Listener category, I'm afraid. Hence" — I conclude with a flourish of a paper towel — "this lecture."

"I'm taking notes," he says after a minute.

Quietly our eyes meet.

Yolanda is furious. We are striding down Eighth Avenue — me in slacks and a cream-colored blouse, she in a purple leotard and translucent purple skirt, black leggings, and chunky heels. Ignoring most of the men who stare at her, nodding curt acknowledgment to a few, Yolanda races toward her verbal destination with fearsome momentum. She's been going for at least ten blocks. It's obvious, though, that she's still ramping up to the worst bits.

The problem: Bill will not eat cauliflower.

"He's like a little boy who doesn't want his cauliflower, and you have to keep jollying him into it. And Tracy, *I'm* the cauliflower." Abruptly Yolanda stops and faces me. "The man cannot commit to an adult relationship."

"But we know that. *He* knows that. He told you so the first day you met."

"Well, you're not going to believe *this*." She starts walking again.

Given the romantic implosion that's already consumed Yolanda's month, I find it hard to imagine anything Bill might have done that I wouldn't believe. Possibly he's had a sex change operation; possibly he's renounced gravity and is floating over Manhattan taunting physicists; probably nothing that interesting. Probably he's been a jerk, which has lost its novelty for everyone except Yolanda, who is still astonished. But foreseeable though this may have been, I feel for Yolanda, who has been earnestly updating me on the details of this particular debacle from the start. The morning Yolanda first heard about the casting call she phoned me in a froth. She was auditioning to play a poet, she could really use this part, did I know anything about someone called H.D.? Five times that day Yolanda called me with questions about Hilda Doolittle — tacitly acknowledging, for the first time in our nineteen-year friendship and despite her long-expressed wish that I jettison my latest paper/grading/reading and join her for disco night at Hot Rocks, that I am indeed a professor. The play, the work of a recent Women's Literature M.A. from N.Y.U., was a dramatization of H.D.'s analysis with Freud. Yolanda showed me the script. It was a well-meant script; that's the best one could say for it. In fact, though I didn't let on to Yolanda, it seemed to me that the author's signature accomplishment was shaping such rich material into something so insipid and politically heavy-handed. But Yolanda took her audition preparation in unprecedented earnest, meditating, doing vocal exercises that made her sound like a gossipy swan, fretting over her suitability. Dozens of women wanted the role — it might have been off-off-off-Broadway, but it was a serious part.

Yolanda needn't have worried. The playwright was adamant that her H.D. have a certain indefinable physical energy — and one look at Yolanda's statuesque figure and no longer fresh face evidently persuaded her that she'd found Hilda Doolittle.

No sooner was Yolanda cast than she phoned with another news flash: Freud was an utter hottie. She and Bill began sleeping together the night of their joint audition. The onstage chemistry, according to Yolanda, was second only to the offstage. Never mind the tiny theater and unknown playwright; this show was the best thing, professionally and romantically, to happen to her in a decade.

Like most of Yolanda's affairs, this one burned bright and blew fast. Now there are two more weeks of rehearsal plus a four-week performance run to get through, and Yolanda can hardly bear to look at Bill . . . which is where Yolanda and H.D. part ways. H.D. trusts Freud with her innermost secrets. Which the brilliant H.D. obviously never would have done had she known Freud was such a big fucking flirt.

"I saw him," Yolanda says. "*With* someone."

"Didn't you say you expected him to go right out and find someone else?" In hourlong sessions earlier this week Yolanda has expressed boundless sympathy for Bill's future lovers, as well as a battle-hardened solidarity with the man's previous girlfriends (until recently viewed with disdain — The Ex-Girlfriend Formerly Known as Snoozan, The Ex-Girlfriend Formerly Known as Mary Queen of Scotch: all now rehabilitated). There is a general amnesty out for all the unwitting females who have ever known or will ever know Bill. Only one woman is excluded.

"The costumer?" I say.

Yolanda looks teary. "I saw them yesterday. Walking on Hudson. Holding *hands.*"

I blow out a long breath. "I'm sorry."

"She is, and I hate to say it but it has to be said, a slut." Yolanda glares at the sidewalk as if she detests every gray inch of it. For the next six weeks she'll have to profess admiration for Freud even as she argues against his sexism. She'll have to refer to him as Professor, Papa, and — endearingly — Owl. It's intolerable. Yolanda believes in vehemence. People she approves of are saints. People she hates are bastards. Other people cry — Yolanda weeps. She does not weigh and reason, which I find, after a long day in academe, a relief. In her midriff shirts and spandex she pronounces gorgeous judgment on the world, and along the way keeps me from taking my professorial self too seriously. Now and then she even gets me out of the library on a Saturday night to join her at a dance club, where I sway simply but contentedly alongside her rubberized friends. I'm glad to have Yolanda in my life. But beneath her rants this month, beneath the obvious agony of having to smile into her costar's romantic indifference onstage, is a fury that has little to do with Bill and more to do with Yolanda still getting blindsided, now that we're thirty-three. Yolanda is the sort of woman people stare at on the street — high-strung, blond, curvaceous. In addition to dance and theater, she studies Pilates, which means she can wiggle her ears using only her abdominal muscles; according to Yolanda, guys find flexibility excruciatingly sexy. Despite being more regally endowed than I in several dimensions, Yolanda wears a small to my medium. But none of this adds up to what she wants. On her twenty-third birthday, Yolanda swore she wouldn't compromise in her search for true love until she was thirty-three.

Now she's thirty-three and can't find a man to compromise with. In the four years she's lived in Manhattan, no man has lasted more than three months. The last serious guy, the one she dumped after she finished her theater degree in Boston, was a rabid Red Sox fan; cute, boisterous, and boring. He cried like a kid when she broke up with him. She moved to New York, traded him in for Yankees fans, and hasn't kept a guy since. The Curse of the Bambino.

I lift my face to the autumn brilliance shedding from the sharp river of sky onto the deep, shop-lined channel of Eighth Avenue. The air is cool, the periodic sidewalk-planted maples spangled orange. "I'm so sorry," I say. "You deserve better."

She doesn't speak.

I lay my hand on her shoulder. "I sometimes think being shocked when romance lets us down is like joining the military and being surprised when people shoot at you."

She sighs. "Promise you'll come to opening night?"

"You know I'm coming. I ordered my ticket last week."

"I'll get you a seat in the front row. I'll get you ten seats. I need you there." She stops. We've reached her favorite health-food shop: terminus for our walk. "I've decided," she says. "I'm going to be like you."

"Celibate?"

"A hermit."

I follow her inside. "You wouldn't last a week."

Yolanda greets the woman at the counter. "I'll take an almond tonic with carrot juice," she tells her. To me she says, "I wish I were gay."

"Do women do so much better with romance, left to our own?"

"Women don't *do* this shit!"

"Suit yourself."

She glares at the street.

"I'm not a complete hermit," I say.

"You're a complete hermit."

I turn to her. "I met a guy. Tuesday."

"Oh great."

"He asked for my number."

"And you *gave* it to him?" She shakes her head. "The poor guy."

"What's that supposed to mean?"

She smirks.

Behind the counter, the woman pours a viscous liquid out of the blender and into a cup. She hands it to Yolanda.

I watch Yolanda count her change. "I think I'd like to go out with this one," I say.

Yolanda stops counting. "What, he's a Nobel Prize winner *and* a Chippendales dancer? But you'll still deduct points for bad grammar. Besides, he'll never survive the fax test."

Yolanda believes I maintain my dysfunctional phone-fax setup to screen potential dates. I've never been able to convince her of the truth, which is that I landed in the situation out of sheer laziness. I have a fax machine that kicks in whenever the telephone line is silent for more than thirty seconds—a defect I discovered the first time I was put on hold without Muzak, when my relief at being excused from Manilow con maracas was fractured by a shrilling in my ear. I decided to take the fax machine back to the shop the very next day. But it snowed.

After a month or so I rationalized: my fax machine provided an outlet for creative expression, a verbal challenge, an avenue for oral improvisation. It was, in any case, beyond the thirty-day return period. Having memorized more literature than I care to admit, I myself have no shortage of fodder for the gaping maw of my fax, no matter how long airline ticket offices keep me on hold. And when I'm forced to set down my phone midconversation to search for a piece of information or take my kettle off the burner, I advise my conversational partners to throw the silence a bone now and then until I return. People recite poetry, whistle, sing nursery rhymes. The less adventuresome count aloud or just clear their throats. I announce my return to the phone with a deliberate, noisy fumble of the receiver, fair warning for anyone confessing secrets into the silence. The conversations after I return are noticeably more fluid—the fax machine has, over the years, earned its keep as a social lubricant.

According to Yolanda, though, I come up with an excuse to put a potential date on hold; then I listen in on his filibuster and subtract points for cliché and poor grammar.

"I have never, ever, put someone on hold unless I had to," I say, as Yolanda takes a sip of her smoothie and turns for the door. "And I'm not that picky with men."

"What about that sweet guy with the flowers?"

"Him? He was a madman. He showed up for our first date with roses."

"He wasn't a madman. He was crazy about you."

"I don't even *like* roses."

"Still, it was romantic. He was the wrong guy, I give you that. But bringing roses is romantic."

"It's the *opposite* of romantic. Romance is careful attention to what a particular lover wants or needs. Giving roses to a woman who doesn't like flowers is not romantic. It's the opposite of romantic — it's generic. And if a woman loves, let's say, auto repair, then buying her a welder's torch is the ultimate in romance."

Yolanda sweeps open the door. "Everybody make way for the love expert."

We step out onto the sidewalk. There is a shout. Just feet from us, a restaurant delivery man and his bicycle flip hard onto the sidewalk. In one continuous motion, the scrawny preteen skateboarder who just shoved him bends, nips two bulging bags of food out of the bike's basket, and is straightening from his crouch — the downed biker and I still inert from shock — when Yolanda knocks one of the bags out of his arms with an impressive kick.

Still holding the other bag, the kid palms the pavement for balance, slams his wheels to the sidewalk, and shoots away, heading uptown.

"You want to know why you piss me off?" Yolanda screams after him.

If I were a zoologist hunting specimens of the indigenous New Yorker, this would be my hunting call. No Manhattanite can resist.

A block away, the kid slows.

"Okay, fine. Steal the food. But at least you could stick around and *acknowledge* what you did to him!"

Holding aloft his middle finger, the skateboarder turns a corner.

From the pavement the delivery guy, a ropy black man with skin so dark he almost shines, looks up at Yolanda as though he's having a religious vision.

"You okay?" I ask him.

"Not English," he says softly, with a thick, eloquent accent. He turns up his palms.

I point to his leg, where a long, painful-looking scrape extends from the edge of his shorts to his ankle. He smiles to reassure me. "Not English," he repeats.

"Denial," Yolanda tells him, setting a firm hand on his shoulder as he stands. "That's the problem with the world."

"Ah," he says with fervor, and follows Yolanda with large glimmering eyes as she hugs me goodbye and strides off, smoothie in hand.

When I get home from work, the number two is blinking on my machine. The first message is Hannah: Adam is back, has already taught Elijah the Russian word for snot, is driving Hannah crazy so nothing has changed. They all want to see me.

I set down my bag and reach for my calendar.

The second message is George. It was a pleasure throwing hors d'oeuvres with me yesterday. Would I care to call him?

I put down the calendar. Then I unload my bag and tidy the papers on my coffee table. I wander to the kitchenette's narrow window and stand for a long while, my eyes roaming a familiar course across the skyline. Uptown, the high rises are a bright, endless filigree. Though I've been hoping for George's call, I abruptly don't want to think about him. I think instead about the city. All those lives. All those individual, earthshaking dramas, and threaded through them the workings of history and poetry and the laws of physics and chemistry and biology, all rushing headlong at the same time and none of it forgetting to work for even an instant. This evening, for some reason, it makes me want to feel religious. The tiles chilling my bare feet, I consider some capacious intelligence keeping it all afloat—a phosphorescent world under an invisible cap of stars. I don't believe in God; I've never been able to convince myself that emperor's wearing clothes. The only faith to which I can comfortably do lip service is an ancestral one, inherited from my grandmother: a petite matron who, when complimenting a family member or voicing her hopes for her grandchildren, would invoke the name of an Irishman ("You should only be happy, Ken O'Hara"). Only in college, in conversation with an Orthodox Jewish classmate—a species as foreign to me as the Amish—did I at last glean the meaning of my grandmother's Yiddish disclaimer. *Kenahora: not to tempt the evil eye.*

I raise the last of my diet soda. Framed mute in my window, the city dazzles. And the hollow sensation I've felt since playing George's message crystallizes into ordinary fear. "To Ken O'Hara," I say, and drain the can. And dial.

George is a consultant for a nonprofit specializing in education policy. On the phone, his voice is friendly and reasonable. He's working on a smaller-schools initiative. Trying to muster public will to fix those overcrowded classrooms. Move the algebra lessons out of converted janitorial closets. Address the thirty-five-kids-per-teacher status quo and the tragic dropout rates. It's not the kind of work where you expect dramatic victory. The idea is to turn the tide one drop at a time. Meanwhile, he likes hiking.

Do I like hiking?

Whatever spontaneity I felt at the reception has deserted me. I do not spill my life story like hors d'oeuvres from a sodden paper plate. In point of fact, I'm practically monosyllabic.

George grew up in Toronto. His father and sister and three nieces, he says, are still there. He just bought a birthday present for his oldest niece. A ragtime recording. He used to play the banjo.

Hasn't touched it though, in two, three years.

His voice trails off, expectant. After a moment he says, "Not a banjo player yourself, I take it?" His voice is kind. As though he's worried for me.

It feels like a decade since my last date. And I'm abruptly and viscerally reminded why I wanted it that way. It was because I detested this exchange — two people reading from scripts, stringing up intriguing details about themselves like bait. Awaiting nibbles.

George jokes easily, posing the usual questions: family, life, work.

My script is blank. "Seattle," I say. "I was born in Seattle."

"And did you always know you wanted to go into American literature?"

This man knows nothing about me. Twelve years' commitment, books and poems into the thousands, paltry stipend paychecks: all bottleneck in my mind and I open my mouth and out pours eloquence. "Yes."

Trying to rouse myself, I force a laugh. "So. Do you have any pets?" I say this in a wry tone. A tone meant to acknowledge our mutual sophistication, as well as the absurdity of two adults starting from zero, gathering information about each other as though we were nothing but gawky kids hoping against hope the other likes our favorite movie.

The line goes briefly silent.

"I once had a hamster," he says. His tone is not wry. It admits, in fact, only two possible interpretations. One: They don't have wry in Canada. Two: We *are* gawky kids.

Dating is — I understand this with thunderbolt clarity — an existential insult.

"Would you mind holding a second?" I say. "I've got something on the stove."

With a stiff apology, I explain about my fax machine. Then, gently, warding off the specter of a cackling Yolanda, I set the receiver on the coffee table, nonplused by my own blundering. Odds are, at this rate, that George will never know me well enough to understand that I have nothing on my stove, ever, except occasionally a teapot. I force myself into a full, slow exhale. I know how to talk to a fellow human being. I talk to humans all the time. Obviously it's been too long since I had a conversation with a man capable of surprising me, even if all he did was throw his food.

Seconds pass. I'm furious at myself. Then, as from a great distance, I hear George through the receiver, clearing his throat.

"*O Canada!*" he trolls.

Even from this distance it's apparent that this is a man who could not carry a tune in a Samsonite.

"*Our home and native land! True patriot love in all thy sons command.*"

I can think of nothing to say to a banjo-playing Canadian named George. After fourteen years' boot camp, I'm a literary Manhattanite. I don't wear pastels. I no longer consider the word "earnest" a compliment. I know that patriotism is just another ethos that needs to be put up on a lift and checked for leaks. I cannot date this man.

It's only when he belts out *True North strong and free* that I start, despite myself, to laugh. As he continues, my laughter swells, grows giddy. I'm afraid he'll hear. Can he? He draws a deep breath, and yodels. "*From far and wiiiide . . .*"

I pick up the receiver gingerly, afraid I'll guffaw. "Hello?"

He keeps singing. Now he's rolling his R's, booming and oper-
atic. *"O Canada, we stand on guard for thee."* He finishes with
a vibrato sufficiently grand to wilt maple leaves. The line goes
silent.

"Encore?" I suggest, more meekly than I intend.

"Not a chance. You have to go on a date with me if you want
the cabaret version. *Ms. New York Sophisticate."* His voice turns
gentle on these last words. I've been forgiven. I'm not sure I
sinned — in Manhattan hard edges are a moral imperative. But after I say yes, my temples pounding, after we agree on a plan and
I set down the receiver, relief floods my apartment so thoroughly
I open a window and lean out onto the sill, sipping the air of the
city that floats and shimmers to the horizon.

The office is in a brick building on Thirtieth Street, with grimy
but dignified stonework and thick, scratched windows. I'm cleared
for entry by a taciturn woman who finds my name on a clipboard
and motions me to the end of the hall. George warned me over the
phone of the irony: his education-policy group rents office space in
a failed school, a building rezoned for business in the 1960s.

The stairs are shallow, covered in speckled tile, wide and echoing. As I climb I bear to the right and hold the rail, cornering ap-
prehensively as though a crush of oncoming student traffic might
knock me backward at any moment. I mount three floors and find
the door propped open.

He sits at a large black desk. A single folder is spread before
him, and he holds a capped pen. He's looking at the folder's contents, but from the set of his shoulders I guess he's not reading.
I step through the door, and stop. The room is large and otherwise deserted, with four cluttered desks arranged conversationally
around the sparsely decorated room. Jazz plays from a small radio
on George's desk, and before greeting him I pause to listen. The
music is a walking bass line, quiet and so low it hardly registers as
sound but rather as a shift in the atmosphere — the change your
skin or inner ear responds to before you take in its meaning: a
rainstorm blowing in from over the next hill.

He flexes his shoulders, stretching. Then, with those just right
hands I remember from the reception, turns a page.

The tingle that runs my spine is the stuff of centuries-old romantic literary cliché; it's accompanied by a hit of pure sexual longing that would never have made it into print.

My shoe squeaks on the floor. George startles.

"Hi," I say softly, an apology for sneaking up.

For a fraction of a second there's a peculiar expression on his face. It's neither sad nor happy, though it's a relative of both. It's something I can't put my finger on, and there's no opportunity to linger over it; as George rises from his seat he's already wearing the bemused smile I recall from last week. He's dressed in a sweater and jeans, and he's just as bright-eyed and lanky as I'd remembered, long-jawed, studious-looking. This time he's wearing a touch of cologne — a faint, warm smell. He greets me with a firm kiss on the cheek.

"Nice office," I say, the smell of him still in my nose.

"Thanks." He tilts his head, appraising the room, then gestures toward the nearest window, which faces into a narrow air shaft of soot-stained brick. "I first fell in love with it for the view."

My laugh comes a second late. I glance at his desktop, which holds a neat pile of well-worn textbooks and thick binders, a notebook filled with sloping script. A crowded-looking desk calendar. A scattering of pens and pencils. Behind his desk a printed sign is taped to the heavily marked chalkboard: GRAVITY: IT'S NOT JUST A GOOD IDEA. IT'S THE LAW.

While he bends to load his briefcase with a sheaf of papers, I concentrate on his face. It's a nice face. Honest. A face that seems incapable of dark secrets. Viewed from above, his lashes are thick, feminine, his forehead wide and vulnerable. There is something about seeing a tall man's forehead from above that invites tenderness. Before me, I say to myself, stands a kind man: bending over a briefcase, packing it with care, traveling the city to work with schools in crisis.

A man who looked hopeful when his date walked into the room. Now that it's had time to register, I realize that that was what played across his face when I startled him: hope. As though he were lonelier than he wanted to let on. Something in me says, Remember this.

We step out onto Seventh Avenue. The air is cool but mild. A perfect evening. We slow in unison. The street is devoid of honking, brightened here and there by yellow-crested trees, lit with that evening glow that sometimes overtakes Manhattan. Every few paces I bump against a vague obligation to speak, but something emboldens me to resist. This silence, unlike those on the telephone, seems to stitch something together. George says nothing. I can imagine us from a vantage point over the avenue: two companionable figures moving unhurriedly downtown. Every now and then I sneak a glance at him.

We reach the restaurant, a cozy affair with green tablecloths and steamed windows. At our table we survey the menu. The waiter arrives with a plate of glistening black olives, takes our order, and leaves.

We both begin to speak, then stop. George lifts an olive in salute, inviting me to go first.

"Tell me what brought you to New York," I say.

He chews his olive thoughtfully, pats his lips with his napkin, and only then answers. "I came to New York mainly to get away from Toronto. Part of a difficult break from the way I was raised. I was, in my younger days, a fundamentalist Christian. In Canada that's a rare and diminishing breed."

"I'm Jewish," I offer, spooning a few olives onto my plate.

He laughs. "I didn't invite you out to talk you into a personal relationship with your savior." Then he smiles a complicated smile, at once bright and mournful. "Getting out wasn't simple. I had to smash some idols, and I'd have to be a jerk to feel good about that. But I'll spare you that story for tonight."

"Sounds like your life is quite different these days."

"Understatement." He winks. "But you meet me now at the pinnacle of my evolutionary journey: I'm a left-leaning die-hard city dweller."

The waiter brings a wicker basket of bread and two glasses of red wine. I offer George the bread and sip my wine. "So what brought you to education policy?"

He pushes back his sleeves, takes a piece and butters it, then sets it down. "My first month in New York, before my business job started, I volunteered in a public school. And I couldn't get over how much potential was going wasted. The kids were so obviously cheated." He rests one wrist on the table. His forearms have lightly visible veins. He rolls open his fingers as he speaks — a calm gesture. "I didn't forget it, though I didn't get into the field for a few years."

As I busy myself with buttering my own slice, something flutters from nowhere into my mind: That this man might turn out to be a lover whose presence I'd carry with me all day — saving up my impressions to deposit in his hands. A man I could laugh with. A teammate. A partner with whom I could rest. Suddenly I realize how deeply I want to rest. The notion is shockingly, alarmingly, seductive.

When my train of thought recouples, George is concluding a sentence. "— so I decided policy work was the thing. It's not the easiest line of work, or the most profitable. But at least I feel I'm of some use."

I sip my wine and nod enthusiastically. I have no idea how he got into education policy but trust in my ability, honed through years of graduate school seminars, to pick this up later.

"So you see, it was either education or the madhouse," he says. I laugh. He seems surprised. Maybe I missed something serious.

"Don't know what I was thinking, going straight into stock trading after college. Someone told me that was the only way to make it in New York, and I believed it. Decisions people make in their twenties — later we can't remember what the hell inspired us. Like Stonehenge."

I nod gravely.

"Like disco," he says.

I form a miniature smile.

"Like leeches and bloodletting. Like putting mercury in hatbands and other follies of world history. Like invading Russia just before the first snows." He folds his arms and looks at me. "I'm not going to stop this until you laugh. Because only that will redeem my original bad joke."

I do. He gives a boyish grin and relaxes back into his chair.

"Tell me about your life," he says. "For real. Not like on the phone."

The waiter brings two steaming plates of pasta; I wait for him to leave.

"Yeah," I say. "That was —"

George shakes his head. "Doesn't matter. Just tell me."

George's hair is straight and flops over one temple. It's thinning, but doing so peaceably, without sticky hair-product comb furrows, or the tufted look of men who curry every precious strand. He gives off an air of unconcerned cleanliness that's undeniably attractive.

"I love books," I say.

"Love them how?" He digs into his pasta with fork and spoon.

"I love the escape. Academics aren't supposed to say that, but it's true. I love to dive into somebody else's vision, nightmare, utopia, whatever. I love how books put a dent in our egos — turns out we're not the first sentient generation on the planet after all. Other people have been just as perceptive, just as worked up, about the same damn human problems we face. I love the theory part — trying to link books together with ideas, like a string of nonidentical pearls."

"I'm with you," he says.

"I specialize in American lit. The interwar period."

"Why?"

I smile. "I like it."

He matches my smile. "Why?"

His teasing unlatches something in my gut — the anxiety I've carried all day without realizing it. A happy laugh escapes me, and I know that this time I won't clutch like on the phone. The relief acts on me like caffeine.

"It wasn't easy settling on a field. Did you know that Christopher Columbus ended up going mad?"

He shakes his head.

"Did you know that a Thomas Paine fan exhumed Paine's body in order to rebury him in England — but the plan fell apart and the bones got lost? *Lost.* So our country's most plainspoken, secular, ahead-of-their-times bones are out there somewhere, floating. I mean, a person could spend her career on just those two ironies. I considered it, for about a week. But early America didn't hold me. There's just no way around the fact that the settlers banished neighbors for 'divisiveness' and 'error,' and I didn't want to spend my life looking at the world through their eyes. The Enlightenment was a little more appealing — all that Puritan stuff eased up enough to let in some whimsy, and by then Ben Franklin had broken the news that individuals were people too. And more women began writing." I hesitate. I hadn't planned to go into such detail. But it feels good. And he's smiling at me over his pasta. "The problem was, Thoreau still got censored for saying a pine tree might go to 'as high a heaven' as a man. And reading past all the slavery-era racism just made me tired."

George has set down his fork and is listening.

"I was too much of a city girl to go for the Transcendentalists. I did get hooked on the nineteenth century, though, and almost stayed. I spent a long time on Dickinson and Chopin. And I think Melville is the greatest American writer, period. He just — he wrote about" — under George's gaze I blush — "the power, the holy terror, of life. Even somebody like me, whose life has been comparatively a cakewalk, can see how *true* his work was, if you know what I mean. I loved Melville so much I almost wrote my dissertation on him. But there was the twentieth century peeking over the horizon. I read Hemingway. And Faulkner. And Zora Neale Hurston." I raise my water glass and drink. "You get me talking."

He reaches across the table and takes my hand.

I let my palm rest lightly against his. The warmth is delicious. I bounce my hand gently. Our palms make contact, part, rejoin: a frank, curious conversation.

"So," he prompts. "The twentieth century was eyeing you over the horizon . . ."

"Before this, authors still addressed the audience as Gentle Reader. The twentieth century is when people stopped assuming the reader was gentle. Nobody could afford to be gentle anymore. The stakes were too high. We already knew what gentility got us: World War I. So now, no more distant third-person narratives. No more blind dedication to principles, noble suffering in silence. Even lovers couldn't be idealized anymore. Everybody had to struggle together to build something honest, even if it was messy. Readers had to pay their ante and roll up their sleeves right next to the authors. It's not that you *couldn't* believe in patriotism, or love, or glory — postmodern pessimism hadn't yet arrived. But you had to build it from the ground up. Europe had failed, the whole world was up for grabs, and America was grabbing. Anarchy, Prohibition, the Harlem Renaissance, radio, cubism, Freud. And in the middle of all that, the writers changed the sentence. They made it growl, if you know what I mean. And yes—interwar America had its uglinesses. But the writing is transcendent.

"So I switched to twentieth century and modernism. I wrote my dissertation on Hurston. That's it. That's my story."

Hand still supporting mine, he sips his wine. "Now what?"

"I'm up for tenure."

"When?"

"This winter. I'm trying not to worry over it." I hesitate, distracted by a glimpse of his collarbone, which is sturdy-looking. "But I'd be an idiot not to make the extra effort these days to keep my ducks in a row."

"And the tenure process?"

"Coming along."

He raises an eyebrow.

"I don't like to burden people—"

"Doubt it'll break me."

"Either I get tenured and promoted this semester, or I'll go on the job market—something I'd rather not contemplate."

"That bad?"

"I'm one of the lucky few Manhattan Ph.D.s who didn't have to move to Boise or Anchorage for a job after graduation. My adviser retired the year I finished my Ph.D. and green-lighted me to fill his spot. One day I was at my graduation, lined up in my robe with a few hundred strangers, all of us with those ridiculous wind socks draped down our backs. The next day I was a prof. I deserved the job: I had good publications and a solid academic record. But so did dozens of others. I'd have to be pretty arrogant to deny the role of luck. Half a dozen smart classmates of mine got nothing but adjunct offers."

He hasn't let go of my hand. His barely restrained smile dares me to continue as though there were no other current running between us. I dare him, in return, to listen.

"And there but for the grace of the tenure committee go I— back into the pit of nonbenefited slave labor over which we junior academics dangle."

"I'm with you," he murmurs.

This, I see, is George's verbal signature. The words mean only *I understand,* but when he says them it sounds like *I'll keep you company.* I'm not only talking — I'm talking to another person, truly talking to another person, the way most conversations aren't. I crack open a window on my life; out come thoughts I've confessed to no one.

"If you want to know what academia is really like," I say, "here it is in a nutshell. I've got a new project in mind, and I'm excited about it — I keep hopping out of bed at night to jot down notes. So I just wrote it up for a few applications, the sort of fellowships that offer a year off the academic grind to just do your own work. I'm not going to win one, it's like an academic lottery ticket. But everyone applies. Now strangers on fellowship committees are going to read my new ideas — yet I haven't breathed a word of them to my colleagues. And I won't, until I'm on the other side of my tenure review. The project is too risky, too easy to snipe at." My words slow. "Dealing with academic politics," I say, "is like reading a book while walking in a rainstorm. You crane your neck like hell to anchor the umbrella's stem while you turn pages. Step over puddles while trying to keep your eyes on the printed words. And pray you're not about to put your foot in it."

A comfortable silence unfurls between us.

Then he says, "You fill a lot of time talking about your work."

My hand goes dead in his. "If you weren't interested in all that, you could have said so."

He shakes his head. "That's not what I meant. Everything you said is interesting. What I meant was that I asked you to tell me about yourself. And now I know a lot about what you think about. But not much about you."

I withdraw my hand. "Is there a difference?"

"Yes."

"So what was I supposed to tell you?" There's no masking the hurt in my voice.

He shakes his head again, watching me. "I don't know."

My words sound brittle. "Give me your best guess."

"Maybe who you used to be. Who you are now. Who you hope to be. What you're afraid of."

"I'm afraid of not getting tenure. Does that count?"

He thinks a moment before answering. "Not really."

I straighten in my seat. He is, once more, a stranger. He's responding as though I haven't just been pouring out my heart, intellectually speaking, for an entire meal. *Do you criticize all your dates,* I'm on the verge of asking. But what I mean is, *How dare you?*

"Water?" he says. He refills my glass from the pitcher on the table. He doesn't, I have to admit, sound like someone who's just passed judgment—but rather someone who's stumbled across something that's piqued his interest. There it is again: that thoughtful, inquisitive look. It's obvious it means me no harm. But I feel harm. I can't recall the last time I felt so rattled.

"What about you?" This time I keep my voice neutral. "Tell me who *you* are."

He opens his mouth and laughs. "Touché," he says. "Okay . . . I have a new theory about the universe. It came to me this week." He watches me. Once more, that gentle dare. "Yesterday, while sitting at my desk, I thought: Life isn't people or animals or trees."

"No?"

"Nope. Life isn't us, though we make that mistake all the time—thinking we're life. But life is really just this big glorious wave, like a wave in a pond—it's the *energy* that moves across the pond. And the thing is, we're insignificant."

"We are?"

"Imagine doing the wave in a stadium. *We're* not the wave—the wave is its own creature. At one instant all the people standing are part of it, the next instant the wave has gone past us forever."

"Unless you're a Hindu or Buddhist, and you believe the stadium is circular."

He smiles—I've taken the dare. "All right. But we can't know the stadium's shape. All we know is, we can't hold onto the wave. It doesn't belong to us any more than it belonged to the millions of generations it already passed through, on its way to wherever it's headed. We're just little bits of matter that get to be the ones in the wave for this particular millisecond." He stops to consider me. "I was sitting at my desk this morning, just thinking how beautiful the whole thing is. And how before we fall back to being nothing—to being just empty water drops—we want to procreate. Send along our descendants, so they can be part of the wave for their own millisecond, too. And maybe their kids and grandkids might each be part of the wave for a flash, when we're already way behind in the wake. It's like we're wired to be sure that the wave goes on. That's our whole" — he hesitates, then his palm describes a low arc over our table — "*purpose*. On earth. To stand up, and flap our arms. And sit down again and wish the wave well. And hope someone else keeps the damn thing going."

I think about this, fork stilled over my plate.

"That's it," he says, sitting back to watch me. "The World According to George."

And George doesn't waste time.

"I like the idea of five billion people standing up at once," I say. "Doing the wave."

"Would look pretty good, eh?" he murmurs.

"More than good. Staggering." I chew a forkful of pasta. "Though — you think maybe we have some other purposes on earth? Any other legacies we leave?"

He considers, then grins. "You seem worth doing the wave for."

I can't help laughing in his face — a high, glad laugh. So he doesn't think badly of me?

He polishes off the last of his pasta.

Or is he just flirting, upping the ante to pass the time?

"Admit it," I say. "You use this routine on all the women."

"I throw food to get their attention, then dazzle them with kitchen-sink philosophy?"

"Well, give me this: There aren't too many men who talk about procreation on a first date. It's a bit forward, don't you think?"

"So this is a ploy?"

I level my fork at him. "You could be a serial food thrower. I hear about that all the time."

He chuckles.

The waiter brings the dessert cart.

And as I watch George mull the selection, a loose feeling overtakes my limbs: the knowledge that something important has happened. I order blindly, echoing George's choice.

The waiter brings two cannolis. I've never eaten a cannoli, never thought I'd like them. But these look delicious.

Across the table, George cracks the shell with his fork.

That's when it hits me: a man who composes theories of the universe, a man who makes me notice things I never noticed — there it is. Right there. This is my romantic.

At the entrance of my building we stop. George smiles right into my eyes. He pulls me into a hug — my head slips just under his chin, and for a second I fit against the surprisingly muscular elasticity of his chest. Then he lifts my hand and kisses it — a warm, soft kiss.

And I think: Did I just lose him?

Wednesday afternoon's meeting has been called by Joanne Miller. According to an e-mail addressed to the entire department — including, in a break with usual protocol, graduate students — it has come to Joanne's attention that the faculty has no consensus on grade inflation. Hence Joanne's e-mail, titled "Time to Clean House."

Grade inflation has come to my attention too — as well as the attention of every major national newspaper, everyone in higher education, and even a handful of enlightened parents. A few intradepartmental resolutions on the subject would, indeed, be useful, and if Grub were a more energetic chairman he'd have convened a meeting on the subject months ago. Instead he's turned the task over to Joanne, whom I once heard him refer to as "bushytailed."

Walking the several dozen yards from my office to the conference room, I try to muster my thoughts on grade inflation. Instead I'm distracted by recollections of last night. Was George, in chiding me for talking too long about my work, dismissing everything I care about? Belittling the dedication and passion I've poured into literature? Or was he after something else; was he coaxing me to peer out of a shell — one I've grown comfortable in? And was I too defensive? And didn't I break up with Jason because he *didn't* challenge me? And was that the stupidest move a sentient human has ever made?

Reaching the conference room, I tuck these thoughts away and focus on the unpleasant business — and colleague — at hand.

The first time I encountered Joanne, during my second semester as a graduate student, she was at the lectern. I'd arranged, as part of a requirement for a pedagogy seminar, to attend four professors' opening lectures of the semester. Joanne's course was titled Sixteenth-Century Literature. At ten o'clock sharp she darkened the hall without a word of greeting to the students, many of whom became plainly uneasy they'd entered the wrong room. Up went a giant projection of King's College Chapel. There was a moment's deep silence. Then Joanne began to recite. "Did not we meet, to Truthe enthrall'd, our Soules enlarg'd in this Hallow'd Hall." Another silence. Several chairs creaked. "Most people," intoned Joanne from the bulb-lit lectern beneath the screen, "approach the great cathedrals with awe. They ought to approach them with relief." The slide changed to a view of the chapel's interior. "These buildings, and the literature that went with them, embody an era in which people weren't afraid to believe what they believed—no matter if that brought glory or suffering." Behind her, the lacy stone vault of the chapel soared impossibly high. "No apology *there*," she said, stabbing the slender shadow of her pointer onto the screen. "Entering this lecture hall, you've stepped into an era that predates doubt. A person might win or lose, live or die—but life was struggle, never paralysis. Moral uncertainty was not in the sixteenth-century worldview. You may think of the sixteenth century as the era of obsessive love poetry, but that's only because our modern perspective has blinded us to the more important aspects of this writing. In fact the sixteenth century was an age of poets like none since. Poets who wrestled with the workings of the world. The capacities and limits of the soul." Joanne gave a swift signal to a waiting TA. The hall lights snapped on; King's College Chapel vanished. Stepping to the center of the stage, Joanne loomed over the dazed students. "They built the moral house you think in."

Another prof might not have pulled it off. Joanne, though, has that magnetism you sometimes see in physically powerful people. She's a big woman—not overweight, just post-college-jock-imposing—with a voice bred on the rugby field and a carriage that hints she might tackle if you resist her interpretation of a sonnet. She has a wide face, faint freckles, and pale-lashed brown eyes that, under rimless glasses, are keen and unblinking. Her prematurely gray-streaked hair, pulled back in a tight bun, gives her face a powerful dignity. In a certain light, caught in a certain becalmed mood, she brings to mind a larger-than-life figure in an allegorical painting by Raphael, or even a Vermeer portrait: her face timeless, her unmasked gaze so thoughtfully penetrating it unnerves.

These days the sixteenth-century gig is staffed either by pallid romantics, drawn by all those sonnets detailing women's features in fourteen innuendo-laden lines, or by morbid souls fascinated with the unforgiving morality plays of an age when life was synonymous with suffering. All those paeans to loss. All those marble busts of dead cherubic children, cold stony ghosts of their former ruddy selves. Joanne's cospecialists are a mousy, bookish lot, even for professors. Among this cohort Joanne is — agree or disagree with her — a standout.

At the end of that first lecture I scribbled in my notebook: *At last! A prof unafraid to show intellectual passion!*

That was then. Since I joined the faculty, Joanne Miller has appeared on my radar primarily as a somewhat self-important colleague a rung higher on the academic ladder (five years older than me, and recently tenured). She's a solid academician and publishes reasonably often. Her papers are persuasive if not lightning-bolt original. I know little else about her, as she never reciprocated the overtures I made when I was first hired. But I've had no problems with Joanne, apart from a few skirmishes upon joining the faculty. (Garden-variety turf battles. Would I *please* ask my students to exit lecture quietly, so their clamor of postlecture liberation won't disrupt Joanne's Spenser seminar across the hall? She doesn't know what I'm doing to them in there, but they sure sound happy to get out. Just kidding.)

It's only her recent push for departmental all-star status that's earned Joanne an upgrade to true nuisance. She's going to climb the academic ladder by sheer bloody-mindedness. She's willing to take on the committee work no one else wants; she's poised to organize and discipline the entire faculty at Grub's behest. Joanne's blunt organizational missives have become a regular addition to the department's e-mail in boxes. Yet when I groused to Jeff he dismissed me. "*You* want to do the work?" he said. "Let her be chairman's pet." Joanne may be tenured, says Jeff, but the sixteenth century is out of vogue. The reach of her work is limited, and she knows it. Every department has a majority whip. Better her, says Jeff, than us.

I join the small crowd assembling in the conference room. Faculty and grad students file in slowly, the grad students pooling just inside the entrance—unaccustomed to attending faculty meetings, they lean against the wall, hesitant to claim a professor's habitual seat.

Entering, Jeff pauses beside me. "This is going to be fun," he whispers. "Joanne's been collecting dirt. I predict a departmental steam cleaning. Alas, I happened to have an unusual number of competent students last term." His blue eyes pop as he mimes the yank of a noose around his neck. He takes his seat.

The faculty is nearly assembled: the theorists intermingled with the Romanticists, our two Medievalists seated beside a clutch of postmodernists, who as usual look depressed. I settle between Jeff and Steven Hilliard, a literary theory specialist visiting this year from Oxford. Steven greets me as casually as though there were nothing irregular about the presence of a visiting prof at a faculty meeting. When Grub enters, Steven rises to greet him with a genial hand clasp, making me recall Jeff's darkly approving commentary upon meeting Steven: *You have to be pulling strings somewhere to get that kind of access to the chair. Even with a genuine British accent.* Maybe so. But you also have to be either a masochist or an extreme political climber to attend another department's meetings by choice—even if some well-meaning faculty member has taken the highly unusual step of inviting you.

The grad students, as sudden and unanimous as birds on a wire, push off from the wall and fill the remaining seats.

Joanne, greeting the twenty-odd assembled faculty and dozen graduate students with efficient cheer, is passing out single sheets of paper.

"Let's see—Tracy . . ." She flips through the pile, extracts a page, and hands it to me. It's a printout from the registrar's office. For a moment, my outrage is stalled by wonder at Joanne's resourcefulness. I have no idea how she persuaded the registrar's office to do this, but some bushy-tailed computer operator in the bowels of that bureaucracy has compiled a list of the grades issued by each professor over the past year.

Joanne — who doubtless pored over the record of each of her colleagues before this meeting — continues distributing printouts until each of us holds evidence of our own handiwork. Then she paces the center of the room, giving us time to digest our sins.

Scanning my page, I see I've given a decent scattering of grades; my average, B, is at least lower than the departmental average, which hovers between B+ and A−. Jeff, however, looks annoyed; clearly he was more generous than he recalled. There's a deep and unusual silence in the room. Looking around, it's easy to guess which of my colleagues have matched or topped the already inflated average.

"I've taken the highly unusual step of gathering all of us in one room," Joanne begins, "because graduate students do so much of this department's grading, and we need to discuss this together."

Silence.

"Some of you may only now be realizing," Joanne intones, "that you've unwittingly contributed to a problem that's hit our university, along with most other American universities. Ultimately this is a problem that can be solved best by following your consciences." So announces Joanne, proud owner of a conscience.

"Jesse," she says.

The room is dead quiet. Jesse Faden glares at her.

"You might want to look at your record." She offers an efficient nod, as though she hasn't just breached a fundamental barrier, chastising a faculty member in front of the graduate students. She continues: "As should most of the faculty." A few of whom look bemused, most of whom look stunned.

"Jeff," Joanne says, "you too."

Jeff meets Joanne's gaze with a look of mild remonstration, then raises his fingers in lazy salute. "Mea culpa," he says dryly.

"You too, Elizabeth," says Joanne.

Some of the graduate students wear expressions of barely disguised horror. Rather than provoking jealousy among her fellow grad students, Elizabeth's peculiarities inspire awe and a touch of protectiveness.

"I believe, Elizabeth, that you've been a particularly egregious offender," says Joanne. "You gave almost sixty percent of your students A's or A-minuses."

Until now, Joanne has always seemed to like Elizabeth. This

meeting has started to feel like a declaration of war, though on whom and for what purpose is unclear. Across the table from me, Elizabeth is flushed hot pink and looks as though she might pass out.

Steven Hilliard raises his hand—actually *raises his hand,* so Oxford is he—and contributes a question. "What standards do we agree upon for grading? How, for example, shall this department *define* a C?"

It's a question that would be eminently reasonable were he an actual faculty member, rather than a visiting prof who shouldn't be in this meeting in the first place. For now, though, no one is in a mood to rebuke him. On the faces around the room, irritation at his presence—at the bizarre format of the meeting altogether—is overruled by gratitude for his civil intervention. Surely when Newton penned his law—for every action, an equal and opposite reaction—he had academic politics in mind. And now that Joanne has bared political knuckles, politeness springs up like a force of nature. A recent hire clears his throat and makes a first modest suggestion. A grad student offers another. The definition of a C billows between the walls of the conference room. C means average. C means no ability but some effort. Speakers defer to one another; those who don't speak wear mainly neutral expressions, in compliance with that basic rule of academia: To survive in the wild, a professor must develop the instincts of a small rock-dwelling animal. When an eagle flies by—or when sniping begins in your presence—freeze. Then camouflage. If you are able to turn translucent, do so immediately.

Only when the discussion has lulled does Victoria speak up. "I don't believe it's necessary to single out individuals," she says. "This is a departmental problem, one in which we all have a stake."

I've always respected Victoria, who speaks her mind in a terse New England manner that invites no closeness and allows no bullshit. With her snow-white pageboy and clear blue eyes, cream blouse and tailored gray skirt, Victoria is my definition of unruffleable. There are nods around the table.

"It is quite clear," Victoria continues, "that we can all benefit by addressing the grading issue."

There is vehement agreement, and the ensuing discussion, moderated by Joanne, rapidly produces a draft of new grading standards and a provision for evaluating our progress as a department. Joanne paces the room's perimeter restlessly. Pausing to make notes on a pad, she towers over Paleozoic, who sits mummified in his chair with lids at half-mast—his pug nose tilted to the ceiling, emitting a slight whistle so it's impossible to tell whether he's sleeping or just listening hard.

I'm silent during the discussion—unusual for me. Something holds me back. I keep my eye on Joanne. I've always found her difficult, but there's something odd about today's ferocity. Joanne wears a look of naked, exhausted triumph that makes me think she's about to crow, or cry.

As the meeting winds down, the older faculty begin snapping briefcase latches and checking watches. Tuning out Joanne's closing comments, I find myself wondering what George would be doing if he were here. For an instant I envision the stuffy room flash lit with his humor. And see his expression as he watched me over dinner: curious, expectant, compassionate, as though I were, unwittingly, making some tremulous and unexpected confession. Even in recollection it makes me feel exposed. Only this time, for no discernible reason, discomfort makes way for a sensation like fizzy water. I stroke the back of my hand.

"What are you smiling about?"

I glance over my shoulder to see whom she's addressing.

"*Who, me?*" Joanne mocks. Her tone is not gentle. "Don't be cute, Tracy. What are you smiling about?"

Holding my smile, I will my face not to become a furnace. "Nothing, Joanne."

The briefcase tinkerers fall silent.

"Why don't you share the joke?" Joanne booms.

There's an uncertain titter from somewhere to my left.

I keep my voice level. "I'm smiling, Joanne, because I'm happy."

Joanne blinks at me, her gaze sharp. "Ha." She actually says the word, like a cartoon character incapable of a proper laugh. She waits another moment, but I neither speak nor duck her eyes.

She turns back to the others. "Any questions?"

Leaving the room I walk apart from my colleagues, a momentary pariah. With visible relief, faculty and grad students break into separate clusters and move off in silence down the hall. Ahead of me, Jeff squeezes Elizabeth's shoulder before their paths diverge.

Paleozoic, newly roused, peers sharply at the two of them. He stares until Jeff turns into his office and Elizabeth vanishes down the hallway. You can see the gears creaking in his mind.

As I pass Joanne, she taps my shoulder. Her face is pale and expressionless. "Don't bullshit me," she whispers.

We jolt along Varick Street. Adam steers with one hand and with the other fishes at the bottom of a bag of potato chips. The borrowed Civic, evidently shockless, enunciates each pothole with jarring clarity. Frowning, Adam turns from the road to scrutinize the inside of the bag. Someone honks; he looks up with a grunt, swerves back into the lane, and tips the contents of the bag into his mouth.

Since his return to New York, Adam has been lackadaisically job-hunting — trolling, according to Hannah, for the lowest possible responsibility-to-salary ratio. Last weekend he moved his duffel into an echoing Boerum Hill two-bedroom he plans to share with a college buddy. He's been eating corn flakes for dinner, sleeping on the floor on a pallet of unfolded laundry topped by a sheet. Convinced that Adam needs a personal shopper in his reluctant pursuit of a futon and other house basics, Hannah promised to shepherd him through the painful acquisition of domesticity. This morning, when Elijah woke with a fever, she phoned me, only half kidding: Could I? Would I? Someone needed to save Adam from himself.

Knowing I was too restless to do a stitch of work, I agreed to fill in for her. A decision I'm beginning to regret.

"Hey," I say. "Could you watch the road? A little bit?" I indicate the looming entrance of the Holland Tunnel, the narrowing lanes of traffic. "Didn't they have driving laws in Russia?"

He crunches chips. "None I noticed."

In the ghostly illumination of the tunnel, Adam consumes the remaining crumbs. Adam's always had that tousled, sleepy look that makes some women want to take care of a guy. Personally I've never seen the appeal. Big blue eyes don't compensate, in my view, for a desire to be an adult. But Adam's got his own brand of magic. In truth I've missed him more than I'd realized. As the fluorescent lights flicker over his face, I watch his jawbones work and see he's lost weight. Most people return from an assignation with Russian cuisine several pounds heftier. But apparently Adam ran himself ragged over there. According to Hannah, between bartending shifts Adam did volunteer work with some of the poorer families. And Gorky had a hard winter.

"So what was it like?" I say.

Adam munches. "Shortages. Ghost towns. The country looks like it's falling to pieces any minute, but it doesn't, or never all the way."

"What did you like?"

"The people," he says, now watching the traffic steadily. "One minute neighbors are cheating each other and the next minute they're bailing each other out. They surprised me every day. I think they surprise themselves."

White lozenge-lights escort the unbroken ribbons of traffic beneath the river. The tile walls and roof shimmer with reflections: watery white headlights, inverted red taillights sailing passively overhead as far as the eye can see. Today the tunnel's mesmerizing length seems merciful, offering the columns of urban drivers a few moments' reprieve from choice. The traffic snakes submissively ahead of us. I watch it for a long time, thinking.

"Also the vodka," says Adam. "I liked the vodka."

"How did you manage bartending, anyway?" I ask. "Last I knew you didn't have a clue how to tend bar."

"I bought a book about mixing drinks."

"You read a *book?*"

Adam pegs me with a long look of contempt. I return the favor. "No," he says. "I just *consulted* one. I did all right except the days I forgot to bring it to work. There was this one time I didn't have it, and this Mafia-looking dude sat down with his buddies and told the waitress to get him a Manhattan. I had no idea what was in one, so I mixed up a stiff blue fruit drink. The waitress took it over, and the guy sent her back in a nanosecond. And she did not look happy. So I had the waitress call him over. He comes over, I swear he's a goddamn ape, and he points at the drink with this fucking huge finger, and he says, 'This isn't a Manhattan.' And all his friends are listening in and grinning because he's going to break my face. So I say to him in my very best Russian, 'Where are you from?' He says 'Gorky.' So I go quiet and confidential, and I say to him, 'Me? I'm from Manhattan. And I'm telling you, this is a

Manhattan.' The guy thinks. He says, 'Really?' And I go" — Adam indicates a solemn nod — "and the guy takes his drink and goes back to his posse. To this day I bet you there's a Mafioso serving up blue Manhattans in Gorky." He snorts. Then sighs.

There's a new flavor to Adam's humor. A mournful half-smile that lingers after he's told a funny story; an abrupt, sun-breaking-through-clouds grin after he's related something difficult. Shocking as this would have been a few years ago, I find myself learning from him.

"Did you feel guilty for being able to leave?" I ask.

"Nope. Everybody in the world who has a chance to live well should jump on it."

I watch him. "You know, you should really write an article about what you saw over there."

He laughs aloud. "Only you could mean that as a compliment."

"It *is* a compliment."

"Why would I want to write about it? That's like suggesting I go stick my brain in the furnace for a couple weeks. Writing is work."

"So forget writing. I'm just saying, you could do all kinds of things. With your experiences. I mean, you've got interesting things to say."

He smirks. "You mean I have *potential?*"

"You *do* have to be really smart to act so stupid."

He looks at me. "At last, a real compliment."

In the years I've known Adam, our friendship's highest accolade has been *you don't suck;* suddenly, though, it seems imperative not to let him mock away my praise. "It's true," I say to him. "You can walk on water when you want to."

Adam seems embarrassed by this uncharacteristic earnestness. As am I. Then, slowly, he shakes his head. "You and Hannah. Did it ever occur to you that maybe I don't want ambition? That I've seen where it gets people?"

This silences me. I've never before heard Adam criticize his parents' choices, or Hannah's picture-perfect life. Hannah and Adam's parents, both intense professionals, divorced a half-dozen years ago after decades of fearsome battles. Each parent is now independently nearing the highest rung on the professional ladder.

Each is consistently miserable. Scrolling back through the years, I'm chagrined by the entertainment Hannah and I found in ribbing Adam for his slothfulness.

Adam pilots us out of the tunnel. The daylight is blinding. We approach I-95 in silence. Adam shifts into fifth gear. "By the way," he says, "I give him credit. It's a classy way out."

"You give who credit?" I turn and look emphatically over my left shoulder at the I-95 traffic, hoping Adam will be inspired to follow my example.

Adam scoots us onto the highway two feet ahead of an eighteen-wheeler. The truck is practically on our bumper. Adam floors it. "Your date. A guy kisses you on the hand when he doesn't want to kiss you for real." Having found a foolproof way to change the subject, he whistles contentedly. I hadn't even mentioned my evening with George. I glare at him.

"Shut up," I say.

He does, which is unsatisfying.

"You're an utter waste of DNA."

He tips his baseball cap.

"And how do you know so much about my date?"

"NPR. Hannah was on-air taking questions about the hand kiss." He gives me a long, wicked smile.

"Jesus! Watch the road!"

He holds his pose another second, then slowly turns back to the windshield.

In truth we're not going fast, and now that we're ahead of the truck the highway doesn't look crowded. Still.

"I don't remember soliciting your opinion about my date," I say to him. Adam: whose romantic résumé includes the time Kim, his college girlfriend, insisted after almost two years on knowing what he felt for her — at which point he assured her that she was *the shit* (end quote) and she broke up with him.

"You most certainly did. You asked me just after you got into the car whether there'd been any interesting women in Russia. And you were *beaming* at me."

"I was not beaming."

Adam reaches across my knees to the glove compartment and pulls out a pair of mirrored sunglasses, which he unfolds and settles on the bridge of his nose. "You're doing it again. I have to wear protective gear."

The Ikea sign appears on the side of the highway ahead of us. When Adam glances my way again, I see my face in the distorted reflection of the lenses: owl-eyed, pale. Hopeful.

How are you supposed to conduct yourself when you believe you've had some kind of soul connection with a stranger, but —being a modern rather than a character in a nineteenth-century play—you still have to suffer the petty indignities of dating? Indignities about which you are, as a habit, skeptical?

"You've got my sister going to mush over this," Adam continues. "She thinks hand kisses are the shit."

Profoundly romantic were Hannah's exact words.

Adam steers us down the exit ramp. "Watch what you do to pregnant ladies. All the gushiness is going to turn that fetus into a girl." We leave the highway for a smaller road, where we sit in line at a light. Above us is an enormous billboard on which a woman's slender hand is practically dwarfed by the diamond ring it bears. "YES," SHE SAID, TREMBLING WITH EXCITEMENT. The image towers over the stalled traffic: iconography of a civic religion. Below the caption someone has spray-painted GET A LIFE. Through the open windows, the warm gritty exhaust of a nearby truck lays siege to our car.

"So," I venture. "You think he didn't want to kiss me? I mean—"

"Whoooooeeeee!" Adam sticks his head out the window and sends a howl to the pollution-tinged heavens. The driver inching forward past in the next lane slams her brakes and turns, with an expression of panic, to find the source of the noise. His head back inside the car, Adam grins at me. "Let me get this straight. You're actually asking *me* for advice."

"Maybe."

"So, what's your offer? What fabulous prizes await me if I share my brilliant—my *walk-on-water*—observations?" His expression—part wry, part barbed—defies me to compliment him again. Traffic begins to flow. He zips us forward. The car ahead of us brakes, and we lurch to a halt just in time to avoid a fender-bender.

"I don't negotiate with terrorists."

"I'll advise you on one condition," he says.

"Which is?"

"Quit driving."

"What are you talking about?"

He makes a bare gesture with his knuckles toward the well where my flexed foot hovers over the floor mat. "You're braking right now. You drive even when you're not driving. If you don't stop you're going to get muscle spasms in your foot."

"I'm not—"

"And if you keep denying it you're going to get carpal ego syndrome."

"Look."

He looks.

"Look," I repeat. "It's just, maybe you could leave a little more following distance."

He makes a face.

"For my sake. I know you're a safe driver." I don't know that he's a safe driver but am willing to make this concession in the interest of peace.

He makes a worse face.

I flex my toes, kick off my flats, and prop a foot on the dashboard.

Adam laughs, a laugh with mercy in it. "Tracy, you want to know what I really think about the hand kiss?" He lowers the sunglasses to the tip of his nose. "If you like this guy, then you must have had, you know, connection. And you're smart enough to be able to tell when connection is two-sided." He brings the car to another juddering halt. "So if *you* think he likes you, then he does. Now the only question is, Why no real kiss? Okay. So. Possibility numero uno: he's shy."

I recall the paper plate on its way down to the carpet, scattering tabouli like a spinning Milky Way. "I don't think it's shyness," I say.

"So that leaves two other possibilities. Either he's into you, but you gave him the vibe that you weren't into him. Or else the chemistry isn't there."

"Hannah thinks it's romantic that he only kissed my hand."

"No offense to my sister, but which of us do you think knows guys better? I'm telling you, you'll know everything on the next date. There *is* the remote possibility he was just doing the gentleman thing for first-impression's sake. But no matter what, lips must lock by date numero two. Nerves or chivalry can muck up date one, but if there's no serious lip mosh by the second date, then forget it. Either the guy's not interested, or else he's *too* much of a gent. In which case you don't want him."

We inch forward in traffic once more.

"You actually like this one, huh, Trace?"

I release my breath. "I think so."

"Well, good luck."

I look at him, silently communicating my appreciation.

With a yelp, Adam punches the sunglasses back up over his eyes. "Jesus, give me a little warning next time you're going to do that."

Later, as an act of appreciation and charity, I dissuade Adam from buying black sheets, a black comforter, black dishes, and black plasticware, on the theory that he will not need to wash them.

George phones at five o'clock to firm up plans.

"You're sure you want to do this?" I say. "Yolanda is good, she really is. But the play itself may not be a winner. You may regret coming. Maybe we ought to hold off, and plan something else."

"I won't prosecute if the show is a flop. Besides, I love theater. And didn't you say you're not free any other evening this week? And that your friend gave you an extra ticket?"

In fact Yolanda phoned this weekend to insist I invite *that George guy* to the opening—a gesture I found brave given her current emotional state. The thought of what George and Yolanda might make of each other, especially with Yolanda poised to vaporize all unrepentant males, makes me anxious. But I'm out of arguments. We agree that he'll come by my apartment and we'll take the subway to the theater. Remembering Adam's caution that I might have discouraged George on our first date, I hesitate before getting off the phone. "I'm looking forward to it," I say.

There's a substantial pause before George replies. "I'll see you at seven."

From the street comes the long honk of an irate driver. The phone line is silent. I rise and, with ripening dismay, shut my window.

"Meanwhile," says George, "I'll phone the Canadian embassy to find out whether it's a violation of international trade laws to give my heart to an American."

My giggle makes me sound like a fourteen-year-old.

At six-thirty I dress. The miniskirt and top are maroon and tight, a gift from Yolanda: *If you've got the body, wear the clothes. If you don't, you'll regret it when you're fifty.*

I turn grimly before the mirror.

Being a proponent of difference feminism rather than equality feminism, I am not in principle alarmed by miniskirts. But I'm accustomed to seeing a scholar in the mirror, not a pair of legs. The outfit isn't me — or rather, it's more of me than I usually display. On the plus side, though, it definitely gives the vibe that I'm into the guy. I add a gauzy black scarf, which produces a more brooding, dramatic look than I'd intended; the effect, a little more Edna St. Vincent Millay than my usual, is definitely bold.

On the other hand, sexual boldness didn't exactly guarantee her happiness.

I exchange miniskirt and scarf for a pair of black pants.

If I were a postmodernist, I'd say St. Vincent Millay never had a chance at what she wanted. I'd say that all love is revisionist history. That totalitarian governments should take lessons from lovers. That I will rewrite this moment depending on the events of the future. In retrospect, it will be the moment I stood in front of the mirror and knew, despite wanting to believe otherwise, that George was a dead end, or worse, a black hole into which I'd pour months of my life. Or else I'll hail it as the moment I understood, in some indefinable way, that George was for me. Either way, though, I'd have to concede that the whole thing was a construct. Postmodernists can't believe in love. It's illegal.

As a modernist I can, technically, believe in love — but only as reconstituted from the fragments of shattered cultural ideals. Facing down the mirror, I remind myself that I was, for most of graduate school, a Romanticist, specializing in the shapely narrative, the honest hero, love as destiny. This seems to brighten my prospects until I recall how in college I once heard my Romanticism TA, when he thought no one was listening, say to another grad student *Love is shit.*

Shit.

I change into jeans. And a slightly snug blouse. The buzzer sounds. I drop my hairbrush, grab my handbag, and, flushed, stride my way through the hall and into the elevator.

At the door he kisses me. It's a soft, long kiss, and when he's finished I'm not. I slide my fingers into his fine straight hair and greet him again. New York City shrugs and looks elsewhere; on this wide concrete stoop two conspirators can query and reply secure in the knowledge that, like children with hands over our own eyes, we've stepped outside the world.

We approach the theater together on the narrow sidewalk, our shoulders occasionally brushing. Fishing the tickets from my pocketbook, I lead George toward the small marquee, brightly lit: WHY THE FLOWER LOVES THE ROD. Below this, in smaller letters, reads: A PLAY OF PASSION POLITICS & POETRY.

"Thanks again for coming," I say to George, and swing open the narrow black door.

The theater is dingy inside. George and I take our seats at the front and wait as the small capacity crowd assembles. I barely glance at the audience, aware instead of George's steady breathing, his expectant expression as he surveys the theater. The difference in our heights even seated.

The theater darkens. There is a long silence. Gradually a vibrant blue light fills the stage. Sound effects of traffic on a rainy day.

I hardly recognize Yolanda when she steps onto the stage. She's regal, worn. Tragic. She taps across the stage swiftly in low heels and a tweed skirt, stopping at its very edge. She faces the audience. Her voice is hoarse like a smoker's. "I'd been through every sort of war. The war of marriage. The war of divorce. The war of childbirth. And the war of wars. The Great War. I let life fling me. Almost break me. But I would not be broken." She pauses to scan the audience. She sees me in the front row, and directs a slow nod my way, like a queen granting audience. "So *he* would be the one. Yes. *He* would understand. He would save me. And I would save him. But not before we'd set each other's worlds on end." She turns in profile. "Up the curved stone stairs to his office. There he sat, like an owl."

Under the stage lights, Yolanda has a ravaged dignity I've never noticed. I understand now why the playwright jumped to cast her. Onstage, Yolanda's grievances are epic. Perhaps, I think, I judged this production too quickly.

A spot comes up on Freud/Bill, seated at the far right corner of the stage, also in profile. And herein lies the first problem. In reality, Freud was old enough to be Hilda Doolittle's father. By the time they met, he was battling illness and apprehensive about the mounting dangers of Nazism. But this Freud is a chisel-jawed hunk. The only concessions to historical reality are a trim snowy beard and wig that manage to look only like accessories on a remarkably pretty man.

Freud/Bill lights a cigar. The smoke he blows lingers in the stage lights.

In parallel monologues on opposite sides of the stage, Yolanda and Bill begin to speak, their lines alternating.

H.D./YOLANDA: "I'd let a man name me once before."

FREUD/BILL: "Not many are able to understand the true depth of my philosophy."

H.D./YOLANDA: "I swore I wouldn't do it again."

FREUD/BILL: "When she came she was a battered psyche."

H.D./YOLANDA: "I was at the end of my rope. I had nowhere else to turn, nobody who understood me."

This isn't twenty-first-century Manhattan; it's Vienna in 1933. And this isn't a self-help show, it's one of the most politically and emotionally fraught meeting of minds in intellectual history. It's beyond me why the playwright didn't use H.D.'s own words— Doolittle wrote beautiful, poetic volumes about her analysis with Freud.

I resist the temptation to look at George. Let him draw his own conclusions without my interference.

Freud says, "The female is of course defined and limited by her biology."

Yolanda turns downstage and eyes Bill. Then she faces the audience. "Despite his views of women I knew he was *brilliant*." She hits the word like a pothole.

"She came to me because she was incapable of understanding her life," Freud intones. "Hysteria lurked in her shadows."

The two continue in this vein, immobile on the stage, long past the point where one would expect this prologue to end and some sort of scene begin. The audience begins to shift in the theater's narrow seats.

I stop paying attention to the words. I've read Yolanda's script and know what's coming: the muddily sketched analysis, a prurient attention to the details of H.D.'s engagement to Ezra Pound, a précis of her failed marriage to Richard Aldington and later the family she shaped with Bryher—all related in dialogue that reduces two passionate human beings to ideological caricatures. In reality, Freud's work with H.D. was hardly the pure misogynist trap this play is about to make it out to be. Freud was of course sexist, but he also thought H.D. was extraordinary. She in turn felt, despite their disagreements, that he'd saved her—and repaid the favor by helping him escape from Vienna before Hitler could seal his fate.

This playwright, though, uses the story of H.D.'s analysis as a vehicle for demonstrating yet again what a disaster Freud was for the entirety of womankind—an axe I'd thought had been thoroughly ground by the time I was in graduate school, leaving feminist scholars free to acknowledge that there may be one or two things to learn from Freud regardless. The playwright has also, ad-libbing off H.D.'s actual poetry, included a scene in which H.D. is transformed, through an onstage costume change, into Helen of Troy, while a double-entendre-spouting Freud narrates her wartime torments against a backdrop of battle sound effects. None of which is as bad as the play's penultimate scene, in which the two share a demeaning and completely ahistorical kiss . . . which would have been at least more plausible between the real Freud and H.D., who actually seemed to respect each other, than between the two speechifying figures of this overwrought play.

I glance at George, who wears a slightly pained expression. He may not know the extent to which history is being abused. But it's clear he knows a bad play when he sees it.

I force myself to focus on Yolanda's voice, which rises and falls with increasingly convincing hysteria and a certain brittle eloquence. And to Bill's smug commentary emerging from the cigar smoke. By intermission H.D. looks like she hates Freud's guts.

Ten minutes until act 2. Yolanda has insisted on a visit during intermission — she doesn't care how colossally unprofessional it looks, let Bill see she's got a social life too. George follows me backstage, where Yolanda grabs my arm and leads us into the single cramped bathroom–dressing room. She locks the door behind us. "That asshole is stepping all over my lines," she says. "He can't bear to listen to me."

George extends a hand. "I'm George."

"Hi," says Yolanda emptily, shaking it. She turns back to me. "Did you see *her?* She was the one changing my costume for the Helen of Troy sequence. I don't want her touching me. Next time I'll do the goddamn buttons myself. Next time I'll punch her in the head."

"I'm so sorry," I say. I squeeze her shoulder. "But you're powerful up there. You're completely convincing as Hilda." It's true: Yolanda as H.D. carries herself with an undeniable, desperate majesty. Despite the script.

"I second that," says George.

"I just wish" — Yolanda shakes out her hands, then her arms, loosening tension so vigorously that George and I step back against the wall — "that he would treat me with goddamn respect."

"I told George the Bill story," I offer.

Yolanda rounds on George. "*You're* a guy. You explain Bill to me." She picks up a program and slaps it down on the vanity. "What an asshole."

"I can't," George says, "though I have a suggestion."

"What?" The hostility in her voice makes me cringe.

But George appears unfazed. "You have to change how you say it," he tells her. "Don't say, 'I wish he would treat me with respect.' It's 'I wish he were the *kind* of guy who'd treat me with respect.' But he's not. So you better go find that other guy."

There's a long silence. Then Yolanda sighs out more air than I would have thought human lungs could hold. She says to George, "Come back to see the show again tomorrow. Make that every night." To me, she says, "Marry him."

There is a single, loud, knuckle rap on the door. It's Freud. "Some of us have to empty our bladders before act two," he calls.

Yolanda fumbles with the lock. "I wish he were the *kind of guy* who'd drop dead." She yanks open the door. We follow as she exits with a haughty glance at Bill, who hardly seems to notice.

The play's final scene, set seven years after Freud's death, depicts the moment of H.D.'s psychotic break. The script, unsurprisingly, implies the culprit is Freud, rather than the two world wars and the personal upheavals H.D. had already lived through. But the scene is brightened by Yolanda's closing recitation of an actual poem by H.D. After, there is sustained applause — more than I expected, even from a friend-and-family-filled opening-night house. The applause crests for Yolanda's bow. George and I don't speak. Neither of us, I think, wants to say a word about the play until we're outside.

We wait until the theater is practically empty, then go backstage to find Yolanda. Taking my arm, a flushed and now grinning Yolanda walks us over to the playwright — a diminutive, elated Jewish woman of about thirty who sets to telling Yolanda how fabulous she was.

When Yolanda can get in a word, she says, "Tracy is the literature professor I was telling you about. I've wanted you two to meet forever."

The playwright turns to me.

"You've done a real service," I manage. "It's about time someone wrote about Hilda Doolittle. It's long overdue."

The playwright thanks me politely and then waits, apparently expecting more. I struggle to formulate some further compliment that's not a lie.

George looks at me for only a second. Then he turns to the playwright and pumps her hand. "Now *that*," he enunciates, "was a play."

She beams.

As I walk out of the elevator, a daytime TV announcer's voice greets me. Eileen is at her desk, mini-television blaring. She glances up at the sound of the elevator opening, sees me, and turns back to her screen, irritated by the interruption. The announcer's excited tones waft through the reception area. "In a dramatic incident at this Hollywood mansion . . ."

Gossip is not Eileen's hobby. It is the food of her soul, marrow of life, milk of paradise. Eileen is a chatty fortyish double divorcée with wavy brown hair, wide brown eyes, and powder pink candied-looking lipstick. She's been the department's administrative assistant since well before I arrived as a graduate student. From her desk she commands the elevator and the stairwell, and, craning her neck, extends her purview to the faculty lounge. When this doesn't provide sufficient data she wheels her cart around the perimeter of the department, trolling for information, slowing flagrantly outside the copy room or anywhere else she might find two faculty members in conversation. Eileen is the Switzerland of the department, accepting deposits from all comers, taking no sides because any alliance might block information supplies from an opposing camp. In her world we faculty are arrested in a submature stage of development, playing smarter-than-thou games while the real matters of adult life go unattended. *You people have your priorities completely screwed up. You don't know anything if it's not in a book.* Despite Eileen's open disdain for our ignorance, or perhaps because of it, a certain segment of the faculty jockeys daily to praise her. My colleagues — most of them trusty straight-arrow sorts, with pale spouses and children with the strangled, overwise look of junior Manhattan literati — admire Eileen's clothing effusively and ask her, with cloying smiles, for the latest tabloid news. They're convinced, as only a group of Ph.D.s can be, that they're charming the sole non–college graduate among them. They think Eileen doesn't notice the smirk behind their questions, the way they use her as a source of see-how-open-minded-I-am points in some intradepartmental tournament. I find it insulting, and suspect she does too; perhaps that's why she grinds her superiority into our faces. When Eileen is particularly irritated, the mini-television comes out of the supply closet. Junior faculty's meek requests for silence and the offended glares of grad students make no difference; on those days the TV prattles uninterrupted on her desk for hours. I once heard Eileen, preening for a handsome new graduate student, say she was the only person in the department who knew how to stand up for what mattered. In truth I've never seen her stick out her little finger, let alone her neck, for anyone. The false heroism of the bored.

As I approach her desk Eileen greets me warily.

As cheerfully as I can, I return the greeting. "By the way," I say, "any chance you've got that photocopying ready?"

She crunches a sucking candy. "Check again later," she says, eyes drifting back toward the screen.

"I'll be in until three. I'll check then."

She shrugs: The fates will decree as they choose. If the photocopying is ready, so be it. As I turn away, Eileen mutters, "*She's got a lot of nerve, asking me to schedule extra meetings during drop/add week.*"

And I've got better things to do than stand here figuring out which of my colleagues ticked Eileen off this time by requesting simple administrative assistance. Turning down the long fluorescent-lit hall, I head to my office. I unlock my door, rereading out of habit and for the thousandth time its single adornment — a one-panel cartoon depicting the tower of Babel under construction, each laborer depicted as a subspecialized academic. I flip on the lights, set my briefcase on the floor below my office's only other decoration — a framed photograph of Zora Neale Hurston — and grab the coffee mug off my stacked desk. As I'm shutting the door I spy Elizabeth, drifting along the wall of the corridor as though forced there by a swift current. The pile of books she's embracing reaches nearly to her chin. She starts when I greet her.

"I didn't see you." Every word an apology.

"How goes it?"

"Fine," she breathes. "Lots of work."

"I can see." I point to the books. "That stack's a spine-bender. You're checking on a new idea?"

"Joanne thought I should do some reading on nineteenth-century English prosody. To put Dickinson in better context. She did a little research for me and suggested these titles."

"Really? To me that seems unnecessary. Do you think Joanne knows your dissertation area well enough to know what you need? She's a sixteenth-century specialist, not an Americanist."

Elizabeth stops walking. Her struggle to formulate an apology looks like a Medieval portrait of agony.

"Don't worry." I give her my most reassuring adviserly smile. "Your dissertation is in great shape. If you just stay on the course we discussed, I think it will be fine. But go ahead and read whatever you think will help."

"Okay," she says. "Thanks."

I glance at the title on top of the stack: *Promethean Poesie*. This doesn't strike me as okay at all — it strikes me as a colossal waste of energy. Elizabeth will read each obscure tome cover to cover just to be sure she hasn't missed something. Then long after I've forgotten about this conversation she'll still be trying to mollify me by implying she did the extra work only to humor Joanne . . . or that the books *were* useful, though not at all in the way Joanne suggested. I don't have time for Elizabeth's curtseys and bows, yet I've already set them in motion by challenging Joanne's advice. Feeling like a jerk, I step into the faculty lounge.

"This is completely absurd," Jeff greets me. He waves a half-empty cheese-pretzel bag in my direction. "Steven left these here. Have you seen the ingredients? I don't know how any intelligent person can eat this crap."

I take the bag and scan the ingredients. "He's British. Maybe he eats it ironically. What's new?"

Jeff half shutters his eyes: his *have I got one for you* expression. "Victoria was finishing her coffee when I got here. She waited until everyone else had left, then asked for a moment of my time. Apparently Paleozoic asked her this morning if I was *courting* Elizabeth."

"You're serious? Did Victoria tell him you were gay?"

"Victoria's too Brahmin to divulge anyone else's business, and too stiff to say the word 'gay' unless it's in a sonnet. All she said to Paleozoic was that she doubted it. But it seemed to her" — here Jeff adopts Victoria's measured New England cadence — "that it would be prudent for me to be aware there are rumors circulating about Elizabeth and myself among the senior staff."

"How could she even keep a straight face?"

"She doesn't have any other kind."

"She *does* know you're gay?"

"Of course. She knew before anyone, including you. The first week I was here she suggested, in a completely uncharacteristic non sequitur, that I stop by and introduce myself to Frank Chanville in Classics. And when I met Frank it turned out he'd just organized the university gay forum. Underneath the granite, Victoria's pretty savvy — unlike Paleozoic, who wouldn't know gay-as-a-goose if it came up to him and —" Jeff makes an obscene gesture.

"But why would anyone believe that rumor?"

"Because straight people are so hung up on the third syllable of 'homosexual' that they think we want to bugger everyone. Plus plenty of them secretly hope—for reasons only their therapists know—that homosexuality doesn't *stick*."

"You really think the faculty is so backward?"

"This faculty is relatively enlightened. Which is why I'm not going to bother correcting the rumor—it wouldn't have legs here. But that's not my point." He lapses into a moody silence. After a minute he says tersely, "Don't believe the commercials. Or our I'm-from-a-town-called-Hope president. We live in a reactionary country. The only way to succeed is to see through the system."

I know better than to speak. I wait until Jeff's irritable expression passes and he takes a long gulp from his water glass.

"Have you considered telling Paleozoic directly?" I ask. "Nipping the rumor in the bud? You're tenured and you're out. It's too late for anyone to label you 'special interest' and stick you over in Gay Studies. Why not be direct?"

"Paleozoic," Jeff says, "is going to figure this one out for himself. I want to see what it will take for him to realize." He stretches his neck, rolling his head from one shoulder to the other. "Besides, Elizabeth is cute, in a Kate Moss kind of way. If I were wired that way, it wouldn't be a bad match."

"Well, I hope you like women with scoliosis, because she's going to have a case pretty soon."

"Because . . . ?"

I drop onto the sofa cushion beside his. "Because Joanne's advising my advisee. She's just given her a last-minute reading list that would debilitate your average grad student. And you know Elizabeth—she's already read everything she needs to, she's practically done writing the damn dissertation. She doesn't need someone making her insecure about irrelevant material."

"You're awfully ticked off. It's just a reading list, right?"

"It's not just a reading list. It's the principle."

"Aren't you being a tad possessive?"

I back off from my annoyance long enough to consider this. Elizabeth is the brightest grad student I've known. It would be natural, wouldn't it, for me to feel territorial? "Maybe," I say. "Still, Joanne could have made a friendly suggestion or two, rather than giving Elizabeth — who is a setup for eleventh-hour dissertation paranoia — a brain-breaking list. It's just inappropriate. I ought to talk to Joanne about it."

"Mmm." Jeff leans back on the threadbare couch. He puffs his narrow cheeks and expels the air slowly. "If I were you I'd be careful about that."

"Because?"

"Something's up with Joanne."

"That was obvious at the grade-inflation meeting."

"True," Jeff says. "Though most people have already chalked that particular stunt up as a power play — more flagrant than Joanne's usual, but something they're willing to overlook, mostly because nobody wants to have to take over the job of organizing these meetings. What I mean, though, is that this week she's jumping on people for the slightest thing. You should have seen the to-do list she gave Eileen this morning."

"I was wondering what was with Eileen."

"And I think Joanne's particularly ticked off at you. When your twentieth-century class came up in a discussion this morning, she pronounced your name as though you'd been caught in a broom closet molesting Spenser."

"What's she got against me? No offense, but you're flip with her all the time. I'm nothing but polite."

"Yes, my dear, but I" — he draws himself up on the sofa, and looks at me sternly — "am a faggot. And straight women let gay men get away with anything. We don't figure into the picture. We're beyond sexism. We're utterly unthreatening. No hierarchy to sort out, no mixed vibes. And don't play dumb about this, Tracy, because it's part of what makes our friendship so easy. No matter how I behave, I am not personally threatening to you."

Checking myself before I launch a rebuttal, I recall my first encounters with Jeff, and the relief I felt sparring with a man with whom there would be no complications. "I see your point," I say.

With a wave he acknowledges victory.

"But what did I ever do to Joanne?"

Jeff takes the copy of the *PMLA* from the coffee table and thumbs it. "If people's biases required rational cause, I could have brought the entire Little League for court-martial when I was eight. I think you ought to let this reading-list thing go and let Joanne climb out of her foul mood on her own. Elizabeth is an adult. She can take care of herself."

As if on cue, the door to the faculty lounge swings open and Joanne and Grub enter.

". . . which sums up how I feel about Gilman," says Jeff. "Did you ever read *Difference and Pathology*?"

"You're good," I whisper to Jeff, as Joanne cuts in sharply from the coffee machine.

"You two are talking about Sander Gilman?"

"We were comparing his more recent output with his earlier books." Jeff twists to face Joanne, his expression completely relaxed: a master at work.

Joanne peels the top from a container of creamer, dumps it into her cup, and stirs her coffee in a tight whirl. She gives a small, competitive smile. "Overrated," she says. "All of it. From start to finish."

Jeff tuts softly. "Oh, I don't think so."

Joanne offers a styrofoam cup to Grub, who declines it. Grub turns to scan a bookshelf, nodding in evident approval of the volumes he finds there. Periodically he lifts the bowl of his pipe and takes a deep draw.

"Are *you* a Gilman fan, Tracy?" Joanne asks.

"To be honest, I haven't read him in a while. Sounds like I need to read his recent work and see what I think."

Joanne shrugs: It makes no bloody difference to her what I read.

"How's life?" I'm not nearly as good as Jeff, and the attempt at friendliness comes out stiff.

She regards me for an instant, her face unreadable. Then she answers airily. "Fine. And how's *your* life?"

Hell with Elizabeth's reading list; Jeff is right. Departmental peace is more important. And Joanne is, in many ways, a colleague I respect. "Good." I offer Joanne a direct, warm smile.

Joanne sips her coffee. "Lovely." Her voice is flat.

After the door has shut behind Joanne and Grub, I rise and open the single window that lets onto the air shaft. I fan my scooped palms in a clumsy sidestroke, but succeed only in urging a few wisps of Grub's pipe smoke toward the ceiling. When I turn back toward to the sofa, Jeff is looking at me mournfully.

"*What?*"

He wags his head. "Now you've really put your foot in it."

"What did I do wrong?"

"You're happy. And you advertised it again."

"Am I missing something?"

Jeff flaps his journal to clear the smoke around the sofa and, with an impatient glance at me, goes back to reading.

"I wasn't advertising," I enunciate. "Besides, that wasn't *happy*. That was just friendly."

"Happy," he mutters without looking up.

"Fine. What's wrong with being happy?"

Jeff lingers over the page another moment, then lays it in his lap. "You'll be shocked how angry it makes some people. Especially people like Joanne."

"Because?"

"She doesn't have a life. She's never mentioned a boyfriend or girlfriend. She may go on the occasional weekend ski trip with old rugby pals, but have you ever heard her mention a close friend? This department is her world."

"Isn't it all of ours?"

"Not like that, Tracy, and you know it. You and I care about lit, and we're ambitious about our careers, but we also have friends and outside aspirations, and now you've got this guy—"

"I *might* have this guy. We've only been on two dates."

"Now you've got this guy—and you're lit up like a light bulb, which Joanne has surely picked up on even if she doesn't know specifics. People like Joanne have nothing ahead of them but ladder climbing. Don't get me wrong, I'm dedicated to Brit lit, sure. But I don't plan to spend my life analyzing someone else's passions without having any of my own."

With a pang it occurs to me that until two weeks ago the circumstances of my life may not have been so dissimilar from Joanne's as Jeff seems to think. It's an uncomfortable thought: Was George right when he said I hadn't told him about myself? Have I truly let the rest of my life atrophy? And how often in the last year have I gone to hear music or see a show, bought something for myself other than work supplies, had *outside aspirations* of my own? I can count the occasions on the fingers of my hands—and two of them date since meeting George.

Jeff is still fixing me with his stare. I stare back, hoping he sees something in me that I can't see.

Jeff stands. He picks up his satchel, slings it over his shoulder, and carries his empty mug to the sink.

I rouse myself. "Hold on," I say. "I still don't buy it as an explanation for Joanne's behavior. People always rehearse that crap about single women, as though we turn pathological the minute we either turn forty or get a cat. As though women's singleness mandates rage at the universe. As a single woman, I've got to tell you that's nonsense."

Jeff pauses mid-step and grins, signaling that this debate now has his full attention. "Aha. So as a gay man I'm *not* immune to charges of sexism."

"Not if you can't come up with something better than the old singleness-equals-bitchiness chestnut. Joanne wasn't always such a rotten colleague — and as far as we know she's lacked close friends and relationships for years, not just a few weeks."

Jeff makes a long, low, ruminative sound — half hum, half growl. "Maybe she's jealous of my torrid affair with Elizabeth." He rinses his mug and glances at the clock: three minutes until the start of his seminar. "Speaking of affairs, how's Mr. Tabouli in the sack? You two rogering each other yet?"

"This would be your business because . . . ?"

"Have you ever met a subject that wasn't?"

I stand and we both walk toward the door. "Things haven't gone that far."

"Good." He pats my cheek. "Mama always said, 'Why buy the cow if you can get the milk for free.'"

"Your mama said no such thing."

"She should have. If I'd waited, maybe Richard would have turned down Emory in the hope of getting in my pants."

"You could as easily have turned down *your* job and gone to Georgia."

He smiles a rueful, soft smile, and for an instant I believe I'm glimpsing the other Jeff — the one he doesn't show at work, even to me. "No blame intended." He shakes his head. "I just miss the guy."

Jeff isn't going to see Richard again until Thanksgiving. I try to think of a consoling response, but he changes the subject first.

"When's your next date with Mr. T?"

"Tonight."

"Tonight, tonight," Jeff warbles, then swats my arm with his *PMLA*. "Stop smiling. You're giving me hives."

He opens the door wearing faded jeans and a lime green sweater with white pinstripes. While I've never much noticed men's clothing, the sweater George is wearing is not a sweater I can feel sanguine about. No Manhattan Jew under the age of seventy would be caught dead in those colors. Shedding my coat, I remind myself I haven't liked most of the Manhattan Jews I've dated, too many of whom have communicated a powerful aversion to getting dirt under their fingernails. As George takes my coat, I remind myself: This is a man who scoffs at all-black wardrobes, sees nothing unrefined about iceberg lettuce, contact sports, dirt. I forgive the sweater.

The place, a one-bedroom, is modest but clean. On the walls are a few posters of jazz greats. Tall shelves hold books, a few low-maintenance plants, a few photos of clean-cut twenty-somethings smiling on mountaintops and scruffier thirty-somethings smiling in city parks. On the coffee table, alongside two beers and a bottle opener, is the video. I've come here, officially, to watch a comedy titled *Topknots* with George. This is, though, our third date: the pivotal date years of experience have taught me to fear. If *Topknots* gets watched at all, let alone before midnight, it's not a good sign.

As George hangs my coat, I notice a framed photograph on a bookshelf. In the picture a wiry, teenaged George hugs a woman who, though she's petite and freckled, can only be his mother: a soft-faced woman with a no-nonsense fringe of straight brown hair, dressed in a comfortable blue cardigan. Her brown eyes are bright. Still, it's not her warmth but something else about the photograph that arrests me. The key to reading a family photo, I realized long ago, is noticing where the hands are. The hands give it all away: who's on the inside, who's left out in the cold, who holds the family together. In my own family photos I generally span an airy breach between my parents, my hands anchoring their semi-smiling likenesses. In this photo George and his mother hug, but it's George's arm that pulls his mother close, his hand on her shoulder securing her in a protective embrace that won't release just because the shutter does. The photo strikes me powerfully. It takes me a moment to identify the feeling as awe. I think: He'd never abandon her.

"She died," George says. He stands beside me, perfectly still, hands folded in front of him. "She was on a train that derailed just outside Toronto, on the way home from visiting her sister in Vancouver. It happened a few weeks after that picture."

I turn around to face him. "I'm so sorry."

He nods acknowledgment, then looks back to the photo. "I like that picture because she's smiling without her hand over her mouth. She had bad teeth, and she learned that habit as a kid and couldn't shake it. I used to try to make her laugh so hard she'd forget to throw up the hand." He smiles, but the smile isn't new — simply a part of a story he's recited dozens of times before. "She tried to teach me to be a gentleman — something I try to hold on to. An uphill battle."

I don't speak. I don't want to say something disrespectful, or pretend to empathize with experiences I don't understand.

He looks at me. "For some reason," he says, his stance softening a bit, "people usually ask whether she was a nervous traveler. I think it makes people feel safer to believe we can have premonitions about these things. But she wasn't."

I take this in. After a moment I ask, "Are you?"

"No." He shakes his head. "I'm not afraid of trains." Then, sounding for the first time as if he's saying something real instead of simply reciting: "I'm afraid of people dying." His face turns, fleetingly, to iron. Then, a half-dozen heartbeats later, to something lighter.

The next thing I know he's stepped behind me, taken my wrist, and is hoisting me onto his back. I resist, confused, his "Relax!" only prompting my body to go rigid, until gravity and his insistence persuade me to stretch my back against his — the white ceiling rotating above me as he pivots, steps toward the sofa, and gently rolls us down. Still facing the ceiling, I somehow land safely, if out of breath, on his chest. He's laughing. I twist to look at him. His face has cleared. He chides, "For contact improv, you need *both* people cooperating."

"I didn't know we were doing contact improv."

"Always." His chest against my back is a sturdy trampoline. He kneads my shoulder, as though I were the one who'd related a painful story. Slowly I relax, my shoulder blades spreading like wings. "I did improv theater for a while," he says. "Part of my detox from fundamentalism. I wasn't very good at it. Compared to most of the troupe, I reacted like molasses. But I loved it."

We rest on the sofa.

"Nice ceiling," I say.

"Mmm," he agrees. His teeth are delicate on my palm.

I roll over and we kiss. We kiss for a long time, and if kissing is a conversation this is one where we both get to talk. His mouth is soft and rich on mine, and all I can think, stupidly, is: *if chocolate syrup could kiss.*

And then it's a hell of a lot more intense than chocolate syrup.

We take a break.

His apartment is quiet. A spicy smell drifts from the Cambodian restaurant on the first floor.

"What else did you do in improv?" I ask.

"Games." I hear him smile. "Exercises. Anything we could come up with to catch each other off-guard—even a regular sit-down conversation, except that the questions, no matter how weird, had to be answered without hesitation. It's amazing what people find themselves saying when they don't have time to think." He sits up, bringing me along, and settles me beside him, our knees touching. "Say something shocking," he says, facing me.

I laugh. "True or false?"

"Doesn't matter."

I hesitate.

"Don't think," he chides.

"I'm in the federal witness protection program. My real name is Lola. This is a prosthetic chin."

"What crime did you witness?"

"Um, there was a 'No Dumping' sign. And somebody took a dump in front of it. Ugh. I don't think I'm going to be good at this—when I panic I just go lowbrow." I shake my head. "Your turn. Say something shocking."

Mischief flickers on his face. "I didn't kiss a girl until I was nineteen."

"Really? Is that true?"

He shrugs. "It was the way I grew up."

"Well, you've made up for it."

He grins. "I'm glad you think so. Of course it's all about having a good partner."

"I do my best."

"What's the most embarrassing thing you've ever done?"

I pull away. "Oh no."

"Oh yes."

"On no."

"Don't stall."

"If we're going to talk embarrassing, then let's open the beers."

He takes one of the beers in his right hand and signals for me to ply the opener, which I do, also one-handed. It takes a while, working together, to open both bottles, but we do it without spilling much. I raise mine. He raises his.

"To embarrassment," he says.

We drink. I set my bottle down slowly on the table, and slowly dry my palm on the leg of my jeans. It occurs to me that if I kiss him again, I may not need to answer.

He watches me, his expression wry. As though reading my mind, he says, "No pressure. And no, I don't usually put women on the spot with stupid parlor games." He sets down his beer. "Just you."

"Because?"

He looks at me simply. "I get a feeling about you. I want to know you."

I stare at him.

His smile is almost apologetic. "As you like," he says. "You can answer the question or not."

I take another draw from my beer, letting my nerves settle. His directness is disconcerting, and powerfully attractive.

It's a sensation like disrobing. "I had a crush on this guy in college," I start. "I got up my nerve to call him. My dorm had this fancy brand-new voicemail system where you could record a message and then preview it before sending it. So — you can guess where this is going — I recorded three separate messages until I had one that felt nonchalant enough. But by accident I sent them all."

"Ouch."

"Ouch." I drink.

"Did he call you back?"

"Nope. And I can't even tell you how he looked at me after that, because I never dared so much as another glance at him. To this day he's probably telling stories about his sophomore-year stalker." I set down my beer. "Your turn."

He rubs his neck ruefully and laughs. "I was in college. I had my first real girlfriend. One Sunday we were, let's say, enjoying the afternoon, and she went into the bathroom to put in her diaphragm. But, as she later explained, it was slippery and the thing sprang open in her hand and flew out of the window and down into the quad. She was mortified. So, like the nice guy I was . . ." George sighs. "I snatched it off the ground just as a student tour group was about to trample it. And two of my classmates saw." He shakes his head. "Maybe that wouldn't have been mortifying to someone who wasn't from my background."

"That I doubt."

He laughs a rich, satisfied laugh. "Something ridiculous you did as a kid."

"Ridiculous?"

"Don't stall."

I take a swallow of beer. "I've never told anyone this. When I was maybe six I forged a love letter to my mother. I signed my father's name."

"How come?"

"I thought it would change something. Isn't that ridiculous?" I smile at him.

"What did you want to change?"

"The silence."

He waits.

"They're just—" I make a futile gesture. "For my parents, conversation is not a set of exotic pigments. Conversation is house paint. Apply enough to cover the subject. Store the rest in the basement." I stop.

He puts a hand on my knee.

"I mean, I do appreciate them."

"What are they like?"

"They're good people. Hardworking, responsible, all that. My father has always had this quiet confidence in me. Unspoken but powerful. When I came to him with a problem, we'd talk it through until I was satisfied. He took me seriously. And my mother left me alone where other mothers nagged. But it's hard to be close to them. My parents, like a lot of people, successfully raised their child to be an adult they can't understand, in a city they find alarming, in a profession they find impenetrable. They weren't thrilled, I think, at my choice to move across the country for college, and then — as though I hadn't already positioned myself sufficiently out of their orbit — pursue a career as impractical as literature. Still, they accepted it. But it's really labor sometimes, keeping a connection going."

"I'm guessing they don't sing to your fax machine?"

"In fact, my parents are the only people who have ever, in all the time I've had that idiotic setup, managed to get shrilled at by my fax. And it's happened to them more than once. I mean, it baffles me that an engineer and a schoolteacher can't occasionally toss a syllable to the line to keep the fax at bay. Still, when I race back to that screaming fax machine I feel frankly shitty. Like it's my fault for trying to stretch their horizons when I should just accept the two of them as they are." I stare at George's window, where the light is fading. "Lately," I say, "when I need to leave the phone for a moment, I just say I'll call them back."

"So that's how you got into literature?"

"Sorry?"

"I mean, is that what first made you go for books?"

I hesitate, then nod. "When I read novels as a kid, I got to see who people really were."

Outside the window, a streetlamp turns on.

Most of the men I've been with would long since have forged ahead to the next act. A conversation that continued into the dark would have signaled détente, the evaporation of sexual tension. But the air between George and me vibrates with attentiveness — the magnified silence of something delayed. The evening has expanded. There is no time, no lecture looming tomorrow, no hurry between us. Only the hushed dignity of moving toward something large.

"What did your letter say? When you were six?"

I gesture faintly. "You know — all the flowery things I could think of. With a lot of misspellings, I'm sure."

"What did they say about it?"

"They didn't. I think they were embarrassed. Nobody ever said a word to me."

"Nothing?"

I open my mouth to speak, but my voice catches. Surprised, I shake my head. "Something ridiculous from childhood," I say to him.

He wraps an arm around me. With my fingertips I caress: his temple, the freshly shaved plane of his cheek, the surprisingly soft skin at his collarbone.

"I'd have to ask Paula," he says. "My sister. She remembers all that stuff." He's quiet for a moment. "Okay—I lied to this really strict teacher of mine because I'd lost a schoolbook. I said it had been stolen. Then I had to lie to my mother. Of course my mother found out, I forget how. But she also knew the teacher was a true son of a bitch—not that she'd ever have used, or tolerated, that expression. So despite her high principles she didn't tell on me. She didn't even tell my father. She made me earn back the price of the book by doing extra housework, and we gave the money to charity. She was like that—she sort of knew how to bend. With everything. The church, and my father, and other things in her life that weren't easy. Plenty of times I wished I could make her compromises." He falls silent. "Funny thing is, I sometimes think she was proud of me for questioning things. For taking on impossible battles. Even when it came to religion. The one time I told her I had doubts about my faith, she didn't so much as rebuke me. She just said I shouldn't worry, it would come to me later." George lingers momentarily over this surprise, still fresh after more than two decades. "She was a teacher before she met my father. And I always had the impression she might not have been as religious back then. She never said she regretted giving up that other life, but I always thought there was that understanding between us." His face is bright with compassion, and innocence.

"Happiest decision you ever made," he says after a minute.

"Moving to New York."

"Me too. Why for you?"

"Friction. Someone's always telling you exactly what they think. If you want human interaction, all you need to do is walk a few blocks. You?"

He smiles, and shrugs. "I love this city." He rises. When he returns from his refrigerator he's carrying another set of beers. "Next question's yours," he says, opening them.

I start my new beer. It takes me a while to think of a question. When I do I set down my bottle and face him squarely. "What's the worst thing you ever did?"

He hesitates.

"I will if you will," I say.

He leans back and shuts his eyes. "The light answer or the serious answer?"

"I'll take one of each."

He smiles gently, eyes still closed. "I used to smoke pot before I went out to proselytize."

"You proselytized?"

He opens his eyes. "I know how foreign that must seem. Just remember, I'm thirty-seven — I left home a very long time ago. I've had more years outside the fundamentalist world than in it. So we're talking ancient history. But after my mother died, my father took things up a notch. Several notches, actually."

"How many?"

"What do you know about fundamentalism?"

"Jesse Helms?" I offer. "That Dobson guy?"

"That's like saying you know the taste of wheat flour from eating Twinkies."

"Then please don't ever ask me what I know about Canada."

"At least you're honest."

The heat switches on with a blast of stale air. After a minute it subsides with a groan. "For someone like my father," he says, "fundamentalism is like a very, very strict love. *A perfect love that casts out fear* — that's Saint John. You're either in or out. You're either faithful, or else you have the wrong kind of heart.

"I was always on the edge of falling — at least that's how I felt as a kid. I don't remember ever *not* having doubts, though there must have been a time. But I used to fight them. It's a nauseating sensation, fishing inside yourself all the time for a feeling that's not there. And even as a kid I knew you can't force faith — no more than you can force yourself to fall in love."

He speaks these last words with the conviction of a man who's tried. I nod firmly, thinking of Jason.

"But." George straightens. "When you finally realize you just don't buy into the whole system, it's like a key turns. And once it turns you can't reverse it."

"What turned your key?"

"My father," he says, "lied." George shakes his head. He continues grimly. "When my mother died he said God had taken her for a reason. She was in heaven, and if we loved her we should be happy. *Rejoice in the Lord always.*" He pronounces the words crisply. "Philippians," he adds. Then he's silent.

"When I cried at her funeral, he refused to speak to me. And I knew," he says, "that that was a lie of the deepest and worst human kind. My father was always rigid, even before my mother died. But that one thing . . ." His voice slows, stiffens. "No one could tell me that I wasn't supposed to cry for her."

The single lamp on in the apartment looks golden in the dark room.

"After that," he says, "my father knew he couldn't control me much longer. And also that my attitude toward the church was becoming dangerous. So he decided that I needed to spread the word. Ironically I didn't mind, because I was still desperate for anything that might pull me back into the fold. It's a true dread, the thought of leaving. So — proselytizing." He gives a rueful smile. "You go out on the street, and introduce yourself to people, and if you're good you can joke with them, and then talk about what matters. I was pretty successful at it — I wasn't shy, and people seemed to like to talk to me. But I was being dishonest too. I couldn't think of Jesus as anything more than a really good person — or maybe even just a useful parable — that had been exaggerated into a god. So before going out I started smoking a little pot, first with a school friend, then alone. And one time I remember meeting some kid on the street who was testifying about how Jesus saved him because he passed a chemistry test he hadn't studied for. And I said — or I'm pretty sure I said — 'Friend, if Jesus gives a flying crap about your chemistry test, then Judas is the man to watch.' "

I laugh, but George waves a finger. "This was no laughing matter to this kid. He reported it to our minister, and I had to answer for it. Which I also" — he grimaces — "chose to do while high." He stops speaking, then looks at me apologetically. "That wasn't exactly a light answer, was it? I'm sorry." He hesitates. "I think it's probably right that I talk about all this, though, because this is the heaviest part of my life. And you may as well see it now. I hope it doesn't freak you out. But if it does, I understand."

I watch him. "So far, so good."

George slips a hand into my ponytail, his fingers slowly juggling curls. He slides his hand higher and softly kneads the back of my scalp.

"Now for my serious worst thing," he says.

"You don't have to," I say.

"No," he says. "I don't mind, so long as you don't mind hearing."

I draw up my legs beneath me and sit facing him.

"The worst thing I ever did was leave my father."

"How do you mean?"

"There was nothing I could have done different. I didn't believe, and he couldn't tolerate that—he couldn't have accepted it before my mother died, and especially not after. So I left. I went to a secular college, which he'd forbidden. I shamed him in the eyes of his community. I'm not absolving him—he did and said some awful things. But I pretty much threw his God in his face on the way out the door. I mean, if you think that Judas comment was bad . . ." He shakes his head at a painful memory. "And even though I had no honest choice—I had to leave—there are some things that are still true, like that it's important to honor thy father and mother."

"How did he react?"

"He didn't. He doesn't react to me anymore. My name is crossed out," George says simply, "in the Book of Life."

I don't know what to say.

George takes my hands and kisses them softly. "But here I am," he says, "anyway." And he winks.

"Do you ever see him?"

"I go back once a year. I stay with Paula's family." He examines his beer bottle. "She's a good person, Paula." He nods slowly, as though affirming this to himself; his expression speaks volumes about the unbridgeable gap between his sister's life and his own. "When I'm there, my father grants me an audience. There's no pretense of interest in me—he's simply modeling charity and good Christian behavior. For me, though, going by his house with my sister once or twice during my visit is a commitment. I'm not going to shut the door with him. Not that keeping it open does much. He just tunes me out like an unappealing radio station. Only tunes back in to ask about my job and whether I've returned to the fold."

He drinks from his beer. Then sets it on the table. "You can tell me if my story puts you off."

I sit silently for a minute. Then with the pads of my fingers I smooth a furrow on his forehead. I take my time doing it. "We come from different worlds. Unbelievably different. But I think I get what you're saying."

He looks at me. "Thank you," he says. "It took me a while to become a person who might deserve that kind of trust." He raises his right hand to the light. Along the knuckles swims a silver scar, which splits off down the backs of two fingers and ends in faint delicate tendrils. "There should be a law against letting anguished young men near walls. Testosterone out of control—plus I was working that idiotic job on the trading floor, where they think rage is just so much rocket fuel. I was in rough shape back then, when I first got to New York. It took me a few years to get out of a job that felt hollow and into work I cared about. And to make peace with my choices." His words slow. "I try," he says, "to remember my mother. And appreciate the people in my life. And not waste my time, or anyone else's. Because you can never be sure someone is going to be around tomorrow. So you'd better go for it. For whatever, and whoever, you care about."

Sounds of traffic rise faintly from the street: laughter, the gunning of a motorcycle engine, muffled footsteps.

"At least," he says, "that's how I try to live."

GRAVITY: IT'S NOT JUST A GOOD IDEA. IT'S THE LAW. The sign, in retrospect, seems not humorous so much as true.

He slips his hand down my side and gives my bottom a gentle, unrushed squeeze.

I lean in and kiss him. He settles against the arm of the sofa, carrying me along. I settle against him. "My worst thing is pretty dumb in comparison," I say.

"Shoot."

"I strung someone along for a couple years. I wasn't brave enough to just follow what I knew in my gut. I kept listening to my head, and to all my well-meaning friends, saying it could work.

Which, technically, it could have. But love isn't technical. And I really hurt him. I mean, he's fine now — he met someone and got married. But I was dishonest with myself for a long time, though I thought my motives were good. I sat at my desk once and wrote on a piece of paper, 'Jason isn't for me.' But I still didn't break up with him for another six months."

"Why?"

"The usual stuff. I knew it was going to be painful as hell to lose him. But also . . . I wasn't sure I had a right to be so picky."

"Why not?"

I shake my head slowly. "It just seemed . . . everyone, including my parents, though they never said so directly, thought I should just marry him. You start to doubt yourself, you know? But that doesn't excuse it, either."

"Most people would say Jason had a responsibility to look out for himself."

I shake my head firmly, remembering the glimpse I once caught of Jason's face after one of our interminable conversations (Jason pushing, Jason willing to fill in nearly all blanks for me, me refusing to say the words that would have soldered us together). After getting ready for bed, I'd stepped into my living room. There was Jason, still seated on my sofa, looking out the window. Wanting to stay, knowing he should go. Trapped. "I know it takes two to tango, George, and I know Jason could have walked. I just think there's no excuse for doing damage when you really know better. It may not have been illegal by social norms, but it was wrong."

To my surprise George starts to laugh softly, and doesn't stop.

"What are you laughing at?"

"Myself," he says, pulling me closer. "For thinking I might never find a woman I was attracted to, whose outlook on the world I'd also respect."

I don't know how to answer.

"You know," he says, "you work at figuring out the world almost like a religious person — except without the God part."

"What do you mean?"

"Religion teaches you to take the world personally. Even if you're someone like me, and you've lost faith in the doctrines you were raised with, you never shake that: that intensity. That sense that the world is a finite system. And every wrong has a cause.

And everyone has a responsibility to understand and counterbalance that cause. There may be lapsed Christians, or lapsed Jews, but I don't think there's such a thing as a lapsed moralist." He sighs. "And you, Tracy, you're constantly grappling with things, from the big to the absurd. I don't ever have the slightest idea what you're going to say next. I love it."

Never in my life, it seems to me, has a man liked me for the same things I value about myself.

"It was one of the first things I noticed about you — after the fact that you made me laugh. And that you were sexy but didn't seem to know it. But what I noticed, after those things, was that you have a way of looking at the world, turning things upside down to sort them out. Maybe that's the Jewish side of you."

"I don't know that I *have* a Jewish side," I protest. "I mean, it's true you don't have to profess faith to be Jewish — with Jews it's sort of don't ask, don't tell, so if you walk the walk you're considered religious. But I don't even walk the walk."

"You *think* Jewish."

I sit forward and look at him, cautious. "What does that mean?"

"I'm not sure I can put my finger on it. You tell me."

I hesitate. "Here's a positive spin," I say. "I once saw a page of Genesis in a Hebrew Bible, with commentary. There was one solitary line of the Bible, embedded in the middle of the page. And the rest was this minuscule writing crammed into every spare millimeter, from the greatest hits of long-gone rabbis. Hundreds of years of speculation and whimsy and meticulous analysis."

"Yup," says George. "Bingo. That's it."

"I'm not sure whether to take that as a compliment."

"An extra-large." He raises his beer bottle, but instead of drinking blows a long, low tone across its top. With a wink he extends it into a tuneless rhythmic riff, then a serenade.

When he's through, I toot a low reply. Then I stop.

I sip my beer. I think over what George said about his family — the strict, grief-leveled landscape he escaped.

I'm not naive. I am thirty-three and I know that a dramatic past isn't just intriguing; it is, in fact, usually an oxymoron. But George also seems, despite it all, like the most grown-up man I've ever met. Happy not because his life has been happy, but because he knows it's important to be. There's a difference, it occurs to me, between easy happiness and passionate happiness.

Sitting here beside him, sipping room-temperature beer, I feel: This place is the center. This sofa is the exact center of the known universe, all neighboring systems quietly reshaping to make way for the heavy pull between us.

"Say something shocking," I say.

He hesitates, and this time I let him. Then he says, "I'd like to know you a very long time."

I pick up his hand. The scar is soft to the touch, bright and featureless and smooth like the skin of some newly hatched creature. I turn his hand in mine, and it looks to me now like a surgeon's hand, unafraid to touch where the damage is worst. I think: Most of the smart people I know would rather talk about why the blood is flowing, and whose fault it is, and what it signifies, than take the risks of actually stanching it. Their intelligence doesn't build up so often as it whittles away. George's choice to walk away from his upbringing, and his refusal to deny the costs of that choice, strikes me at this moment as the most honest thing I've ever heard of anyone doing.

I rest his hand against my breastbone. He kisses me softly, then pulls me down onto the cushion.

"Say something shocking," he says after a minute.

But instead we drift into a long, breathing silence. I stare at the ceiling, and think about the sacrifices I've made to do what I love. I think: A woman's independence is a hothouse flower. Improbable; rare; requiring vigilance. Millennia of patriarchal history argue against it. A quick review of my coupled girlfriends' lives reveals that there are few that appeal to me. Of the relationships I've seen, even the better ones, almost all seem claustrophobic. I've seen too many girlfriends who started out jauntily definitive about what they wanted end up with cheerless smiles. I've seen too much marital sniping followed by embarrassed jokes to dinner guests; too many acquaintances who tell me they're happy, yet sacrifice so much (career, friends, children) that I don't trust their happiness. Too many relationship compromises that seem to gut the person I once knew. My father at the window. My mother coming alive over the crossword puzzle, then lapsing into silence. Forster was right when he condemned novelists for "that idiotic use of marriage as a finale." Love, too often, is the start of the trouble. Men, at least, have the excuse of needing it; statistics show that their life spans are lengthened by marriage. Women, on the other hand, bathe at their own risk.

What, I ask myself, might love wreak on my life? Somber thoughts occupy me, counseling caution. Then I alight on the words of Adrienne Rich. *I choose to love this time for once / with all my intelligence.*

Into the dimming apartment, the sounds from the sidewalk and the aroma of Cambodian spices, I say something I know to be true only as I pronounce the words.

"I have been alone," I say to him, "as long as I can remember."

Morning.

"Yet this critical response, you have to remember, was contemporaneous with the emergence of London's Bloomsbury group."

A sophomore with a long brown ponytail whispers to the girl beside him. Flipping the page of my lecture notes, I glance pointedly at the two, who gaze at me from their back-row seats with the blank expressions of hardened criminals.

"So why this initial resistance to modernism in the American context?"

The two students smirk, still facing forward, their gossip all the more delectable for being interrupted. Surely they were talking about a classmate, a crush, a weekend keg party. Unless, of course, they were snickering about me: their professor who is wearing her bra on the outside of her blouse.

I defy you to find a female professional who, having had this thought, can resist a quick downward glance. With a rapid duck of my chin, I continue: "And what links can we see between this and the reception received by American postmodernism several decades later?" Blouse firmly fastened, bra out of sight; obviously they're laughing about something else.

My next thought makes me blush hard. As I consider the likelihood of my own transparency, I forge ahead with my lecture, continuing steadily if more emphatically. Students have love radar. It's their specialty. I eye the ponytailed kid, whip-thin and wisp-bearded, and his neighbor, a sweet-faced girl with multiple piercings. Their expressions are studies in bland interest. But they, like most students, are smarter than they act, and possibly they've spotted the signs: Unusual levels of energy. Cheerfulness in the face of literary theory. My tendency, today, to distraction.

Love. If it can happen to me, anything can. The square inch of Brazilian rainforest I bought in a ninth-grade environmental campaign holds the fabled mother lode; the rangers have been searching for me for years. My dental records confirm that I am Princess Anastasia, and my dentist has been waiting until my thirty-fourth birthday to tell me. I have won the office pool; I have been exempted, refunded, recognized; my long-lost sister is entering stage right. *Tracy?* she cries, clutching her gorgeous hands to her supermodel face. *Is it really you?* She is my identical twin.

Until last Saturday I'd never been to a spa. But Yolanda, in need of a post-opening-night debriefing and keen for news of my potentially budding love life, wouldn't hear of me refusing her invitation to Félicité, where two day passes awaited, payment for a recent gig modeling spa wear. After a hard workout, Yolanda led me to a glass-doored room, indicated I should sit on a slatted wooden bench opposite her, and nodded greeting to a trio of shiny-faced women. The door closed behind us and there was a moment's silence, long enough for the heat to make an impression. Then, startling me nearly out of my towel, steam shot up through floor vents. Yolanda, smiling like a giddy yogi, vanished in a thick, rising cloud. The whiteout wreathed me. The steam I inhaled was as hot as the air I exhaled — so hot I couldn't tell where my body ended and it began. I couldn't breathe. In fright I stood to grope my way toward air, but the door, along with Yolanda and the other women, was invisible. Disoriented, I stood trembling, taking the air in small sips. Then bigger.

I sat. The air was strangely full, but breathable. I closed my eyes. And noticed, as I gave the weight of my head to the wooden wall, that I didn't care anymore where my skin ended and where the air began.

That is what sex is like with George. My head tucked beneath his chin, our bodies bearing toward some unknown destination, I'm blind, claustrophobic, certain I won't be able to breathe. And then with a shush of skin my body declares itself: no longer a collection of disparate elements, arms and legs and breasts, but a simple whole. Alive, all breath and want, eager to touch, meet, fathom. George is impish and soothing, gathering me. The dark room absorbs our greetings, sounds of surprise and assent, the crush of my hair in his hands. An unfamiliar, girlish timbre in my laugh, and George's hands moving with the precision and delicacy of a paring knife slipping under the fruit's skin. Then a long, breathing silence. George, intent, turns my face to his. His eyes stop me. When he says the words I reply with a swiftness that surprises us both. I cling to his shoulders; he doesn't flinch. I roll into his chest, sleep like a baby.

And walk to morning lecture shaken down like a tree, leaves and cones scattered. Leaves and cones, my dear love-besotted students, all over Sixth Avenue.

"Before I conclude," I say to the sun-blanched lecture hall, "I must emphasize that there is little point studying postmodernism unless you acknowledge what it is the writer truly asks of the reader." Several students lift their eyes to the clock, whence will come their release in another minute forty-five. With my copy of *The Complete Short Works of Samuel Beckett* in hand, I step back from the lectern and consider the echoing distance to the back row of the hall. "Postmodernists want you to *interact* with the text. Question how it comes to you. Be skeptical. Vigilant. Above all," I say, "active." And with a lumbering skip forward, I heave the book into the empty air over the heads of my students. The angel of gravity is merciful and the book, pages roiling, sails straight toward the back row — toward the shocked upturned face of the kid with the ponytail.

"Catch!" I command, and he does, he traps and cradles Beckett in his narrow chest and hugs it with a great grin as the sweet-faced girl with the nose rings utters a quiet "wow" into the silent gallery and I, knowing there are moments whose glory must not be squandered, stride out of the room.

"Hi, Tracy." Elizabeth greets me in the dim corridor with a trapped expression I recognize from our last encounter. This time she carries a sheaf of student papers under one arm.

"How's it going?"

"Okay, I guess." Her mouth quavers: a fluttering ribbon of a smile.

Down the hall, Eileen steers her loaded cart majestically into the photocopy room. I wait until she's out of earshot. "Ever get through that gargantuan stack of books?" I ask.

Elizabeth nods, her laugh tight. She glances at her watch. "I've got another stack, though. Joanne recommended more reading. I guess I'll need to move back my dissertation-defense date a few weeks. I just talked to Eileen about the rescheduling."

"You're joking."

She shakes her head, then looks at her watch once more.

From down the corridor a beam shines across the sill of the copy-room door, then sweeps the hallway and walls like the sudden interrogation of a lighthouse. Eileen is copying with the machine's top open. A brief pause; then the light sweeps the hall again and continues in regular rhythm, a long, diagonal bar of brightness swinging across the far wall, up our bodies, across our faces, scaling the walls nearly to the ceiling, where it snaps off. Slide . . . clunk. Slide . . . clunk. The heartbeat of the department. Elizabeth shifts her papers to her other arm, and as she does there is an instant's desperate communication from her wide black eyes.

"You know you don't have to do all that, right?" I offer gently. "Joanne isn't even your adviser. *I* am. And the dissertation draft I've been reading is wonderful. It's going to make some waves in the Dickinson world. Elsewhere too, I'd bet."

Elizabeth watches me. The light slides up her face, illuminating her mouth; her nose; her eyes; her forehead. As it passes onward and leaves her in darkness, I have a disturbing image of her pale face looking up at me from under water.

"What are the books Joanne recommended?" I ask.

Elizabeth lists them, or starts to; after four titles I've had enough. "That material isn't even relevant, Elizabeth, and we both know it."

"It might be, if—"

"Look, Elizabeth, I'm sorry to cut you off, I really am, but this truly needs to be examined." Pausing to listen for movement from the offices down the hall—there is none—I continue with lowered voice. "You could be nearly finished with your dissertation by now. It could be on its way to publication. But you're getting caught in second-guessing, and I think Joanne is having"—I check myself—"a certain amount of trouble keeping in mind the best interests of your project and career."

Elizabeth says nothing.

"I don't mean to be hard on you. I'm just concerned."

"I'll think about it," she promises. She turns on a bright, professor-pleasing smile.

"But why do the reading, Elizabeth?"

"It's okay," she soothes, stepping backward so the light sails off her shoulder and her face is shadowed. "I'll just skim, in case there's something in there I need." Her voice is steady now, and carries a clear request to be left alone.

Jeff greets me in the faculty room with a raised glass of seltzer. "I hear you blew them away in Twentieth-Century Lit."

It takes a moment to figure his meaning. I blink dizzily at Jeff, and at the sofa and the bookshelves and magazine racks of the faculty lounge, as though I've just tried on someone else's glasses and can't yet trust the world's normal proportions.

"I didn't think you had that kind of stunt in you," Jeff continues.

The world reasserts its proper dimensions. Feeling loose-limbed, I pour myself coffee and stir in half-and-half. "I was possessed by the spirit of Beckett," I say.

"Bullshit. You were possessed by the spirit of Mr. Tabouli. You didn't throw that book, you levitated it with pure sexual energy."

A grin steals onto my face, torpedoing any chance for a deadpan comeback. I sip my coffee, the usual coal-and-chalk departmental brew. "What's that, anyway?" On his lapel Jeff wears a small button emblazoned with a picture of a smirking Brad Pitt.

"This," says Jeff, eyeing his lapel as though a turd has inexplicably appeared on it, "is from Richard. In honor of our seventh anniversary. He worships Brad."

"You're wearing that to lecture?"

"Richard dared me," Jeff says dryly.

I find it hard to imagine anyone daring Jeff to do a single thing he hadn't already deemed was in his best interest. "He thinks you need more Brad in your life?"

"No. Not more Brad. Less *dignity.*" He pronounces the word with an expression so baleful it implies this seventh anniversary will be their last. He sets down his seltzer. "On a brighter note," he says, "maybe it will help Paleozoic get the idea." He opens his laptop.

"Trolling airfares again?" I ask.

He nods without looking up. "Download them every morning along with my e-mail, and look at them when I have a chance." Jeff and Richard's commitment to visit every three weeks has hit a stumbling block since fares jumped with fuel prices. "A pointless way of biding my time until the new job listings come out next month and Richard and I can scheme."

"Again?"

"I'm serious this time. It's not worth it to keep doing things this way. My grad school classmates who couldn't find jobs may tell me what a lucky fuck I am to be tenured in Manhattan, but it's rather irrelevant given my situation."

"Can't Richard just move to New York?"

"You know how much harder it is to find an academic job here. Plus, in other parts of the country a person can actually live well on an academic salary."

"But doesn't it —"

The door opens and Jeff hushes me with a tiny slice of his forefinger against his jugular. Victoria steps in, followed by Joanne, who on this warm late-September afternoon looks as sour as any winter-bitten, devil-fearing Hawthorne churchwoman.

Victoria looks displeased to find the faculty lounge occupied. "Good afternoon," she says vigorously and with the barest of smiles. Crossing to the cupboard, she offers Joanne a coffee mug, but at a sharp shake of Joanne's head returns the mug to its place.

I draw a deep breath. Jeff may disapprove, but it has to be done. "Joanne?"

She turns.

"At some point, when you've got a few moments free, I'd like to speak with you about Elizabeth."

"What about Elizabeth?" She regards me, pale-lashed eyes unblinking.

"I was hoping you and I could discuss it in private."

She sets a neat manila folder on the coffee table between us. "I don't have time for secret tête-à-têtes."

As though the rest of us loafers do.

In a heartbeat, Jeff has turned into a set of green sofa cushions, Victoria into several volumes of *The Collected Works of Dante*, softly sipping coffee.

Joanne lifts her chin. Goodwoman Miller, with the authority of the church behind her. The only thing missing is a bonnet.

I measure my words. "Elizabeth has been working on her dissertation for several years. She knows Dickinson inside and out, and her scholarship is first-rate. I've read her draft and it's phenomenal. I'm sure if you read it you'd agree. I don't think it's necessary for her to do deep background reading on subjects that are tangential. Yet every time I see her she's bent under another stack of books you told her were essential."

Joanne's reply is swift, spring-loaded. "I thought that was the kind of scholarship we prize in this department. *Rigorous.*"

"I have nothing against *rigor.*" The word is, despite my effort, splashed with sarcasm. "But don't you think Elizabeth has done enough? She knows more about Romantic poetry than all of us combined."

Joanne's expression is mocking: *Speak for yourself.* "No one's forcing her to do the extra reading."

"Joanne, I know your aim is to help. But you've been a graduate student. If a professor on your dissertation committee strongly suggests a book, you're going to read it. Perhaps you're unaware that because of your suggestions, Elizabeth has already requested to have her defense date pushed back?"

Joanne offers a noncommittal shrug.

"You and I know Elizabeth is one of the brightest sparks to come through this department in years. She ought to sail through the dissertation process. She should be in the downhill stage by now. Instead she's getting more and more anxious. We've all seen students who are burnt out by the time they get their Ph.D.s. Most recover, but some don't. Let's not put Elizabeth in that position. I'm her adviser, and at this point any time I ask her about her progress she looks as though I'm with the torture squad."

Joanne's smile is icy. "I'm sorry you don't have a better relationship with your advisee."

From the book-lined wall behind Joanne, Victoria looks up, her face heavy with disapproval and a strange kind of pity.

"Joanne." I keep my tone deliberate. "If this is something between you and me, let's settle it, rather than playing it out through Elizabeth."

She takes her folder from the coffee table and centers it, almost lovingly, under her arm. "My dear," she says, "maybe everything isn't about *you*."

"Joanne," Victoria says in a low voice.

Joanne's words have lifted me to the balls of my feet, where I balance, calves trembling. "I'm not going to be dragged into a contest of insults. Elizabeth is an adult and free to choose her own course. I simply ask that you consider whether your advice is in her best interest."

Joanne presses her lips into the form of a smile. "You've made your point."

Exit Joanne.

Victoria, frowning, follows her without a glance at me or Jeff.

I face the shelves, bouncing lightly on the balls of my feet, scanning book spines blankly. From the sofa pillows behind me comes a soft yowl.

"Jesus!" I wheel to face Jeff. "Don't give me that bullshit about women's arguments being catfights. This is serious."

Jeff emerges from the sofa like a Cheshire, sardonic grin first. "*Why* is it serious? Elizabeth may be timid, but surely she can take care of herself. And if she can't, she'll need to learn. If she wants a career in academia, she's got to develop some basic political survival skills. You can't do it for her. Your five-alarm response is uncalled for."

"I disagree."

"Why? Tracy, Joanne can't take criticism. She never could, and this semester she's got a bug up her butt, who knows why, and nothing you or I do is going to change that. Is she obnoxious? Of course she is. Plenty of people are. Why is this worth fomenting World War Three?"

"You think *I'm* the one fomenting?"

He blows me a kiss.

I have no rebuttal. What appeared logical a few moments ago now seems foolish. But I recall the cold blue light sliding across Elizabeth's face and I know that Jeff is wrong. "I'm not trying to belittle Elizabeth's ability to take care of herself," I say. "But she's got the worst case of good-student compulsion I've ever seen. And it's going to get her in trouble."

"Does it occur to you you're being a bit controlling about this?"

Eileen's cart rattles by the faculty-room door at an excruciatingly slow pace. Stubbing the toe of my shoe into the carpet, I wait for it to turn down the far corridor.

"You think I am?"

Jeff's hands hover over his keyboard. "Life will be much easier," he says, "if you let this be Elizabeth's problem." His gaze returns to his laptop. I watch his eyes move down the screen. His fingers tap restlessly. "Great," he murmurs. "More e-mailed excuses from my worst student." He fires off a reply. Then his hands stop moving. "What's this now?" He falls silent. In the space of a minute his expression changes from skeptical to stunned to boyish. I wait for him to speak.

"The chairman makes his move," Jeff says softly.

"What chairman?"

"Emory." His eyes are still on the screen. "They've been given a line for a senior hire. They're inviting me to apply — give a job talk, meet the deans, the whole thing." He blows out air, as if exhaling a long draw of cigarette smoke. "Richard told them last month that he was considering leaving to be with me, but we didn't think they'd move so fast. Coca-Cola must be doling out that cash." He lets out a sharp laugh. "So Emory is going to try to cherry-pick me." He looks up. "I like the sound of that. I can be the cherry-cola prof of Brit lit. Of course they'd have to offer me tenure. That's going to require playing some serious hardball."

"You'd leave me here with White Fang?"

"In a heartbeat," he says. His eyes drop back to his screen. He types rapidly.

A few moments pass before he looks up. "Oh, did I miss that cue?" He shuts his laptop, sets it on the sofa, stands, and regards me gravely. Then he startles me with a strong hug. "You're the one thing about this department I'd miss."

"Honestly?" I say, my chin on his shoulder.

He speaks the words slowly, his narrow chest thrumming. "You make this place marginally human."

"That, Jeff, is the nicest thing anyone's said to me in all my years in this department. Pathetic, but true."

Pulling back, he chucks me under the chin.

The door opens and there's a hoarse gasp. "Oh. Terribly sorry." Paleozoic, pipe in hand, actually throws a hand over his eyes to prevent himself from seeing whatever untoward acts Jeff and I might be up to, standing here fully clothed in the faculty lounge. Ash scatters onto the carpet. Paleozoic looks confusedly at it, embarrassment stamped on his face.

Jeff snorts. "No call to be sorry."

"I don't need to know," Paleozoic wheezes, warding off enlightenment with an airy, panicked wave. And is gone.

Late at night, lying on my back with one leg close enough to feel the warm fuzz of George's, it strikes me: I am, for all the advice I have dispatched on the subject, utterly lacking in rules about relationships. During the three and a half weeks I have known George, I have been on drugs. Experiencing Technicolor flashbacks to here and now. Prone to fears and euphorias, not responsible for my actions. Love, as far as I can make it out, is contiguous with panic.

The digital clock glows green by the bed. George is fast asleep. I flip my pillow, adjust the covers.

I know a few rules of life. There is the Statute of Irrelevant Authority, which holds that if you shoot a crumpled paper across the room in the middle of a meeting, and if it drops right into the trash can, then your comments will instantly and thereafter be heard with more respect. *If she can do that, what else can she do?*

Then there is the Cookie Thief Paradigm: Sometimes it is better to ask forgiveness than permission. *I'm sorry, I didn't realize I wasn't supposed to eat those.*

Beside me, George sighs. Who ever heard of anyone sighing in his sleep? I rest gingerly on the pillow and wonder whether this staggering weariness portends disaster. *A weary man,* I think. *A man exhausted by his choices.* My eyes open in the dark room, I conjure the bleakness of his gaze after a demanding day at work, and try to fathom what inner darkness it might signify. And remember a long-ago March weekend Hannah and I spent in Boston. It was evening; Hannah and I paused on a footbridge over the Charles River to look over the frozen, glinting surface, and it was then that the world came apart. Without warning there was movement all around. What should have been solid fractured and shifted; the horizon spun toward me in slow motion. I was twenty and recognized immediately that there was something wrong with me — a stroke, a heart attack, surely there was some terrible clinical name for this dizziness that set me clinging to the bridge's stonework. Only as the world's peculiar motion accelerated did I understand that I was fine. That my panic was due not to disaster but to the simple fact of change. The river had, at that very moment, broken. Chunks of ice turned, swirled deliberately, entered widening channels of black water. Hannah and I ran from side to side of the bridge as the jigsaw that had been Boston's winter spun and floated downriver, faster, irreversible, heading for the bay. Spring.

At two in the morning, with a man I've known only twenty-four days sighing in his sleep beside me, this metaphor is utterly unconvincing.

The Grocery Checkout Proviso: The more things you care about, the more vulnerable you are. If you are part of that epicurean minority in this country that is still offended by violations of the English language, you will be slapped in the face every time you stand in line at the market. FIFTEEN ITEMS OR LESS. Caring passionately about grammar—caring passionately about anything most of humanity doesn't care about—is like poking a giant hole in your life and letting the wind blow everything around. Is like walking out your door with a big sign that says PLEASE FUCK WITH ME. The villain will seize the advantage, take hostages. For every single new thing or person you love, your vulnerability increases by a factor of precisely three billion. Falling in love is absurd. I am an absurd person.

Afternoon. Turning to Hannah for sanity, I find her in her apartment wiping vomit from the toilet seat.

Hannah is in her seventh month, beautiful, and head-turningly pregnant as she fills me in on the latest: Elijah, now napping, has mostly recovered from his bug, but the cough still makes him throw up. Refusing my offer of help, she finishes wiping the toilet and douses the area with air freshener. I sit on the sill of her tub —a perch where I've been advised through more troubles than I wish to recall. Hannah flips a wrung-out sponge onto a shelf, washes her hands, then flicks droplets of water onto my upturned face.

"Can you clip my toenails?" She sits on the closed toilet lid and grins saucily at me. "Don't worry, I washed my feet. I can't reach them over my belly, but I'm pretty sure I squirted liquid soap down there sometime in the last month."

I make much of wrinkling my nose. "You're lucky I like you." Then I kneel on the bathroom mat, remove her thick socks, and take her broad and perfectly clean feet in my hands. She passes me the clipper and leans her head luxuriously against the rolls of toilet paper stacked on the tank of the commode. "Adam was by yesterday afternoon, to drop off a CD he pirated for Ed."

I survey her pale, overgrown toenails, then probe delicately with the clipper. Adam has a new job, with a company that does something with software marketing. Fortunately the work—which Adam has refused to describe to me in detail, calling the very description a waste of breath—hasn't cut into his music-pirating time. Most afternoons he drops by Hannah's en route to his Ultimate Frisbee practice to help himself to leftovers and overstimulate Elijah. According to Hannah, she's now living the life of Penelope, but with a twist: each day she works to raise her child right, and Adam comes along and undoes the day's lessons.

"Turns out he and Kim are off again," she says sleepily.

"Did I know they'd been on?"

"They were more on than ever before. They were free agents while Adam was abroad, but they got back together as soon as he returned. Adam wanted to live with her."

"He wanted to *live* with her?"

"Yup," says Hannah. "But Kim said she wasn't ready to stop dating other people."

"Is he having a tough time about it?"

"Well . . ." From my position, I can see only Hannah's belly and her upturned chin, which bobs lazily as she speaks. "He's sad. But he's also okay. He says Kim is a *neat girl*." Hannah's imitation of her brother is gentle. "And he knows she cares about him. He says a commitment is something you have to be ready to make. And if Kim isn't ready there's no point quizzing her for explanations." Hannah rolls her head forward off the toilet paper spools. "He says he's not psyched to just keep dating her, not unless it's for real."

"You know," I say. "Adam can be impressive."

"You planning on clipping my nails?"

I've been holding Hannah's feet as though they were eggshell china; now I work the clipper around calluses and do my duty in silence.

"I can't get over how great George was with Elijah," she says once more.

I brought George over for a spaghetti dinner with Hannah and Elijah on Wednesday night. We've already discussed Hannah's impressions of George by phone, Hannah's voice radiating approval. But it's a pleasure, I admit, to hear her rehash in person.

"He's such a good guy, Tracy. I really like this one. Of course, Ed now says *he* should have been here on Wednesday to give his stamp of approval. But if I'd said the least word of encouragement about Ed joining us for dinner he'd gladly have skipped out on his plan to work late that night. Then he would have spent half of this weekend in the office to make up for it, and I'd have been on my own here, with Elijah sick."

I wait to give Hannah a chance to say more about Ed, though I know she won't. Out of respect for her I make it my policy not to pry, though it seems to me that Ed could do more to help her. Back in college Hannah never seemed to think Ed withholding; rather, she was grateful for his every utterance. Barely complaining, she put up with the dozen ways he kept her waiting. She thought his humor wry, while I privately found it careless of her. When, just after graduation, he finally broke up with her to go trekking, I thought it was all over but the cleanup; cautiously I began to voice some of what I'd thought all along. But Hannah couldn't stop grieving. A full year of Hannah's grief passed before Ed returned to the United States, humbled by malaria and the thunderbolt conviction that Hannah was the one. And he's been devoted ever since, placing himself in Hannah's hands with almost childlike trust. I can only assume this was what Hannah wanted — a man she could shepherd along. When they got engaged, I had to eat my words. I promised her I was thrilled for her happiness. Besides, I said, how would *I* have the slightest idea what made a good marriage? I'd never seen one. Neither, Hannah admitted reluctantly, had she. Neither, for that matter, had Ed, whose parents had divorced when he was ten. Hannah planned the wedding in a square reception hall; that way if things heated up between the exes someone could blow a whistle . . . and each parent (Hannah joked until the joke wore thin) could retreat to his or her corner.

The quiet thud of the front door signals Ed's return. Finding us in the bathroom, he kisses Hannah lightly — one hand gripping his briefcase, the other resting on the rise of her belly. Then he greets me with a dry peck and a grin. Ed has sprouted a few gray hairs around the temples, lessening the slightly pampered look that's always seemed incongruous alongside Hannah's sweet competence. Hannah fills him in on Elijah's condition, and Ed seems so downhearted at the news that Elijah won't be able to go to the playground that it's both laughable and endearing, and I recall once more what usually brings me around to Ed: his open adoration of his wife and son.

Ed vanishes into the bedroom to change his clothing. I start Hannah's other foot.

"So how *are* things with George?"

I stop what I'm doing and look at her. "I think," I say, "that this could really be the guy for me."

"Tracy, that is fantastic! I've never heard you say that about anyone. This is great!"

I focus on her toes and don't speak until I'm through. "It *is* great. It is. It's just . . . remember when we saw the Charles River break?"

"I'll never forget it."

"Well." I drop the clippings into the trash. "Change is fucking terrifying."

She gives me a quizzical look. "I never thought seeing the ice break was scary, Tracy. I thought it was just cool."

Cool.

Midnight. I curse as I set down my pen; the cartridge has ruptured, black ink staining the indents of my knuckles where I've gripped the last two hours. George and I agreed I'd work this Saturday night after we returned from dinner, so all of Sunday would be ours. Now he waits in bed, magazine in hand. I set the pen on my desk, grimace at the stack of undergraduate papers still untouched, and head to the sink to wash up.

I've just finished undressing at the side of the bed — still a self-conscious act in front of him — when he touches my shoulder.

Opening his hand, he shows me the broken pen, ink feathering into the creases of his palm.

He works carefully. The tiny prints proceed like silky animal tracks along my breastbone. Like a message slowly, finely telegraphed.

Body as text, smirks some restive part of my brain.

The tracks progress, a foreign alphabet of touch — a question? a promise? — along the curve of my side. A dot of ink slips and blooms on the cool sheets. Gingerly I stretch alongside him.

Down my hip. Down to my thigh, where he lays his heavy head, before beginning to blow the ink dry.

Aunt Rona has just phoned my cousin Gabby with tragic news. A neighbor's son — a son Aunt Rona has had her eye on as a match for Gabby for two and a half decades — has gotten engaged to a non-Jewish woman. The couple has decided to raise any future children Protestant. The parents are in shock.

Rona is — so she announced to Gabby — beyond shock. She is stunned. Rona, unlike my mother, is an officer in the Sisterhood; throughout our childhoods she insisted that Gabby attend our Reform synagogue for every holiday, including some I'd barely heard of such as the tree birthday — for which the Sisterhood had the synagogue's progeny cavort under cardboard trees heavily festooned with green Christmas lights Rona purchased off-season.

Aunt Rona loves her religion.

This morning, on one of the gossip tears that used to prompt us to speculate that either she or my taciturn mother must have been adopted — there was no way they could be sisters — Aunt Rona phoned Gabby to expound on the disaster. *I've known Jonathan since he was a boy. His poor parents. All those years you raise your child, you teach him and look after him . . . what a waste.*

Gabby is incensed. A waste of a life? Just because Jonathan isn't raising his own children Jewish? What about all the wonderful qualities Jonathan possesses, all the reasons his parents treasure him? Have these things suddenly vanished? Won't he pass some of them on to his Protestant children?

My ear still aching from the pressure of the telephone receiver and Gabby's outrage (her heated defense of Jonathan's choices hinting that she might not have been entirely indifferent to him), I find

George seated on a stool in my kitchenette, bent over the newspaper in bright autumn light. He's unshaven, dressed in a faded blue T-shirt and sweatpants. As I relate the telephone conversation he passes me my coffee. It's delicious: the coffee, the day-old garlic pizza in its soggy box, my indignation. Both of us tousled. Smelling, frankly, like sex.

Brushing the hairs on his forearm with my fingertips, I let out a yawn. "Aunt Rona is a bit extreme that way."

He swallows a mouthful of coffee and considers. "I wouldn't call her extreme."

I sit on a stool beside him. "Well, okay. I know that compared to fundamentalists she's mild. But in the context of my almost totally nonobservant family, you know."

"What I mean is, I think she's right."

"Right about what?"

George lowers his mug. "It *is* a waste when someone walks away from his upbringing. I'm a waste to my father."

"How can you say that?"

"No need to prettify my situation, Tracy." He studies the mug in his hands, then looks up at me. His voice is dead calm. "I'm not afraid to call it what it is: I failed my father."

"Your father failed you too," I offer with a heat I don't entirely understand.

"Okay, true." He pauses. "Yes he did. But I'm through blaming him — he's not capable of understanding me. All I'm saying is, there's something important about sticking with your kin and upbringing. I had to get out, but I'm no shining example of virtue. If I could have stayed, I would have. That business about honoring your parents is a good idea, no matter whether it was a person or a deity who wrote it." He offers an apologetic smile. "Family is the center of everything. Speaking of which" — he turns his stool and positions himself to face me — "do you want children?"

I laugh.

"What's so funny?"

"That was just — abrupt."

"Was it?" He shrugs.

In the quiet kitchen, George waiting, I find it difficult to enunciate my feelings. I've always thought I might like to have children. In theory. In truth the alchemy of love has always seemed a more pressing question than its byproduct. Kids — how many and when — are not a subject I've given sustained consideration. Do I want children? I assume I will. Most people eventually do.

Don't they?

"I think I do," I say.

"Because I'd like a pack of them."

"A pack?"

He nods.

"How many come in a pack?"

"It's just a wish," he says.

There it is again. That hopeful look. It washes powerfully across his face. I watch, uncertain, caught for a moment in its undertow.

He presses on. "How would your parents take it if you married a non-Jew?"

I shrug. "They'd get used to it." In truth my parents are so obviously relieved that I'm dating anyone — so quick to forgive George's failure to be Jewish — it's a bit insulting. "They'd respect you, and be a little shy around you and . . ." I can't help smiling at this image. At the fact that George and I are — aren't we? — hypothesizing about a future. "They'd love you. Judaism not mandated."

His brow is furrowed. "I'd convert so we could raise our kids right."

Three responses collide in me: euphoria at his directness; anxiety at his directness; confusion.

"Why would conversion be an issue?"

"Clarity," he says.

I wait. He doesn't elaborate.

"Who says kids have to have a homogeneous religion," I say, "or any religion for that matter, to grow up well?"

"Structure is important. Stability. Clarity of morals. People's roles in their community."

I can't help laughing. "But look how you and I live: like loose atoms bouncing around Manhattan. Now we're bouncing together, and that makes me happy." I hesitate. "Happier than I've ever been, George."

His smile lights his face.

"I'm sure there's a lot to be gained from religion," I say. "Sometimes I suspect the difference between someone without a clear faith and someone with may be the difference between a stick of wood and a cello. But I can't overlook all the harm religion does. And I don't think we need some big structured community to have meaningful lives."

"It's important, though," he argues, "when you start a family. Community plays a part in a stable life, and gives everyone a distinct role to play."

"How do you mean?"

"Well, for example, in a healthy community, men and women have contributions to make . . . *different* contributions." He rubs his head, musing. "That's the problem I have with American feminism — it tries to make everything unisex." His hair lifts at the passage of his hand, then slowly fans back into place. "It tries to upend everything. Plus it lacks humor."

I am daily falling more deeply in love with this man. He makes me laugh. He is a grownup. He is good-looking, considerate, sexually generous. And he's speaking a language I don't recognize. It is at this point that I realize how profoundly I want him not to turn out to be a closet reactionary. My hand, resting on his forearm, looks yellow against his pink-toned skin.

"Feminists have great senses of humor," I say. "I for example think everything is funny. I think sexism is hilarious."

"You consider yourself a feminist?" He looks genuinely startled. "I thought your whole complaint about Yolanda's play was that it was feminist."

"No. No, no, no. My complaint was that it was bad art. That it was so busy making a political point — which happened to be a somewhat tired feminist one — that it blotted out all nuance." As I say this, I have the vague sense there was something beyond the play's hackneyed politics that spurred my condemnation of *Why the Flower Loves the Rod*. The unbearable spectacle, perhaps, of a woman deliberately turning over her trust to a man who would not treat it kindly? It occurs to me that what bothered me most was not the play's obvious flaws . . . but that sitting in the theater next to George, watching a woman risk her heart, was intolerable.

A line of thought I do not, at the moment, wish to share with George. "I don't have to agree with every feminist on the planet to consider myself one — which I do, George. I'm garden-variety, mind you. I'm no Dworkin and I'm no crusading castrator—but then almost no feminists are. That's a peculiar cultural fantasy, this business of the man-eating feminist. Mostly I want things like equal job opportunities. And huge international pressure on those countries that do horrible things to women." I pause. "But can we take this back a step? What were you saying just before, about women's roles?"

"Career is fine," he explains, his voice friendly. He rests a warm hand on my knee. "Career is great. Of course it is, Tracy. So long as a woman isn't so ambitious she puts it ahead of family."

"All right. Can I assume the same is true for men?"

He wags his head. "Women have a special role in the family. A lot of women make the mistake of not realizing that. Listen, I think it was pathetic that my father refused to learn to cook after my mother died—that we ate macaroni until Paula and I took up the challenge and learned how to cook. But when my father used to say 'a woman makes a home,' he wasn't entirely wrong. When my mother died, it wasn't a home anymore. It just wasn't."

I hesitate. "Don't you think that had something to do with how your father acted, though? I mean, wouldn't it have been a home—even if there was nothing more than macaroni to eat—if he'd approached his kids with warmth, instead of . . ."

George watches me. "Judgment?" he fills in.

I nod.

He purses his lips, then shakes his head. "I can't imagine it."

I can't ask George the next question that pops into my mind: Does he think his mother got a fair deal, stood up for herself, felt she had choices? But it's too delicate a query for a heated moment. And too soon for me to touch that subject with George. I retrench. "Forgive me for saying so," I say, "but 'special role' has always sounded like a sugarcoating for stay at home and clean up everybody's mess."

He stops to consider this. "Why are you so suspicious of traditional structures?"

"Because women have traditionally gotten screwed over."

"Why are you so angry about motherhood?"

I stare at him for a full minute. I'm trying to sort out whether he knows how he sounds . . . or whether he's simply innocent of experience with this sort of conversation. "If you want a history lesson in misogyny," I say softly, "I'll give you a mind-boggling reading list."

His jaw flexes. "Are you an angry woman?"

It's with effort that I stay seated. "I am not *an angry woman,* George. I am a reasonable person who happens to get angry for a few specific and compelling reasons. Because if I'd been born thirty years earlier, or into a different kind of family, I wouldn't be doing the work I love now. Because most girls in the world don't have my opportunities. Meanwhile, be careful when you chastise a woman for political anger — you should be glad to be with a woman who can *say* she's angry, as opposed to all those women who never admit to being angry. Who say *fine* when they mean *fuck you* and spend their lives emotionally pretzel-knotted, depressed, and untrustworthy."

He tilts his head. His face, the face that's become, for me, synonymous with welcome, catches the warm light from the window . . . and he laughs aloud. "Let me get this straight: I'm supposed to be *glad* you're angry at me?"

"You bet."

"That's —"

"But what's more important is that you know who I am. I'm moved that you offer to convert. I'm touched. More than touched. But I don't want you to. And I'm a professor, George, and serious about my career. If you have other requirements in mind for your mate, or if you want someone who's going to march in lock-step with some community or religious mores, then I'm not the woman for you." There is a sour taste in my mouth: garlic, coffee, fear. This man lifted me in his arms last night, and my mind stopped — actually ceased contradicting and observing and made room for something new. We made love like some impossible sailing Calder sculpture barely needing to touch ground. Gentleness and force in balance. Now I experience full-body confusion. Somehow we've pivoted from unprecedented tenderness to what sounds like the verge of a breakup. I speak his name. Anyone stepping into the room unaware might think the quaver in my voice is anger.

His face is still bathed by the window, his brown eyes flecked with light. Leaning forward on the stool, he addresses me slowly. "I love you, Tracy. Of course I don't have a problem with who you are. These are small differences. They're not worth worrying away a beautiful morning." He gestures toward the street, the fenced golden-leafed park. The city that awaits our complicity.

"Okay," says Yolanda. "First of all, calm down." She taps a sugar packet on the surface of the diner's table, her dark red fingernails making nauseating contrast with the speckled-salmon Formica.

I glance up at the mirrored walls where Yolanda's neighborhood watches itself calorie-count. A couple of anorexic-looking preteens from the nearby Joffrey Ballet studios, hair in murderously tight buns, sip tall glasses of water and pick at salads. A flagrantly beautiful young man studies his reflection as he sips something with lemon in it.

"It was just such an awful conversation," I say.

"So he has a couple old-fashioned ideas," says Yolanda. Accepting her plate, she addresses the waitress. "Oh, did you see the witch they gave that walk-on part to?"

The waitress, so thin her mute, bitter smile seems to carve channels in her face, hands us napkin-wrapped silverware.

Yolanda salutes her. "Courage to us all."

"Courage is a dime a dozen," says the waitress in a flat voice, refilling our plastic cups of water. "So's talent." She thunks down a metal pitcher, splashing water over the rings of condensation that already decorate the table.

I watch her stride off. "So much for friendliness."

"No," says Yolanda. "That's how I feel after I lose out at an audition, too. There's no justice. That's why I do yoga — it keeps me from dwelling. Yoga, and vitamins." Yolanda pulls a plastic sack from her gym bag and offers me an assortment of pink, green, and brown-speckled pills, which I decline. Yolanda is dressed in workout clothes: a pale orange spandex leotard that leaves no curve unexploited, and perfunctory black shorts that would turn heads anywhere other than here in the Village. She wears little makeup this morning, a rarity, and her hair, pulled back, is currently dyed H.D.'s pale brown — close to Yolanda's natural shade, which she last wore in high school. The effect is to leave her face unexpectedly exposed. She looks older, and, though she'd probably disagree, more beautiful than usual. The critics, I know, would take my side on this one; one reviewer called Yolanda "a devastating and devastated beauty." Reviews of the play itself have been mixed, with the harshest asserting that the script was "a politicized retread and a bad case of approxa-history" (a comment Yolanda dismissed with a shrug: she didn't care *who* Freud was in real life — in this play he was a dickwad to H.D., and that was all she cared about). But the praise for Yolanda has been universal and lavish, and it seems to be drawing audiences . . . a fact that hasn't been lost on the playwright or on Bill, who have responded with varying degrees of gratification and pettiness. Yolanda herself, unaccustomed to critical attention of even modest proportions, seems irritated by too much mention of her good fortune — as though that would jinx this unprecedented career boost. She mentions the reviews only sporadically, with awe, before moving on to her latest grievance against Bill. Though even that litany has seemed perfunctory of late. She's getting her say every night onstage, and even if Freud won't really listen to her, it's clear the audience does. Today she'd much rather settle my problems than rehash Bill.

"So your guy has traditional ideas about family or religion or whatever," continues Yolanda, dry-gulping two vitamins and dropping the rest back into her open gym bag alongside water bottles, rolled towels, exercise bands, and a pair of magenta thong underwear. "Doesn't sound like the end of the world to me."

I sip at a mug of coffee and watch without appetite as Yolanda wolfs her cottage cheese–special plate. My stomach hasn't unclenched since I left George this morning.

Yolanda sets down her fork and pats her lips with a napkin. "This is perfect, Tracy. You're a professor. You love to tell people what's what. You can teach him your worldview as you go along."

"But why the offer to convert, even though we've already talked about how we're both agnostic? And what is this stuff about traditional roles?"

"Ooh, sounds like an axe murderer. Okay, so the guy has an old-fashioned streak. And maybe he's got a few sexist assumptions. Does he treat you badly? That would be the only red flag for me. Tell me, Tracy, does he respect your professor-ness?"

"He read Kafka last week, so he could understand a paper of mine that he'd asked to see."

"Okay. Listen to me. I know you're used to giving me advice, so now take some. How long have I known you?"

"Nineteen years?"

"And remember how we used to speculate about what kind of guy we wanted to meet? And remember how you were always so picky?"

"No more than you—you had eye-color specs, and a height cutoff."

"Right. So, nobody gets exactly what they expect. George comes from a conservative background, so of course he's going to sound traditional sometimes. And most men have a few creepy ideas about women. Most women also have some creepy ideas about men. And by the way, I've been meaning to break this to you for years: most people, men *and* women, think 'feminism' is a dirty word. Saying feminists are humorless has nothing to do with whether this guy respects women."

"No?"

"Sometimes I can't believe they let you be a professor, Tracy, no offense. There are plenty of ways to show respect. Breaking a woman's heart isn't respectful, and so far he hasn't done that to you, has he? At least he's open about his tradition thing. Most of the guys I deal with are A-pluses at political correctness and ball-room dance. They play dads on Home Depot commercials, they're sensitive, they massage their girlfriends' bellies every month. And then if you look at the way these same guys flirt and swagger and cheat it's obvious they don't respect women. They just like being heroes—and in the circles I travel you're a hero if you're politically correct. The ones who *aren't* jerks—the truly honest-to-God sensitive arts-guys who actually *like* women—are so confused about what might possibly be left of guy-ness once you take away the swagger that they can't handle the whole scene. So they go on four magical dates with you, they inspire you to drop your defenses along with your pants, and then on the fifth date they think they might be gay."

Yolanda has flung her arms wide. Even in this clattering diner, her emphatic delivery is turning heads. Ignoring onlookers, she fixes me with that in-your-face stare that is the sole province of stage actors and cult proselytizers—the kind of prolonged eye contact that makes adults develop facial tics and dogs attack. Grimly I nod affirmation. I've seen Yolanda through two of these tormented actors.

Slowly Yolanda lowers her arms, head bowed. After several seconds, she raises her head. "Be glad you found one who is straight and wants a woman in his life. And if he's cool with you being Professor Tracy in her full glory, marry the guy. And if he wants to be Jewish for you, that's the most romantic thing I've ever heard. Meanwhile, take my advice?"

"Yeah?"

"Don't push him."

"I'm not going to pretend agreement if he says things that bother me."

Yolanda leans forward, hands splayed on the tabletop. Her green eyes look tired, spidery lines radiating from their corners. "Fine, be as blunt as you like. Go on some big protest parade against traditional statements, conservatism, sexism, whatever. And you'll lose half the good ones who come down the pike. Men are like . . ." Yolanda turns her eyes to the ceiling, searching. "Coral reefs. Brush them the wrong way and that's it. Finito. You have to be delicate, otherwise you'll chase away the best ones."

I'm not naive. Every relationship between two humans involves censorship; I have, of course, excised from this afternoon's recounting the part of the argument where George and I disagreed about precisely why we hated Yolanda's play. But there is small, ego-saving censorship, and then there's the big variety: the kind that's dishonesty. "If a guy runs away when I speak my mind, how does that make him the best? Besides, how can you say you respect men if you insist on expecting so little from them?"

Yolanda takes a long sip of ice water, then sets her glass firmly on the table. "All I'm saying, Tracy, is that you've got to live in the real world."

It's been just over a month since I met George. The smell and feel of his skin are with me when we're apart. Sitting in this absurd overpriced diner, I imagine losing him, and it prompts a sensation I've had only once before: jumping, on a dare, from the high cliff at the quarry near my high school. The approach, the launch, then the drop: endless, wrong, dreadful. Long enough you had time for regret.

"I know you think my reaction is overblown," I say. "It's hard to explain, Yolanda. But the conversation worried me." *Worried* is too ordinary a word for what I felt, leaving George this morning after a Sunday spent strolling the city and a night's uneasy sleep; packing my school papers and stepping out onto the street with coat buttoned high and my arms tight across my chest, as though to defend myself against assault. Something about George's matter-of-fact assertions — something, as I replay the conversation in my mind, about the eye-of-the-storm calm with which he said he'd failed his father — made me ask whether this might be a dangerous love.

Gazing past Yolanda's shoulder, I locate myself amid the array of the diner's clientele reflected in the wall mirrors. Ballerinas and black-clad students; the pierced, the hair-gelled, the suburban high schoolers playing hooky. The crowd simmers in bright reflection, eating, gossiping. And there I am, drab and professional opposite Yolanda's ponytail and upright posture. In my slacks and navy blouse, satchel of papers by my feet, I'm the out-of-place detail Magritte might have added to spice this tableau . . . yet, all the same, just another figure in the crowd. Talking about love.

And weighing, now, another question: Is every love, every real one, dangerous?

"So this is the guy's first flaw." Yolanda zips her gym bag. It's time for her yoga class. Reaching across the table, she grabs my forearm. "It's taken a whole month to find one. You're going to balk over some minor thing? The guy is calm. He's polite. He's thoughtful. He's in *love* with you, Tracy. And you with him. This is just panic." Yolanda's grip is so tight it hurts. Abruptly, she lets go. "And you two are the only thing giving me a fucking ray of hope for God's sake, so don't screw this up. Okay, talk values and religion and all that crap with him. Speak your mind, Tracy, fine, just don't ask him to call it feminism. Call it 'Bootyism.' Call it the 'International Movement to Be Nice to Your Favorite Pair of Tits.' Every time he makes a feminism-friendly comment, just give him a blow job and watch how fast he changes his tune, only do not screw this up over some professorial debate about gender roles or whether a religious conversion is *necessary*. Don't you dare. I'll never speak to you again."

With this last, all the force of four years' romantic exile weights her voice and I have not an iota of doubt that she means it.

• • •

Propelled by the weight of a black canvas backpack, Elizabeth practically hurtles into my office. She wears the pack over both shoulders, the thick straps crowding her breasts. There are small greenish scoops under her eyes. Her mannish button-down shirt is rumpled and bears a coffee stain over the left pocket: tattoo of the academic heart.

She's right on time for our eleven o'clock appointment, and after greeting me she digs in her backpack for the paper we're to discuss — a reconsideration of the contemporary critical literature on Hawthorne's *Blithedale Romance*. Twisting in her seat, she works at the task, her back as slim as a child's. It takes a full minute's wrestling for Elizabeth to extract the paper from her bag. I watch her unwrap it from around the spine of what could be a hardback Manhattan phone book: more sixteenth-to-eighteenth-century prosody, I'd bet.

I lay her paper on my desk and scan the opening lines. I haven't had coffee this morning, and the prodigious headache that bloomed during my morning lecture leaves little room for patience. Let Elizabeth run herself into the ground if she can't stand up to a bully — Jeff is right. There's no need to babysit a graduate student. Furthermore, Yolanda's advice the other morning in the diner only confirmed what she and Hannah have been telling me for years: I overreact, take things too seriously, prophesy trouble where it doesn't exist. In the days since my argument with George, the hesitancy between us has receded, leaving only a faint residue, the high-water mark from a nearly forgotten flood. Tonight George and I are going dancing. I've got more important things to concentrate on than a grad student's inability to defend herself.

Before I've read two sentences of Elizabeth's paper I'm distracted by the lettering, obviously not the product of a computer printer. Though I know my reaction is unreasonable, the idiosyncrasy seems an affront: a call for the very attention I've just decided to withhold.

"Where in the world did you dig up a manual typewriter?"

"Eileen had it in storage. I asked for it. That's all I did."

I glance up. "I didn't say you stole it."

"Okay, okay," she murmurs.

Here and there a line runs off the paper, words sailing into the void. I drag my eyes down the page as though reading against a current. "I see the margin bell wasn't working." I've never been this sharp with Elizabeth.

"I got tired," she says absently. "I typed it this morning at home. I was in the library all night." A nostalgic smile spreads across her face.

There is a thin tapping from the hall: my excuse for a moment away from Hawthorne, Blithedale, and Elizabeth, all mired in romanticisms irrelevant to mine. With a brisk "back in a second" to Elizabeth, I rise.

In the hallway Jeff is hanging a framed photograph on his office door. The black-and-white image appears to be a picture of the nave of an enormous church, but its wooden arches and shadows stretch and twist in a way that subtly defies gravity.

Jeff gives the nail a final tap. "It's by a local photographer," he says.

I move closer. The photograph is indeed an image of a church, but projected onto a man's naked shoulder and back.

Hammer in hand, Jeff eyes the poster. "Is it straight?"

"On *your* door?"

He folds his arms: Very funny.

"Why don't you just tell him you're gay?"

Jeff tuts. "Too easy. I want to see how long it takes him on his own. I considered hanging a gay-pride flag on my door, but I didn't think he'd know what it meant."

"What is it about toying with Paleozoic that so appeals to you?"

"Tracy, my friend, I have selectively played straight more times in my life than you'll ever know. Now I've got tenure. I'm entitled to the small pleasure of fucking with the emeritus. Besides" — he lowers his voice even further — "I go down next week for my job talk."

"To Atlanta?"

He answers with a slow-hatching grin.

My headache, momentarily forgotten, returns with a hard throb above my right eye. "You're serious about this?"

With an expression of barely attained forbearance, he slides the hammer back into his briefcase and sets a hand on my shoulder. "Yes."

"I hate you."

"Hate you too." He blows me a kiss. "Did you hear the latest from Eileen?"

"You're diverting me."

"I think you'll like this diversion." He glances down the hall, then his thin lips form a smirk. "Joanne's furious. Some student was entering those summaries of student evaluations into the undergrad course guidebook, and instead of typing a description of Joanne's lectures as 'lucid' the kid typed 'lurid.'"

"No."

"Oh yes."

"That's terribly unfortunate." My poker face holds for a millisecond, then dissolves under Jeff's blue stare. "It's also the funniest thing I've ever heard."

"There are seven hundred copies out. The head of the student committee came to Joanne's office to apologize, and she told him he could save his breath. She called it, and I believe this is an exact quote, 'a puerile act of sabotage.' The world is conspiring against our dear Joanne."

"I want to take that student out to lunch."

"Now, now," sings Jeff. "It's childish to bear ill will against a colleague." He pins me, momentarily, with a disapproving frown. Then the Cheshire cat grins once more, leaving me with the familiar queasy sensation of lagging a step behind Jeff. And wondering yet again whether Richard, too, finds it impossible to be certain of Jeff at times like this — or whether he's able to step inside the perimeter that separates Jeff from the rest of us mortals, fathom the well-oiled gears, wind and unwind the highly polished clock that is his lover.

Back in my office, I find Elizabeth snoring, her head tilted against the wall. I consider waking her, then decide against it. She wouldn't take my advice about rejecting unnecessary work — now she's exhausted. If she's late for a class because she was desperate for a catnap, let it happen. I wash my hands of this. I slide her paper to the side of my desk, open my laptop, and turn my attention to the statement I'm composing for my tenure packet. I've been given a December tenure meeting date: relatively late in the season due to some faculty scheduling conflicts, but Jeff thinks I'll be all right. "Just make the packet as thunderous as God," he said. I've taken him at his word, shaping every publication and official kudo into a dossier that is, to my pleasant surprise, intimidating.

When Jeff comes to rouse me for lunch I don't hear his approach, so engrossed have I become in blending confidence and modesty in a proportion designed to impress anyone on the tenure committee who hasn't yet formed an opinion of me. I can compare Faulkner to Fellini using only my abdominal muscles. I can balance everything Henry James ever wrote on the tip of my nose. I like Gertrude Stein.

"Hungry?" Jeff swings my door wide.

I glance at the clock. Over an hour has passed since I installed myself at my desk. Elizabeth hasn't stirred.

Jeff crosses his arms and slumps his lean frame against the doorjamb, in his black-on-black outfit looking more than ever like a hieroglyph for boredom. With an amused nod, he indicates Elizabeth. "What's with her?"

"She's sleeping it off. She was in the library all night."

"How could she have been in the library all night?"

At which moment I realize what pique and undercaffeination blinded me to earlier: the library closes at eleven.

"She was probably just out clubbing, having a hot night with a half-dozen bodybuilders," says Jeff. "Mousy grad student by day, street troller by night. Let her have her rest."

But I'm embarrassed: for letting a student sleep in my office; for failing to catch the contradiction in her library story; most of all, for being made a fool of. I defended Elizabeth to Joanne, and in doing so worsened an obscure enmity that's reared its head just as my tenure review process is beginning. For thanks I get an idiotic, undergraduate-level lie about a library all-nighter.

It takes several repetitions of her name and a firm shake to wake her. My hand on her shoulder feels like a violation, and I withdraw it the instant her eyelids flutter. "Elizabeth," I repeat.

"Yes, I'm sorry." She struggles upright.

"I've got a question for you."

Her gaze lolls around the office, lands on my desk, my computer, me. "Oh shit," she murmurs, and her pale cheeks flush a hot red. From the doorway Jeff watches with a smirk.

"*How* were you in the library all night last night?"

She answers me with obvious relief at not being asked a more difficult question. "I broke in."

With a low whistle, Jeff steps inside and closes my office door. "Beg your pardon?"

Elizabeth looks from me to him. Then her dark eyes come home to rest on mine. I feel their tentative weight.

A powerful, irrational sense of responsibility turns my voice hoarse. "Tell us," I say. "It's okay."

"The bell had already rung, and I hadn't left, and the guard found me on his last round through the stacks. He was pretty mad. So I pretended to leave, and while he was on his walkie-talkie I jumped the barrier and slipped back inside." She pauses, then utters a soft hiccup of a giggle. "He didn't even see me. I spent the night in the rare books room." She laughs again, louder this time, and with edge.

I picture the lithe form of a cat burglar sailing over the barrier, leaping balletically between shadows to claim the orgiastic delights of two-hundred-year-old volumes. Elizabeth's slim figure suddenly looks a good bit less sickly.

"Wasn't it dark?" asks Jeff, sounding mildly impressed. I shoot him a look: we ought to be expressing concern, not fascination.

Grinning at Jeff like a co-conspirator, Elizabeth plunges an arm into her backpack and fishes out a small plastic contraption, which she straps onto her forehead. She reaches up to flip a switch and the headlamp glares blue-white into my eyes.

"I got it at an outdoor goods store."

Jeff and I squint in turn as she looks at each of us for approval. "Oh, sorry." She shields the bulb until she's able to find the switch.

As she twists to return the extinguished headlamp to her backpack, the words run through my head: *canary in a coal mine.*

I turn to Jeff. He gives me a mocking salute: *this one's yours.* With an exaggerated flourish, he bows to Elizabeth, now watching us expectantly from her seat. "I'd love to stay and chat with you ladies, but I've an appointment with the Queen." He leaves, closing the door firmly behind him.

"Elizabeth," I begin, and then don't know how to continue. To gain time, I make a show of pulling her MLA paper toward me and lowering my head as if reading. For a while I stare blankly at the first page, considering: Is this just the mild mania of an over-taxed graduate student? Or is she losing her grip? And if she isn't, and if I make a fuss about protecting her well-being, how badly will I shoot myself in the foot? Absently I flip to the second page, and scan the opening paragraph of an entirely new paper.

It has been asserted (see Farrell and Gray's <u>Crying After the Moon: Calvino and His World</u>) that Italo Calvino's magical universe had primarily Cuban and European antecedents. Yet a brief look at some nineteenth-century American texts — texts available in both Cuba and Italy during Calvino's youth — may indicate that his literary influence also included, to a significant degree, American Romantic writers.

I raise my eyes. "I thought you were writing about Hawthorne."

"Oh, sorry. Did I leave the opening page of the Hawthorne draft there? You can throw that out. The new paper, the one I want you to look at, is about Calvino. I changed my mind last night."

I read on, flipping pages slowly. Fifteen minutes later I look up to find Elizabeth nibbling dreamily on the nails of one hand.

The paper is gold. Once more Elizabeth has taken a common critical assumption, documented its origins, then provided enough counterevidence to flip it on its head. Whatever is going on with Elizabeth, her mind is obviously as lucid as ever, faulty margins notwithstanding. It occurs to me that with some sleep this might be fine. Straightening the pages under Elizabeth's gaze, I ask myself what Victoria would do if she were here. It's the kind of situation she would know how to handle graciously: attending to her younger colleagues' needs while giving their emotional lives a respectfully wide berth. Expressing concern without being nosy.

I don't ask Elizabeth why she broke into the library. "Go home," I say in as firm and kind a voice as I can muster. "Get some sleep. You've written a terrific paper. Now call in sick."

"But I've got work to —"

"Go home, Elizabeth. Sleep deprivation is for political prisoners. Go home and get yourself back on track."

She stands and swings her pack across her shoulder. There's an audible thud as it connects with her back. I wince, but she doesn't seem to notice. As she shrugs her way into the straps I rise and open the door for her.

"Thanks," she breathes. Leaving my office, she accelerates to a rapid stride, the echoes of her footfalls crowding the hall as though one step at a time were not enough for her.

"Sleep," I say, as she rounds the corner and disappears.

The breeze whips the deck of the ferry. This is our fifth consecutive joy ride between Manhattan and Staten Island — a full afternoon's cruise for free, New York's most accessible thrill for low-budget lovers.

The ferry churns through sparkling water, the day so bright I regret leaving my sunglasses at home. George balls the wax paper from his picnic sandwich and stuffs it into our makeshift trash bag. "How's Yolanda?" he asks.

"Much better, I think — despite the extension. She'd been counting the days until closing night, so I thought she'd lose it when she learned the play is reopening in SoHo next month." I squint at the water. "But maybe it's therapeutic, having to face the kind of guy she falls for and act out the consequences every night. She got hit on by some dancer at a party this week, the smooth-operator sort she usually flips over. And she refused him. Never, in all the years I've known her, have I heard of Yolanda saying no to a well-polished bad apple." I turn and watch the horizon of Staten Island recede. "This Bill thing has been worse than her usual, which is saying a lot. Yolanda has had a rough go of it."

He grimaces. "I sympathize. The world can be a forest of wrong people."

"And she lets her hopes soar for each one. Which is part of the beauty of Yolanda."

"Well, didn't you?"

The wind picks up; I brace myself against the railing. "Not the same way," I say. "I hoped to fall in love. But I was pretty content in the meanwhile."

He tilts his head, studying his orange juice container. "Still, haven't you been hungry to meet the right person and get started with life?"

"I've wanted to meet someone, yes. But I think my life has already started."

Inverting the container, he takes the last swig, then wraps an arm around me and pulls me close. "I've lived for it."

"What about everything else going on in your life?"

"It's so much water treading. Important water treading. But not the real thing."

". . . which is finding someone, and making that life wave go forward?"

He laughs, but his face is earnest as he answers. "That's how I feel, anyway. Love, kids, the future. That, and taking care of the ones who raised you. If you're able." He hesitates, watching me. "I think it's important to understand your priorities, and try to steer so you don't end up sorry. Life is finite."

The ferry chugs heavily through the harbor. The Manhattan terminal, blanched by the autumn sunshine, comes into view. We near the dock.

For me, moving forward has meant writing the next paper, putting together a tenure packet; debunking, subverting, inverting. I've committed myself to a life of service to literature. The quotidian is a waste of time. I don't send holiday cards — it only encourages people to expect them next year. I don't darn socks. People need to eat? Hence the discovery, in 1645, of takeout. My salary is largely sub-investment-level, my parents give no indication of needing or desiring help, my future is abstract, and health is not something that occupies my attention. I think about my responsibilities to my "family unit" as frequently as I think about taxes — which is to say only as often as necessary to stay out of trouble.

"You've thought about some topics more than I have," I say, leaning against him as the ferry slows. "You think about mortality. Personally, I like a little denial. I concede I have a bladder; it's made itself evident. I suspect, though, that I might not have a liver — it's never so much as cleared its throat. I certainly don't have islets of Langerhans."

George absorbs this without comment, but his smile says, *What a beautiful fable.*

The notion that he might think me immature catches me off-guard. As the ferry bumps gently into its dock, I argue silently in my own defense. So what if we'll all get sick and need help and die? So what if things can end badly with no appeal? The beauty of life is in denying mortality, not arranging your life around it.

Soaring has everything to do with amnesia about the ground. Why shouldn't we do it as long as possible?

"Do you think I'm fatuous?" I say.

"Nope," he says. As the dispersing passengers fan out around us, he stops on the landing and takes me by the shoulders. "Tracy, I think you're very slender."

We walk north in a silence relieved only by the sounds of traffic. I tread the cracked pavement as faintly as though I'd just received a body blow. When at last I venture a glance at George, I'm greeted with the burst of laughter he's been reserving since Whitehall Street. Stopping in the middle of foot traffic, I have only two words for him.

"Come on, that was worth it just for the expression of horror on your face." He hugs me, not the way you hug a person to jolly her out of a bruised ego, but long and hard, cradling my head. "No," he says after a moment. "I don't think you're fatuous. You're a fantastically thoughtful person who has just had different life experiences than I. Plus you're fun to be around."

"Yeah, well. Watch you don't get pulled over for crimes against the language."

"Just what are the language police going to do to me?"

"Suspend your poetic license. Slap a writer's block on you."

"I'm frightened."

Which is precisely where two A.M. finds me, alone in my apartment, an October rain dotting the windowpane. It's the first night I've spent alone in recent memory, and I bicycle my legs slowly in the cool sheets, feeling George's absence, knowing he's forty blocks uptown prepping for a seven A.M. conference call. Before I met George I was untouchable. I was a sprinter looping a track, lapping those slower runners set back by love, by breakups, pregnancies, by their insistence on living life as though it were a one-way street full of personal opportunities that would not come again. Me, I jogged blithely past. It strikes me now, insomniac under the faint luminosity of my clock radio, that nothing spectacularly new has happened to me for twelve years. I've moved along a preset course, from undergrad to grad student to teacher. I've published articles, a book of criticism, and an anthology, accomplishments that were praised but not unexpected. My image in the mirror has shown little alteration through Ph.D. and salary negotiations; my ovaries, I believe, aren't aging; I will be thirty-something for several decades at the least. I've known myself to be — loath as I am to boast — immortal. Last winter, when the surgeon who'd performed my appendectomy stopped on his rounds to tell me all had been normal, my relief was marred by the tiniest sting of betrayal. I found it neither entirely comforting nor entirely plausible, this assurance that my insides were ordinary plumbing and tissue readily incised, retracted, oxygenated. Already the memory of the stabbing pain, the stack of books I'd dropped, the blurred taxi ride to the hospital, was fading. I waited — don't most of us wait? — for the surgeon to tell me: You were not in the least bit normal, not ordinary and vincible flesh and blood at all. Inside you are exceptional. Inside you are gilt, frescoed. You are driven not by the muscle beating in your chest, but by a pump of alabaster, ether, quicksilver.

I try out a bit of melodrama: *Nothing will ever be the same as it was before I met George.* Spreading my arms, I slide them slowly along the sheets, simultaneously reveling in the solitude of my bed and understanding that I like it in part because I know he will be here tomorrow. George has become a pillar of my happiness. If we broke up there would be no easy recovery, no untouchability in being alone. Life has become a one-way street.

A thought not at all conducive to sleep. Because if love can happen in my world, anything can happen. The choices I make matter, and can pilot me irrevocably toward better or worse. Life is not infinite. Carpe diem.

Even Jeff, I register, knows this.

Even Adam. Adam — who broke up with Kim rather than continue without commitment — knows what I have been too dumb to realize. This thought is so sobering I actually register gratitude when sleep relieves me of it.

On the morrow I wake with a new knowledge: I have come to a crossroad in my adult life. I decide to roast a chicken.

I dial the number. "Mom," I say.

Her voice is faint on the telephone, as though Manhattan were not across the continent from her kitchen counter, but in another solar system. I picture her in her school clothing: a vest buttoned over a pale blouse, dark slacks, pumps. A tall woman with a raspy voice that never seems to rise, with straightforward friends who don't demand much, with students whose crises and triumphs don't penetrate the walls of her house — students who passed anonymous through her classroom each year of my childhood and never offered hints. The only romantic counsel my mother ever extended to me was a consoling, if uncertain, *Tracy, you're one in a million,* followed by the advice *You shouldn't be so picky.* I never did work up the energy to point out her mathematical inconsistency . . . or what it stood for. The simultaneous blessing and curse tendered to a daughter who's made a very different choice: the stated desire for my success, the hobbling passivity about its likelihood.

"Buy a small chicken," she says. "Three or four pounds." It's clear, from the puzzlement in her voice, that there is more she'd like to ask. That she suspects my telephone call means this George I've mentioned is serious. But we have no signal for this kind of conversation in our family semaphore. My mother is unpracticed at prying into my personal life. If she did, if she asked a single pointed question right now, delight and fear would tumble out of me whether or not I thought it wise. But I've learned not to volunteer information on my own. I've poured water onto dry sand too many times to expect anything to germinate. All you're left with are an empty pail and a somehow shameful stain.

"Baste every twenty minutes," she says. "And don't forget the paprika."

There is a long, awkward silence.

"Do you know how to light your oven?" she asks.

I buy the chicken — Perdue, because that man wouldn't lie. I carry it back to my apartment, wash the rubbery insides, and plop it in a foil pan purchased for the occasion. There it sits, naked in the pan. A dead chicken.

The slaughterer has left a small flap hanging where the chicken's neck once was — a frail tube, an airway or perhaps a blood vessel, nearly translucent.

I stare without touching. Then, following my mother's instructions, I dress, sprinkle and dot, and land the chicken in the oven.

During the initial round of basting I consider, for the first time in my life, becoming a vegetarian. Then I consider something else: We're all going to die. There's no such thing as existence without change. While my moral logic is admittedly unclear at this point,

I gradually become privy to another, higher truth: The chicken smells fantastic. I have a vision of the future — of myself as a mortal, vulnerable, loving, one-way-street woman literature professor. I will cook chickens with (useless as this is to the chicken, foolish and politically void) *respect.*

"You two are making me nauseous," says Adam, digging into a drumstick with his knife.

George grins and wraps me tighter. He and I stuffed ourselves on chicken over an hour ago. Adam, who dropped by with his roommate to return the CD player I'd lent him, showed up, with the uncanny timing of a practiced freeloader, just as we were about to clear the table. Leaning together against my double-stacked bookshelf, George and I watch Adam and the roommate, whom he's introduced as Worms, eat. Adam is sporting the Beer Pong shirt and blue jeans he wore to work. Worms, round-faced and unshaven, wears his baseball cap so low on his forehead that his gray eyes are barely visible. From that zone of privacy the world must appear heavy-domed — a television screen Worms watches out of the corner of his eye while he drowses on the sofa.

Shifting the plate on his lap, Adam raises his leg and, with the toe of one sneaker, nudges a book to the near edge of my coffee table. He picks it up and glances at the author photo on the back jacket. "She looks like a housewife in a floor wax commercial," he says. "Except she's just had a nervous breakdown."

George takes the book and holds it next to Adam's cheek. "Actually she looks a little like you."

Adam blows a kiss.

George scans the back of the book, then the inside flaps. "She probably had reason to be tired."

"Why?" says Adam. "She had to wax everybody's floors for real?"

George shrugs, and sets the book back on the coffee table. "Could be. She was writing back in the nineteen-thirties. Can't have been easy for a woman writing then."

And though I've always disliked Dorothy Parker, though I'd have been much more interested in her work were she not sardonic by reflex, unable to stop playing to the audience long enough to let on that anything actually moved her, I now look at her photo — a deliberately unglamorous shot taken long after the Round Table years — with sheer love.

Adam glances at me. Then he turns to George. "You are such a kiss-ass," he says. "I'm taking notes."

Worms sets down his plate. Slowly he looks from Adam to George to me, considering. At length he speaks. "Dude," he says.

Thus shall he be entered into the Book of Deeds. George: a thoughtful man. Paying respect to feminism in his own way. The jury may still be out on long-term compatibility, but initial signs are promising to say the least. In retrospect, our sole argument seems — doesn't it? — a foolish panic over semantics.

He rolls onto his side, dragging the sheet with him. Sunday morning, Sunday afternoon, who cares. I slide into the lee of his back and drape a hand over his bottom. His ass. His butt. The words are either absurdly leering, or else childish — our literary heritage may go into paroxysms over breasts and thighs, but has declared itself too dignified to dwell on this part of the anatomy. Lightly furry. Warm. Tracing a path up his side with my fingertips, gliding, hushing — is there any word for that sound skin makes on skin? — tucking my chin over his shoulder, I inhale. You cannot be with a man if you don't like the smell of the spot where his neck meets his chest. There it is: a new Rule for Love. You must like the smell of that place. Also, the face he makes in bed just before he lets go. No matter how foolish it might be. That face is a secret, a light flashed into a well's depths. I have my own, too — a face I've never seen. George knows it. I entrust it to him.

I fall back into sleep planning a day spent at a museum; at a street fair; in a library; in this bed. Wondering — as I shed each thought into the vanilla light that's soaked through the window shade — whether this is how a person might start thinking about a lifelong commitment: there are so many things I'd like to do with this guy it could take a lifetime to do them.

"Hey." I rap my knuckles on Jeff's door as I open it. "Did I leave my *Complete Hurston* in here?"

He sets down the phone receiver and gives me a smile I don't like. "I don't care about your Hurston. I scheduled my job talk."

He puts on a light Southern lilt. "Fixing to head down next week."

"You've dusted off that accent awfully fast. How long did you live in Georgia as a kid?"

"Ages seven to nine, before moving to scenic New Jersey. Long enough to pick up a prêt-à-porter accent, which came in handy on the phone. The guy in charge of scheduling asked me right away if I was, and I quote, 'one of ours.'" There is a pen lying flat on Jeff's desk; he gives it a satisfied twirl. "Ah most *suh*tainly am."

"You're shameless."

"The word is 'hirable.'"

I make a face. "Where's my damn book?"

Flashing me another brilliant grin, he shrugs.

There's a knock on the open door. Joanne stands stiffly in the doorway, waiting to be invited.

"Hi, Joanne," says Jeff, without gesturing her forward.

She steps into the office. Ignoring me entirely, she addresses him. From my seat I watch her profile: chin taut, shoulders hunched forward. A boxer entering the ring.

"Have you heard about the rescheduling of today's faculty meeting?" she says to Jeff. "It's been moved half an hour later."

Jeff glances down to his desk calendar. "It's four-thirty now?"

"Yes."

"I'm going to have to leave early, then."

"We need you there," says Joanne.

"I'll be there only for the first half-hour."

Taking a small step closer to Jeff's desk, Joanne slaps down her trump card. "We're going to field proposals for the new core curriculum," she says. "And summarize the flaws of current offerings. I don't need to tell you how much is at stake. Our recommendations go to the Humanities Committee, which reports to the Coordinating Committee, which writes the summary for the Academic Committee. And they'll be determining the new standards. We need to discuss the English Department's position and philosophy."

Jeff gives the pen on his desk another spin, and, while it's still a silver blur, leans back in his chair. "In lurid detail, I'm sure."

Joanne stands in front of his desk. Stock-still.

I have no idea why Jeff is doing this. The hairs on my arms rise to attention: an animal instinct, right here in the sacred precincts of Literature. For an instant I'm actually frightened Joanne is going to step around Jeff's desk and knock him cold.

Instead she turns and faces me. The words are lead. "I trust you'll be there too, Tracy."

Nobody here but us office chairs. "Sure thing," I say.

"*I trust you'll be there too,*" Jeff mimics when Joanne's gone.

"Are you nuts? Why provoke her?"

Placidly, Jeff pens something onto his calendar. Only when he's finished does he answer me. "Joanne will let it go in a couple days."

"You're so sure?"

"I'm not a threat to her."

"Will you *stop* with that?"

"It's true. Never underestimate the faggot factor. She's still hoping I'll be an ally. It would take something bigger to put me on her permanent shit list."

"I've got to tell you, I think you're off-base on this one."

"Just watch. I'm still under the threshold. *You,* my friend, don't have that luxury."

I refuse to engage this.

Jeff leans back in his chair. "Maybe it's that acne that's making her so mean," he muses. "She's looking like a teen all over again. Who do you think is making her hormones act up?"

"I pity him."

"Or *her.*"

"You think?"

Jeff weighs the question for only a heartbeat. "No," he says. "Not gay. Not the type."

I consider, and shrug. "What's on your schedule this afternoon that can't be moved?"

He taps his silver pen on the fresh marking on his calendar. "It says here I have a plan to go to the gym. Get a workout."

With these words I finally understand that Jeff is leaving this department.

"Want to know a secret?" he says, standing and stretching his veined arms overhead. I glance at Jeff's wall clock: a spare, polished silver disk with twelve faint marks etched around its face and only one hand, indicating the hour. It's nearly two, time for his next seminar.

"Sure," I say, following him to the door.

He speaks quietly. "If Emory doesn't work out, I'm going to Atlanta anyway. I'll edit journals or hoe peanuts. And fuck Richard happily every night and massage his buns when his department stresses him to distraction."

Still inside the door, I face him. Seminar or no, Jeff cannot simply present this scenario and sail glibly out the door. "You would truly *leave academia altogether* for Richard? Jeff? Come on. I understand you'd leave New York, but drop your whole career?"

He steps into the hall, and only there does he face me. He closes his eyes for a long moment, as though reminding himself of a need for restraint. When he opens them, his expression is serious. "It baffles you, does it?" he says. He pulls his office door shut.

Twenty minutes into the faculty meeting, Steven Hilliard takes up arms against the core curriculum proposal that has been backed by both Joanne and, we are led to assume, Grub — a proposal that would focus the mandatory writing courses heavily on the classical canon, steeping undergraduates in *Beowulf* and Behn, Surrey and Spenser, Wordsworth and Keats and Shelley and Wilde and the Brontës, and presenting Woolf's 1927 *To the Lighthouse* as the outer limit of progress.

"What the hell is *he* doing here?" someone whispers behind me. I turn to find Jesse Faden, our pale, long-haired aesthetics specialist, looking peeved. Jim Lakes, seated beside him, is nodding. "Since when do visiting faculty get invited to curriculum meetings," Jesse adds, including me in his audience. "Or does being from Oxford mean you can just invite yourself?"

I turn back to Jeff, who looks irritable. For once, I see, he doesn't know the answer. He watches Steven keenly.

Directing his comments at Marion Lewis, the latest mouthpiece on behalf of the Joanne-Grub proposal, Steven sharpens his assault. "I've got to say," Steven begins, "I'm stunned to hear these arguments here, of all places. I thought the furor over canon definition died down a few years ago, even on this side of the pond, and right-thinking people conceded a few changes needed to be made to accommodate modernity. Why would you want to undo that progress?"

Steven is one of those young academic Turks who makes cockiness his signature. By reputation he's got the intellectual firepower to back it up. And in this case I believe he's right. But the brash delivery, combined with his unaccountable involvement with this department's politics, raises brows around the room. Eyes turn to Grub. Yet Grub, despite his known stance on the canon (epitomized by his view that there's no need to include Native American literature in American lit syllabi, as *surely comparative literature can manage that*), is as mute as if such outspokenness were normal behavior on the part of visiting faculty. Gradually the scattered expressions of scandal among the older faculty abate.

Marion Lewis is a gray-haired eighteenth-century specialist with a repertoire of brown and gray cardigans. He doesn't socialize with the twentieth century — never offered anything beyond a collegial nod once he learned I'd passed up Melville for Hurston. He's one of those professors with the irritating habit of requiring students to fill in the blanks in his own sentences, endlessly coaching as they steer grudgingly down the narrow corridor of his own thoughts: *The word you would expect here is what?* [long silence] *What word? You would expect the poet to use the word 'morning.' Instead he uses the word 'dawn.' Well, is this telling us something?* [long silence] *Is it?*

Now Marion glances at Joanne for support. Fortified, he sheds upon Steven a tolerant smile implying a consensus that modernity is a passing fad. As are visiting Oxford men.

Steven continues, unperturbed. "I'm here for only one year," he says, "but I can promise you that if you choose this route, you'll be pointing a terrific department backward."

At five o'clock on the dot, Jeff rises and steps out the door, Joanne nodding tersely in his direction as though she herself had authorized his departure.

Selecting a less confrontational phrasing, I support Steven's point. I then list the justifications for a more flexible set of requirements, incorporating the classics but offering undergraduates the opportunity to take one of their writing seminars on a spectrum of topics including African American literature, postmodern text, Bible as literature, literature of the American South, gender and text, Native American orature and literature, contemporary literary theory, and a new syllabus proposed by Ginny Jones titled "Literary Evolutions." And half an hour later, this is the approach that wins by a narrow margin, though the vote is close enough (and a Joanne-enforced and tacitly Grub-backed plan intimidating enough) that a compromise is decreed: both suggestions will be presented to the Coordinating Committee. "And will be judged by their merits," asserts Joanne.

Just outside the conference room, Grub corners Steven. "Hilliard," he says, tapping a suddenly discomfited-looking Steven on his sternum. "You're the sort of man who speaks his mind about aesthetics."

"I try to," says Steven, with bite — as can only a visiting prof with nothing to lose. The end of the meeting has left him inexplicably riled. With his wavy, dark hair, rosy cheeks, and flared nostrils, Steven looks like a nineteenth-century painting of Youth Confronting Falsehood. This place is getting to him.

"Tracy?"

I turn reluctantly from this tableau to face Victoria.

"Do you have a moment?" She gestures me toward her office, only a few doors away.

I follow her, noting along the way that I've never seen Grub buttonhole Victoria. It's difficult, in fact, to imagine anyone trying to manipulate her; Victoria seems capable of staring down any member of the department.

Inside Victoria's office, a single wood-framed Edward Hopper graces the wall opposite the desk. Within the austere sweep of choppy gray waves, a white sailboat appears so isolated that, though a rocky New England coastline is clearly visible in one corner of the picture, I'm reminded of Melville's accounts of the Nantucket whaling-man's terrain. *Alone, in such remotest waters . . .*

Not what I'd hang on my wall to make me feel at home. Clearly, though, Hopper's vision has a different effect on Victoria.

The rest of her office is sparsely decorated. Two wide shelves are lined with books whose spines declare her specialty in Irish literature. A photograph of two beaming, leggy children occupies a small corner of the lower shelf beside the window.

"Yours?" I ask, careful, despite her age, not to assume the boy and girl pictured are her grandchildren. I seat myself opposite her, my back to the Hopper. Other than the fact that she's a widow, I know nothing about Victoria's personal life.

"My sister's grandson and granddaughter. My husband and I never had children."

A silence fills the office.

"There's a small thing I want to say to you, Tracy." She speaks deliberately, with a thoughtful pause as she composes each sentence, and an air of finality after its utterance. "I'm hoping a brief word to the wise will suffice."

If I didn't respect Victoria's intelligence, I might be revving off my seat by the time she rounded the corner of this second thought. Instead I study her reserve: an ability, anomalous in this city, to say far less than she knows. *The dignity of movement of an iceberg*, wrote Hemingway, *is due to only one-eighth of it being above water.*

"I am not unaware that Joanne has been difficult lately." Pause. "I believe, however, that it's important to show sympathy."

Victoria sets her hands lightly on her desk.

Silence.

"I do try to be sympathetic," I say. I'm conscious of slowing my speech, lest it sound flippant by comparison. "Is there something particular that's upsetting Joanne?"

Victoria looks at me gravely, then shakes her head. "That's not mine to say."

The next long pause is my refuge, as I try to find an angle of entry that doesn't pressure Victoria to take sides.

"It's been rather difficult," I say at length.

She nods.

"I believe Joanne has been inappropriate with Elizabeth, and that concerns me. And" — I can't help pointing this out — "I feel she's been gratuitously nasty to me on several occasions."

Victoria gives another deep nod. "I'm sure your points are valid." With startling directness she meets my eyes. "And I am aware that Joanne is not an easy personality."

The relief I feel at this last statement is prodigious, and utterly out of proportion to Victoria's words. It's as though she's taken my hand and consoled: *My child, you are understood.* While I wish she'd offer to set Joanne straight, I can't help reacting to Victoria as I sometimes react upon meeting former soldiers, women and men now immersed in civilian life, whose vestigial military bearing seems to mandate my trust in a way I don't completely understand.

"I wanted to tell you I'm aware of Joanne's behavior," Victoria continues. "You don't need to wonder whether everyone else is blind to it. What is visible to you is visible to others." A long stare past my head, then that same direct gaze. "I've told the same to Elizabeth." She registers my appreciation with a nod. "The only thing I would ask of you at this time is to show sympathy."

Sympathy.

Victoria smiles: a limited but friendly, tough-times smile. This conversation is over.

"Thank you, Victoria." I'm not sure precisely what for, but trust I'll sort it out later. "I'll bear this conversation in mind."

I exit the office, Victoria already flipping a book's pages as I pull the heavy door shut. I step down the hall, aware that a part of me that had been clamoring for justice has, for now, been quieted. A voice of calm has spoken from the edge of the wilderness.

Sunday noon, George is distracted. He's taken it upon himself to make brunch — a complicated omelette involving fresh herbs and a redolent cheese that's a clear violation of his usual budgetary austerity. When the omelette is finished, George covers it, sets it in the warm oven, and disappears, looking tense, to the shower. He takes so long under the hot water that he practically oozes steam by the time he joins me once more, dressed in jeans and a T-shirt. I greet him with a burst of political commentary about the newspaper articles I've read in his absence: a summary of the effect of AIDS on women in Africa, a piece about Clinton's travel schedule, another depressing article about global warming, and more about the decline of national education standards. "You might want to read the education article," I murmur as I pop my cool coffee into the microwave. "Or maybe not — your blood will boil."

"Hmm."

"What's most amazing to me in that global warming piece is the statistics."

He doesn't speak.

The phone rings. "That's probably Gabby," I say, rising. "I told

her she could call here, I hope you don't mind. I won't be long."
As I carry the phone to the other room there is a tight look on
George's face.

Ten minutes later I return. "Sorry again," I say, pressing the button to reheat my coffee once more, "for the interruption." I settle
beside George. He says nothing. "Big news on the family front."
I take a forkful of the omelette George serves me. "Aunt Rona,
remember my aunt Rona? She who kvetches about her daughter's
allergy to Jewish men?"

George is silent.

I take my coffee out of the microwave. "Don't worry, as I've
said my mother's cool about you."

He nods.

"Hey," I say. "This is delicious."

George nods again, more curtly this time. His nods are slightly
out of sync. Conversing with him is like trying to track the mouth
movements on a dubbed film. I continue, though his distraction
is starting to make me nervous. "Back a couple years ago, when
Gabby told Aunt Rona about her college boyfriend, of course
Rona's first question was 'Is he Jewish?' Gabby said, 'No, Mom,
he's not Jewish. He's Indian.' Long pause. Aunt Rona, in her most
hopeful voice, then said: 'Is he Brahmin?'"

George doesn't laugh as much as I do.

"So now here's today's news," I say. "Gabby just told me she's
dating a rabbinical student."

George nods. Then nods again. "Is he Jewish?"

When I don't answer, George blinks at me.

"What's going on, George?"

"Tracy. I have to ask you something."

"Shoot," I say, sounding spunkier than I feel.

"The thing we've talked about. Us. Being together."

His toweled hair arcs in darkened sheaves, and the bits of pale
scalp visible in between remind me of sun flashing between corn
rows as you drive past. My New York self, that endlessly unrav-
eling spool, is abruptly spent, and I'm homesick for the Pacific
Northwest. I understand that George is about to break up with
me. Being a gentleman, he's abandoned his usual frugality for a
farewell brunch, over which he will explain: my tentative visions
of the future don't inspire him.

This is not only absurd, it's tragic. Can he truly deny the strength of this attraction? The odd, happy eddies of our conversation? The sense that we *match?* Simply because I'm not on overdrive toward a future with children? We've had just shy of two months to learn about each other. Surely each of us still has surprises to divulge, yet unanticipated tendernesses or shoals. But George is a man committed to moving forward. He doesn't waste his own time or anyone else's. It's one of the things about him I respect.

Forcing myself to sit straight, I settle my hands on my lap: a calm posture utterly at odds with the sensation that my chest is being flooded with cold air. I ready myself for one of those conversations that plays out like emotional Twister. Right hand on yellow; left foot on blue. The strain becoming clearer with each move. How many will I sustain before collapsing?

"For, as we've said, *a long time,*" George continues. "Having children if we're so lucky. Supporting each other in every way, even if it's hard. Do you" — George looks at me hard — "do you see it?" Dots of perspiration adorn his upper lip. He sits straight-backed on his stool, a furrow of tension between his brows.

"Yes . . ."

"Do you see supporting one another through ups and downs?"

If he's not about to drop the axe, then what? Could he be asking me to move in with him?

George — suffering, wet-headed, and as handsome as I've seen him — waits for my response. There is some kind of choreography to this conversation, and while I don't understand it, I can follow a lead: it's clearly my turn to provide reassurance. Because I love this man. Because I'm hoping this new improbable untested glorious high-wire structure bears weight, too.

"Yes, I see it," I tell him emphatically.

"Do you see learning to live together? Being a pair, Tracy? I know we haven't known each other for long, but I think we know each other well. And I see it."

"I see it, too," I say.

A grin breaks on George's face like a tsunami.

"You know," he says, "we'd have to sort out all that Jewish-ceremony stuff."

George and I could get engaged soon. This idea is absurd. Colossal. And entirely ordinary.

I wink at him. "I think," I say, "we could handle that." Because we've now declared that this love is as serious as I think it is. As suddenly as it seized me, the dread falls away. I laugh aloud. I'm not crazy: George and I are contemplating a future.

With George's eyes practically pelting joy into mine, I think of the hurdles I'd want to clear first: I'd want to speak seriously with George, of course, about our ideas of the future; about where we agree; and how we might metabolize our disagreements; and whether we'd want to live together for a while before making the leap. I'd want to have a conversation with Hannah about timing, and whether I'm ready to choose this man — whether I even know what marriage means. And with Yolanda, whose emphatic honesty is like oxygen. And with my parents; though I haven't consulted them about my life in years, I have an urge to bring them, however awkwardly, into the circle of such a decision. Most important, I imagine a few long solo walks in Central Park: tranquil assessment of my own life and hopes.

George rises, encircles me with his arms, and kisses me sweetly on the mouth. "I love you, Tracy," he says. "I love you so much."

To the flank of his neck, I confess. "I thought you were going to break up with me."

My rib cage shimmies with his laughter, which grows to an unexpectedly wild song of celebration. Then he looks into my face, and my confusion dissipates. I think, See. See how lucky. And may I never forget it.

George kisses me on the forehead and leaves me in the kitchen grinning stupidly at the newspaper. The sound of his voice drifts through the wall. A moment later he steps into the kitchen. "My sister wants to get on the phone with you."

"Your sister?"

"You bet." George brushes my bottom as I pass him in the narrow hall.

I pick up the bedroom phone. "Paula?"

"Tracy?" The voice on the other end of the line is young and unexpectedly energetic. "George has told me about you." She enunciates carefully, but with real warmth. "I want you to know I'm so glad. Even though it's fast. But George has never done things the regular way. And sometimes good things don't need time to become clear. Heaven-sent things. I've been hoping for this news. It's about time George found someone he cares about enough to make a life with."

She pauses for my reply. George is standing behind me. "Um," I say.

There is a clatter on the line, and a murmur of surprise from Paula.

"Earl speaking," says a flat baritone. There's a deep pause. "Marriage is a blessing. If entered in the proper spirit."

There is a brief silence. Then Paula intones, her words buoyant, "Welcome to the family."

It is at this moment that something happens that I don't fully understand—something I will puzzle over for months to come. A voice inside me, clear as any voice I've ever heard, says: *Say thank you.*

And I do. The "thank you" I utter is a gift to George. It is the greatest gift I have ever given to another human being.

There is a click: George's father has set down the receiver. Paula begins posing questions. Tell her about myself. About my family. "I'm . . ." I hesitate.

"Jewish. I know. George explained. But"—her voice turns solemn—"he's not exactly Christian, as you know."

In the silence that follows I realize she's waiting for a reply.

"I know," I say.

I don't register what she says after this, or what I answer—all I know is that she fills in my pauses with *You must be overwhelmed right now,* and brings the conversation to a graceful end with another obviously heartfelt congratulation and a solemn *May God bless you.* And I find myself off the phone.

"George?"

"I know. Paula can be pretty direct about religion, though not as bad as plenty of the people I grew up with. I assume she mentioned it?"

Dumbly I nod.

"But she's extremely excited about you. She knows we're going to live a different life from hers, but she's all right with it. Even glad."

"Your father said marriage could be a blessing." My voice is hollow.

"He got on the phone? I didn't even know he was at my sister's house — I was going to write him a letter." George looks impressed. "That's progress. For my father, that's surprising, given his son isn't entering a Christian marriage." He falls silent, considering. Then his hand slides around my waist, pressing something cool and hard into my palm. His free hand curls my fingers around the glass of pale, effervescing champagne. "I gave my sister your parents' number, but I told her not to call for twenty minutes, so we can call them ourselves first."

"George." I set my champagne glass on the night table. "Okay. I've got a silly question."

"Anything." He sets his glass on the windowsill and turns his full attention on me.

The words make me feel ill. "Did we just get engaged?"

His grin thickens. "Why, is there a better term for it?"

"That was a . . ." I grip his hand, which does not grip mine in return, telling me I'm on the thinnest of ice. "That was a proposal?" I whisper.

George's face stiffens as though he's smelled something bad. "That was the best and only attempt at a proposal I've ever made."

I grip his hand harder. Nothing is making sense. I replay the last five minutes. "You said *we would* need to figure out a Jewish ceremony. I didn't know you meant we *will*. As in, let's-get-married-*we-will*."

He breathes. "Is this a grammar discussion, or a discussion of whether you want to marry me?" His voice breaks slightly on the last words.

"It's — how did you get my parents' number?"

"It's listed in the Seattle directory. I called them last night."

"You called them?"

"I called to ask your father's permission."

"My —"

"I know it's old-fashioned, but I wanted to make sure they felt included. I wanted to do this right."

I sit on the bed.

George speaks in a normal voice but watches me with extraordinary intensity. His face is naked, poised between purest faith and apostasy. "They were lovely. I think they appreciated the gesture. Your mother was practically effusive. She kept me on the phone a good long while, asking about my family and my work."

"My mother . . . ?"

He turns up his palms. "It surprised me too."

The world has unhinged.

"I'm in shock," I say. Wasted words, a pointless plea for more time to think. The ball sails toward me and gravity cannot be dissuaded. Everything depends on what I do now.

"Did you want something fancier?" George stands like a statue beside the bed. "I thought you wouldn't want some public, sky-writing-type proposal. Did I guess wrong?"

"No, you were right about that. It's just . . . a surprise."

"Well, we *have* been talking about it, haven't we?" Tension rises in his voice; he clears it with a forced laugh.

"Yes, but I wasn't expecting this now." *Do not push him too hard. Do not push him* — the directive seems to come from the marrow of my bones — *because this is a moment when everything could burn to the ground.* He's watching me. In the severity of his expression I read fear.

I stand and put my arms around him. After a few seconds he reciprocates.

"I'm rattled by your response," he says. "Just tell me, are you cool with this?"

"I love you, George. And I'm" — the last word I'd choose, my head is about to explode — "cool with this." It hangs in the air: the first lie I've ever told George. "I just . . . thought there would be a little more time. For us."

"I'm right here," he says. "And, Tracy, we have all the time . . . well, all the time we're given, to work out our ups and downs."

"I just" — each word tentative, as though I'm trying to make myself understood in a foreign language — "wanted some time to think. To . . . I don't know. Talk this over with friends."

He absorbs this. His face softens. "Talk." He points to the telephone. "Take the time you need." He kisses me on the lips and steps away. "I'll be in the kitchen. I'll play music so I can't hear you. Run up the phone bill."

That is absurd. "George —" He's gone.

The telephone looms on the nightstand like a poorly lit prop in a thriller. As though I, the heroine, ought to know what to do with it.

Hannah answers on the second ring.

"What's wrong? You sound awful."

"George proposed to me," I whisper. Hannah's end of the line goes silent. Shivering, I drag the bedspread over my legs and tuck it around my knees.

"And?" prompts Hannah.

"I said yes. Sort of."

"So you're engaged?"

"He's sitting in the next room."

"I don't get it."

"He's waiting because I said I needed . . . time."

"But you said yes, right?"

"I said yes, but I didn't know that's what I was saying. I'm" — I draw an uneven breath — "I'm seriously freaking, Hannah. This is crazy. This isn't the way people get engaged. Is it? I didn't know he was asking me, I thought we were just talking in general terms about our relationship, then suddenly he's got me on the phone with his family."

"All right. Try to calm down." Hannah's speech, already breathless from pregnancy, takes on a peculiar force. "This is going to be okay, Tracy. It really is." In the background Elijah begins, uncharacteristically, to whine. His rising cry tells me — for I've long understood that Elijah is Hannah's emotional weathervane — that despite her steady words Hannah considers this an emergency.

"You told me last week" — breath — "you thought this was the guy for you" — breath — "so did something change?"

"I feel . . ." Stunned. Ill. Homesick, but for what home?

"I know it's fast," says Hannah. There is a long pause.

"Mo-*mee!*" Elijah shouts.

Hannah ignores him. "Yes, it would probably have been better if he'd waited another month or two. Or made things clearer. But do you want to be with this guy?"

"I think. Yes. But how well do I know him?"

"Tracy, I'm still getting to know Ed. There's no endpoint to it. There's no 'enough,' no point of safety where you can predict everything about a person. Okay" — she draws another deep breath — "so I know this is a bit unusual. So this isn't ideal. But jump into this, Tracy. You've already said yes. His family knows. Just" — breath — "jump *in*. If you decide it's a mistake you can always break it off. We can talk about this tomorrow, we can talk about this for the next six months or six years. Just don't keep him waiting now. This is not men's strong suit. Their egos aren't built to stand this. I'm telling you something important, Tracy. Do not keep that man waiting now, because if you spend the rest of your life with him you will never be able to remove the scar that will result from spending the next hour on the phone with me. Never."

My voice climbs to a panicked falsetto. "What about the scar this will leave on me? Shit, I didn't even know what I was saying when I said yes. This engagement wasn't even a conscious choice. I don't know what the hell happened, George and I are usually" — words flurry — "this isn't how we *are*."

"Okay. But who do you think can handle the stress better right now, you or him? Men are terrified when they propose. Ed was shaking. After I said yes he went to the bathroom and vomited. Okay, maybe that's not typical, but I also think it's not as unusual as people might guess. George may be acting calm now, but he's as revved as he's ever been. Go back to him. Tell him you love him. Talk about whatever worries you have. Tell him you need a long engagement, and then over the next few weeks you can sort out how you feel. Just get back in the room with him."

"My God." There is a long silence, during which God patently fails to intervene. "If you truly think guys are so fragile they can't handle the truth, Hannah, why marry a man?"

"As opposed to a what?"

The solid wall of it looms before me: Hannah's shrugging acceptance, her infinite protectiveness, the untouchable mystique of Ed's fragility. I've never understood how little Hannah asks of men. I have known men my whole life. I have a father, quiet but steady. I have male friends. I have male colleagues. They are not fragile. If you ask something of a man, he will rise to the occasion as often as a woman will. Men, in my experience, do not need to be shielded from emotional truths.

But I am not dealing with Men. I am dealing with one particular, irreplaceable man. And if Hannah is right, George will never recover if I balk this afternoon.

"Tracy," Hannah says. "We can discuss our views on gender

relations some other time. He's out on a limb. Don't leave him there."

Thus my best friend takes me by the shoulders, turns me around, and sends me back to the lions. I leave the bedroom, stepping charily toward the love of my life.

"George?"

He looks up at me from the sofa, his eyes dark and undefended.

Straddling his thighs, I kiss him firmly. I draw him to his feet and bring him to his bedroom, where, hugging him with one arm, I reach with an icy hand for the telephone.

"Tracy," says my mother. To my father, presumably in the next room, she announces emphatically, "It's Tracy."

Drawing George with me, I sit on the bed, receiver against one ear. My temple rests against George's neck. His steady pulse radiates peace.

"George's sister called ten minutes ago," says my mother. "She was very pleasant. We figured you two were off celebrating and had forgotten to phone us." My mother, ascetic among her kind, manages to say this with only a minuscule dollop of reproach.

"Mom." I clear my throat. It remains tight. "I'm going to marry a wonderful man."

"We know that." The last time my mother's voice had such lift in it I'd brought back all A's on my first-grade report card. "George sounds terrific. You're very lucky."

"I am lucky," I say.

A long pause follows, during which a petty, childish neediness raises its hand and will not be ignored. Reluctantly, with the sensation of dredging ancient history, I voice it. "Do you maybe also think *he's* lucky?" I ask.

"Of course he is. I'm going to call Rona. She'll want to help plan the wedding."

"Whoa, Mom." Hearing my voice rise, George puts an arm around me. I pull away from him. "No plans. Not yet. No Rona."

"Nobody's making plans. Rona and I will just talk."

"*No planning.*" I don't understand. I have never in my life heard my mother enthusiastic about planning a social event.

"Your father wants to speak with you."

My father gets on the phone, his voice oddly constricted. "Tracy, we're proud of you," he says.

It's a physical relief to hear him on the line: the father who tele-graphed unspoken trust in me all my life, pursed his mouth with satisfaction each time I took up a new challenge, tacitly urged me toward my goals. Who helped me reason through bungled geom-etry exams, dropped softballs, the mysteries of parallel parking. "Dad," I say, "I—"

"Hi, Tracy." My mother is back.

That's it?

"Your father and I want to say hello to George," my mother says.

George holds the receiver to his ear. Twice he starts to speak, then demurs. He nods vigorously at one point, and thanks them three separate times. Clearly my parents have saved up thirty-three years of parental advice for a son-in-law. Every mystery they never revealed to me they are now imparting to him. They are crooning ballads of derring-do, reading him the secret codex of their mar-riage.

When George speaks at last, he says only: "I'll take good care of your daughter."

"Yes," I mumble. "She can't cross the street by herself."

George doesn't hear me. He listens for a while longer before saying a warm goodbye and setting down the phone.

"Put on your jacket." His words brim with pleasure. He looks as though he might levitate.

"Let me clean the dishes—"

"Later!"

There is a midafternoon jazz hour downtown. The music tastes like cardboard. I can't finish my mimosa. George holds my hand, only letting go of it to applaud hearty approval of the soloists. We stroll along Broadway. I receive his solicitousness like a zombie. My voice sounds, to my own ears, strangled. High-pitched. For the first time since we met, George seems oblivious to my mood. He treads beside me on the bustling sidewalk, his gait unsteady, struck down by happiness. He leads me to the door of a jewelry store and sweeps it open.

"I picked out a few favorites," he says. "They're all pretty sim-ple—as you know, my salary isn't princely, and we've got to have something left for the wedding. But I'm hoping you'll like one of them. I didn't want to make a final decision without your approval."

The row of velvet-lined cases shines in the depths of the store. I balk like a mule: head down, legs planted on the sidewalk. "I can't think about a ring yet," I manage.

"Okay." Disappointed but good-humored, he lets go of the door. "It's been a big day already. You're looking a bit glassy-eyed." He takes my hand. "I'm sure I am too."

Dinner is at Pequod, a crowded, elegant restaurant. George has reserved a corner table and the champagne arrives as soon as we do. The waiter finishes pouring and leaves. George, watching me, wears the fervent expression of the man in the movie who's just pledged to defend his wife and kids against the invading armies, even if it means forfeiting his life.

"We know only a little about each other," I venture in the same tight, vacant voice I've heard all afternoon and evening, speaking from somewhere just behind my head.

"True. We know only the most important things." He raises his glass. "Don't we?"

I let my confusion bloom on my face. But for once he doesn't seem to see it.

"And I can't wait to spend the rest of my life getting to know you better, Tracy Farber."

If our glasses make a sound, it's lost in the restaurant's din.

We settle in for the night at George's apartment. There are phone messages from Aunt Rona and Uncle Ted. Rona's congratulations are strained.

"She'll get over it when I convert." George chuckles.

It is shockingly easy to get by without replying. Nothing seems to require an answer beside the one I gave this morning. Our conversation is a frictionless surface. George hasn't yet come down from the day he planned for us: music, dinner, romance. A palette of experiences offered to seal his pledge. He's lit from the inside, drunk on our future. We make love with the lights out. I try again and again to pierce the darkness, to apprehend the man caressing my body, whispering my name. But it's as though some passivity bomb — ticking away silently in my innards through girlhood

and years of education and competent professionalism — has deto-
nated. Afterward we don't speak. I slow my breathing. I might be
asleep.

George kisses my shoulder. Then, one arm cradling my head, he
lies still for a very long time, facing the ceiling. An hour seems to
pass, the quiet unrelenting. Then George whispers slowly, tasting
each word. "The best day of my life," he says.

At first I think he's speaking to me. Then I understand he's
speaking to himself. To the hope that suffused his face on our first
date. To the path ahead of him, embodied in my sleeping form.

His breathing deepens. Tears slip down the sides of my face. I
love him. Save that, there's no room for a single clear thought.

During the night I wake three times. Once to a feverish hope
that dashes about the dark room like a moth. Once sweaty, with
heart pounding from a dream of some dizzying terror. Once to
grief: I never thought having a romantic engagement mattered to
me; yet accompanied by the quiet rhythm of George's breathing,
I mourn the surprise, and the glimmering velvet jewel cases, and
the champagne, that had nothing at all to do with me.

PART II

"YOU'RE WHAT?" says Jeff. He sits back, palms flat on his desk. "You want to get married to a man you hardly know?"

I lean against his closed office door, barricading it. "I love him," I say miserably.

Jeff's brows form an offended V. "Irrelevant. You don't *know* him. You don't know how this relationship will weather. You don't know what this guy is like when the novelty wears off, or what moods he gets into in the dregs of winter, or whether he turns into a werewolf after the first six months. This relationship hasn't had time for the warranty to wear off. This is what, five days you've been dating? Look at you, you're seasick."

"Just under two months. There was this . . . voice. I don't know. I just knew I needed to say yes—I mean, go along with it, the engagement, the phone call with his family." I gesture uselessly. "Does that mean it's right? Even if my rational mind is taking awhile to catch on?"

"A *voice?*" He folds his arms. "I make decisions with my rational mind fully engaged, and this, my dear, is not rational. It's heterosexuality-induced madness. What's the big rush toward matrimony? What is this, nineteen-fifty? Next you'll be dropping babies." He leans forward, setting his elbows on the table and steepling his hands. In someone else it would be prayer position. In Jeff it is a posture for argument: the greater the tension in his precisely aligned fingertips, the fiercer his points. "I take no issue with your making a commitment. I just don't think a person — especially a straight woman — should ever rush into anything. Tracy, we all know heterosexual marriages are unhealthy. It's Western culture's open secret. You've read the stats, correct? The ones that document how married women are more depressed than single women? That shit is real. If you want emotional health, your surest bet is to get away from the old gender game. Women are happier with women, men with men. The healthy straight marriage is possible, but a rarity. And takes time to develop. In sum: I've got nothing against Tabouli, but what's his rush? And speaking of which, what the fuck is yours? Seems goddamn suspicious." His argument complete, he sets his chin on his fingertips. "Has 'danger' written all over it."

There is a long silence. I don't budge. "I love George," I say carefully. "He and I love each other. That's very clear to me. It's just . . ." I draw a deep breath. Each word is an island. "It's just fast."

"You want to know what I think you should do?"

I open my mouth. Then, firmly, I shake my head.

Jeff goes immobile. He is a bust of the Academic at His Desk: cut in marble, perfectly posed, aghast. "There's something very nineteenth-century about you," he says.

He turns back to his papers. I don't imagine he's reading — the tension in his jaw belies his calm flipping of pages — but he doesn't look up again.

Back inside my office, door closed, the tightness in my throat is so painful I let out a whimper. What is supposed to be my happiest moment, the start of the rest of my life, has gone dreadfully wrong. I know what this means. I've seen it in movies, read it in novels: I'm cursed. I'll marry him and it will be disaster. Or we'll break up and I'll grieve for George forever. My breathing gets uncontrollably louder — surely Jeff can hear through the wall? — my chest shrugs, my chin rises as though there might be better air in a higher stratosphere. Small black spheres begin to bobble through my vision.

Professor Dies of Un-Broken Heart in Bizarre Office Incident.

Having no paper bags, I seize a hardcover volume of Mark Twain from my shelf, open it on my lap, and sink my face into the tent of pages.

In a short time the hyperventilating subsides. I take a first normal breath, then another. My wet eyelashes bat the black lettering that parades across the creamy page, each letter bold and expansive as though seen through a magnifying glass: the last paragraph of "My Literary Shipyard." I raise my head slightly. *To start right is certainly an essential,* says Twain. I slam the book shut.

"Professor Farber?"

At the second knock I open the door. A sophomore from my twentieth-century course, a sleepy-faced, dimpled late-teen in sweatpants, steps inside and hands me a paper.

"I'm here for our revision conference? About the Didion paper?"

"Ah yes," I say, with such force that she startles. Sniffling as I settle into my chair, I gesture at the box of tissues on my desk. "Allergies," I explain.

"Oh my God, that *sucks,*" she declares.

Thereby proving once more that students are smarter than they seem.

Before venturing to the mailboxes I wash my face and apply makeup. I pass down the corridor without encountering a soul, collect my portion blindly from the honeycombed mail slots, and scan the bulletin board for new announcements. I'm quick, but not quick enough.

"Congratulations, Tracy," calls Eileen from her seat, the greeting a lasso to hold me until she's free for an interrogation.

Victoria, standing at Eileen's desk, turns.

As I expected, some offhand comment of Jeff's has already radiated from the faculty lounge to the central gossip artery of the department. I wave to Eileen, make a vague gesture at my wristwatch, and start toward my office. But Victoria calls my name and signals for me to stay put. I wait with mounting agitation while she accepts a folder from Eileen and files it in her briefcase.

When Victoria steps toward me it's with an approving smile. "Who's the lucky fellow?"

"George," I say. "Beck," I add, then don't know what else to say.

"Oh?" prompts Victoria.

"Yes. George. He's . . . great."

"I should hope so." Victoria's amusement expresses itself in a slight compression of her lips. I don't know whether to be embarrassed or laugh along.

"I wish you a long life with Mr. Beck, full of great happiness." Victoria's voice drops; behind her I see Eileen lean forward over her desk on the pretext of watering a plant with a mug I'm certain has no water in it. "My husband and I were lucky with the happiness part," Victoria says. "We didn't have so very long together, but what we had was good. We kept each other on our toes. Marriage can be a wonderful, mutually energizing arrangement."

I don't know how to reply to this, but, bless Victoria, she's said her piece and with a firm pat on my shoulder — the first physical contact she's offered since a welcome-to-the-faculty handshake five years ago — she leaves.

"Well," sings Eileen, smug as a clerk catching a customer shoplifting. "Who's been keeping secrets?"

The first door off the corridor opens and Joanne emerges from her office, a small stack of pages in hand. "No secrets," I answer sharply.

"When's the date?" prods Eileen.

"No date yet."

"Where's your ring?"

"No ring yet."

Eileen's brows shoot toward her hairline. Her fingernails tap a polished disapproval on the surface of her desk.

"The photocopying for the CC," says Joanne, dropping the pages on Eileen's desk. *Core Curriculum,* or maybe *Coordinating Committee.* If you have to ask what Joanne's acronyms stand for, you're not part of the club.

"Tracy's engaged," says Eileen slyly, paper-clipping the pages.

"I know," says Joanne without a glance at me. She pokes the top of the stack. "This one goes to Manning, and I want these in triplicate to send out with individual notes."

As Eileen pencils these instructions on a pad, Joanne swings her head toward me. For a second she looks nauseated; the very sight of me, I am given to assume, makes her ill. Then, in a voice calibrated for broadcast, she offers her own congratulations: "Jeff says you hardly know the guy."

After lecture, during the fifteen-minute break between student conferences and seminar, I will murder Jeff.

"Maybe what Jeff said is I haven't known George for long," I correct Joanne. "Maybe that's what he said. But I know George well enough to be sure he's the guy for me."

"That's *beautiful*," chimes Eileen, with the sort of lascivious spectatorship that reminds me why certain types of romance novels deserve a spot on the porn shelf.

"Sometimes you just know," I add. And sometimes you are piercingly terrified: a piece of information neither Joanne nor Eileen needs.

"Good, then," declares Joanne. "Good." She folds her arms, consigning me to my fate like a C-student who has just informed the university of her decision to drop out. "If it were done when 'tis done," she says, with an abstracted gaze past my left ear, "then 'twere well it were done quickly."

"That was nice," says Eileen after Joanne is gone.

Though I hate to play into this obvious fishing expedition — Eileen's attempt to divine my feelings toward Joanne — I have to set the record straight on this account. "It certainly *wasn't* nice. That was a quote from *Macbeth*. It's Macbeth talking about committing a murder."

Eileen's flat brown gaze meets mine, and I register a flicker of recrimination for my failure to deliver my personal romantic gossip gem directly to her desk. "Still," she says doggedly. "It was nice."

"And?" says Yolanda.

"And it's like we're on some satellite audio-link since he proposed. There's just this . . . gap. Between me and him. Between what I say and what he hears. It's like dealing with a stranger. It's like having a Mack truck driven over our relationship."

"And?" says Yolanda. "Don't hold back now. Give me your worst, sweets." Both arms braced on the table, she goads me with a nod, ready for any hurricane-force wind I might unleash in the mirror-spangled diner.

I'm too tightly wound for irony. "How could he have proposed so fast?"

Hands to her skull, Yolanda pantomimes Munch's *The Scream*.

"Yol, George obviously doesn't even know me well enough to know I'd need time to think about marriage. To talk a few more things through with him, and live together, and learn how we fight and make up, and get used to the whole idea. He doesn't even know me that well yet, and he wants to marry me. What does that say about him?"

"Maybe that he's in love with you?" She unfolds her arms and grips the tabletop. "You two are just doing this the old-fashioned way. You got engaged, and now you'll get to know each other."

"Maybe," I breathe. "But I didn't want to do it this way. I lie in bed next to him and spend half the night quietly freaking. And he and I have barely spoken in the last forty-eight hours, because we're on the phone all the time with our public. I didn't know we had a public, but evidently we do. Mostly our parents' cousins. And they're very gratified about this engagement. I don't even *want* to be engaged, I just want to be with George, like it was before Sunday. But I can't get un-engaged without bringing my life down around my ears."

"Which is fantastic. Tracy, I've got to tell you, I see that you're suffering, I see that for you this is catastrophic, but I have no idea why. I'm trying to comprehend that you think this is the worst thing that has happened in your life, when it looks to me like the best and most romantic, and frankly I'd like to be in your shoes."

"You'd like to have unknowingly pledged your troth to a man you're crazy about but have known only eight weeks?"

"If he was cute," says Yolanda. And then, more fiercely: "If he loved me."

There's a long silence.

"How's it going with Bill?"

She blinks. "It had been easier for a while."

"Now it's shitty again?"

"Not according to the audiences. *They* like us onstage. By closing week, people were even starting to say nice things about Bill's Freud, and our *chemistry*." The word is a curse. Her face goes blank, restless. "Maybe if I didn't have to kiss him in that one stupid scene, maybe I wouldn't be reminded all the time. But when he kissed me at the last three performances, suddenly it was like he was *into* it again. You know what I mean? It's like he's trying to fucking torture me. I can't *believe* we have to reopen in two weeks, even if it's just for a short run."

"I'm sorry," I say.

Yolanda doesn't answer. She scans the café. Without lifting her hands, she stretches a long finger toward a man crossing the room. "What do you think?"

I track him in the mirror opposite our table. Lean, reddish hair, nice face. "Not bad," I say, with as much encouragement as I can muster.

Yolanda crows. It is an unattractive sound, stripped of wistfulness or optimism, and it tells me Yolanda is turning some corner — though onto what path I don't know. "Gay," she pronounces. "Or if he isn't yet, he will be as soon as he meets a nice woman."

She falls silent. Then, still silent, begins to cry.

I can't remember the last time I saw Yolanda cry. Not, it seems, since we were girls. Through these past years of disappointment, and even with Bill, Yolanda has so steadily broadcast rage that it's been easy, I suddenly see, to miss the magnitude of her distress.

I take both her hands, and hold them. The café's clatter waxes and wanes.

She stops crying and closes her eyes. We sit holding hands. Then she draws a shuddering breath, and looks at me. "I'm going to be okay," she says. There's a long silence. She puckers her lips into a fish mouth, crosses her eyes. With a decisive laugh, she lets go of my hands and digs in her gym bag. She offers me a vitamin. "Keep up your strength," she says.

I take it with a sip of ice water that freezes my throat. Swallowing, I'm hit with a recollection of Joanne's face in the instant when, turning toward me, she faltered. Was that dislike, as I assumed? Or is Jeff right — was it envy?

"Tracy," says Yolanda. "You've got to relax."

"I can't even sleep," I murmur. "I don't know how to talk to him. I've never had trouble talking to him before —"

"And you need to stop."

"Stop what?"

"Going through life like a deer in headlights," she says. "Because let's just assume everything's going to be okay — which it probably will be. Think of all the time you'll have wasted worrying. And if everything is *not* okay, is there anything you can do about it now — since you're going to marry George anyway? Because he's great, and because you love him. I mean, you're here in this café with me to tell me you're terrified of being engaged to him, right? But you're not actually considering *not* marrying him. Right?"

"I *am* considering it. I am. I can't marry a man who acts like a stranger. Who —"

"This is just nervousness. And it's also very Tracy." Banished are the tears; Yolanda's voice gains volume. She is, once more, on stage. "You're worrying about things in advance, so if everything goes wrong you'll be able to claim you saw it coming. You'll be able to say Tracy Was in Control Even if She Got Married Against Her Better Judgment. Am I right?"

Yolanda is, with her fuchsia leotards and chunky heels and disaster of a love life, an archangel of commitment. And she does know me.

"That's possible," I offer.

She winks, gives a last, dismissive wipe at her eyes, and sips her water. "At least you can admit it." Setting down her glass, she lays a hand on my elbow. "Tracy, call me any time you need. I have no fucking idea what to say. But call me any time."

At home I drop my briefcase, survey the blinking answering machine with gimlet eyes, and press Play.

He is a wonderful wedding consultant. I was given his name a year ago and held on to it because, you know, maybe Gabby, but oh well, soon maybe, right? It could happen, God willing, if Gabby made the least little effort. She's terrific, Gabby. She only shouldn't be so picky. Suddenly out of the blue sky she tells me she's dating a rabbinical student — now, five minutes later, no more rabbinical student. Don't ask me why because she tells me nothing. Here's the information, Tracy love. Use it in good health. I know this is a Seattle business, and you're in New York, but I'm sure they can give you advice. I'm so happy for your news. I am. All right, I wish George were Jewish, but I'm glad for you because it's wonderful.

I stand over my answering machine as Aunt Rona's voice spells out the name and phone number of Herb Levine's No Ordinary Wedding Express and closes with three loud kisses.

A key turns in the door. It might as well turn in my gut. In the five minutes I've spent in my apartment, my need to see George has grown so keen the click of the tumblers lifts me to my feet.

"Ready?" he says.

Only now do I remember: This morning George offered to get tickets for an evening movie. *The phone can't reach us in the theater,* he said with a laugh. Not that he's seemed to mind it: the stream of congratulations, the awkward greetings from long-lost relatives. George has hailed each — even the fundamentalist cousin who didn't return his calls for years — with warmth, welcome, a hearty clean slate.

He sets down his briefcase and loosens his tie. His arms wrap my waist. "Of course, we don't *have* to go. We can order pizza, and eat it in bed, and get crumbs everywhere, and practice for our honeymoon."

My jittery laughter reminds me, for an instant, of Elizabeth. "Let's not waste the tickets," I say. Suddenly the prospect of a cool, pitch-black theater — a blank space in which to think, George beside me — promises salvation. "I've heard great things about this movie."

In the theater my hold on George's hand grows so faint he gently anchors it with his other hand to keep it from slipping. Instead of fostering meditation, the dark, cavernous room inspires vertigo. We sit side by side before the film's lush panorama, my hand loose in the warm trap of his palms. On the screen a feast of colors sways, and the beautiful, sad faces of the actors grow still more beautifully sad as *Crouching Tiger, Hidden Dragon* reaches its denouement and love ends tragically.

We leave the theater amid a thick crowd. George looks serious. As we walk down Broadway, I ready myself for confrontation. I dread his interrogation about my distant mood, and am eager for it — for the true contact that will follow my confession of turmoil.

After several blocks he speaks. "I did some thinking during the movie, Tracy. I'll be in Buffalo next week for that state educators' conference, and I'm thinking I ought to take an extra couple days and go on to Albany for some meetings."

When I don't speak he continues. "Yesterday I was on the phone with Paula, and my father actually asked to get on the phone with me, for the first time in years. He didn't say much other than 'Your sister says you're well.' But from him that's a big step. I doubt it'll mean much. The breach between us is far too big. But Paula says she'd like to come to meet you, and there's a chance my father may actually come with her. Paula says they'd like to come in two weeks." He tilts his head, skeptical. "Anyway, I'd been planning to go to Albany that week, but I figure I ought to get that travel over with now . . . so I can give my full attention to bracing you for my father's sermons, or deep freeze — whichever comes." He squeezes my hand. "But it means I'll be out of town all next week. And I wanted to check that with you, because so much is going on right now."

I can think of little I want less than to meet Earl Beck. But no one's asked me. A bubble of indignation rises, only to be extinguished by reality: engaged women are, aren't they, expected to meet their future in-laws? I feel sick at the thought of all that might be expected of engaged women. As for letting go of George for a full week? A desperate desire for a few days alone vies with an equally desperate desire to wrap my arms around George's neck and insist, *Don't leave me.* But pleading with my lover not to take a weeklong trip seems incongruent with self-respect.

Is it?

Nothing's clear. Except that a weeklong business trip is not the matter he and I need to discuss. I open my mouth to unburden myself; then, with George watching me, shut it.

I want to turn back to the theater and bury myself in the movie's heartbreaking vistas.

"Okay," I say.

He stops walking and faces me. "It's okay with you?"

I nod.

"You seem tired," he observes.

Too tired to stay out late. Or debate the movie's symbolism. Or match George's ardor, or his sleepy, quizzical touch.

"Congratulations," says Elizabeth, running a finger along the folders on my shelf.

"Thanks," I say.

She stares at a stack of files, now tapping her fingertip on her pouting lower lip. Relieved at her apparent lack of curiosity about my engagement, I sit back in my chair. Fatigue laps at me, drawing my head back until I'm looking at the ceiling. The night's sleep hit a shoal at two in the morning and spun in fragments until dawn. George slept soundly beside me, one leg stretched across my thigh.

"What are these?"

I tip my head forward to see what Elizabeth is looking at. "Nothing," I say sharply.

" 'Tolstoy and the Big Lie,' " she reads off the tab of a file. She fingers the others in the stack. " 'Literary Gloom, European.' 'Literary Doom, American, Nineteenth Century.' 'The War Against Joy, Modernist.' 'The War Against Joy, Postmodern.' 'A Conversation with Palcy's Father.' "

I have no idea when Elizabeth assumed this almost proprietary comfort with my office. It's like having a kid sister rummaging in my things. "Notes," I say. "For a project."

Now I have her full attention. "It doesn't look like your American surrealism research."

"That's because it isn't," I conclude with asperity. I wave her toward her seat.

She doesn't move. "Well, what *is* it, then?"

Noting that this emboldened Elizabeth is considerably more irritating than her spooked predecessor, I pick a pencil from my desktop, examine the tip, and insert it in the electric sharpener, which makes a whining sound. "It's a new book I'm considering. One I'm researching on the side for the moment."

"What did Tolstoy lie about?"

I click the pencil down onto my desktop and feel its needle-sharp point. In truth the project could benefit from a little airing in the company of another mind. Elizabeth is an incisive intellect. She's rigorous and thoughtful. Most importantly, she's not on my tenure committee.

"This is absolutely confidential."

"Of course." Her face is bright with concentration.

"It's not going to win me tenure. It's a book I hope to start writing next year."

"Got it," she says, conspiratorial.

I hesitate. "It's just this," I say. "I think there's a deep, long-running bias against literature about happiness. A cultural mistrust of anything but tragedy. The only happiness a writer can allude to without risking his reputation — and then only briefly — is that sort of false Happiness in Perpetuity that wraps up Dickens novels. You know — marriage between two characters who can be expected to go cross-eyed with contentment and stay that way until they die." As I speak, my voice gains confidence. I sound like myself. "It's as if our whole literary tradition, which has been unsparing on the subjects of death, war, poverty, et cetera, has agreed to keep the gloves on where happiness is concerned. And no one has addressed it. I mean, shame on us all — readers, critics, writers. Anybody who tries to take happiness seriously is belittled. The writers who pen happy endings risk getting labeled 'regionalists,' which is like a paternal pat on the head and a nudge back to the children's table. Or worse, they're called 'romance writers' — the literary world's highest insult. In fact, I wonder sometimes whether some of the most obnoxious dismissals of women writers, which feminists have interpreted as sexism, are actually part of something else. Women talk about happiness more freely than men do, and that's one major reason why they've gotten slammed. Men are in the Romantic tradition; woman write romances. Had Grace Paley not included some tragic stories in her mix, her whole oeuvre might have been ignored. If Eudora Welty had written more tragedy — if she'd used humor only to take people apart, rather than allowing them to remain stitched together — those last idiots still calling her a regionalist in the seventies wouldn't have had a leg to stand on. In fact they'd probably have crowned her an Epic Writer. And if Edwin Arlington Robinson hadn't been so depressed, you'd never have heard of him. There's this cultural fear of thinking seriously about happiness — I'd go so far as to say it's a cultural debility. People talk about culture wars over sexuality and race. But we're in a culture war over the nature and feasibility of happiness. And no one even acknowledges it."

Elizabeth is nodding.

"Tolstoy," I say, "is just my symbol for the problem."

She's still nodding.

"I sometimes think the only writers who've gotten away with writing seriously about happiness with their reputations intact have done so on the sly. Sort of sneaking it in at the margins. So that's what I want to look at. Writers who do that. Welty, Bambara, a dozen or so others. And I want to look at how they do it, and how the critics read them, and how it all plays out over their careers."

Elizabeth stops nodding and falls silent. For several minutes she scans my bookshelves, tapping again on her lower lip.

"I like it," she says. "It's daring."

In a heartbeat I've forgiven her nosiness. "The idea isn't fully worked out, of course," I say. "It's in the early stages. But I think it's worth exploring." For the first time in days, I feel energized. "Let's get coffee. Then we can catch up on your dissertation progress."

We walk silently through the hall. Outside the door of the faculty lounge, Elizabeth pauses. "How will you set up a conversation between Tolstoy and Bambara?" As she speaks the door swings open and Steven exits.

Stepping inside, we're greeted by Jeff, who is seated on the couch marking a student paper, a bored expression on his face. "Who's trying to span Tolstoy and Bambara?"

"Whoops." Elizabeth giggles and drifts to the bookshelves without another glance in my direction. I stop in my tracks, staring at her.

Jeff frowns at me. "Too broad."

"You don't even know what the project is," I say sharply.

"Don't need to. Too broad."

Elizabeth is absorbed in the bookshelf. I fill my mug with the last of the pot, reach into the cabinet for a clean filter and load the coffee for another run. Jeff and I haven't had a substantive conversation in four days — not since the morning after my engagement. Ignoring the heat in my face, I turn to him. "Don't you ever pause before you pass judgment?"

Jeff flips a page of the paper he's marking. "What's the point?"

I watch him finish the paper, toss it onto a stack by his feet, and start another one — the last of the pile. With a giant sucking sound, the coffee starts to brew.

"Have you heard, by the way?" says Jeff, pen poised. "The Coordinating Committee is supposed to release its initial recommendations tomorrow." He sighs deeply and rests his head against the back of the sofa. "So now all await the first poke from the finger of God. Which subspecialty will be rewarded with dozens of TA's; which will suffer fiery torment." Opening his eyes, Jeff makes a swift mark on the paper he's been reading. "Grub is so excited he's been incontinent four times."

"Who's Grub?" says Elizabeth.

Jeff looks at her blankly. "Did I say that aloud?"

Elizabeth's hand flies to her mouth and stays there a moment. Then, dropping her hand, she lets out a guffaw. "Who *is* it?"

Jeff yawns. "So how's the work?" he says.

"Fine." Elizabeth speaks airily, and with a barely restrained, private-joke smile I don't like. "I wrote two more papers. And I'm finishing up another round of note taking for the dissertation. I'm going to focus more on the era's political and religious tropes as filtered through imagery and argument. Less on romance motifs. Joanne thought I'd do better to concentrate on the more universal themes if I'm going to make my argument about Dickinson precipitating a shift in American literary culture."

Unreal. I open my mouth, but Jeff is quicker.

"Interesting," he says. "Joanne may, by sheer coincidence, have a point."

"That change," I say, "could set Elizabeth's dissertation back a full year."

"But focusing on something other than romance motifs may better position Elizabeth for the job market."

Elizabeth watches us as she might fish in a tank, her lips curling in a smile of amused curiosity.

"This isn't about job positioning," I say. "It's about intimidating a graduate student out of the dissertation she wants to write. This is crazy."

"Not crazy at all," says Jeff. "Just politics. If you want to get published, write about literature of political strife. Analyze the hideous things poets said to one another a hundred years ago. Chart literary power struggles. That's what's hip. Joanne has a point. If you focus on romance these days, you're passé."

"Jeff," I say. "Forget whatever disagreements I have with Joanne. You actually think Elizabeth ought to defer her Ph.D. and labor for peanuts another year in order to become more mainstream? You're advocating that?"

"Of course I am. I tested the waters and built my own publica-

tion record on the set of standards that was current. Right now romance is out, poetics of politics in — so Elizabeth should write the
necessary dissertation."

"Academics are supposed to be intellectually independent. I
know you advocate realpolitik. But what's the use of freedom of
speech if everyone aims for the middle?"

"Elizabeth can find a way to express her unique interests in a
way that conforms to current trends. It's simply a career move."

I don't answer.

"I would think," he says, "you'd recognize the merits of self-
preservation."

He turns back to the paper on his lap, frowns over it briefly,
then scribbles something in the margin and tosses it to the stack at
his feet.

Moving deliberately, I step toward my only friend in this department. The tightness of my throat is out of all proportion to the
subject we're discussing. I understand that he's baiting me, in this
week of blinding confusion, not just to make a professional point
but to underline my folly: my thralldom to emotion, my passivity,
my failure to control my life.

Jeff's posture hasn't changed — arms wide on the back of the
sofa, relaxing as assiduously as any undergraduate — but I know I
have his full attention. Behind me I hear Elizabeth breathing softly.
I say to him, "You spit in the temple of literature."

Elizabeth lets out a fresh guffaw.

Steven Hilliard opens the door. "Am I interrupting?" he says.

"Thank God," I say.

"Tut," says Steven with a wicked grin. "Don't quarrel. We need
stout yeomen. The Coordinating Committee made a last-minute
request for some paperwork, and Eileen is gone for the day. Joanne
needs volunteers to help with the collating."

"I'll be there shortly," I say. At the moment I am too wrought-
up to be in the same room as Joanne Miller.

Elizabeth slips out the door behind Steven.

Jeff doesn't move. I look at him, accusing.

"Collating gives me a rash." Jeff hoists the pile of marked papers from the floor to his lap. He loads them into his satchel and
tucks it under one arm. "Besides" — he shuts the metal latch with
a one-fingered tap — "I certainly don't have to worry about mak-

ing friends here anymore. By New Year's I'll be the most popular guy on campus."

I don't speak.

"I'm going to give all A's." He strokes his satchel as gingerly as if it contained a bomb. "I've got thirty-six students. That's enough to throw the grade average for the department — in a display of the most spectacular grade-inflation Grub and his bulldog have ever seen." He smiles broadly.

"What is *with* you? You take potshots behind Joanne's back, but you can't be bothered to stand up for what matters. You can't even be bothered to stand up for a friend."

The grin evaporates. For a moment Jeff looks tired. "On the contrary, Tracy," he says. "I absolutely do stand up for my friends. I just happen to have a different definition of what's truly in a friend's best interests, as opposed to lovey-sounding bullshit. And I stand rock-solid on my principles. You can trust me on that. Among my principles, however, is playing the game so I don't get played by it."

"Unlike naive suckers like me?"

He cants his head. After a few seconds I turn from him in contempt. I direct my hostile gaze toward the softly steaming coffeemaker.

From behind me I hear Jeff sip his coffee, then set the mug on the table. "Your naiveté is refreshing."

"If you like it so much you might consider backing me up next time."

"Tracy," he says. Turning, I'm met by the serious eyes of a Jeff whom Richard must know. "I think people should be practical. In career, in politics, in love. Naiveté" — he pauses for emphasis — "is suicide. I wish it weren't true." He falls silent. A long time passes. Neither of us moves. Then he nods reflectively. "Atlanta made me an offer," he says. "A strong one."

"They did?"

"Mm." His smile is wistful.

"Aren't you going to try to get Grub to counteroffer? Come up with something for Richard here?"

"Already did. Though I knew it was going to be futile. He just gave that smile he uses when he thinks someone's bluffing — he doesn't believe I'd leave this place for Emory. And talking up Richard was never going to have much effect — you can imagine how stiff his face turned at the mention of yet another queer theory hire."

I take this in. "Richard's going to be thrilled," I say at length. "And I'm glad for you."

He holds up a cautionary palm. "It's not final."

"Why not?"

He seems disappointed that I have to ask. "I'm playing hardball with Emory on the details."

Footsteps sound in the corridor and I hear Joanne's voice commanding the troops. Jeff scrutinizes me.

"And you?" he says. "Are you playing hardball with your man, Tracy?"

I have no answer.

Jeff's sigh comes from the depths of his lean body. "I wash my hands of this."

I ride the shuttle bus to the airport with George. It seems imperative not to let him out of my sight a moment longer than necessary. When I'm with him my dread thins and some crude compass points unsteadily forward. I love this man. Everything else is up for grabs. My speaking voice has risen a register. I sound winded. I sound like one of my damn students, every sentence ending in a question. Secrecy, heretofore absent between George and me, burgeons.

What are you thinking?

Nothing particular.

Engagement has been, so far, the worst thing to happen to our relationship. According to Yolanda, this is all in my head. According to Jeff, I ought to refuse George outright until he comes to the table with an endorsable deal. And according to Hannah — the only one with a livable track record where relationships are concerned — I need to sort it out without George's help. I need, according to Hannah's womanly wisdom, to approach a man like a bomb defuser approaching an unexploded ego. Never mind that this parses with nothing in my experience of men. (And why, after all, have I felt so certain I understand men? My years disappointing Jason? Jeff's harsh tutelage? A camaraderie with Adam—whose primary food group is pizza? My father who can't, it turns out, stay on the phone with me?) This is the big time. This is playing for keeps. If George knew how compassless I feel, according to Hannah, he would burst out from between the airport's magazine-and-candy racks, sprint down the Terminal 2 concourse, clear the jetway in a single grand jeté to the tarmac, and lift off for Buffalo under his own steam, flapping his way northwest beyond the runway until he's nothing but a contrail of wounded pride on the horizon.

There goes another good one, the travel pillow saleswoman says wistfully in my ear.

Note to self: Investigate whether development of surrealism was concurrent with moments of intense psychic torque in individual authors' lives.

I insist on walking George to security, my arm wrapped tightly with his, stepping through the fluorescent-and-tile jungle of LaGuardia Airport. At the end of the snaking line, he takes me by the shoulders. His eyes are a vibrant brown that makes me want to cry. "Tracy, since we got engaged you've been very quiet. What's going on?" He brushes my face with a warm, dry palm. "You all right?"

Oh, George. If I could only roll out my heart for us to salve together. But I'm afraid you'll spontaneously combust. "I'm just a bit freaked," I say. "But I'm okay."

His hand stops moving. He looks stricken. "*Freaked?* By being engaged to me?"

"But okay," I urge. "You know. Freaked-but-okay?" I bob my head, willing him to sign on to this diagnosis.

The line advances. Walking backward, his bag rolling between us, George moves with it. "But you're good with this, right?" he says. "With us?"

Hannah's urgent coaching blasts in my head. Before me lies a minefield of language. Gingerly I set down one foot, then the other. And how long, and what will it take, before it feels safe to step freely? "I am," I say. "I love you."

The lines of tension on George's face break into a beautiful, dazzled smile. His voice slips, loses its footing, after a short struggle regains it. "It *is* strange, isn't it? I mean, we're *engaged*." He grins, wraps one arm around me, then waves to catch the attention of a passing flight attendant.

"We're engaged," George tells her. "And I'm the luckiest man in the world. I'd like to tell everybody. Think maybe you could, you know—announce it? On one of those?" He waves vaguely at the wall, where a speaker has just finished thrumming its rote security announcement.

The attendant dimples, calls a "Congratulations," and continues on her way. A few people in the security line clap. "Good luck," calls a grandmotherly woman at the head of the line. She smiles at us for a full half minute while the security officer waits impassively for her to turn back to business.

In fact, a good third of the line is smiling. This is an airport. They're supposed to be irate. Instead they've gone mad with satisfaction. Our relationship has had its IPO, and all these nice people own stock. We've made a deposit to the social security fund of love. We're good for America.

He bends and kisses me. "I hope you won't feel too freaked while I'm gone," he whispers.

I press my cheek to his jaw, hook my elbows around his neck, and cling. "I won't, I just need . . . a little time."

At this moment I am committing a relationship sin. I should tell George the depths of my confusion. I should inform the security officers that I'm not at all sanguine about this engagement thing, ask the flight attendant to announce that I have doubts about how George and I might fare within the institution of marriage. I should insist that George stay with me and hash this thing out until everything makes sense again, until we understand each other, until it seems safe once more to speak my mind. But the guardian angels pummeling my head with their wings tell me to kiss George sweetly and send him off to Buffalo. Which is what I do.

And let me make note here: I am not the only one behaving abnormally. The usual George would be inquisitive. He would chase after my doubts, address *me* rather than a passing flight attendant, even miss his flight to make sure I was truly all right.

Or would he? The doubt balloons too quickly to be contained: How well do I know him?

Engagement has made us fragile. Only the passengers and weary-looking security officer are sturdy. We shuffle to the head of the line. I hold his hand. A paunchy businessman slaps him on the back. Lovingly, the fiancé kisses his affianced.

Leaning forward on the edge of Hannah's bed, still dressed from my lecture, I drop another sodden tissue into her trash. As I straighten my head spins; it's been more than a week since I had a reasonable night's sleep. "I just don't know," I repeat.

"Maybe you do," says Hannah. "Tracy, why do you think you said yes?"

"Because I was too shocked to do anything else?" I rub my eyes with open palms.

"Maybe because you *wanted* to." Hannah, fresh from her office and poised to launch into the afternoon with Elijah, digs into this crisis as efficiently as she might cut her son's food. "Maybe because you have a stupendous *hunch* about him . . . which is all *anybody* has to go on, anyway." Balancing on one foot, she bends over her belly in an attempt to take off her stockings. When this doesn't work she squats, clutching the bed for support. "I think it was just a misunderstanding, the whole timing thing. It doesn't mean he's the wrong guy. Yes, he rushed things. But that's because he's ready. Plus, from what you say he's really lost his whole family. He's eager to start fresh."

"Hannah, you think I haven't thought of that? But if being pushed into an engagement I wasn't ready for is part of helping him make up for bad voodoo in his past, what else is he going to need? What exactly did I say yes to?" As I talk, George's image thins and recedes, begins to resemble the outline of a man, vaguely menacing. *As we stray from love,* Amichai wrote, *We must multiply speech,*

Words and sentences long and orderly.
Had we stayed together,
We could have remained a silence.

Hannah puts on socks.

"Listen, if you choose not to go ahead with this" — her voice gains a sudden, self-exculpatory vehemence — "it's okay. I mean, I have no real opinion on this. Yes, it's a bit worrisome that he rushed you. I like George a lot, but that doesn't mean he's your fate, or that you *have* to get married, even. The right thing is whatever you choose. Only you can choose."

I want to insist, *But what should I do?* but I know better.

Having issued her message of neutral support, Hannah peers into my face for confirmation of delivery. "Look, anyone would be a little shocked in your position. Anyone would have fears. Do some thinking while he's gone, Tracy. And give it time. You love him. He loves you." She glances at her watch. Her mouth forms an unhappy *oooh,* and I realize, with the outsized terror of a child, that I'm about to be dismissed. "I've got to wake Elijah ten minutes ago. Today's his art class." She rocks forward with a peculiar rhythmic motion that I don't recognize as an attempt to rise until she reaches for my arm. I help her to her feet and then continue clutching her smooth, cool hand. She squeezes back. "Call me any time," she says.

As I step into Hannah's elevator, the thought of the full answering machine I will surely find in my apartment makes me balk at going home. I'm awash in well-wishers, and I've never been so isolated. Everyone wants to share the frisson: whirlwind romance, surprise proposal; the tide of romance that's swept me off my feet. Everyone asks eagerly about plans, no one about how I'm feeling now that my feet can't touch bottom. Great-aunts interrupting hours I've set aside for Faulkner. UPS at the door with engagement gifts: distant relatives cementing the edifice of our romance with nonstick pots. The tiny hints I've made: *a bit sudden . . . got to catch my breath . . .* are glossed over. Only Jeff and Yolanda have declared opinions, with Yolanda calling twice in the last twenty-four hours to quote articles from *Glamour* and *Modern Bride* in which experts discuss prenuptial panic and its treatments. But Yolanda and Jeff represent two sides of an ideological battle: marriage partisans and soldiers of the resistance, for whom ideology runs as thick and hardens as fast as glue.

And of course Hannah doesn't want to touch this decision. If she advises me to marry, and I'm miserable? No friend would want to be responsible. If I break off the engagement on her advice and die lonely? See above. If I marry, and she's advised me not to? The friendship takes a staggering blow. Remembering the argument in which I once blurted to Hannah that I worried she was compromising with Ed, I'm shocked at my foolhardiness, and more shocked our friendship survived.

In the elevator's rattling solitude I think: A freaked-out engaged person is a grenade with the pin pulled. No one comes near.

The walk to my office is only fifteen minutes. The street is chilly, a few last leaves scuttling, the daylight draining from the November sky. It's late and the department is quiet. I unlock my door and drop into the chair opposite my poster of Zora.

In this portrait she might be thirty. She's dressed fashionably in a belted dark dress, thick necklace, and a black hat with a sloping brim. She's a big-limbed woman with powerful-looking shoulders, a relatively flat chest, and a large-boned face. She sits erect, but with shoulders rolled slightly forward, as though she were trying not to be as big as she is. Her eyes are averted.

Of all the literature I read in graduate school, Hurston's work was what spoke to me. It moved me, literally — from a specialty in nineteenth century to twentieth. Hurston mixed delight and majesty and humor as few writers do; but it was something else that riveted me. Traveling from Manhattan under the sponsorship of curious white patrons, Hurston reported on her Florida hometown — its beliefs, colorful characters, tall tales. The book she produced was an anthropological account that informed and obfuscated in the same sentence, delighting in frustrating outsiders' attempts to understand.

I spent years poring over those wild yarns and lies she reported. She made it seem riotous, that extended jaunt to Eatonville to collect folklore. And maybe it was. But sometimes I swear I can feel a jagged loneliness behind Zora's blithe sentences. Sometimes I'm sure that behind the anthropologist's mask she's trying every trick she can think of to hurdle her isolation, split the difference between the clashing worlds she inhabits. Am I wrong to see, underneath the shiny surface, an urgent, reality-bending scramble for answers?

I open my copy of *Mules and Men* to the first page and, supporting my head with my hands, scan it.

First place I aimed to stop to collect material was Eatonville, Florida.

The expression on Zora's face is unreadable. She has shut herself off against prying eyes and is patiently waiting for the portrait photographer to leave her alone.

Folklore is not as easy to collect as it sounds.

It seems, however, my best option.

"I had doubts all along," says the fitting room attendant, hoisting a pile of Levi's to her shoulder. "But I was too intimidated to express them. Stupid me. That marriage took five years out of my life."

I shake my head in sympathy.

"Not sure I've recovered yet." She holds a pair of jeans to my waist and gauges its length against my legs. "Try these."

"Honey, when I got engaged, you think it was perfect?" The cashier glares at me. I'm the only customer in the crammed market, which smells of sour milk. Holding my purchase — a plastic bag of bananas — above the counter, she pauses, bananas just out of my reach. "He proposed on the stage of a club full of my friends. On my birthday. He was so nervous he hardly looked at me the whole time, just talked to the crowd. The instant he popped the question, they started cheering. I never said yes. For years, every time he ignored me or fell asleep over dinner, I thought: *I never said yes.* Except at the altar, but what I really meant was *Jeezus, I hope this works.*" She thuds the bananas down in front of me. I practically hear the bruises forming on the yellow skin. "It hasn't been a bad marriage, mind you. I've seen worse."

Settling my Caesar salad in front of me, my waitress says, "The whole *point* of being engaged is being terrified. When *I* first got engaged, I knew Stan loved me . . . you know what I mean? But what I wasn't sure of was — if I got in an accident and my face got burned off, would he still love me then?" Distressed by the memory, she rests a plate of butter pats atop a steaming teapot, where they liquefy as her hands rise to cradle her peaches-and-cream cheeks. "You learn a lot about each other during the engagement. By the time we got married I knew he *would*." Her kohled eyes turn dewy.

"That's right," says the waitress at the next station, swiping coffee rings off the countertop with a damp rag. "Engagement is when you sort it all out." She folds the wet rag into the belt of her fanny pack. "Plus, now you've got *leverage*. You can fight all the fights you want, and you won't have those dating nightmares where you don't see him for a week and don't know what he's thinking and you're petrified he might run away. Engaged people don't run away. It's too embarrassing. You've planned this perfectly — *every* woman should be engaged while she's deciding whether to get married."

"Maybe," I say. Before me is a white packet of sugar covered with tiny hearts. I open it, spill the contents, form the sugar into cocaine-lines on the tabletop until the family at the next table stares. "But engagement is intimidating, don't you think? Makes it harder to be honest?"

"Intimidation is *fabulous*," says my waitress. She's levitating near the ceiling, checking her makeup in a small handheld mirror. "Without peer pressure, who would ever go through with the 'I do'?" She snaps her compact shut. "When I was engaged, if I'd thought no one would have noticed, I would have hopped off the wedding-planning assembly line and bolted. And I'm so glad I didn't. It's been two years, and I'm nuts about him."

The police officer previously sipping her coffee at a table near the window is on her feet. "Bullshit," she barks. "Bullshit to leverage, bullshit to intimidation. And *why* is it considered romantic for the man to take the woman by surprise?" She thumps her fist on the tabletop, splashing coffee to the floor. "Don't you think the most important decision of a woman's life is one she should *not* make when she's been caught off-guard? Why would *any* woman like the idea of being shocked by a proposal? Why would *any* man trust an on-the-spot answer? If you're going to start a relationship in that system," she says, glaring ominously at the wait staff, "all bets are off."

"As goes the engagement," says the cashier, looking glum as she hands me my change, "so will go the marriage. I'd turn back if I were you."

Entering the elevator along with a half-dozen students drifting their way toward eight-thirty A.M. classes, I'm greeted by a grinning Steven Hilliard, who installs himself beside me with an impish thumbs-up. Before I can utter an automatic *Thank you, George is wonderful,* Steven addresses me in a whisper. "Things look good," he says. "Seems the Coordinating Committee is leaning heavily toward a pluralistic curriculum. Their report goes as far as to stipulate that students' writing-requirement classes *must include at least one 'older' text.* If they have to say that, it means the traditionalists are on the defensive."

"That's great. I've got nothing against older texts, though. I just want balance."

With a sharp wave he dismisses balance. "Serves them right to get a taste of their own medicine. And it certainly won't hurt you in December."

The elevator ejects us onto the ninth floor, and Steven takes his leave with a clap on my shoulder. I've been dubbed a team member — though this promotion seems more about Steven's political vindication than about camaraderie.

I stop at my mailbox. As I flip through my mail, dropping leaflets into the cavernous metal trash bin stationed here for this purpose, my gaze lights on Paleozoic's box, situated directly above mine. Lying atop a curled stack of departmental notices is a postcard sporting Jeff's handwriting. Tilting my head, I read the message Jeff has penned to Paleozoic in black ink: *Tuesday faculty meeting delayed until Thurs 4 P.M. Wanted to make sure you knew. Best — Jeff Thomas.*

Since when does Jeff take it on himself to notify the chairman emeritus of changed meeting times? With a swift glance confirming that I'm alone, I reach up and flip the card. On the glossy side is an enormous pink triangle.

In my office I check my voicemail. There are two messages, the first from six A.M.

Hello, my dear freaked lover. George's voice is husky. He clears his throat. *I've got sunshine on a cloudy day . . .* For a full two verses his serenade tackles Smokey Robinson and wrestles him to the ground. *So I'm here in Buffalo,* he says. *I'm doing a little research on the Web before the day's meetings start. And I've been looking into conversion. Reform, Conservative, or Reconstructionist. Which flavor do you favor? Call me at the hotel.*

The message service cuts in with its pleasant female accent. I breathe again. *Next . . . message . . . received . . . today . . . at eight . . . A.M.*

Tracy, says a voice to which I definitely never gave my office telephone number. *It's Aunt Rona. Your mother said I might catch you in. Just a couple thoughts about your wedding. I'm thinking buffet would be nice, if you can find a caterer with variety. Your uncle Ted lives for buffet.*

I open a page of Flannery O'Connor. For an hour I try to haul my brain into an examination of her lushly perilous world, but every story frightens me — desperate men and women scanning the universe for a miracle, only to get thrashed by the very people they thought their saviors. The notes I make are scattered: *illness as catalyst, humanity, capacity for grotesque, for grace.* I give up and mark student papers. Shortly before noon I permit myself to go for a walk, heading downtown this time.

The afternoon is damp and cold, the few leaves on the sidewalk sodden. It's impossible to get warm. Each cozily lit storefront or warm café I bypass soaks me with regret. At Houston Street, I'm seized by an urge to telephone my parents in Seattle and demand to know the truth — any truth — about their marriage. About anyone's marriage — about what augurs doom, what happiness. Fingering my cell phone, I discover the battery is dead. Just as well.

"Never marry a man," says the boutique owner in a soft Virginia caress of an accent, "whom you have not seen angry. Goad him until he gets angry: that's what I tell my daughters. Then see what he's made of. If he's a gentleman to you even when he's spitting mad, then marry him."

("George," I will peremptorily summon the most loving man I have ever known. "You know that cap you wear? The wool one?" I'll sneer. "It's incongruous.")

"Marry the ex of a friend," says the woman trimming my hair at Horatio's Hair Design. I close my eyes as slippery trimmings rain past my nose. "It's a pre-vetting service."

"A relationship is a building," says the gardener, rake poised in the churchyard's meager garden. "Marriage is just the ivy that grows on it. It tells the world the building is old and respectable. But if you're not careful" — a scrape at sodden leaves — "that ivy can crack the stone." He straightens. "Live in sin, if you ask me. You may not look as respectable, but your building will stand or fall on its own merits."

In Battery Park, inside the wooden barricades erected for his demonstration, the balloon operator releases a final jet of flame into the multihued dome overhead. "For men," he shouts, "marriage is a dirigible. They don't really understand how it works, but they like the view. The fact that they're not sure how to steer the thing doesn't trouble them, because now that they've gotten up so high there isn't really anywhere particular they need to go." He hops into the balloon's basket and works at the knots that tether his bucking vehicle. "For women, marriage is a car with bad alignment. It has to be urged constantly in a particular direction just to avoid meandering off into the woods and crashing." The last knot gives; the balloon operator recedes into the sky with a beatific grin.

"Marriage?" says Anna Karenina, pausing on the edge of the subway platform to gather her skirts as the express thunders nearer. "Yeah. Everybody does that once."

I re-enter the department carrying a paper sack of sodas and cookies: enough fuel to power me through my afternoon obligation, an American Women Writers seminar I usually enjoy but today have no appetite for. As I exit the elevator I am summoned by Eileen, who beckons, a stack of papers in her hand.

Reluctantly I approach. She's holding a copy of my tenure packet, which by now must be in the hands of more colleagues and external reviewers than I care to think about.

Eileen hefts the pages in her open palm. "Feels like tenure-weight." She smiles perkily, today's lipstick augmented by tiny silver sparkles.

"Only the committee knows," I answer as spookily as I can, which succeeds in making her laugh. I start away from her desk.

"Ah, the committee." Eileen murmurs, attaching a label to my file with a hot pink paper clip. "Committees, committees." A few paces from her desk, I wait for her to emerge from this clumsy conversational roundhouse, new grist in hand. "Committees rarely come up with sensible solutions for personal issues, don't you think?"

"I don't know," I say. "I've never gone to a committee with a personal issue."

"I suppose not," says Eileen with approval. "Anyway, I don't know who they think they're going to get to cover classes when Joanne's on reduced hours this spring."

"Where is Joanne going?"

"You mean which hospital?"

I meant nothing of the kind.

"Whoops," says Eileen.

"Whoops *what?*" My voice crests with anger: a momentary stay against the awful understanding overtaking me.

"You did know, right?" says Eileen. "I thought everyone knew."

This time I keep my voice steady. "What's wrong with Joanne?"

"It's not official public knowledge," says Eileen primly. When I don't take the bait, she relents. "Joanne has lupus, love. She was diagnosed at the start of the term. You professors, I swear. I expect the *men* to be oblivious, but I thought at least you women would have noticed how ill your coworker looks. For heaven's sake, Joanne's been on steroids for two months, and *no one* here has had a clue? Only Victoria picked up on it, and she came to me to talk."

More likely, Victoria did her best to deflect Eileen's suspicions until some bureaucratic necessity required bringing her into the loop. "Joanne's going on leave?" I say.

"Part-time medical leave, for the spring. She'll give up two of her three courses. I'm handling the paperwork." Eileen wags her head with a sympathy that's hard to believe. Even she can keep a secret of this gravity. If she chooses not to, it's because she can't stand Joanne — a fact that had escaped my attention until now. It's obvious Joanne would not want me, of all people, getting inside information on her health problems — making this revelation a perfect dollop of revenge to mix with the more public support Eileen will surely offer Joanne. I'm being used, but also — even in my shock I can appreciate this — protected. For a few seconds I contemplate the limitless array of missteps from which Eileen has just saved me.

"Now why did you *think* she got so sensitive when it sounded like the students were making fun of her in the course catalogue?" Eileen's habitual defense: it's not rumormongering if everyone should have guessed.

I accept my penance. "I couldn't figure it out."

"Not that Joanne always makes sense." Eileen giggles. "Except to herself, of course." Sobriety wafts over her. "It can be crippling, you know. And she used to be a big athlete. People can die from lupus, too. Though I hear that's rare. But Victoria seems to think it's a serious case." A final glance at me; then she casts down her eyes and wags her head, the picture of empathy.

I find Jeff sitting at his desk with one hand draped over the telephone, as though he hasn't yet disconnected from a conversation that ended moments ago.

"I just learned something important," I tell him.

He flitters his fingertips: my news can wait. "Richard thinks I've been an ass," he says. "He thinks that when you first told me you were engaged you needed support, rather than my real opinion." He screws his pale lips into a small, pained-looking rose. "I *was* harsh."

In the eight years I've known Jeff, this is the closest thing I've heard to an admission of error. Lowering myself into the seat opposite him, I loft a thank-you across windy, highway-threaded miles to the mysterious Richard. So that's who makes Jeff tick: A man who isn't afraid to stand up to him. Who values friendship over principle. Who's chosen a specialty in Queer Theory, as out as can be, while Jeff coolly chooses when to divulge each crumb of information. I take a moment to imagine their fights: long Sunday checklist versus lazy brunch, tidy desk versus photo-cluttered surface. The thought of these two torturing each other makes me like Jeff a good deal better.

"You *have* been harsh," I say. "You know I value your opinion. Sometimes it's simply a question of how it's voiced."

Jeff's raised eyebrow knocks aside this olive branch. I've misunderstood; he wasn't apologizing, just mulling. He sweeps something invisible from his desk and deposits it in the wastebasket, his half-mast eyelids flickering with perturbation.

Joanne's knock at the door spooks me. Guiltily I meet her owlish stare. Her broad face looks poreless, nubbled and not quite clean — something I've noticed for weeks without noticing. Now I realize her skin is in fact overlaid by a hearty coating of peach-brown — the thick makeup of an actor stepping from swaying curtain shadows onto glaringly lit boards. How long has she put on that mask before coming to work?

"A word?" says Joanne.

Jeff nods her in.

"Two of your undergraduates had the bad judgment to hold an extremely loud gossip session outside my office door. They made it impossible not to overhear. But it was lucky I did. It turns out some joker is raising false hopes in your class."

"Really?" says Jeff, his voice betraying not the slightest interest.

Joanne pauses, slightly, to catch her breath. She continues. "According to your students—who of course tried to squirm out of any confession the minute I cornered them—some attention-starved classmate of theirs claims to have overheard one of your TA's telling another that when he flipped open your roll book to check a student's attendance record, he saw column after column like "Substance: B-plus; Presentation: B-minus; and then in the space for semester grade, an A already filled in.""

Jeff doesn't answer. If he's surprised, his face does not betray it.

"So now," says Joanne, "the rumor has spread. Of course, it's up to you whether you want to disabuse your students of their fantasy that A's are guaranteed. Or let the lazier ones skewer themselves on it." She stops, breathes. Leans, as if casually, against the doorjamb. "But I felt you ought to know. About the fabrication."

Grading sheets aren't due for over a month; Joanne and the others weren't meant to discover Jeff's grading mischief until late December at the earliest—by which point he should have received his countersigned copies of the Atlanta contract and given notice to Grub, effective at the end of spring semester's paid leave. I anticipate Jeff's handling of this ripple in his plan: the charade of laughing off the rumor, only to submit an unblemished list of A's in December. His parting fuck-you will be postmarked, impersonal, and after the fact.

"There's no fabrication," says Jeff. His delivery is as cool as ever, but the muscles of his forearm, as he massages his jaw, are tight. He knows this is impolitic.

Joanne looks puzzled. "One hundred percent A's isn't a student fabrication?"

I stare hard at Jeff, but he doesn't so much as glance my way. I understand what he's doing. He doesn't approve of my choices, he cannot apologize for speaking his mind, but he values my friendship, and he will, with implacable flair, commit this small political suicide for me—reparation for the dozens of times he's watched his own back while I took heat from Joanne. Bearing the standard of our friendship, he gallops off to a mission I desperately want aborted.

Jeff's sigh speaks of regret admixed with awe. "It was an act of God."

"An act of God," Joanne repeats.

He takes off his glasses and folds them, the soft dual clicks the only sound in the office. He rubs his brow, then speaks softly. "God"—Jeff points upward—"came down"—a gesture toward the carpet—"and put the A's in the roll book." His eyes, steady and calm, dare Joanne to demur.

Joanne's throat emits a strange cluck: the sound of something giving way. As she tips up her chin, drowning, I see that she has considered Jeff her friend.

Her words hit the air like tacks. "I wish I'd been in this office," she says, "to witness the theophany."

"You missed it," says Jeff in the same patient voice, "because you were too busy making life miserable for Elizabeth."

Beneath the healthy tint of her makeup, Joanne's face darkens with fear, and it hits me that her look of nausea at our recent encounter was neither dislike, nor envy of love. It was envy of life.

"I see what's going on here," she says, though it's obvious she cannot see, she cannot see at all. She leaves the office brushing the doorjamb with her fingertips, blind.

Jeff blinks at me. Then one corner of his mouth lifts in a tight salute of a smile: no thanks necessary. With a pointedly unhurried motion he turns a paper on his desk. His cheeks and forehead are pale, his lips compressed. He could as easily be the one with a grave illness. Or Elizabeth. Or me, I think. The whole department is drawn, poised for some terrible outburst.

"Jesus, Jeff," I breathe.

He rolls his head briskly from shoulder to shoulder, the movement an alloy of adrenaline and release. Stopping abruptly, he releases a long tunnel of air. "Yeah," he says. With the single syllable his face opens, and he wears the frank, grateful flush of a man warming his hands over a stove.

It hurts to break the news.

"How sick?" he asks after a silence.

"Must be bad, for her to take off from work."

He chuckles, waves a hand in acknowledgment of the inappropriateness of this, and is quiet again. I consider leaving.

"It's a shame," he says. "But Joanne had it coming." The equation having been solved cleanly in his head, he seals it with a nod. "Fuck, though. Richard is going to give me hell."

George phones from his hotel room in Buffalo. The meetings were productive. He leaves for Albany at six A.M.—an early start, but the only flight he could get. He's longing to see me, isn't it amazing how hard it is to be apart. Paula, by the way, has started asking about wedding plans.

"How about a small ceremony?" he muses. "Maybe next month. The less time we leave for planning, the less the details can drive us crazy. Then we can take a few months for just us, maybe to ride waterfalls in barrels, or go on a low-budget camel trek, or maybe just recover from writing all our thank-you notes, before we try to start a family."

The phone offends my ear; I move it an inch away. *I'm not even certain I want to have kids.* The statement is an incendiary I will not toss, though I finger it in my pocket, along with its companion: *I don't even know if I ought to marry you.* "Who says we'd start trying right away?" I say.

From this distance George's voice is preshrunk, unreal. "It's just a suggestion," he says gently. "We can wait a few more months if you like."

The upstairs neighbor's vacuum cleaner thumps its way across my ceiling.

"You okay?" he asks.

"I've had a lot on my mind." I hold my breath.

"Work going okay?"

The saga of Joanne and Jeff offers itself, ready explanation for my distress.

After I'm finished, he's quiet for a few seconds. "Jeff is a bit of an asshole, isn't he?"

"He can be."

"He's right that Joanne brought it on herself—bad behavior is bad behavior. It's just a shame no one knew she was ill. Things could have been handled differently."

"I have no idea now how to conduct myself with Joanne."

"Sounds like Victoria had it right. Be as sympathetic as you can. Also give a lot of C's. No, I'm joking — just grade fairly. Jeff's sins shouldn't fall on your head."

"*Shouldn't.*" My voice is clipped.

There's a silence. "You sure you're okay, Tracy? You just . . . sound like you've had a hard day. With Jeff and all."

George, who's never seemed the sort to mince words, is being oddly circumspect.

"I'm okay," says my script.

HE: "Okay? And . . ." [beat] ". . . okay with everything else?"

Do not — urge the stage directions — *waltz into explosive territory over the telephone.*

SHE: "Getting used to all the changes in my own way."

HE: "That's good. I think. Is it?"

SHE: [a laugh] "It's good."

HE: [decisive] "I think it's great."

The music blares and turns brittle. I look down and notice the stranger I'm dancing with has two injured feet. I want to pull him closer, but every step risks breaking him.

SHE: "Me too."

"Just so you know," George teases, "any time you want to stop using birth control I won't object."

The clock radio spits static and love ballads. My head still welded to the pillow, I work my hand onto the snooze button and silence it.

With rapid strokes, my high school algebra teacher chalks the formula on the board: *Tracy times x equals y.* "Now," she begins, underscoring with her chalk, "*y* equals marriage. And *x* equals the changes you will make in your life in order to make this marriage thrive." She stands back to survey the equation. "Whatever the problem is on your side, whatever the disagreement or disparity of vision, it has to get balanced. You just solve for *x*."

I scrutinize the chalkboard. "What if I'm not sure about *y?*"

She dusts a hand on her skirt, leaving a ghostly palm print. Then, with a practiced glare, she hands me the chalk. "This," she says, "is what grownups do."

I'm dreaming.

"Just listen to your inner voice," soothes the used-books dealer, tucking a hank of her skirt into her belt as she climbs the ladder to retrieve a volume.

My inner voice. Was *that* it — the voice that said that *thank you* to George's father, those two words that meant *Yes, I will marry George Beck?*

"Indeed," says Freud from the high shelf, passing the woman the book. "That, child, was your unconscious: your psyche, speaking up after thirty-three years of silence with two decisive syllables." He exhales a wreath of smoke and taps ash off his cigar. "Your kishkas."

"Hardly," H.D. counters irritably from the base of the ladder, which she steadies as the book dealer descends. Cigar ash rains down on her head. "What you heard was a million years of culture. Ballads and folktales and fairy tales, all conditioning women to speak these two words and nothing more."

"Why are you so passive?" screams the truck driver, leaning out his window as he barrels down the avenue. "Just tell him what you think."

Swimming up through sleep. Soul singers swoon. Lewis Carroll rows his boat across the lake, Alice at the prow. They wave at me, smiling. Their hands grow enormous; their oars turn to flowerpots; their voices are as tiny as mouse prints.

When George phones from Albany, his voice is ratcheted a notch tighter than usual. "I can't talk long now," he says. "I've got a meeting in an hour and I haven't prepared. But I needed to hear your voice."

I sit down on my sofa. "You okay?"

He lets out a long breath. It drops, ripe and trusting, into my ear. "I've had better days," he confesses. "I spoke with my sister this afternoon, and my father got on the line. It took about twenty seconds for him to get to the point. Which was that marriage may yet propel me back into the fold — Jewish wife and all. Assuming, that is, that you convert — otherwise we're not *equally yoked.*"

Oxen laboring through the mud, slipping and struggling to their feet, raising dumb eyes to the unremitting heavens.

I hate my brain.

"Apparently," says George, "there's hope for both of us, but only on Jesus' terms. I told him I thought it likelier we'd be equally yoked under Judaism." The laugh he emits is hollow. "Turns out it wasn't even my father's idea to reach out to me now, but the minister has been reminding him no trouble is too stubborn for the Lord. Only it seems the Lord is used to more obedient sons. My father announced, after three minutes of conversation, that he knew I wasn't worth the effort."

"I'm sorry," I say.

I listen to his silence. I imagine George in my bed. George in his apartment, rolling me over his back, settling me on his sofa, raising his beer bottle. Daring me. The man I'm risking all of this for.

"Hey, lover," I say softly. "How you holding up?"

His voice yields, warms, readmits a trace of humor. "Managing," he says. "In accordance with time-honored tradition, I borrowed a car this afternoon from one of my less nosy colleagues, and I drove until I'd driven the knots out."

I finger the telephone cord. "I can't imagine that."

"Driving doesn't soothe you?"

"Of course not," I say. "You know me —"

But of course, he doesn't. He doesn't know me at all, doesn't know simple things my best friends know — like the fact that my single recurrent dream involves piloting a car along the highway and looking ahead, only to see another car come tumbling across the divider: head over tail, a silent ballet of metal and glass. That as the other car rushes toward me there's no overcoming the passivity of my hands on the wheel. And I drift wide and sail off the curve, my own car now tumbling, rushing toward the verge, the rocky cliff, and, far below, the surf: the endless, dark, frigid, impossible weight of the water, and I call out *no* as though the word were not a command or request but a state of being.

"You don't like driving?" George repeats.

I stare into the blank air of my apartment. I can't answer his question. Neither can I say without doubt that I know a single thing about him.

"Tracy?"

I'm numb. "My parents reserved their flights for Thanksgiving," I murmur. My parents, who have been east only three times in all the years I've been here. "They didn't want to wait any longer to meet you. They want us to plan a quiet getaway, something out of the city." I'm dangerously distracted, still lost in my dream. "I'm sorry," I say, "that you're having such a tough day."

"That's fine about your parents. I'm looking forward to meeting them. Any place you want to go is fine." He hesitates. "The weirdest part, with my father, was that at the end of the conversation he said we'd speak further about my life choices. This, after telling me I wasn't worth his time. I'm guessing the only thing that's keeping him tuned in is the prospect of grandchildren soon."

I rouse myself. "George . . . leaving your father out of this for a second, don't you think it's early to plan children? I mean, do you honestly think we're ready for that?"

He's silent.

"Besides, what sort of lifestyle changes would you make — to accommodate these children you want to have so soon? What on your busy schedule are you willing to give up?"

He's still silent.

"George?"

"These things work out," he says with emphatic innocence.

"They'll work out better," I say, "if we take them slowly."

"But why not dive in? Doesn't it all go together? Getting married, maybe buying a place for the sake of stability, having kids?" George reasons like a traveler who's signed up for the package deal. "If we're going to do it, we may as well —"

"Why are you pushing me?" I snap.

There is a deep pause, a pause that goes on and on. I hear George breathing.

A shrilling pierces the silence. Beneath the dire cry of my fax machine our "damn it"s mingle, indistinct sounds of dread.

He arrives from the airport angry. His suitcase hits the bed, jolting the mattress. His kiss is brief. On the shuttle bus he had two calls on his cell phone. One was his boss, Joel, and George has promised to call back.

He goes into the kitchen. His voice is low and heavy. The conversation lasts several minutes. When it's over, I hear the refrigerator door.

"Joel thinks I need to be drumming up more business," George says, opening the beer bottle as he drops onto my sofa.

While Joel is technically the head of George's consulting group, he and George interact more like college roommates, playing Nerf basketball in the office and notching the results of their rivalry into a wooden paperweight on the office's center table. From what I know, they've never had more than mild differences of opinion, easily patched. Now Joel is suggesting that George raise the number of his consulting engagements in the next few months.

"I'm starting to think it's time to move on," says George. "The salary is too low for the long term."

"But you manage fine as you are. And this job is what you love, right?"

"That may be, but it's no excuse for Joel to treat me like a workhorse. I don't get paid enough to go running all over the country."

It's the first time I've heard him voice dissatisfaction with his salary. "Can you talk to Joel?"

George shrugs, then yawns, eyes averted.

The second phone call on the shuttle bus was from George's father. Civility didn't last three city blocks. For the first time in years, George's father berated him. George flared as well. An utter waste of energy, excepting whatever thrill the other passengers got from hearing a grown man say *Let's leave Satan out of this*. The two went head to head for about half an hour, then lapsed back into their customary silence. Perhaps a bit worse. Pointless to expect more. Pointless to stir that pot. Nothing more to say on the topic.

Paula is excited to meet me.

After George falls asleep I lie with my head on his chest. The angle of my neck is uncomfortable, but I don't move. I wait, as though listening for direction. His sleeping pulse enunciates a steady, unseen labor. In the dark, I set Woolf's words to its rhythm.

. . . *she* [Orlando] *lay content . . . Indeed, she was falling asleep with the wet feathers on her face, and her ear pressed to the ground when she heard, deep within, some hammer or an anvil, or was it a heart beating? Tick-tock, tick-tock, so it hammered, so it beat, the anvil, or the heart in the middle of the earth . . .*

I want to sleep seven days and seven nights and rise a new person. New thoughts, new hopes. A perfect love that casts out fear.

"Can't you just close your eyes," says Yolanda, "and jump? I mean, can't you just *ignore* his talk about kids? You're not going to have one until you decide you're ready, right? So why confront him on it? It will work out over time."

I trail Yolanda between the racks of feathery apparel like a pet begging scraps. This is her favorite dress shop, where she tries on outfits she can't afford and lies in wait for sales. I've met her here on a quick break between lectures. Already I'm checking my watch, gaming the subway route back to my office and how much of my prep time I can skip without the students noticing.

She hands me a black cocktail dress, which I hold for her while she searches out another. "Because something's different," I insist. "The words are the same, but the music's changed. Yolanda, if we love each other, shouldn't it be okay to tell each other the truth?"

Yolanda pauses, one hand sunk in a bloom of aubergine taffeta. "All these years, Tracy, I've thought *I* was the flighty one, and *you* were the pragmatist. I never dreamed I'd say this to you, but you're completely unrealistic. Nobody's totally honest in relationships. Okay, so you're terrified—you'll deal with it. I mean, *we'll* deal with it—I'll help you. But you need to flow with romance, not dissect it."

"Maybe romance is the enemy of love."

"Then fuck love," pronounces Yolanda. She rifles the rack for a long while, leaving me empty-handed.

Abruptly she pulls a low-cut spangled number from the bar, sweeps it in an admiring arc, gathers it against her body. She sashays to the mirror, where she tosses her head like one of those haughty magazine models you'd never want dating anyone you know. Then she lowers her chin and scrutinizes her reflection, its lovely face etched with spider lines and craving.

Posters featuring a black-and-white photograph of Yolanda alongside a review quote in which a critic called her "haunting" have already gone up outside the theater where *Why the Flower Loves the Rod* is due to reopen in a few days. She's getting calls from casting agents who never before gave her the time of day. Bill, however, is still Bill.

"Maybe you ought to try therapy," she says.

"It sounds as though you're experiencing some difficulty adjusting to the concept of marriage." The therapist nods so steadily she reminds me of the wave tanks used in high school physics experiments. Ripples of all-purpose compassion emanate from her bobbing head.

She stops nodding. From beneath her glossy blond bangs she evaluates my expectant silence. She fingers the slim gold band on her left hand. "Maybe you ought to say more about that."

The clock strikes three. I write a check for one hundred and fifty dollars.

Tuesday morning my office phone rings. It's an outside line, a relief: I'm dreading a reprimand from Joanne. I've been skipping meetings, neglecting nonessential departmental duties, barely keeping up with book-order forms for the spring term.

"Aha!" says Rona. "So she *does* answer the phone."

My head swimming with fatigue and irritation, I glance at the clock. "Hi, Rona. I've been busy. Listen, calling me at my office isn't actually so good."

"Of course. But we do need to talk planning. Time is ticking."

I finger the top sheet on the pile of untouched work on my desk. "This isn't a good time to talk about weddings, Rona. I'm at work. I'm in the middle of something."

"Just tell me, have you set a date?"

"Not yet."

"Well," she says. Her voice drops. "Honey, it's natural you would hesitate."

I rest my hand on the stack of papers. "It is?" I ask.

"Well, of course it is, Tracy love! After all, you're making the bigger commitment."

"But George is making the same commitment I am."

"Tracy sweetie, you're the woman. Believe me, you're making a bigger commitment."

Have I just learned more than I ever wanted to know about Aunt Rona's marriage? Or is she trying to tell me something about marriage in general?

"Anyway," she says, "we should talk flowers."

Jeff appears in my doorway. I raise a hand to hold him.

Rona is still talking. "Your mother asked me to think about flowers and food. You know your mother never had a big wedding."

"Rona, I—"

"So I think a big, beautiful wedding could be important to her."

I signal Jeff to wait another minute, but he shakes his head, indicating my clock. Striding to my desk, he pulls a silver pen out of his breast pocket and writes for a moment on my notepad. By the time I spin the pad to read, he's gone.

Signed w. Atlanta. Moving in 2 wks. Grub's shock a thing of beauty for the ages. Joanne choking b/c bailing right after a paid leave Simply Isn't Done. 'Tis. Bequeathing you coffee mug / Brad Pitt button / antacids / Joanne. Congratulate me.

"Okay," says Rona, "so I'm not pressuring you about a date now. Just one thing. Do you like tulips?"

I grip the notepad.

"I've always thought tulips were *lively*." Rona caresses the word like a lucky pair of dice. "You *will* want floral arrangements, right?"

"Rona. We don't even have a date."

"Well, I was just thinking, and I had this idea. Tulips aren't traditional, you know. But I think they're lively."

"Rona, I'm at work right now. Tulips are just fine, for whenever the wedding happens. I'd just need" — this conversation is surreal — "to ask George."

There's a long pause. "I don't see what anyone could have against some nice tulips."

"I'm not saying—"

"Well, you ask your George if you like."

Her hurt reverberates in my silent office.

Outside in the unremitting rain, I curse the weather, my balky umbrella, my aunt, myself. Rona, I know, will echo my mistake back to me into the indefinite future. Rather than indicating my personal tulip friendliness, I should have punted the question, asked George what he thinks of fucking tulips, and come back with a united-front response. If this man and I marry, and if the ceremony does not involve tulips, years from now Rona will still be asking what sort of man — callous, unwholesome, obdurate — doesn't like her beloved tulips. The relationship between my husband and aunt will begin strained, burdened by Rona's offense.

We. I was supposed to say *we.*

George's father and sister spend one night in New York. We arrange to meet at a midtown restaurant: a tasteful, moderately priced sample of a Manhattan that Earl and Paula indict in George's kidnapping. George spends the afternoon with them. When he phones from Paula's room at the Mayflower to fill me in on dinner plans, he greets me with a tense "Hey" that makes me want to carry mace along to the meal.

When I meet George at his apartment he's alone; his father and sister, who wanted to rest after the afternoon's walk in Central Park, will take a cab to the restaurant.

"I didn't expect them to embrace New York." George rubs the back of his neck. "But I expected some expression of appreciation. Even if they do think it's the den of iniquity, et cetera. Even Paula just sort of glanced at the skyline, and then her eyes zeroed in on all the dirt, and she didn't say a damn word. I'd have expected her, at least, to be more open-minded. But both of them just stared at the gritty buildings and gritty people. The things that are only atmosphere when you live here." He blows out air. His face looks uncharacteristically gaunt. Then, after a moment, it's softened by a smile. "But I've got something for you." He opens his briefcase and removes something. Gently he unfolds my hand. On the center of my palm he sets a small and lightweight green velveteen box.

"I couldn't wait anymore," he says in a quiet voice. "If you don't like it we can pick another. But I've been saving up, and I borrowed a bit too."

"You borrowed? But you said—"

George nudges me to open the box.

The ring is a small square gem set in a narrow gold band, two dark green stones on either side. The diamond is exquisitely bright, a fragment of life dancing against the emeralds and green flocking. The stones look like stars.

The ring is beautiful. The gesture is beautiful. The whole moment is as beautiful as a frigid pristine night that silences speech. I stare. "George——" I have no idea how much such a ring costs but the expense is a dreadful heaviness in my gut. My voice is unrecognizably girlish. "Thank you," I whisper.

He slides the ring up my finger. "I love you," he says. "With everything I am." Then, pressing my hand between his until the too loose band digs into the neighboring fingers, George unfurls a sigh as long as all the miles he's traveled in the last thirty-seven years, and I hear it: the watermark left by his loss.

I love you, too.

A battered yellow cab wrests us downtown.

At the restaurant they're already seated. Paula stands as we approach the table and beams up at me: a diminutive gentle-faced woman my age, with her mother's straight brown hair and soft brown eyes. I recall what George said on the way over: *She was always a serious kid. It was like she knew life was going to be hard, and she took to the Bible like an instruction manual.* Trying to open his sister to different ideas—something George attempted in his twenties—was futile. He respects her, though. Now and then when he's in Toronto, after her kids and husband go to sleep, the two of them sit up and talk—something they both look forward to, though their worldviews are barely in the same galaxy. From time to time one of Paula's daughters asks if George believes in Jesus. When George says no, his niece asks why he wants to go to hell.

Paula takes the hand I offer, but instead of shaking squeezes, then kisses me once on each cheek. When she's finished we're both blushing.

The resemblance between George and his father is breathtaking. Earl is a tall, spare man, good-looking in a chiseled way. His cheekbones are prominent and his color high; his forehead shines where the cropped silver hair has receded. He and Paula look like white middle-class relatives from central casting. Not, I am forced to concede, the glassy-eyed fundamentalists a liberal education has trained me to expect.

We sit, Paula beaming, Earl looking dispassionately patient, as though this dinner were a business obligation he'd been unable to avoid.

The waitress brings menus. We read in silence. When she returns, Paula, George, and I order. The waitress, a lean brunette with a crewcut and a nose ring, scrawls on her pad. Earl watches, his gaze decidedly unfriendly.

He snaps his menu shut. "Nothing for me," he says.

"Dad," Paula coaxes, but Earl raises his hand.

Paula smiles ruefully at George. "Interesting menu," she says.

Earl's hand settles back on the tablecloth. I watch it: the dry lined skin of the knuckles, the fingers thickening with age. Its inert weight on the tabletop.

George, beside me, says nothing. Beneath the table I lean my knee against his. His leg sways away under the pressure.

Paula is watching me. Her warm eyes, apologizing into mine, welcome me, caution me, and telegraph a request: keep the conversation flowing. Turning to the waitress, she interrogates her closely about the preparation of the seafood dish she's ordered, receiving each answer with an expression of enthusiasm.

After the waitress leaves, the table is silent.

"So, Tracy." Paula stirs her tea noisily. "Are you kosher?"

It depends how I'm killed.

"No." I offer the sugar bowl, which Paula declines. A quick glance at Earl—who looks away—confirms that I am to address myself to Paula alone. "The truth is that I've never been very religious."

Earl's jaw tightens.

Paula tucks her own opinion into a long sip of tea.

"George tells us you're an English teacher," Earl says abruptly.

Beside me George stirs.

"That's right." The warmth in my own voice shocks me. Earl's surliness is his power. In the space of minutes I've become willing to applaud this man's every nonaccusatory utterance. I lower my voice to a less welcoming pitch. "I teach English literature to undergraduate and graduate students."

"It's a very good job for a woman," Paula chimes in with pleasure. It's obvious she and her father have discussed this. "It makes it easier to have a family."

At this reference to my future childbearing, Earl turns his gaze on me. His brown eyes traveling slowly, he looks me over in a frank appraisal that's unlike any I've ever been subjected to. I hunch forward for a sip of water, then sit back with my arms crossed over my breasts.

"Tracy is an English *professor.*" George addresses his father as though they were the only two at the table. His cheeks are pink, his face alive. He looks like the man I fell in love with. "Her students are lucky to have her. Whatever she decides to do about work and family, she'll be great at it."

The waitress, suddenly Paula's best friend, arrives with bread.

George lays a palm on my thigh. Whatever current pulled him away from me earlier has subsided. He squeezes my leg: wordless assurance of solidarity. As his sister busies herself with the bread basket he reaches for my left hand and caresses the ring, running the pad of his index finger over the three stones as though they were worry beads. His breathing slows. Before eating he turns to me with an expression that makes full apology for his faults, and declares humble appreciation for my companionship at this painful cornerstone of his life, where he's taken no lover before.

That night I dream we scuba-dive through caverns, hands tightly clasped. George, moving gracefully beside me, is more beautiful than I could ever have imagined. His eyes are filled with wonders; his face, shed of mourning, is radiant in the depths. Pulling me forward through the cool water, oblivious to my dwindling air, my repeated attempts to make my hands execute the signal to surface, he dives ever deeper.

I wake with my hands urgent on his body. We're making love, our breath sharp in the dark room. We pause only long enough for a condom, then knock pillows to the floor, tumble across the bed's surf of white sheets, lie still.

It's as good as ever. So why, as I slip back into sleep, do I grieve?

I exit the elevator and am greeted by Steven, who is positioned beside the departmental mailboxes with coffee in hand and an insouciant expression. He raises his mug in salute. "How's it going?"

Nearby, Elizabeth is absorbed in study of the faculty bulletin board.

I nod. "And you?"

"Couldn't be better." Steven gestures toward my mail slot. "I think you'll like what you find in there."

I draw the stack of envelopes from the slot, irritated at this further confirmation that the contents of faculty mailboxes are no secret — not to those who loiter in Eileen's presence.

From her desk, Eileen, who has awaited this moment, preempts my good news with a loud singsong. "Look who's gotten an invitation to *the* holiday party."

I glance up at her, then down at the top envelope on the stack. The paper is thick, cream-colored, and the flap bears the gold-embossed crest of the university. I open the stiff envelope with some difficulty and draw out a single card that begs my presence at a private holiday gathering, hosted by the president of the university, to be held in three weeks in the Howard Perry Room of the faculty club.

"What's the Howard Perry Room?"

"Holy of holies," says Steven. "Only the deans and provosts and such use it. This is the inner-circle party."

I look up. "How do *you* know this stuff?"

Steven smirks.

I study the invitation. "Since when do junior faculty get invited to these things? Or visiting professors, for that matter?"

Steven takes a conspiratorial step closer. "I've made some friends here. My chairman at Oxford roomed with Dean Hopkins at Andover. I was introduced around in September. Word must have spread that I was a thoughtful bloke" — he punctuates this with a grin — "and that you were an up-and-coming. You and I championed a contemporary curriculum, and that approach is winning. These things get noticed. You and I are invited. So are Manning and Judson, of course" — a.k.a. Grub and Paleozoic — "but nobody else from the department."

"I didn't champion a contemporary curriculum. I just asked for balance."

"This is great for you," he says. "If the people whispering in the president's ear start tapping you for the Perry Room, you're untouchable. Things are changing here. The traditionalists are in for some unhappy surprises." He doesn't look the least bit sorry for them.

I study Steven. "Thanks," I say.

He winks.

"Wear something *elegant*." Eileen draws out the word. "Not like you wear to teach."

A quick mental catalogue of the contents of my closet finds them inadequate. Filing away the wearying prospect of dress shopping,

I slide the invitation into my briefcase for later scrutiny. I hesitate, then address Steven once more. "I just don't want to give the impression I'm siding against anything written before nineteen hundred."

"Aren't you?" he teases.

"No." I fumble. "I mean, I'm the biggest Melville fan there is. I'd teach him — and some earlier writers, too — if my schedule allowed it."

Another wink. "No worries," Steven says.

I give my best inscrutable smile and start for my office.

"No!" Elizabeth's ferocity arrests me midstride. I turn to find her facing Steven, fists clenched by her sides, her forehead knit with fury. Steven steps back. His elbow bumps the mailboxes and a wide slosh of coffee hits the floor.

"Tracy isn't ignoring earlier writers at all!"

A half-alarmed smile curls on Steven's mouth. "Whoa," he says. "Relax there, friend."

"She's got a ton of respect for earlier works! Her whole new project is about Tolstoy. And taking on the whole idea of tragedy. And considering American literature within and against that paradigm. And she's going to break open the whole question of happy endings in American literature."

My face is burning.

Steven no longer looks alarmed. He looks amused. He slides the sole of his shoe into the spilled coffee and taps a pale dotted arc on the linoleum floor. "Really?" he says. He looks at me.

I make a noncommittal gesture.

"Isn't that a bit broad?"

"Not the way she's going to do it," says Elizabeth. "She's picking all the right examples. It's going to be really big."

"Elizabeth!" I cut in. She stops speaking, gives me a frustrated look, and turns back to the bulletin board.

"That's enough on that subject," I say, although Elizabeth no longer seems interested in the conversation. I turn to Steven. "It's just an idea. Just in the beginning stages. I talked about it vaguely with Elizabeth."

Steven pats the toe of his shoe in the coffee. It makes a faint plashing. "It's bold, all right. You're probably crazy." Stepping to the verge of the corridor, he grinds his shoe into the rug, drying it more thoroughly than it could possibly require. He stares at me. "Or maybe you're incredibly canny. If you could pull that off, it would be colossal."

In a confusion of alarm and pride, I nod. Steven leaves, presumably for his office.

"What's so controversial about this project of yours, Tracy?" asks Eileen.

"It's . . . complicated. Okay if I tell you some other time?" Before Eileen can respond I turn my back on her and take Elizabeth's elbow.

Leading her down the hall feels like ushering a reluctant schoolchild to the principal's office. At one point she literally drags her feet, and I have to put my hand on her shoulder to coax her forward.

"You're angry at me," she says when I've closed my office door.

"You bet."

She looks miserable. Then, from some heretofore dormant depth of Elizabeth, defiance flares across her face. "It's stupid to be ashamed," she says. "It's a great idea."

"I'm not ashamed. I'm prudent. At least I was, until you decided to out my project to the entire department."

"I'm sorry," she bats back. It's obvious she doesn't mean it.

"Elizabeth, what's going on? Don't you remember promising to keep my project under wraps?"

She picks up a pen from my desk and clicks it repeatedly.

"I've known you for a few years now," I say. "Elizabeth, something's changing. What's going on?"

She sets the pen sharply onto the desktop. "I'm all right. Yes, I used to get a bit flighty. But I'm fine now."

"What do you mean, *flighty?*"

She watches me. "I get stressed-out, that's all. I've got a lot of stress. You know all about that, you're the one who's been standing up for me."

At this overdue acknowledgment that I've tried to protect her, I soften. The clock on my wall indicates I've got only fifteen minutes to prepare for seminar. "You getting any rest?" I say.

She doesn't answer.

"Please, Elizabeth, don't talk about my project in public again."

"I promise." This time she sounds sincere.

She leaves. I settle into my chair. Before forcing myself into *The House of Mirth,* I indulge myself in a brief replay of Steven Hilliard's voice pronouncing the word "colossal."

My mother, who does not buy outfits, has bought outfits for this holiday in the Catskills. She fusses with the buttons of her new sweaters and is painfully shy around George. With me, she is abnormally voluble.

The grassy, starlit parking lot is deserted. The air smells of woodsmoke. In the dark beyond the parking lot the hills roll on for miles, beckoning me with a blunt, chilly clarity I trust. There's no sound but the wind in the bare trees around the inn. No evidence, other than a half-dozen parked cars, of the mountainside inn's other patrons, tucked away in their lamplit rooms, presumably readying themselves for tomorrow's Thanksgiving feast.

Still, my mother, suddenly a font of gossip, whispers. "You remember Theresa and Watson from next door?"

"The ones from L.A.?" I can't help whispering in reply.

"They have a *terrible* fertility problem."

I hoist my weekend bag higher onto my shoulder.

"The problem is Watson's," she continues. "They're seeing a specialist."

The injustice of it stuns me: now that I've made a life choice she understands, she's eager to provide a map of the world.

Silhouetted in the inn's lighted doorway, my father claps a hand to George's neck and waves. I follow my mother toward the entrance.

Since George and I greeted my parents at the airport this afternoon, my father has hardly spoken to me. Instead, he's peppered George with questions and nodded vigorous approval of every answer. And George — I couldn't help noticing as I sat speechless in the back seat — was perfect. Courteous, solicitous without being smarmy, funny without crossing any lines of propriety. The two of them fell into a hearty friendliness that continued as George piloted us north in the rented car, the tension of their postures easing in the front seats as their conversation grew steadily more genuine.

Do fathers always greet their future sons-in-law with such grim cheer? Do they always shift their gazes from their daughters with that suddenly preoccupied expression? *If you're going to choose another man then I'm going to grit my teeth and make best friends with him and ignore you until you have children.* My father, who always said I could be anything I wanted to be, doesn't seem to have planned for my becoming a wife. He is taking my engagement personally. It is obvious I need to say something to him about this.

You tell me what.

Here is my recollection of adolescence: You grow breasts (even if they are not particularly significant breasts), and everyone changes overnight. People you used to count on suddenly find you uninteresting. Other people — ones who never had much to say to you — are abruptly unshakable.

Engagement, I am coming to believe, is a second set of breasts.

"How's work, Dad?" I say when we join them in the inn's foyer.

"Fine," says my father, smiling as though he's trying to remember my name.

"How about some hot soup?" my mother interjects.

I want to curl up in her arms.

We settle into our rooms, separated by a discreet distance. At this juncture it seems pointless to mention to George that these are not my parents. And in any event he doesn't look as though he'd want to believe me. His face is animated. He undresses slowly, like a man who's finally, after a despairing search, stumbled across a club to which he belongs, and he hates to let go of the day. Only one thing seems to perturb him. He settles beside me on the mattress. Wrapping his arms around my waist, he says, "Just one thing, Trace." He nuzzles my neck. "And I'm sure you didn't mean anything by it. But I didn't appreciate your mentioning my job trouble in the car."

Holding loosely to his arms, I sift my memory of the last few hours' exchanges, at last unearthing the small conversational nugget. "But all I said was you've been doing a lot of travel. And that you may have some tough negotiations ahead. I didn't say anything about trouble."

"I don't want them to think I'm not a good provider." He sits on the bed.

"But I didn't mention money. I just said *tough negotiations*. They wouldn't —"

"You made it sound like I was struggling."

"George." I settle against the wooden headboard. "I don't get it."

He sits in silence for a long time. When he speaks he begins heavily, reluctant. "I didn't tell you about my conversation with my father," he says. "Just before they left for the airport on Thursday. There wasn't time to tell you. And I honestly didn't want to." His face colors slightly. "My father says I don't have a clue what it takes to support a family."

"I'm sorry, George. I'm really sorry." I watch him. "But really, we don't have to care, do we? Your father's opinions are back in Toronto, and they can stay there."

His voice turns adamant. "He's right. Joel hasn't given me a raise in years."

"But that's because money is tight. It's not a sign of disrespect. And you love your work. You've told me you're all right with the money."

"That was before."

"Before what?"

He looks at me as though I am being obtuse on purpose. "Before we got engaged. I'm ready to move forward with life. I want a family salary."

"Don't forget, George, I earn a salary too."

His expression sours: this was the wrong thing to say. He rises. As he speaks he paces the length of the room. "I want to move forward. I want to start our family." He stops by the door and faces me. "I'd like to set a date, Tracy."

I draw a deep breath, and stumble off script. "You're freaking me out."

George looks unstrung. He returns to the bed and settles beside me. He lies on his back, hands beneath his head. He doesn't touch me, but stares at the ceiling. "I know I've been difficult."

"You do?"

"I've been preoccupied. And . . . revved." He falls silent. Then he props himself on one elbow and, taking my hand, cradles it in both of his palms, considering its bejeweled architecture. "I don't like to admit this, Tracy." He looks into my eyes, questioning.

"Go ahead," I say.

"And I hope you won't think less of me, although I know you might."

"Tell me." At the prospect of some heretofore untold secret, an explanation for the way George has been acting, my pulse races.

"Sometimes," he says, "I doubt myself."

I wait in vain for him to continue. "That's it?" I say at length.

He chooses his words with care. "I doubt my ability to live the life I've hoped for. I doubt my ability to make the grade in the daily grind. I think there are some things — good things — my father accomplished that I may not be able to achieve."

"But of course you feel that. Everyone worries about those things. Don't you think?"

"Not everyone," he says softly. "Sometimes I think I'm just not going to measure up." A moment passes. Then his gaze leans into mine. Relief washes his eyes. Slowly the tension in his body seems to drain. "It's good to trust you like this, Tracy."

I'm not sure he should.

For years I believed I understood men. I was comfortable teasing Adam, jousting with Jeff, critiquing male authors whose texts I mined in an intimacy known only to scholars. Now it's clear to me that all along there was some core impenetrable to me: an untouchable, red-hot male region of shame.

I do not understand men. I understand only that George has just opened his heart to me in a way he hasn't for weeks. And that my job is to place suddenly awkward arms around this one man I've loved. To cradle his head, gingerly, in my lap.

"George," I say after a long time. "I'm sorry your father doesn't have faith in you. I have absolute faith that you can *measure up*. More than measure up . . . whatever that means. And as far as I'm concerned your job is just fine." I hesitate. "Also, listen, I know my parents, and they're not going to think less of you for a mention of difficult negotiations. *Everyone* has difficult negotiations, about one thing or another. There's no shame in that. Everyone has difficulties."

George raises his brows: not, apparently, future sons-in-law. "I'm just making a request," he says. He smiles to soften the impact of this conversational trump card. "If you want we can talk about it more tomorrow. I'm fried." Then he kisses me, squeezes my hand, and, sliding beneath the covers, turns out the light. At first I think he's going to reach for me, but his breath slows so quickly I know sleep's ambushed him.

The low-ceilinged room is silent.

Is that part of the marriage contract? Wives pretending their husbands have no troubles?

George begins to snore.

If so, then every married woman is the keeper of a secret: her husband's vulnerability. This is absurd. I will not be married if it means lying to everyone close to me. Isn't the best thing I have — despite a thousand faults and obstinacies — my honesty? Isn't pretending men have no doubts the very thing that keeps all the stupid macho stuff going? I'm certain my parents wouldn't flinch at something as ordinary as *tough negotiations*.

Unless they would. Unless they all adhere to an unspoken patriarchal code: my parents, George, the married set, all conspiring to keep the world safe from the least tremor on a male emotional Richter scale.

I recall my conversation with Hannah, the day of the engagement — only this time the phrase that pops into my head is: *the day I lost George.*

Is that it? Is it all lost — the delicate fun, the lightness, the companionship between us? Did its heart stop beating that day?

At breakfast the next morning I leave the scrambled eggs on my plate and can't get down my coffee. George and I aren't going to make it. I cannot be a wife: his, anyone's. We're leading my poor, game, color-coordinated parents through a social charade we'll all regret.

Midway through breakfast, my mother falls silent. As we rise from the table to prepare for the day's hiking she gives me a quiet, intimate look I don't understand.

We spend the day hiking gullies of boulder and pine. The fresh air is bracing, the vistas austere and lovely. George and my parents comment on the landscape and share safe family stories. I'm light-headed from hunger, tightlipped. All day my mother's eyes seek mine — concerned, empathic, reassuring.

Baffling.

Yet I can't recall a moment since childhood when I so longed for an audience with her.

After dinner George and my father step out to the inn's reception area to consult maps for tomorrow's hike. My mother and I settle in front of the fireplace.

"So, Mom." I stretch first one calf, then the other, then roll onto my side, deliberately casual as though dealing with a flight-prone animal. I want so much from her it frightens me. I don't know how to say all I mean. A minute passes; George and my father won't be gone long. "Tell me," I say, "about marriage."

She nods gravely—as though she's been waiting thirty-three years for me to ask. "Well," she says carefully. "Two people just get along."

I stare. "Okay. But I mean—you and Dad. And the other couples you've seen. What makes marriage succeed? In your opinion?"

She looks into the fire. For a moment her face works. When she turns to me her eyes are clear, her words quick with the thrill of confession. "Sometimes you have sex more often than you feel like it."

The fire emits a loud pop.

"That's it?" I say.

She nods. She sits back, visibly animated at having divulged this secret. She takes a long drink of her wine.

I stare, incredulous. Exposed yet again, years beyond the point where my childhood hopes should have expired, as a fool.

As though he'd been watching from the hall, the inn's burly waiter comes in to offer a refill of her wineglass. She accepts. Once more he offers me a glass, and once more I decline. He leaves. I turn back to my mother. She's not looking at me, but watching the fire with an expression of wonder, and sorrow, and fulfillment. It's then, and only then, that I understand her flushed solidarity for the falsehood it is.

"I'm not pregnant," I say.

She offers a slight, knowing smile. Disbelieving.

Without another word I get up and head to the kitchen, where I tersely obtain a cigarette and a light from a bored busboy. Returning to the inn's fire, I manage to smoke without coughing, despite the fact that I haven't touched a cigarette in years. She turns back to the fire. I watch as her expression ranges from shock to an almost heartbreaking disappointment; then to a stony sort of relief.

By the time she turns back to me, her face is once more blank. A blankness in which I recognize my own paralysis.

The men return, amiably silent. George sets a tray of hot cocoa on the table and brings me a mug, then settles behind me and begins to knead my shoulders. My father summons my mother to the hallway to consult the map. Alone in the room with George, I glare at the fire.

"You didn't tell me your father was into fishing," he says. "We're already talking about a summer trip."

The dry heat hurts my eyes.

"You know, Tracy," he says, "I've waited so long for this. For you. I waited so long for someone I *recognized*, Tracy. Ever since I left Toronto for college I thought, I left home and now I'm cursed: I'll never have that whole life."

His words bounce off me.

"The love, the sense of family, the kids, the house. I thought: that's the price I have to pay for freedom. Then I met you, and it just, you know . . ." His speech falters; he takes my hand. ". . . grabbed me. That I *can* go back to that dream. It's just . . . the most clear, the most compelling . . ." His voice trails, regroups. ". . . *vision*. As though I can be forgiven everything."

His words scatter among the embroidered pillows and crocheted throw blankets until they're silenced by my parents' return.

My father settles onto the sofa opposite me. His gray, curly hair is silver in the firelight, his face kind. Concerned. "Tracy," he says.

Slowly I blow across the scalding surface of the cocoa.

"Have you considered mutual funds?"

"This is where the bride would come down," says the assistant events coordinator as she strides along the bare pavement between the dark, barbed-looking shrubs of the Botanical Gardens. I slow, falling behind Yolanda, who has locked step with our hostess.

This foray was, needless to say, Yolanda's idea. "We'll have our walk today," she said this morning. "I promise. We'll just do it someplace else that I have in mind. It'll be like homeopathy. Try a teeny dose of wedding planning. You'll see it's not toxic. You might even start to imagine yourself walking down the aisle with him."

"And here," continues our hostess breathlessly—she of shining countenance, the sort of girl who loses sleep worrying that she'll cry at her own wedding and she's not sure waterproof mascara really holds—"is where the guests would sit."

We stand in a paved clearing. Silvery tree trunks and bare metal trellises surround us, the winter beauty of an urban garden. One might almost forget the city bristling a few hundred yards away—except for the beeping of a truck, backing up somewhere beyond the circular drive.

I have to be at a faculty meeting in fifty minutes. "What about the traffic noise?" I say.

Yolanda rolls her eyes. I'm not opening my heart to the wedding spirit.

Our hostess's smile is all sweetness: I've made her day by asking. "In the spring," she breathes, "when the leaves are put on, they really break the sound barrier."

*Whhhoooooooshhh*BOOM! Here comes the bride.

"That'll be perfect," says Yolanda.

"Congratulations," I say to Jeff. "Richard must be thrilled. And I hope the department there is as good as it sounds."

He purses his lips. "Mad at me for leaving?"

I sigh.

"How's your work, O bride?"

I shrug.

He raises his coffee for a toast. "Keep your pecker up, as the Brits would say. You're going to get tenured. I'll fly up from Atlanta to lead the voting parade next month."

I nod my thanks. "I hope you can persuade them. I suspect you've lost a bit of political clout."

"Don't be absurd. Yes, I've lost clout—I turned into a ghost the instant I announced my resignation. No one's going to invest in camaraderie if they know you won't be around to reciprocate. But my status isn't going to hurt you. You never needed my help for tenure."

Eileen appears outside Jeff's office doorway. "*Good* afternoon," she sings. "I thought I'd hand-deliver these." In her hand is a stack of photocopies.

Jeff sips his coffee without glancing at her. "You know," he says to me sotto voce, "how Thomas Pynchon's never been photographed, or seen in public? America's mystery author? Well, I've solved the mystery." Almost imperceptibly he tilts his head toward Eileen. "It's *her*."

Eileen approaches his desk. And then, as if she's just noticed me, "Oh, Tracy!"

Jeff leans back in his chair, arms folded.

"So have you set a date yet?" Eileen prods, still holding Jeff's photocopies.

"Not yet, Eileen."

"*Really?*" She plants her broad bottom on the edge of Jeff's desk and, hugging the photocopies to her bosom, faces me. "Why not?"

Jeff laughs aloud.

Yolanda leads me into the photographer's apartment. "She's supposed to be the best," she whispers. "I had to call in a favor to get this appointment, so behave yourself."

"You said we were going to your yoga class."

"We are. After."

"And you said you just needed my company on a quick errand of *yours*."

"That's right. This is my errand. It's my *mission*. It's not like I have much else going on in my life these days anyway." Patently untrue — *Why the Flower Loves the Rod* is a week into its second run, and Yolanda has had a surge in audition callbacks for other projects. Still, since my engagement she's never been too busy to let me trail her, miserable company though I've been. "I'm going to show you," she says, "that wedding planning isn't too clichéd for an intellect like you. And it *doesn't* have to be terrifying. And this way if you like this photographer's work, you can call her the minute you set a date."

On the walls of the photographer's apartment are large color wedding portraits and soft-focus hilltop picnic scenes. Most are shots of the photographer's own family — the women straight-backed and tailored, the men trim-bellied and hair-gelled. The photographer — a woman in her mid-fifties with frosted hair, designer glasses, an impeccable mauve suit and matching manicure — settles her sample album on the table.

Glancing to my right, I indicate a photo hanging on the wall:

a generously sized portrait of a bride and groom surrounded by a half-dozen others, including the photographer herself in a gold lamé dress. "Your children?"

"That's my son," says the photographer with pride. Her finger-nails click briskly against the tabletop. "He's divorced now. But we all look so good in that portrait I couldn't discard it." She smiles fondly at the picture. "So I lasered in one of my cousin's daugh-ters. The body in the wedding dress is Steve's ex-wife, but the face is his cousin Emma."

Emma's plump, freshly scrubbed face looks somewhat disori-ented atop a slim, lovely figure, about to be wed to her second cousin. And it is under Emma's glazed smile that I am led, page by page, through the perfect pictorial story my wedding could be. Price tag: $4,200.

Yolanda, doggedly attentive, looks like she's in pain.

"*Everyone* marries under false pretenses." The deli cook slams down her heavy pot. "Why do you think they bother making the vows so binding? Doesn't matter if you've known the person your whole life, you're still in for a rude shock."

"So what?" Her husband brandishes a cleaver. "After a few years your spouse is just a force you maneuver around." He takes aim at a chicken breast.

Stepping out of the deli onto the sidewalk I take refuge in my headphones. The radio is tuned to an R and B station. "*Wedlock,*" Laura Lee wails into my ears,

> *is a padlock*
> *when you're married to a no-good man.*

I try to cross the street, find the traffic signals unintelligible, freeze amid the flow of pedestrians.

> *Girl, when you cut the cake don't make a big mistake*
> *Make sure of who you love*
> *Honey, I'm telling you it's easy to get into*
> *But hard to get out of*

A sledder whizzing down the snowless avenue slows to offer me a lift. It's Ethan Frome. *Hop on,* he says.

• • •

Adam strides along Riverside Park, bare hands jammed in the pockets of his jacket.

"Thanks for meeting me in the middle of the day," I say.

He shrugs, then blows on his hands and slaps them together. "What's going on? I've only got twenty minutes 'cause we've got some damn meeting." Pulling a pair of drumsticks from his back pocket, he breaks stride and raps a sharp riff on the metal-pipe fence. "How's the fiancé? He still the man?"

"I'm not sure, Adam." I slow my words: a vain attempt to steady my voice. "The way I fell in love with him was just different, from everything else before. But so much feels just *wrong* now." It's the last of November, the air snappy. I shiver despite my gloves and coat. "And there's a ton, a ton I don't know about him. And I wasn't ready to get engaged. And now this last month has been Invasion of the Body Snatchers. Suddenly I'm supposed to just leap into a wedding gown, beaming. Nobody's acting normal. Including me."

Without glancing at me, Adam drums along the fence.

"I just don't get why he proposed so soon," I add.

Adam strikes a sharp chime on a post, then resumes a tattoo on the top rail. "He thought you two had an understanding."

"But listen—" The mountains laid low, the valleys upraised: I am turning to Adam Freed for advice. "How could he have missed the fact that I wasn't ready to get engaged yet?"

"He thought you were just being shy."

"*Shy?* Why would I be shy about my own engagement?" But even as I protest I see Adam is right. I *was* shy. George raised the issues of children and long-term commitment for weeks, and I kept myself ignorant for fear of overreaching. I was afraid—this a full generation after feminism was declared victorious—to break the magic by being too assertive. I was cowed by love, terrified I'd want more than he was willing to give, terrified I'd want less.

With a whirl, Adam brings down his sticks and crashes them on the roof of a trash bin; this proves so satisfying that he braces his sneakers against the bin's broad base and executes a solo loud enough that two patrolling police officers stop to listen from a distance.

I raise my voice. "He's acting just . . . not like George."

It's hard to make out Adam's words over the din. "Something must be up."

"Yeah," I say. "Suddenly he says he's self-doubting or something. He's afraid he won't be good at supporting us, or some damn thing. It makes no sense. Plus, all of a sudden he's wrapped up with his father again—he's got this icy fundamentalist father he'd given up on, only now George seems to care what he thinks."

Adam shrugs without missing a beat. "All that could flip a guy out," he says. "Married guys think they have to know how to run the farm. And fight off intruders. And do CPR on the manual transmission. The dinner check's gonna get handed to them for the rest of their lives. They think they have to be action heroes. That's why I'm marrying"—a crash on the metal bin—"a weightlifter millionairess."

"But why wouldn't—" My words are drowned out.

"Is the deal that you're not sure about George altogether"—three enormous crashes followed by a drumroll crescendo—"or is it that you know he's your guy, but you just don't want the whole marriage deal yet?"

My voice deflates. "I don't even know," I say shakily, doubtful Adam can hear. "All of a sudden he's like another person. He gets where he's not even talking to me . . . it's like he's talking to this . . . *agenda.* I can barely remember who he is."

Adam stops drumming. "Then you should break off the engagement."

I search his face: he's not kidding. "I don't want to," I shoot back, surprising myself. "I don't want to lose him. I don't know what to do."

"Jeez, Trace, you sound fucking scared. You seem to be under the impression that George can just *marry* you."

"Can't he?"

"Not without you marrying him back. You have power. What's this with the sudden wet-noodle act? You can tell him you want an eight-year engagement, and you want to get married on Lake Serenity on the moon, and"—his eyebrows bounce—"you want *me* to perform the ceremony. You can tell him anything you like. I mean, he'll either go for it or not, but you get some say in this too. This is *your* damn engagement, right?"

I hesitate, then nod.

"What does George say about this freak-out of yours?"

"He doesn't exactly know how bad it is."

Adam looks appalled. "You're joking."

"Everybody said not to push him too hard, or he'd bolt. Everybody said it would leave a scar."

"Everybody. You mean, women?"

I nod, suddenly embarrassed.

"You mean my sister?"

Another nod.

"Crapola. My sister's smart but she's also a moron. She thinks men are made of glass. If this guy loves you, it's not going to break him in half to hear you're fucked over by the engagement. I mean, *he'll* be fucked over, but he'll deal. And if he doesn't, you're better off knowing that's the kind of life you'd of been signing on for. Besides, if you don't tell him what's up, you're doomed. Either you'll start foaming at the mouth and you'll break off the engagement the day before the wedding, or else you'll be, like, Mrs. Robot Wife."

I start to cry, but it feels like relief. I feel like hugging Adam. He seems to know this, and resumes walking. I say, "This is the most helpful conversation I've —"

He flings out his arms to form a great Y, drumsticks piercing the heavens in acknowledgment of the multitudes' adulation.

George meets me at the entrance to the park. He wears a navy sweater under his black wool jacket. His shoulders are broad, his cheeks rosy, his breath a white plume in the new-hatched cold. He looks indisputably, wondrously solid. I tell myself: trust this man.

He takes my gloved hand. Our fingers, too thick to interlace, settle into a loose, insensate hold. We set off along the edge of Sheep Meadow, past a scattering of pedestrians dressed in dark colors, collars raised against a chill deep enough to make your ears glow with pain.

"I'm lost, George," I say.

"I know," he says. His voice is strained. "I don't understand what's gone wrong."

Squeezing, I find his hand in the depths of his glove. "These last weeks have thrown me. I can't breathe."

We walk for another moment before he answers. "I assumed going quickly was the best thing."

We pass a steaming pretzel cart. A man whirs by in a wheelchair, propelling himself with long scoops of his arms. With a synchronous absent-mindedness we turn deeper into the park, past the shuttered façade of the carousel. We walk in silence. George doesn't speak or look at me. His glove clasps mine so loosely it hardly feels like his hand is inside.

"George, I'm asking you to tell me honestly. What's your rush?"

He does not answer. We pass the dairy, pausing to allow a few rosy-cheeked toddlers in moon suits, shepherded by their stunned-looking parents, to amble across the path in front of us. When they've passed I start forward, but George hasn't moved. He gestures wordlessly after the toddlers. I turn to him; his face is tense with longing.

"Yes. I can imagine it, too," I say. "But we haven't even figured out the marriage thing yet. We haven't even learned how we solve problems together. Why jump ahead? Since you started pushing, it's like you're a stranger."

He emits a strangled sound: the sound of someone about to override his better judgment and say something he shouldn't. "Tracy," he says. "Life is a lot easier if you don't overthink everything. If you just take some leaps."

I speak softly. "Imagine the leap I just took for you."

"We both took a —"

"George, like it or not, this is who I am: someone who wants to consider each step she takes. I can't quite understand why you're so surprised by my taking marriage seriously. I start to worry about how unseriously you seem to take it."

"Tracy." He turns to me. His face wears the loneliness I've glimpsed there before. This time, though, it is distilled into a plea for my understanding. His gaze leans into the words as though he's struggling with a foreign tongue and doesn't trust his speech to communicate all he intends. "There has never been anything more serious in my life."

I set my hand on his arm, and nod.

He continues. "I think, Tracy, that this is harder for men than you realize."

I touch his cheek with my gloved fingertips. "You know," I murmur, "that's what Adam said."

George's expression solidifies. "You talked to Adam?"

"Just about how I thought engagement was affecting your outlook—"

"You said that?"

"I told him a little about our recent conversations, but—"

He pulls away. His silence is more alarming than any retort.

After a minute he says, "You talked about what my father said? And my concerns about finances?"

"Why is that bad?" I ask. "He thought it was totally understandable. We're talking about *Adam* here."

His words are clipped. "That was a confidence I entrusted to you. You repeated it."

"I'll keep secrets for you, George. I'll keep any secret, anything at all, if it's reasonable. But I won't keep the secret that you're a human being."

He shakes his head roughly, then takes a step away from me. He wears a look of pure shock—as though he's undergone a sudden amputation without anesthetic. "Tracy, this throws our trust into question."

"It's not a matter of trust, George. It's just . . ." My hands rise to plead my case but have nowhere to go. "It's just that I don't think you need to feel shamed. I have a different sense of—"

"Don't tell me what to feel." His voice quakes, his face registers vertigo. "Don't try to control me."

Some red line has been crossed. This man may be my soul mate, but something is holding him by both shoulders.

We walk. As we near the back of the zoo I picture them as though they were right before me: the polar bears in their concrete arctic dioramas, and their dirtied fur raises inchoate objections in my throat. Slowly I'm filling with rage at marriage: the alien language in which George and I now struggle to communicate. Trailing George, I shut my eyes and try to imagine myself without him. I discover that I can. I can picture going back to a solitary life, a life of predictable comforts, intimate friendships, and invigorating projects.

But I don't want to. And there is only one way to restore breathable air to this abruptly suffocating park. Every love—I see this as clearly as if it were written across the frigid sky — comes down eventually to the issuing of a dare. *Try to change me, and I will leave you.* And everything hangs on how this challenge is played out.

I stop walking, as does he. "You know what I want?" I say. "I want you to be with *me*. Not with some hypothetical blushing bride. You're acting like you've gotten engaged to an idea, not a woman." I look to the park benches, the passersby, the little children in snowsuits, as though to corral them as witnesses. When I continue my voice is softer. "I want to be with you more than anyone I've ever known. But not if we've got to be two figurines on a wedding cake." I hesitate. "Remember, George? Remember what we're like together?"

His lips are pursed in thought, his face turned down. My hand floats to his shoulder and then, when he does not respond, to his cheek. I do not pause to consider what I'm about to do. There seems, at this moment, nothing to consider. "We've got to start over," I say. "I can't do it this way."

I pull off my left glove. There is a sharp, buzzing sensation in my head, like the loud protest of a loose wire. I finger the ring — sparkling, understated, exactly what I would have pictured had I ever dreamed myself an engagement ring. "This is beautiful. And I want to wear it because it's from you. Please give it to me when you want to be my partner."

I unfurl George's gloved fingers. With a quick prayer that Adam is right and Hannah a moron, I set the ring in George's motionless palm.

"Until then," I say, "let's spend every day together. Let's move in together, George. My place or yours, I don't care. Let's figure out every step together as lovers and best friends."

He looks up. His eyes are quiet and clear, as though something has at last penetrated the fog of the past few weeks.

"I love you," I say.

He shuts his eyes and keeps them shut. I have a long time to read his face, which seems more handsome and honest than ever before. He breathes evenly, as though relieved of some great weight.

After what seems like minutes, he opens his eyes with an unreadable expression. He pockets the ring. Then, without another glance at me, he turns his back and walks away.

PART III

I STALK MANHATTAN for hours, fueled by a tumble of urges, turning east, west, south, or north as WALK signs dictate. If I stop moving — so goes my thinking — something terrible will happen. In this manner, following Broadway and its tributaries into the mid-Nineties, I ignore the fact that something terrible already has. I watch the sidewalk, noting as for the first time Manhattan's topography. *How easy it is* — the thought seems to take several blocks to form in my mind — *to forget that there's geology under all this concrete, until it rears up beneath you.* I stride the hills and contours of Manhattan's scarified face. Crossing Broadway, I fall in behind a teenaged boy walking two huskies. An old man crossing opposite us glares as he nears the trio, then points a finger at one of the huskies in ferocious accusation. "You owe me a beer!" he shouts.

If George were here, he'd think this was hilarious. And this — the picture of George wagging his head with laughter, squeezing my hand as we make our way down the sidewalk — is what rends the spell that has held me together since afternoon. The cabdriver listens without comment as I sob for seventy blocks. I stumble into my apartment, its white walls liquid, and fall asleep on the sofa with a comforter pulled over my face.

I wake at five in the morning, my head ringing with silence. Lying still is intolerable. My apartment is stifling. I dress in sweatpants and sweatshirt, throw on my coat, and take the elevator to the street. The morning is cold and cloudy. I make my way to Twenty-first Street and lap Gramercy Park with the bundled dog walkers and insomniacs, pausing at random, drifting mindlessly around the locked fence. The sun inches higher in the white sky. Schoolchildren and their parents begin to appear, lunch bags in hand. I wheel at the sight of a tall man walking down the sidewalk toward my building.

Not George.

I continue my circuit.

Seated on a bench along the downtown side of the park is an ancient-looking woman. Her face reminds me of melting wax, and her chin and neck—if they can be said to be two separate features—exhibit the same glacial flow downward as the mound that is breasts and belly. Her cheeks are soft with wrinkles; her eyes rheumy, suggestive of some capacious sympathy.

Drawn to her slumped figure, which looks as if it's traveled the earth, I hesitate beside her bench.

Her eyes meet mine, their soft gaze sampling my face. She works her jaw for a moment before speaking. "Welcome to the patriarchy," she snaps.

Maybe Tolstoy was right. We're doomed.

Hannah prepares tea in my kitchenette. She arranges mugs and spoons on my coffee table deliberately, saying nothing until I reach the bit where I mentioned to George that I'd spoken with Adam. Then her hand flies to her mouth.

"Okay," she says. "Okay."

Which clearly means it isn't.

"I think, Tracy, that the mistake was to tell George you spoke to Adam."

This makes me feel so sick I can't answer.

"Did you apologize?"

Reluctantly I shrug: I don't exactly recall.

"You're dealing with a man, Tracy. Men might talk to women about their doubts. But they don't tell each other. And they can't bear being outed to other men as unconfident."

"Oh right, I forgot." I sound hysterical. I sound bitter. "Not unless they're drunk and have just survived being gored by bulls while escaping a sinking ship. Or unless they're on the battlefield and at least one of them is bleeding to death. And even then they can only refer to each other by last name and they have to pound each other on the back until someone cracks a rib. Is that it?"

Hannah sets a soft hand on my shoulder.

Jeff leaves me three phone messages, two on my office line, one at home. He needs to speak with me. Urgently.

I wait until an hour when I know he won't be at his desk, then telephone his office and leave a message. "Been a little busy here. Nothing much, you know. George and I seem to have broken up." I draw a ragged breath, irony failing. "I think I ended it, but . . ." I hesitate, then set down the receiver.

I lie in bed, watching the ceiling. In my head rings my useless protest: *I don't understand why he won't even return my calls.* And Hannah's gently meant eulogy: *You didn't let him be the man.* I think: I am not competent to navigate this world, a world in which kindergarteners apparently know what I failed to realize: You can't give a ring back. It's against the rules.

I sleep fitfully, waking to dial George's number and leave another rambling message. Rising to go to the bathroom, I bump walls. I reach into a cabinet for a dish, misjudge the height of the shelf, and scrape my hand so it bleeds. Proportions confound me. My body is undergoing a transformation, turning foreign. Like Peter Parker getting bitten by a radioactive spider only in reverse: a night of nausea, dizziness, flashbacks, followed by the early morning discovery that my skin is chalky, my breasts cold, my leg muscles too weak to carry me. I think of my undergraduate Women's Studies professor and briefly consider looking her up, to inform her. To accuse her. To tell her that evidently those women's studies courses were like vocational training in technical support for Betamax. Teaching me the perfect skills to navigate a system that never took hold.

Would she laugh at me, set me straight? Does she live in a universe where men and women behave rationally? Or is she homeless and unemployed, urging her clamoring shopping cart down the sidewalk? On the back of her coat a sign, WILL WORK FOR FOOD.

"Quite a week for you to phone in sick," says Eileen. There's an unmistakable edge to her voice. While I sort the mail in my cubbyhole she sits back and regards me with the glittery gaze of a predator licking its chops. "Quite a week," she says, "what with everybody worked up over losing Jeff, on top of the letter incident."

I look up from my mail only long enough to nod. The only thing that persuaded me to leave my apartment today was the patent need to put in an appearance in the department and somehow, otherworldly though it feels, conference with half a dozen students on the bibliographies for their final papers.

"Of course," Eileen says, "we understand your calling in sick the last two days . . . *if* you were really sick?" She eyes me hungrily. "I asked Jeff if you were off somewhere making moon eyes with your fiancé. He said that was no longer likely." She leans forward. "Did you *really* call it quits?"

I turn my back, leaving her at her desk to simmer over my failure to explain the breakup or ask about the letter incident, whatever that might be. The flak I'll catch for my absence during whatever minor political earthquake this represents is of no consequence to me. In two days, my image of academia — its elaborate castles, dungeons, and balustrades — has been redrawn in two dimensions. There is a limit to how much energy I can spare for the morality plays of this department.

En route to my hallway, I wish for the first time that Jeff weren't my office neighbor. An I-told-you-so from him will shatter what little composure I have. I consider circumnavigating the department, allowing me to reach my office without passing his door. But that will mean walking past Eileen again.

"Tracy." Victoria's summons is sharp as I round the corner. Standing in her office doorway, she looks severe, and — insofar as Victoria ever displays this emotion — agitated.

She doesn't speak again until I'm seated opposite her in her office, door shut. As she opens her mouth to begin, the telephone on her desk rings. With a deliberate gesture, she turns off the ringer. In the silence she regards me.

She speaks with a crisp formality unusual even for her. "I am seriously worried about this department."

"Jeff's resignation?" I say dully.

"Jeff's departure, though a blow, is the least of it." With her barretted white hair, blue eyes, and deep green sweater, Victoria is as perfectly put together as ever. But her posture is unaccountably stiff. Her eyes search me. "I hope you feel you can work to keep things together, rather than pulling them apart."

"Of course." I nod, impatient for a hint of what's troubling her so I can address it and retreat to my office, where only a few student conferences will intrude on my dreadful mood.

"There are people inclined to pull departments apart," says Victoria even more slowly, "and sometimes they succeed. I hope you're not one of them."

With a jolt I realize the meaning of Victoria's formality: she's angry. "I don't know what you're referring to," I say. "I certainly would never do anything to harm this department."

This statement only makes Victoria look cross.

"Victoria?" My voice sails into a higher register. Victoria: who is the paragon of reason in this department; who is one of the only colleagues I completely trust. Whom I've tacitly counted on to speak up for me at my tenure meeting. "If there's something specific going on," I say, "maybe you can fill me in."

"I'll leave that to Joanne."

"Victoria, I know Joanne is sick. Eileen told me. I feel terrible for her, and I regret that there was friction between us this fall."

"Frankly that sympathy surprises me in light of your recent action." Again, her gaze searches me.

"I don't know what action you're talking about."

She hesitates. Then she stands. "I'll suggest to Joanne that she speak with you about it."

I don't budge. Anger, in my voice, is not formal. It is unstable, lightning flicking across the sky. "I would really appreciate a hint, Victoria."

Victoria compresses her lips. "I understand you've been under stress. Jeff tells me you broke up with your fiancé."

I don't speak.

"Jeff was trying to be helpful, Tracy. He was trying to explain your oddly timed absence." Victoria's face tightens with indignation. "Joanne did not, I can assure you, take kindly to the letter."

"What letter?"

Victoria takes my measure. "I don't think anyone could forget writing this sort of letter."

I lower my voice, dogged. "I did not write any letter. I have a right to know what I'm being accused of. This letter I supposedly sent to Joanne, I assume it wasn't kind?"

Victoria nods.

"Why do you think it was from me? Aside from the fact that I was absent this week?"

"It arrived the first day you called in sick. And it contains, shall we say, a *forceful* expression of opinions you've voiced to Joanne multiple times."

At this answer my gaze scales the walls of her office. *Elizabeth*.

My own words dizzy me. "Well it sure wasn't me who signed it, because I didn't write any letter to Joanne."

Victoria sits. She looks past my head to Hopper's cold blue sea. Gently she lifts the bunched fingertips of one hand to the center of her forehead and, with lowered lids, presses as though this delicate touch might relieve the flower of a headache. The gleeful children in the bookshelf photograph are, I'm reminded, someone else's. The family in which Victoria invests her pride and mounting years is this department.

She speaks. "A serious offense has been committed. Someone has incited and possibly threatened another faculty member. Not to mention denigrating her pedagogical skills and personality. If it's true that you didn't write it—"

"*If* it's true?"

A quick, decisive nod. "I believe you, Tracy. I recognize, just from this brief conversation, that though you might endorse some of the opinions in that letter, you wouldn't have written it yourself, even under stress. The tone is too—well, you'll see. You had better ask Joanne to discuss it with you, and you had better explain things to her. Word got out fast that the feud between you two—which, I'm sure you know, had already attracted attention—has reached a new level. Having people believe you wrote a hate letter to Joanne is not good for you."

People. Meaning our departmental secretary, who is at this moment surely delivering news updates door to door. Yet would my colleagues truly believe me capable of such self-destructive, irrational behavior? It doesn't seem likely.

Nor does anything that's happened in the last forty-eight hours.

"I'll do what I can to clear your name," says Victoria.

I sit back. The wooden chair creaks. "People here know me, Victoria. They know I wouldn't do something like that. I'm not everyone's best friend, but I've got a reasonable track record."

She doesn't answer.

"How about telling Eileen I'm innocent," I blurt, "but making her swear not to tell a soul? That ought to do it."

Victoria doesn't laugh. "Tracy," she says, "the day you and Joanne had your argument in the faculty lounge, she was carrying the folder with her doctor's notes, as well as some articles from medical journals that she'd found through her own research. She'd come in expressly to share her concerns with me, and to consult with me about the smoothest way — the way least disruptive to the department — for her to take time off. I'm aware you didn't know this at the time, but there was a reason Joanne wasn't responsive to your concerns about Elizabeth. Joanne is quite ill, Tracy. I'm amazed in fact at how well she held herself together in public. She's broken down in this office more than once. She didn't want anyone to know about her illness for as long as possible. Now apparently the word is out among the faculty. Joanne had hoped for a few more weeks' privacy. On top of that, this letter she's received is" — here Victoria's voice betrays a tiny quiver of outrage — "astonishingly poor timing. I trust you understand why we need to determine authorship as rapidly as possible." She inclines her head. "I apologize, Tracy, for assuming you were responsible. The letter — at least the parts Joanne was willing to read to me — does make reference to complaints you've made." Victoria taps her desk softly. "Who do you think wrote it?"

In my mind's eye, Elizabeth hunches silently over a piled library desk, laboring away: pencil behind one ear, tongue peeping out the corner of her mouth. I allow my shoulders to drift upward with a bewilderment that is not a lie.

Joanne sets it all down when I enter: pen, headset, Walkman. Surrounded by neatly arrayed shelves, framed posters of Mary Herbert and other sixteenth-century poets in neck ruffles, Joanne draws herself straight in her swivel chair. On her desk, the open tape case is the only hint of disarray: Gregorian chant, the plastic box lying open as though flung there. Her broad features are flushed.

"One would think you'd be savvier," she says. Pushing aside the Walkman and cassette case, she lays her hands flat on the desktop. They are pale, cold-looking.

"Can I have a piece of paper?" I say.

She doesn't move. On my own I take the pad from her desk. My hand jerking slightly, I sign and hand it back to her.

"*That's* my signature," I say. "Not whatever is on your letter."

"Very funny. But given that the letter is signed *Herman Melville,* maybe we should get *him* in here for a handwriting test? Or maybe we should dispense with the bullshit and go with the obvious: you wrote it."

"I didn't write it, Joanne. Whatever the message is, I didn't write it. Victoria implied it's insulting. I would appreciate it if you'd let me see this letter, because if I don't then the rancor around here is only going to get worse."

She doesn't budge. "You did a pretty good imitation of Melville's style," she says. "I'll grant you that. But then, American lit *is* your specialty. It can't have been too hard."

"I'm sorry you've gotten a piece of hate mail, if that's what it is. But I didn't do it." I draw a deep breath. "And even so, even though I didn't do it, I want to say I'm sorry for the hurt this clearly has caused."

At the word "hurt," Joanne stiffens. "Why should I let you re-read your own handiwork?"

I keep my voice low. "I'm not responsible for it."

"And I wasn't born yesterday." But as she speaks she lifts a folder and slides a single sheet of paper from beneath it: a concession to reality. Whatever disagreements I've had with Joanne in the past, I've always expressed them directly. Sending an anonymous missive would be out of character and she knows it. The page trembles in her hand as she holds it out over the desk. Her expression is peculiarly intent.

The letter is single-spaced, typed in a percussive black that left slight indentations on the creamy letter stock. It begins without salutation or date. Halfway through the page, the lines begin to run off the right margin with increasing disorder.

Whence come you, Joanne Miller? By what right do you drink
from my flagon of life? And when I put it to my lips — lo, they are
yours and not mine. I feel that the Godhead is broken up like the
bread at the Supper, and that we are the pieces. In me divine mag-
nanimities are spontaneous and instantaneous — catch them while
you can. The world goes round, and the other side comes up. So
now I can't write all I felt when you entered my world. Your heart
beat in my ribs and mine in yours, and both in Literature's.

You were archangel enough to despise the imperfect thoughts,
and embrace the soul. You heard the ugly Socrates because
you saw the flame in the mouth, and heard the rushing of the
demon, — the familiar, — and recognized the sound; for you have
heard it in your own solitudes.

But for the soul that sees is reserved the greatest burden. Have
you upheld yours?

I charge you with misdeeds. Disdain for our fellow scholars;
intellectual extortion; holding a degree like a carrot before a laboring mule; bullish commandeering of faculty gatherings; zero-sum
politics; pugnacious and juvenile manners; toadyism melded with
disdain (of which G is unaware but others, many others, know).
You have woken the rage of those who love the book; those whose
temple must not be desecrated.

Perhaps you ought consider the consequences.

This is a fiery letter, but you are not at all bound to answer it.
Possibly, if you do answer it, and direct it to Herman Melville, you
will missend it — for the very fingers that now pilot this typewriter
are not precisely the same that just rolled into it this page. Lord,
when shall we be done changing? Ah! It's a long stage, and no inn
in sight, and night coming, and the body cold.

My dear Miller, the atmospheric skepticisms steal into me now,
and make me doubtful of my sanity in writing you thus. But, believe me, I am not mad, most noble Festus! But truth is ever incoherent, and when the big hearts strike together, the concussion is a
little stunning. Farewell.

I have written a wicked letter, and feel spotless as the lamb.

Goodbye to you, with my blessing,

Herman

The signature is penned in blue ink, with a great flourish, at the
very bottom of the page.

"The only person who would accuse a colleague of *commandeering* faculty meetings, Tracy Farber, is someone who doesn't

have the guts or charisma to run them herself." Joanne glares at me, but it's clear she's bluffing. "*Now* will you confess who wrote that letter?"

"Herman Melville," I murmur.

Joanne gives a sound of disgust.

My eyes drift back to the letter. "It's Melville, Joanne — at least most of it is, and it's verbatim or nearly so, with alterations for the sake of modernity, like substituting *typewriter* for *pen* and so on. It's from a letter Melville wrote to Nathaniel Hawthorne."

"So says the woman who claims she knew *nothing* about this letter?"

I look up long enough to make eye contact. "American literature *is* my specialty."

Joanne relents.

I reread in silence. Brushing past the lofty praise and peculiar theological imagery, I focus on the central paragraph cataloguing Joanne's misdeeds — the only passage not lifted from Melville. It is a seven-line, scathing summary of my quarrel with Joanne Miller. The opinions are mine, the *temple* reference a clear allusion to my rejoinder to Jeff. Blessedly, Elizabeth didn't bother spelling out Grub's full nickname.

"*For you have heard it in your own solitudes,*" Joanne recites. She watches me fiercely, daring me to say what seems obvious: that this line, with its disturbing intimacy, has unsettled her. Melville meant it as praise for Hawthorne's art; but in this context it could easily be an unflinching reference to a lonely struggle with illness.

"*The body cold,*" Joanne continues. "*Farewell.*" There is a long silence. Joanne appears to be reading the posters on the wall behind my head. "Victoria wanted to call the police," she says, "based on the parts I read to her. She said the letter sounded like a threat. By the way, you might be amused to know she initially insisted that something so florid couldn't possibly be from you. Until I explained about the sense of so-called humor shared by you and Jeff." Her expression darkens as she pronounces his name. "And your recent erratic behavior. And of course, *Melville*. You and your Melville."

She waits for me to acknowledge this. When I don't, she continues.

"But I wouldn't hand over the letter, to Victoria, or the police, or anyone else. Its author didn't have the guts to address me directly and" — she gives me a bullish look — "I'm not intimidated."

Perhaps. Perhaps, too, Joanne recognizes truth in the letter's accusations and fears their public dissemination more than she fears any letter writer's potential ill will.

Might Elizabeth have intended to threaten Joanne? Nineteenth-century prose is full of morbid phrasings and allusions to human frailty. Quoting Melville one naturally runs across references to cold bodies, madness, mortality. Still, if I received such a letter, such a mix of worshipful tenderness and accusation along with ambiguous phrases of farewell, I would call the police. I consider whether I ought to call them myself, right now, and let them take over the matter. Then I picture pulling dusty volumes off my shelves and trying to illustrate, while the cops drag Elizabeth away, that the words Melville penned to Hawthorne were consistent with nineteenth-century prose, and do not necessarily constitute a death threat.

"Are you denying authorship?" Joanne charges.

"You know I didn't write it."

"You didn't *write* it. Is this a semantics game? Did you hire a typist?"

She's playing for time — beneath the repeated accusation is fear. I drop the letter onto Joanne's desk, where it slides to within an inch of her blouse. "Why," I say slowly, "would I do anything so crazy? For God's sake, even if I had a desire to, I'm up for tenure. This would be the stupidest move I could make."

A small muscle works in Joanne's jaw.

There is a step behind me, then a soft rapping at the open door. "Joanne," says Victoria. "I hope you'll excuse my intrusion. This is surely a difficult moment. I wanted to tell you I'm certain that Tracy didn't write that letter. It would be an absurdly self-destructive thing for her to do. I have full confidence in her innocence, and I hope you will too."

Victoria ex machina.

Joanne's expression is utterly neutral.

Victoria addresses me. "Elizabeth wrote it. Didn't she?"

Looking only at Victoria, I give a shallow nod. "I think."

Joanne lets out a small sound of protest.

Victoria steps toward the desk. "May I read it, Joanne?" she says softly. "I promise I won't divulge its contents without your permission."

Joanne doesn't answer. Victoria takes the letter from the desktop and scans it. Her frown deepens: the letter is crazier than she'd thought.

"Is that Elizabeth's typewriter?" Victoria asks me, indicating the letter.

"I know she borrowed a typewriter from Eileen."

"Stole." Victoria shutters her eyes. With a sorrowful mien, she executes some inner calculus I'm not privy to. "Eileen noticed a few weeks ago that it was missing from its shelf."

For an instant Joanne's eyes, too, are closed. When she opens them she wears an expression I did not expect.

Some things in life are like shooting stars. A fragment of the cosmos streaks into the atmosphere and sears its trail across the sky. By the time you free your hand from your pocket to point, by the time you say, *Look, there's a shooting* — it's gone. Either your companions have seen it, or they haven't and never will. So no one else will ever see what I see at this moment — the expression on Joanne's face that is there, then gone: satisfaction.

"I'll be in my office," says Victoria to Joanne. "Please stop in later, and we'll discuss an appropriate response to this."

Victoria is gone. Joanne's eyes are focused somewhere beyond this office, her gaze luminous, her face alive, mobile, eager, as though she's waiting for the answer to an astonishing question. Seated motionless at her desk, she is arresting in a manner that frightens me: the manner of an eighteenth-century consumptive euphoric with her own demise.

"Joanne," I say.

She looks surprised by my continued presence in her office.

My head feels as if it's going to explode. "I've been told," I say, "that you're grappling with an illness. I know it's your personal business. I have no intent to pry. But I do want you to know I'm sorry for any extra difficulty the recent tensions between us have added to your life. If there's any way I can help — covering your classes, anything — I hope you won't let our past troubles stand in the way of asking. I'm your colleague. This department should be a resource for you. I'm committed to doing my part."

Joanne's clipped "Understood" directs me out of her office.

In the hallway Grub stops short at the sight of me. He assumes a chairmanly half grin, which he holds in one cheek like a wad of tobacco. Approaching, he pats me confidingly on the arm. "You're the kind of person," he says, "who is smart enough to mend fences."

My voice quakes. "I didn't write that letter to Joanne."

"Of course you didn't." His smile ratchets up to a higher setting: he doesn't want to know whether or not I wrote the letter. "*And* you're smart enough to mend fences." With another firm pat on the arm, he strolls to his office and shuts the door.

Jeff stands before a row of half-empty bookshelves, a volume in each hand. On the desk behind him sits an open cardboard box labeled OFFICE — BOOKCASE.

He turns at the sound of my footsteps, relief lighting his blue eyes.

"I didn't do it," I say dully.

"I know. You wouldn't." He wags his head. "It's about time you showed up here to put a lid on the rumors."

"Does anyone seriously believe I did it? I know Victoria had to take Joanne's accusation seriously, because that's Victoria. But why would anyone else?"

"Tracy." Jeff shuts his eyes, and shakes his head as though mourning my obtuseness. "There are people in this department who've been trying to get a fix on you for a while."

"Meaning what?"

"Meaning you're different. You're not a political player, and you don't socialize within the department. You've got original ideas and have had a lot of success, and have managed not to become a completely political animal. People haven't a clue what to make of you. That hasn't been a problem, until now. Do you understand envy, Tracy? Now they've got something to chew on. In fact they've got a couple things. They now believe they understand your motivations, and not only are your motivations drearily mundane — professional competitiveness, made more virulent by private romantic failure — but your choice to write Joanne a hate letter was idiotic. You've been brought back to earth. That's very satisfying to certain people."

228 ⌣ Rachel Kadish

"You want me to believe" — I gesture beyond his door — "they're ready to assume the worst?"

He lays one book, then another, in the box. "You seem to be laboring under the perception that these people are your friends."

I watch him take a roll of packing tape and seal the box. "Jeff, that letter is patently insane. They'd have to believe I was psychotic."

"No, they wouldn't. No one's seen the letter. Joanne is refusing to divulge anything but the briefest quotes — which of course are being amplified and distorted through the grapevine. Joanne has been calling it 'character assassination of the most cowardly sort.'" He pushes the full box to one side and sets an empty one beside it, then stops. "It was Elizabeth, wasn't it?"

My hand rises to my forehead. "I think."

"I'm sure." He sighs, then begins to load books into the new box. "I already told Steven and Eileen it wasn't you. I'll keep spreading the word."

At this assurance, some inner strut gives. I don't lean so much as sag against the doorframe.

"Good lord, girl." He stops working. Folding his arms, he whistles, taking his time at it. "I'm glad you're back," he says finally. "This was getting out of hand in your absence."

"This is" — I make a feeble gesture — "unreal. I don't have energy for this shit. I've got bigger things going on in my life at the moment."

Jeff steps closer. Gone is the nonchalant exterior. "Tracy, listen carefully to what I'm saying to you. You're in personal hell right now. That's plain. I'm sorry to see it, though I think you've just saved yourself a world of heartache. But there will be plenty of time for licking those wounds later. I have seen a lot go down in this department, and this smells like smoke. You'd better drop everything else and deal with this letter business."

"But I didn't write —" I don't bother finishing the sentence. I can already hear Jeff's response: that I need to find Elizabeth before my colleagues' images of me solidify. I need to learn what the hell is going on and stop her before she puts other opinions of mine on display in her next burst of departmental pyrotechnics.

If there were ever a moment to take Jeff's counsel, this is it. I feel, though, as if I've donned a lead apron. All I want is to settle into Jeff's swivel chair and savor its familiar contours, along with the relief that Jeff has, after all, no need to bask in I-told-you-so's.

"I'll do spin control," says Jeff, and his keen expression tells me that he will be fierce in my defense with what departmental clout he still possesses. Setting down his books, he takes my shoulders and steers me, not ungently, toward the hall. "You go find out what else she's doing to screw you over." From his doorway he watches me go. When, unlocking my office, I glance back, his face is a study in worry. Pausing, I turn and survey the long corridor of faculty doors. All save Jeff's are shuttered.

From my office I dial Elizabeth's home number. She doesn't answer. Holding the receiver loosely, I allow the phone to continue ringing while I consider my next move. Repeatedly I come up blank. The phone rings on in my hand, twenty, thirty times, a hollow sound. Then, from a distance, I hear Elizabeth pick up.

I press the receiver to my ear.

"I'm sorry," she whispers before I can say a word. She sounds drugged.

"Elizabeth, what in hell is going on?"

She cannot speak over the phone. She will not explain why. Each syllable seems to require effort. She agrees only to meet me at a Tribeca café.

It will take Elizabeth at least half an hour to reach Tribeca from her Brooklyn apartment. I phone my students, offer their answering machines rescheduled conference times, post a sign on my office door, and set off downtown. At first my fury-lengthened strides gulp the city blocks. My feet slam to the rhythm of *how could they think,* which transforms itself gradually into *how could he think,* and then—blocks later, my pace slowing—a one-word riddle: *belonging.* Confusion eclipses rage. I drift along Broadway, peering into storefronts. The world has tilted. Taking out my cell phone, appealing to it to break the obscene silence between us, I dial George's number.

In measured, impregnable tones, George's answering machine fields my call.

"George?" I say, stalling in the middle of the sidewalk. Pedestrians swerve to avoid me. "George, I need to talk to you. I miss you. And frankly things are all going to hell right now. I don't understand anything. I don't understand why just being true to what I think, being true to *you and me,* means the bottom drops out. Call me. Please. I'm asking. I didn't mean to hurt you. There's also this thing happening, at work, it's crazy, I mean really crazy, not that that's important right now, but I could — I just refuse to believe everything can be so easily shattered. Everything. It's this crazy distorted broken mirror of who I think I am. George, don't we know each other? Don't you know me? Don't you know I'd never —"

George's machine cuts me off.

I fold my cell phone and consider flinging it into the nearest trash bin.

She is seated at a table. Though it's easily seventy degrees in the tightly packed space, she wears a heavy coat and scarf. The air is waxy with the ghosts of dozens of candles. The table where Elizabeth sits — and where I join her, settling straight-backed on a flimsy metal chair — is coated with overlapping patches of colored wax. Without looking at me, Elizabeth carefully scores another line down the table's center with a thumbnail. The line joins tens of others; scar by scar she is laying a fine grid across the table.

"It was the only letter I wrote," says Elizabeth to the tabletop.

"You woke up and realized the consequences?"

Startled by the anger in my voice, she raises her head. Dully, her wide black eyes meet mine. She is pale, and, if a face can be said to be closed, hers is sealed. It is the face of a refugee. Of someone preoccupied by fear and exhaustion, expecting no salvation.

"No." The word is a sad hiccup. Her chapped lips separate in the specter of a laugh: the possibility of consequences hadn't crossed her mind. "I couldn't write any more letters, not real ones."

"*Real* ones?"

She doesn't answer.

"Elizabeth. Do you realize what you've done? To your career?"

At length she shrugs.

"Why isn't that important to you?"

She doesn't answer.

The waitress brings water and silverware for me. I order tea. The waitress leaves. I stare blankly at the menu's gritty columns, trying to gather my thoughts. Elizabeth's letter has already strewn political shrapnel about the department; even in the best-case scenario I'll never know the full extent of the damage to my reputation. I consider my upcoming tenure review and feel ill.

When I look up, Elizabeth is reclining in her chair, yawning, looking for all the world as though she's about to take a nap.

"Did it occur to you, Elizabeth" — my voice is tight — "that people would assume I'd written that letter?"

This question seems to engage her interest for a moment. She thinks about it, then shakes her head. "That's not very perceptive of them," she says.

I couldn't agree more. But when Elizabeth blinks sleepily and nests back into her chair, I can't help sounding like a piqued schoolteacher. "Isn't there anything you'd like to say to me about that?"

After a moment's consideration she gives the kind of sheepish shrug with which she might acknowledge borrowing a friend's favorite skirt without permission. "Sorry," she says. Then she waves a hand: there's something different on her mind. "I started the letter as a joke," she says. "I thought Melville could help express some things to Joanne. The things you're always saying Joanne needs to hear."

"What made you think that kind of letter would be taken as a joke?"

"At first I wasn't going to send it. But then I saw it was a good thing and I ought to. Anyway it wasn't my decision."

"I think you'd better explain that last comment to me."

A smile wafts slowly over her face. "Okay." Her speech is so soft I edge forward to hear her. "I'll tell you. Because you've always been really nice to me. And I know something amazing, and you deserve to know too. But I need you to promise it will be our secret."

"At this point, Elizabeth, I don't believe I owe you any promises."

This seems to shock her. Sorrow washes visibly over her thin body. "That's true," she whispers. "I guess you might be mad at me."

"*Mad* doesn't begin to cover it, Elizabeth. I'm shocked, and confused, and alarmed. I'm goddamn furious. I'm also frightened for you."

She slides lower in her chair. I am seated opposite the loneliest person I have ever seen. Her expression is utterly desolate. It stirs in me an unfamiliar, uncomfortable sensation.

"I'll keep your secret only if it doesn't compromise me."

She rouses slowly. "Oh, no," she murmurs. "No, no, no." She pauses, attentive. "No, it definitely wouldn't."

I spread my hands on the tabletop, feeling the fine grid lines soften under my fingers.

"Okay." She fills her lungs, and lets out a long, breathy sigh. "There are people," she says.

A few seconds pass.

"Inarguably," I say.

She looks confused.

I fold my arms across my chest. "Go on."

"There are people who aren't people." She gazes at me meaningfully.

"I don't follow."

"Tracy, I *understand* them now."

The heavy smell of candles blankets the room. "Who?" I say.

"Herman Melville and Emily Dickinson. And sometimes a few others. Most of them are writers, but some of them aren't."

"Herman Melville?"

"And Emily Dickinson. It's incredible, Tracy. You've been such a good friend to me. So I want you to know this." Her eyes have shed their dullness and shine now with gratitude, and something more. "You know how when you work, you feel sometimes like the writers are speaking, and you really *hear* them? And your job is to understand their message more fully than maybe even they did at the time they wrote?"

She waits until I give a grudging nod.

"And sometimes you think the writers didn't know everything they meant when they wrote it, because nobody ever does, not even God knows what he means when he writes." She waits for another nod. "Well, it may be true that they don't know completely what they're writing *as* they write it, but it turns out that they realize it later, I mean once they're dead. Then they wait around for someone who's really listening. And I was in the library a lot so they started really telling me what they thought."

Very slowly, I take a sip of water and set the glass back on the table. "Which was?"

"Oh, *things*. All kinds of things. They showed me the whole world, they showed me how it's all laid out in the most beautiful words. Orderly and dazzling, and it just goes on forever, Tracy. The whole world, every part of it, is just a shining stream of words, and they can recite it by heart. They showed me what books to look at in the library, and how to make sense of everything through them. At first I didn't know it was them, but then I saw they were guiding me."

The waitress sets my tea on the table and disappears. Watching Elizabeth, I think of reading Tolstoy at two o'clock in the morning, my mind hopping so it's nearly intolerable to sit at my computer. Of burying my own confusion in Hurston's tongue-in-cheek prose. The lure, the warming light, of books. How delicious it might feel to follow that beacon, farther and farther from shore, until there remained no hope or desire to return.

"And then Melville helped me write a letter to Joanne, and once I started I saw it wasn't a joke at all, because he was helping me tell Joanne how much I admire her but how much she's also wrong, like you're always saying. Melville" — she turns a soft, beneficent smile on me — "agrees with you."

I weigh the bowl of a teaspoon in my palm.

"He gave me the words to say what I needed to Joanne."

"Elizabeth." I dread her answer to this question — a last hope of connecting her to reality. "Who signed that letter?"

She looks puzzled. "Herman Melville. He was talking to me every day last week. Only, he's stopped." Her pale fingers curl on the tabletop, looking abruptly lifeless. "Just a few days ago. I don't know why. And Emily has stopped too. All of them stopped. They got tired of me, or maybe they think I'm not listening hard enough. That's why I can't write any more letters." She bites her lower lip, chews it. Her teeth are white, even, heartbreakingly perfect. "I miss them so much, Tracy." She falls silent. Slowly she closes her eyes.

The thought of George is an updraft in my chest. Shutting my own eyes, I sample all that was delicate between us. All that was warm.

I force myself to sip my tea, barely registering its pungent smell of orange rinds. "Elizabeth." I set the cup in its saucer. "Has this happened to you before?"

"A bunch of years ago. When I was in college. Then they stopped talking to me. And this fall they came again. But now they're gone." Her voice is the voice, slow and sad, of a woman speaking alone from a fathomless pool of grief. I feel a sickening drag to follow her into the depths. "They would come at night. It made it hard to sleep sometimes. But I didn't mind. I never, ever, *ever* minded." Her face gathers, and then she's crying, her constricted throat producing a high, whining noise that she's unable to stop despite visible effort.

"All right," I say. "All right." This is the only thing I can say that is compatible with nodding, and it seems imperative that I keep nodding until my thoughts regroup, though it's obvious that what I need to do right now is stand up and stride out of this suffocating café, dragging Elizabeth with me into clear, sensible daylight. "Let's go over this, Elizabeth." As we have gone over every chapter and theme of her dissertation. Adviser and advisee. "The writers you talk to."

"They're not from here," Elizabeth says with effort.

I don't want to hear what she's about to tell me.

"It's true!" she protests, suddenly defensive. She's stopped crying.

"Here, New York?" I pin hollow hope to this shred of logic: Emily Dickinson was from Massachusetts.

Elizabeth shakes her head.

"Here, Earth?"

She nods vigorously.

Slowly, with the fingertips of both hands, I rub my temples. "Isn't it a *good* thing, Elizabeth, if these voices . . . these aliens, just . . . you know." I flutter one hand. "Go away? Leave you to your normal life?"

She addresses me with reproach. "Herman Melville said you'd *appreciate* my writing that letter. Since we knew you agreed with everything in it."

"Then Herman Melville is an asshole."

Elizabeth recoils. With the indignant flush of a woman in love, she corrects me. "Their coming is the most beautiful thing that's ever happened to me. It's what I've been put on earth for. You don't understand what it's like to hear a voice and just know."

I shake my head violently, banishing the recollection this prompts. "Elizabeth, have you ever been on some kind of medication for this?"

"Yes."

"Did you stop taking it?"

"Yes."

"Why?" I demand.

A martyr before the Inquisition, she replies with head high. "I chose not to dodge the intensity of literature."

"The *intensity*? I think this is more than—"

"It's beautiful. Books. People have no idea how beautiful books are. How they taste on your fingers. How bright everything is when you light it with words."

The waitress comes to the table. I send her on her way with a rude flick of my hand. Across from me Elizabeth waits stubbornly for acknowledgment of the truths she's bestowed on me. The wreckage ahead of her terrifies me. I'm frightened not only for her, but—in a way I don't fully understand—for myself.

Surely there is a script I ought to be following, some clarifying, therapeutic question I ought to pose; but nothing has prepared me for this. At length I ask, "Have your visitors done anything to hurt you?"

"They read my *Moby Dick* paper. And tore up a page of it."

"Why?"

She doesn't answer.

I think of something very intelligent to say. "Why that particular page?"

"I can't figure it out. It was about the figure of Ishmael." The hollows above and below Elizabeth's eyes are dark, her chest concave. Slowly her mouth dimples. She blinks rapidly. "I just want to understand why they're not talking to me anymore." The high whining cry begins again, and this time shatters into wracking sobs.

For a moment I take refuge in inane consideration of why Ishmael might draw the ire of Elizabeth's visitors. I'm about to ask Elizabeth exactly what point she'd been making on the page her visitors desecrated, when the ache of my own clenched fists— bearing down on the waxed tabletop like twin mallets—becomes plain to me. And I do something I've never done with a student. I take Elizabeth in my arms and hold her slim, birdlike figure, and feel, in the shifting of her bones beneath my uncertain hands, the world reshaping around this moment.

"She says this has happened before." I keep my voice low, though it doesn't seem anything could wake Elizabeth, curled in a blanket on my sofa and to all appearances getting her first solid sleep in weeks.

Jeff's end of the phone is silent. Beside me on the carpet is Elizabeth's crammed backpack, from which — averting my eyes from torn, script-crammed pages — I've seined a black cloth wallet. Thumbing past loose cash and crumpled receipts, I extract a neatly lettered card.

"There are two telephone numbers here," I tell Jeff.

"Don't do this," he says. "Things are just starting to quiet down here. I've been on counter-rumor duty all day."

Twisting the phone cord around my fingers and glancing at Elizabeth's motionless form, I leave my thanks unspoken. "Under 'emergency contacts' it lists her mother as Mary Archer of Chicago. And there's a number for a Dr. Thomas Haley."

"If you feel compelled to contact her mother, then do so, but extract yourself from this situation immediately."

There is a sound from the sofa. Elizabeth shifts, her peaked face flickering. Her pallor, even in sleep, is unbearable. I force my gaze away. And turn my attention to the single thing in this entire day I'm sure of.

"Jeff." I rest my forehead on the heel of my hand. "Joanne is responsible for this."

I hear Jeff's desk chair creak as he lowers his legs to the floor. "You're being —"

"No," I tell him. "I am not being melodramatic. There is such a thing as moral responsibility."

"Your logic is flawed. How was Joanne to know Elizabeth was crazy?"

"She's not crazy!" I whisper.

Jeff's silence is a laser pointer underscoring the absurdity of this statement. I try again. "What I mean is, Elizabeth's mania — or whatever this is — had been under control for years. She hadn't

had an episode since college. Why should it flare now? I'm not saying Elizabeth bears no responsibility, only that there's something
else going on. We've all seen how Joanne's been torturing Elizabeth."

"*Torture?*" Jeff mocks.

"Yes. Sustained intellectual and psychic baiting is torture. In academia this is the surest way to undo someone, and you know it."

"You fail to realize how off-base you sound. No one made Elizabeth go off her medication. If she was working so hard that she
forgot to take her pills, that's her own responsibility."

"I can't prove what Joanne did. But I know it's real. I know it in
my gut."

"Ah."

"Don't be that way. You'd believe me if you'd seen Joanne's face
today, when she learned Elizabeth was responsible. She was *glowing*, Jeff. The look on her face was practically indecent. It's like
Joanne's been grinding down Elizabeth on purpose."

"Why?"

"Fear."

"Your conspiracy theories are not—"

"*Why* not? Maybe Joanne is terrified of being disabled. Maybe
she needed someone to free-fall with her. Chillingworth did it to
Dimmesdale in *The Scarlet Letter* without lifting a finger. Salieri, if
we're to believe the movie, did it to Mozart. You can destroy sensitive people's equilibrium—disturb their *souls*—by gaining their
trust. Making them dependent. You never have to lift a finger. And
before the eyes of the world you're innocent."

"Number one," says Jeff, "stop talking about souls, and get
Elizabeth out of your apartment this minute. You're going to be
seen as an accomplice. I appreciate your act of charity, Tracy. I do.
Don't think I've missed that you're being noble here. Elizabeth is
ill and needs help. And yes, the faculty will extend their thinking
far enough to acknowledge that this is a disease, and not a reflection on Elizabeth's basic character. But give them a few more
bits of bizarre behavior to chew on, and they'll snap back into
judgment—next time for good. You do not want to be tarred by
that brush." He pauses. "Number two, don't breathe a word of
your Joanne theory to anyone. That includes Victoria. As far as
you're concerned, Elizabeth's manic break occurring in the middle

of her dissertation troubles is pure coincidence. Number three, it wouldn't hurt for you to be visibly involved in determining the appropriate departmental response to Elizabeth's actions. Make it known that Elizabeth tried to pit you against Joanne. And drop these three words as often as possible: *She used me.*"

"I am not going to turn on a woman having a breakdown."

"Do not screw around with this, Tracy. She wrote a threatening letter."

"You can't really think Elizabeth is dangerous."

"On the contrary."

"You actually think she's a danger to Joanne?"

"Don't know about Joanne, and don't care. Elizabeth is a danger to *you.*"

"You're missing the point. I didn't write the letter, and thanks to you, people now know that. Correct?"

"Yes."

"And they believe it?"

"Immaterial. Once the public sees a person brought in in handcuffs, they will in some part of their minds always think of that person as a criminal. Doesn't matter if the person's name is cleared."

I rise from my chair. "I've got a track record in this department. I'll mend the necessary fences. And yes, once Elizabeth is in safe hands I'll take your advice to the dot. But you didn't see what I saw today." Joanne, seduced by her own power, hooked into some strange intimacy by her effect on Elizabeth. I can't yet articulate this in a way that will persuade Jeff, but I know it's real. "Joanne is going to crush her," I say. "This isn't about me."

"You're wrong."

Behind me, Elizabeth startles. For a moment she breathes rapidly, locked in her dream, pursued or pursuing.

"I'll call you later," I say.

I fill my kettle. While the water heats I keep my back to my bedroom door. Indulging for just this moment the fantasy: George is here, George is asleep in my bed, is sighing in his sleep, the pillow smells of him and his clothing is strewn on my floor but I won't have time to notice because he will wrap me in his arms before he even opens his eyes.

The water boils. I resist the temptation to go to my drawer and finger the one shirt he left there, the one I don't dare put on for fear I'll dissolve. Instead I brew my tea and try to explain my strategy to myself. I will do only this one thing for Elizabeth, and then I will keep my involvement with her minimal. I've never flown in the face of Jeff's advice before. But, I reason, what choice do I have? To abandon Elizabeth?

After all—I speak the words aloud in the quiet room—*I'm her adviser.*

I pour my tea and return to the telephone that I have used, of late, primarily for bereavement calls: *The engagement is off. No, I guess it wasn't right. Where shall I return your gift?* I pick up the receiver and wait for the dial tone. Framing the card between thumb and forefinger, I dial the number for Elizabeth's mother. On the second ring, Mary Archer answers: a pert Midwestern voice that turns serious the moment I introduce myself. She listens wordlessly. When I have finished I hear Mary breathing. She's terse as I spell out details. The scratch of pencil on paper comes faintly through the line.

Before setting down the telephone I hear myself make a promise —one Elizabeth's mother, whose questions are practical, has not solicited. "We're not going to let her down here," I tell her over the telephone. "We're not going to isolate her."

Mary's *thank-you* is so brief I wonder if she didn't understand what I was pledging.

I lay down the receiver and walk through the kitchenette to the bathroom mirror, where I find my uncombed hair and stilled face.

Elizabeth wakes, eats canned soup that I heat over the stove, and sips hot cocoa drowsily. She asks no questions, and seems neither surprised nor grateful to be cocooned in my apartment. Her silence is a relief. I have no desire to speak; am obscurely frightened of her; am painfully attentive to her every move. I minister to her awkwardly and in near silence.

An hour before Mary's flight is due from Chicago, when Elizabeth is asleep once more, I telephone Victoria.

"She's at your apartment?" Victoria's voice is crisp with incredulity. "Don't you know we've been trying to track her down for hours?"

"She's in trouble. The thing she wrote to Joanne is just a symptom."

"Of?"

"She's had some kind of breakdown. It's severe. I've contacted her mother, who's on the next flight in."

"Tracy. When I interviewed Elizabeth for this program, I naturally questioned her in a private meeting about the one-year gap on her résumé. At the time she indicated that she'd had some past psychiatric issues. She was not specific on the subject. And I didn't pry, beyond ascertaining that she took responsibility for maintaining her own equilibrium. She said her condition was completely under control with medication, and there was no reason to fear a relapse so long as she kept her life balanced. I should think she needs to reach out in some fashion, face up to what she's done, and communicate to Joanne that she means her no harm."

"Victoria, do you have any sense of *how* unwell Elizabeth is?"

"Tracy, Joanne has, of her own generosity and against a preponderance of advice, decided not to bring this before the faculty senate until she's had a conversation with Elizabeth. That may or may not be wise, but it's her prerogative. If Elizabeth can't come in to the department right now, then she can at least get on the telephone with Joanne. Either she is capable of being a nondestructive part of this department, or she is not. Don't forget, Tracy, that there is, at this very moment, a seriously ill member of our tenured faculty who is being placed under unnecessary stress. This department does not have time for hide-and-go-seek with a graduate student."

"There *is* one ill faculty member right now. True. There's also one ill graduate student. I know the department's priorities are with the faculty, but we can't ignore the other side of this."

Victoria doesn't answer. I realize I'm millimeters away from directly accusing Joanne. Even in my anger I know enough to tack. "When you saw Elizabeth going into dangerous waters," I say, "with her dissertation, weren't you worried?"

"I had a word with all three parties involved — Elizabeth, Joanne, and yourself. That should have been enough. We are all responsible for our own equilibrium, Tracy. This department is composed of adults."

On the sofa behind me, Elizabeth shifts. The pillow that's slid, inch by inch, from beneath her head over the past several hours escapes now and drops to the floor without waking her. Her face is an eclipsed moon, empty of desire.

"I think," I say, "that getting on the telephone with Joanne right now would be very bad for Elizabeth, and not productive for anyone."

"I appreciate your concern, Tracy, but you were not the one on the receiving end of that letter. Do not forget that there is the possibility, however remote, of a physical threat to Joanne. Do not forget that mentally ill people who are deranged enough to write menacing rants to colleagues may be deranged enough to do more. It needs to be established right away whether Elizabeth is a danger to Joanne. Joanne wants to speak with her."

It takes a physical effort to slow my speech and punctuate it with silences, translating my bucking temper into Victoria's native tongue. "I believe that if you heard what I've heard today," I say, "you might see this matter differently. Elizabeth's world is so removed from reality at this moment that I think it would be a waste of everyone's considerable energy — in fact it would be pouring fuel on the fire — to confer with her now. It's true I'm not in Joanne's shoes. And I'm not an expert. But I'm convinced that if you saw Elizabeth you would agree she needs, before all else, immediate psychiatric help. I'm asking you to trust me. Any conversation prior to treatment will bear no fruit. And I think Joanne's outrage, as justified as it is, will fall on deaf ears." Or shatter whatever of Elizabeth remains intact. "Elizabeth — the Elizabeth we know, Victoria — is lying in pieces on my living room sofa. Her mother will be here in an hour to take charge of her care."

There is another roomy silence. Then Victoria, in her own flinty way, relents. "I can't promise that there won't be consequences if Elizabeth doesn't answer for her actions soon." She pauses. "I expect Joanne will be patient enough to wait a few days more, once I explain the situation. And I will extend myself to keep this matter from getting out of hand. But in the meanwhile, rumors will continue to proliferate. And rumors make people anxious. I can't do anything to prevent that. This is the sort of issue that ends up on the chairman's doorstep."

We both know what will happen if it does. Grub will swing

open his door, sniff an unpleasant problem, and make it — and
Elizabeth — go away.

In my imagination, my chairman's door shuts. The click echoes
along a silent corridor lined with literary cartoons, brochure-laden
bulletin boards, and the closed doors of my colleagues' offices. The
brochures float momentarily in the breeze and are still.

Mary Archer rings the buzzer near midnight. When I open the
door, a petite, black-eyed woman in boots and a no-nonsense winter coat nods briskly at me. Beneath her wool cap, her lined face
is so chiseled with resolve that, as I step out of her way, I nearly
falter with an outsized longing to curl up on the sofa and receive
her ministrations myself — this woman who has appeared out of
the frosty dark and from halfway across the country to save her
child from a nightmare. Without a word to me, she steps over the
stacks of books and magazines on the carpet, kneels, and kisses
her daughter's forehead. Like a princess in a fairy tale Elizabeth
wakes at the kiss, and with an alacrity that leaves me breathless
tosses herself into her mother's arms.

"Don't worry, love," says Eileen. She holds out an unsealed envelope.

Opening it, I find confirmation of the date for my tenure meeting, a week and a half hence.

"You had great chances already," says Eileen, "and now with
Jeff leaving and Joanne going part-time, they can't afford to lose
another prof."

I tuck the letter into my pocket.

"It'll be fine," prods Eileen. Today she's in earth-mother mode,
and I'm failing to be sufficiently appreciative.

I'm about to turn for my office; instead, I linger. Eileen, it suddenly occurs to me, is not only the chief purveyor of departmental
gossip, but the best gauge of public opinion. "Unless," I say, "people still blame me for Elizabeth's letter."

She clucks her tongue. "Everyone knows Elizabeth wrote it. And
no one could possibly blame you for that poor child's troubles."

Mother Earth lays it on thick, but this morning she does seem
sincere.

"Word has it she's gone completely loony," she lilts. "I hear they've got her in some kind of lockup ward, and her mother's waiting on her day and night." She searches my face for a response. When I give none, she takes a draft of coffee from a YOU GO, GIRL mug on her desk. "Now, tell it true, Tracy. Aren't we having a wedding?"

I draw a deep breath. I see no point in dodging this one any longer. "It doesn't look like there's going to be one." I meet Eileen's gaze and don't look away. "You probably want to know why. Things didn't feel right. I couldn't go so fast. I asked him to slow down. He walked."

Eileen's eyes widen. The effect, accentuated by her blue eyeliner, is startling. She looks genuinely concerned. For a full minute I think I've silenced her.

"Go ahead," I say. "Tell me I'm stupid."

Thoughtfully, Eileen balances a tape dispenser in her palm. "A girlfriend of mine did something like that. She never regretted it — though everybody said she was dumb for losing the guy . . ." Eileen sets down the tape. "I thought she was brave."

I don't know how to answer this. Eileen is watching me, for the first time, with what looks like respect.

I gesture at the clock. "Meeting," I say.

In the faculty room most of the seats are already filled. I step past the empty chair by the right wall; Jeff is in Georgia, house-hunting with Richard. Steven Hilliard — present and accounted for as usual, his attendance now grimly accepted by the faculty — gives me a collegial wave. I make my way to a free seat, weaving past faces that hold more than the usual quotient of curiosity. Fortified by my exchange with Eileen, I am able to see beyond the inquisitive glances and understand that I'm a sideshow to the larger tensions animating the room. Elizabeth's letter has palpably spooked this assembly, but there's something more. Final grade sheets aren't due for another few days, but Jeff has already submitted his; I detect his glittering farewell confetti of A's hovering in the room. There is a jumpy excitement of the sort that animates a high school cafeteria just before a promised fistfight.

Anyone wandering into the room who hadn't known Joanne six months ago would see only a somewhat bulky woman, shoulders rounded, face plump, pacing heavily while the others settle into chairs. Her colleagues greet her with a blank, preoccupied politeness, as though the change that's overtaken Joanne these last months were invisible to them. Joanne, expert in sixteenth-century poets who took the measure of mortality in sonnets full of chilly graves, scans the gathering with thunderous disdain. Her colleagues' gazes flee.

The fall term is all but over, exams winding down. This is the time when academics wrap up grading and pray to be left alone. But Joanne has been in high gear. She's given up two of her classes for the coming term, yet if anything seems to have taken on more committee work. She's been particularly solicitous of the junior faculty, taking them out for preholiday drinks: jokey, confiding, abruptly interested in their personal lives. It may look like friendship. More likely it's empire expansion. I've played into it at the flurry of end-of-term meetings, gritting my teeth and voting Joanne's side wherever doing so does not directly betray my principles. My hand was the first in the air for her grading-review proposal last Friday, and I voiced immediate and emphatic approval of her motion for the creation of a new fifteenth-century post, leaving the meeting trailing unacknowledged at the rear of her retinue. I'm not stupid. Surely some of the faculty — including any senior colleagues undecided on the question of my tenure — are still watching for confirmation that I meant every word Elizabeth penned.

Joanne, who hasn't deigned to comment on my support, appears nonetheless mollified; at Tuesday's meeting she even went so far as to second my nomination of Jesse Faden for the Admissions Committee.

Now Joanne paces alongside the table. "I'd like to submit that we draft a departmental letter to the deans, requesting that student course recommendations no longer be distributed on the university's dime unless first reviewed by a faculty member. It may be an uphill battle, but I believe it's important to make an effort to institute this policy. I'll draft the letter this week, and I hope for your support and cosignatures."

No one with a stake in peaceable departmental relations will touch this one. Let Joanne tilt at her windmills.

"They meant well," says Steven Hilliard.

Joanne whips to face him. "A damning praise if ever there was one! Undergraduates aren't trustworthy, and you know it."

"Well." Steven chuckles, pointedly unfazed. He speaks so slowly he might be deliberately trying to infuriate her. "*Most* of us aren't trustworthy, if you're going to count honest mistakes as treason. The students who wrote your course description made a simple error. It wasn't intentional."

Joanne's finger slices a broad arc in the air. "The difference between the *almost right* word and the *right* word is really a large matter — 'tis the difference between the lightning-bug and the lightning." She drops her hand. "Mark Twain. Look it up."

Steve's voice tightens. "You're out of line."

Even though I'm braced for it, Joanne's fury is dreadful. Her voice is so loud it seems to leave a backwash of static in the still air. "I fail to see," she says, "why a bunch of students who clearly have trouble respecting women in academia deserve your defense." She stops, as though taking aim for her next blow.

Steven laughs and is silent.

The room is dead quiet. "All right, then," says Joanne vaguely. Flushed, she thumbs her notes. Then, in a manner that brooks no challenge, she sweeps the agenda along to the difficulties with the bookstore's new computer ordering system.

Outside the faculty room the assembly disperses. Halfway down the hall, the new Colonial Lit hire Elliott Harrell huddles with Joseph Yee, our resident anti-Marxist.

"Sometimes I hate feminists," Joseph is saying as I pass.

My step falters. Elliott and Joseph watch me, amused. "No offense intended," says Joseph.

Before I can continue on my way, Elliott says, "What do *you* think, Tracy? Were the students being sexist?"

I hesitate. From Elliott the question may be sincere. And I am tired: tired of letting the rumor mill speak for me, tired of feeling isolated within this faculty. I would like, just once, not to be misunderstood, caricatured, my ideas and beliefs slotted into dismissible categories. Even if the discussion is only about politics. "I don't think this is about sexism," I say softly. They move apart, making room for me. "That last zinger was just Joanne's way of getting Steven to stand down. I think this is about Joanne's other . . . stresses."

They acknowledge this with nods. "Poor thing," says Joseph briskly.

"Feminism," I say carefully, "isn't the issue here. It's a shame she felt compelled to invoke it."

"I see," says Joseph, with the same tolerant smile he might level on a die-hard Marxist who insists that — setting aside its practice — there's still a lot to be said for the *theory* of Communism.

It's almost hopeless: an aggressive woman who speaks her mind is everywhere assumed to be a feminist. Yet Joanne has just targeted the department's most promising female graduate student. She offers friendship to female colleagues only if they're well below her on the food chain, or vastly senior. She plays the men's game harder than the men, admitting to no known relationships, no outside interests, taking no prisoners. It's my belief that Joanne qualifies as an antifeminist.

I keep my meditations to myself. Elliott and Joseph may be free to dish on Joanne; I, for at least the next week and a half, am not.

Joseph glances at his watch; the two nod their goodbyes. As they depart for their offices, Joseph stage-whispers to Elliott. "Yeah. Maybe she's not a feminist. She *could* just be a bitch."

They disappear down the corridor, Joseph snickering.

I turn for my office and find Victoria in my path.

"How are you, Tracy?" Last week's indignation is gone. In its place is a genuine if reserved concern.

We take a few steps together in the direction of our offices. "I was sorry to hear about your breakup," she says. "But you surely have your reasons. I wish you well."

"Thanks."

"I recognize that your tenure review is also approaching. And you're doubtless feeling taxed by this whole ordeal with Elizabeth . . . a difficult situation, and one that we're all handling in good faith."

I accept this recognition with a grateful nod.

"That's a big load to bear," she says. We've reached Victoria's office. She reaches for the doorknob. "But you're going to be fine. Just lie low and do what you're doing." She hesitates, hand on the knob. "Steven tells me there's a new book in the works. Something *brash,* he said. He was vague on details."

I can't refuse Victoria — even when she's too genteel to ask directly for information. "It's about happy endings as possible acts of resistance in American literature. A different kind of truth-telling in the face of a prevailing cultural trope of tragedy."

She's silent for a bit. "Are you certain you want to take that on?"

"Yes."

She looks askance at my sharpness. "It's an awfully big thesis." She pauses. "Of course, theses used to be bigger, in my generation."

I know what she means: the academic bandwidth has shrunk over the past decades, with minutiae gradually elevated over sweeping concepts. It's a relief to be standing in the hall with Victoria, speaking not of loss or of madness but of books. A profound sense of sanity warms me. I tell her about Tolstoy, and the arc of my argument.

When I've finished she says nothing, only frowns with concentration. There is no rushing Victoria's thoughts. Her dignified, stodgy consideration makes me feel safe.

"I disagree," she says. She twists the knob, and her office door opens silently. She gazes into its quiet confines. "Our stories are tragic because we are. Happy endings aren't acts of resistance to cultural imperatives. They're simply exceptions—and not always believable ones—to the overarching human rule."

Victoria's desk telephone rings. She smiles briefly and closes her door.

The hospital room is barren. It takes me a moment to realize the barrenness is the absence of books. I've so rarely seen Elizabeth without books. The walls are free of shelves, there is no desk, no backpack loaded with tomes, and the tabletop on which Elizabeth's meal tray rests is free of papery clutter.

On the windowsill is the room's only patch of color—the ivy plant Mary bought in the hospital store last week while I lingered, making unnecessary offers of assistance, mysteriously incapable of returning to my apartment. Drinking in the spectacle of Elizabeth bearing her head high in the presence of her questioners: a martyr going to the scaffolding, her faith intact. Mary, fluent in the routine of hospital admission, shepherded Elizabeth smoothly between interviews with nurses and doctors . . . only once turning to me, as I numbly repeated my offer of help, with a look that sized me up — my blouse and wool slacks, my overstuffed briefcase, my uneasy expression — and found me lacking.

Now Mary sits in the corner. She nods when I greet her, then turns back to Elizabeth, whom she watches with a calm I cannot fathom.

Dressed in a shapeless T-shirt and sweatpants, Elizabeth floats on the wide hospital bed beside the window: a captive animal carelessly docketed in the wrong artificial habitat. A television, its gray eye blank, floats mute on its perch near the ceiling.

Seating myself, I think of Dickinson. *This is the Hour of Lead.*

Elizabeth stares through the pane. Watching her motionless form, I'm unfathomably attracted, unfathomably repelled.

Slowly, she turns to me. "What's happening?" she asks.

Of the possible answers to this question I choose the simplest. "The department is calming down."

"They put me on probation." Elizabeth's eyes linger on my shoes. In the last week she's gained color. Her movements are less agitated, yet there's a dullness to every gesture, as though body and thoughts drag chains. The effects of medication. Or, perhaps, loss. "Joanne left a phone message. She says if I write a letter of apology she'll consider dropping the issue, so it won't have to go before any committee that might terminate my degree candidacy." She's silent. Even her breathing seems to stop. Then she stirs again. "My mother won't let me write the letter yet. She says it's too early to think of anything but my health." Without warning she looks directly into my eyes. Then away to the window, stranding me.

She's made no mention of alien voices or literary revelation, leaving me to guess that her visitors have receded further under the drizzle of medication. Yet she herself seems, if anything, more remote than before. The offense I feel at this makes no sense: as though her breakdown were a deliberate betrayal of some unspoken trust between us. I want to shake her frail frame until she wakes.

Instead, chiding myself, I manage a kindness. "It's okay," I say. "We'll find a solution."

A nurse comes in to change the bed. Elizabeth, roused, proceeds to the ward's day room. I follow her. She settles on the sofa.

"Anything good?" I say, gesturing at a stack of colorful magazines on the coffee table as I lower myself into an armchair.

"I can't read."

I bend nearer. "What do you mean?"

"The words get inside my eyes, but they just" — her hand makes a slow eddy in the air — "swim."

"You can't read even a little bit?"

She sighs.

"Do you need me to read to you?" I glance at the magazines. The covers advertise recipes and home décor advice.

"My mother will." She fingers a small stain on her T-shirt. Her voice is loose with trepidation. "I leave this place in a few days. My mother says she'll stay with me."

In the day room are two other patients, neither of whom acknowledges our presence. Both are middle-aged women. One drifts aimlessly about the room's circumference, trailing fingertips along the flocked wallpaper. The other sits in a rocking chair with eyes closed, perfectly motionless.

"What about the letter of apology?" Elizabeth asks with abrupt energy. "I have to write it."

Speaking these words in a place designated for healing seems hypocritical, yet I'd also be failing Elizabeth if I didn't give her the truth. "It may be important," I say, "to make some gesture to Joanne as soon as you feel well enough. I've got something bad to report, Elizabeth. Joanne is ill. Word has spread only recently. I think it's going to affect your chances for forgiveness. People who know are very protective of her."

"Oh, I know she's sick," Elizabeth says absently.

"You know?"

"She told me. Months ago. Even before she told Victoria. It was our secret." Elizabeth's smile goes in two directions at once, pride and pain welded in the tight curve of her lips. "She's known about my problems, too. I told her about the time in college when I zoomed and then crashed and was in a hospital. She had asked me about the year I took off from academia, and I didn't want to lie. I trust her."

Elizabeth's voice flickers: these last words are a question. I don't answer it. An unfamiliar sensation floods me so powerfully I can hardly sit. It is the potent, pure understanding of a forest animal smelling smoke: Joanne *knew*. There are only two things that need to be done in response to this woman. Sound the alarm, and run until the forest is a memory. I can shun Joanne Miller and survive. I don't need her approval for my own happiness or productivity. I don't even need her vote — I feel suddenly sure of this — to make tenure. But there behind me, a dim speck on a smoky horizon of trees, is Elizabeth. Standing right in the fire's path.

"I'm worried about Joanne," she says.

I don't open my mouth.

"Is she all right?"

"For now," I say stiffly.

"Did you tell her? About Melville and Dickinson? About them talking to me?"

"No." My voice is clipped. "I didn't give details. But the department knows you're not well, Elizabeth." An understatement. Only yesterday I overheard one of the grad students refer, with a not quite apologetic snicker, to "the wacko in the stacks."

"Thanks for not telling," Elizabeth says. "People wouldn't understand." For several minutes, she picks meticulously at knobs of lint on her sweatpants, collecting the tiny navy balls into her fists like a precious harvest of seeds. Gradually the speed of her picking slows. She watches them come to rest on her thighs: open, senseless hands, spilling nubs of fabric. "Except you," she says.

Now it's my turn to look away.

Mary steps into the room and settles next to Elizabeth.

Checking her daughter into this hospital last week, Mary seemed all-capable. Her short gray hair and plain speech and her determination to safeguard her daughter's dreams answered a stubborn, unspoken hunger in me, and I was riveted. Yet now Mary asks me nothing about Elizabeth's precarious departmental situation, or Joanne's demands, or the ways I might help. She only picks up a magazine and begins to read aloud. It is an article about fall styles, and she enunciates each description of color and line as though it were of importance. As though she hadn't just hurtled across the country to answer a distress call. As though her daughter, her brilliant scholar of a daughter, were not seated beside her with flattened hair and rumpled clothing, in immediate danger of losing everything she's worked for over the past five years. Mary's seeming lack of concern confounds me. I can't say what, precisely, I need her to do. Only that the contrast between the mother I witnessed last week and the one I see now shocks me. I sit a long time, past the hour when I ought to be back in my office grading papers. Parched for something—a word, a gesture. For Mary to rip off her civilian costume and transform into the hero Elizabeth so needs—I so need—her to be. Instead I watch her sit on the sofa, reading her daughter fashion magazines with an unfathomable passivity. I leave tightlipped, freighted with an inexplicable, titanic anger.

I've nearly forgotten the evening's obligation when I spy it on my calendar: *Why the Flower Loves the Rod*—closing night.

I glance back at my computer screen, scanning my e-mail to Jeff. I've tapped in my worries about Elizabeth's condition, along with a transparently plaintive paragraph about my approaching tenure review date. I make no reference to Victoria's comments about my project, or to the unutterable void where George used to be, or to a thousand other signs proving Jeff right.

I hit Send, grab my bag, and rush to the subway, cursing at my watch as though it were to blame for my lateness. I promised Yolanda . . . but I can think of little I'd enjoy less than spending ninety minutes watching Hilda Doolittle unravel under Freud's analytic eye.

The lights are just going down as I drop into my seat in the packed house—a small theater, only slightly less shabby than its predecessor. My dash from the subway has left me breathless. It's a moment before I can hear H.D. over the racing of my heart.

"I'd been through every sort of war." Yolanda's taut, regal presence quiets me. "The war of marriage. The war of divorce. The war of childbirth. And the war of wars. The Great War. I let life fling me. Almost break me. But I would not be broken." She pauses to scan the audience. She sees me in the front row and directs a slow nod my way. "So *he* would be the one. Yes. *He* would understand."

The words, denatured when I first heard them, now accuse. Do H.D.'s grandiose hopes—her faith that she can, after all, reveal herself, rest her weight on another — echo mine? I shift in my seat, commanding myself to quit thinking about George and focus on the play.

"He would save me," Yolanda continues. "And I would save him."

The trust in H.D.'s voice — in Yolanda's — is an indictment. How could I have been so deluded? How could I have placed such a colossal bet on love, believing — despite all I'd seen before I'd met George, and all I saw once we began to unravel — that George and I would last? How is it that I'm still, even now, unwilling to disabuse myself of the fantasy?

The danger in the theater is suffocating. Love is an ecstatic compulsion to madness. I don't think I can bear sitting in this seat, watching H.D. give up control. I remind myself: *This is a terrible play.*

It doesn't help. As H.D.'s monologue ends, tears run down both my cheeks.

I'm counting on Bill's disinterest and incongruous youth to break the spell. But when Freud/Bill speaks, nothing is as it should be. The dialogue is the same, but Bill has changed. He's no longer indifferent.

"Not many are able to understand the true depth of my philosophy," he says. But this Freud doesn't look certain he understands that philosophy himself. He looks at H.D. as though he thinks she might. When he says, "She came to me because she was incapable of understanding her life," he sounds skeptical. When he says, "Hysteria lurked in her shadows," he looks apologetic. The exchange between H.D. and Freud proceeds in all its grinding, over-politicized detail. But Bill, onstage, finally looks at Yolanda as if working with her has gotten to him, too. As if he does long for her, but is powerless to do anything about it. When, halfway through the Helen of Troy scene, H.D.'s robe catches on a piece of scenery, Freud releases it with a gesture so tender that Yolanda actually stops to stare.

Hell with ideology. These two people *see* each other. There is a tragic chemistry between Yolanda and Bill that unmakes the heavy politics of the script.

I can no longer recall why this play is terrible. It doesn't even feel like a bastardization of history . . . or maybe it's just that, if you ignore the words and watch, underneath this H.D. and Freud's declarations is real respect, and an honest passion — not the incoherent one that the playwright penned into the script, but a deeper, gentler, more heartbreaking one. It's electric. There are two plays going on simultaneously in front of my eyes: the literal script, which tells a predictable feminist story of betrayal . . . and another story, far more complex and tragic.

The lights drop. Intermission.

It's not just me. The audience looks dumbstruck. Fully half the crowd stays in its seats. The woman seated next to me stares at the empty stage.

I, too, sit still, to take this in: Yolanda wasn't crazy. Bill *did*, in some loopy impossible way and despite all his outer indifference, love her. And she knew he did. Which is what was driving her nuts all that time.

When Yolanda re-emerges onstage, the clarity in her face is stunning. Gone is the last of the heavy rage that's fueled her performance. In its place is an airy sorrow. Something, some long-delayed exchange or conversation, happened backstage.

She turns to Freud. "We'll never be together," she says. A line that is not in the script. "But," she adds, "I wasn't wrong."

Freud/Bill is trembling visibly, a palsy of exposure and revelation.

"There's a difference," she says, head high, "between what you know in your heart, and what you think is acceptable to know."

Bill looks at her as though if he had an ounce more to give, he'd give it. Then, with a line the real Freud actually spoke, he brings them back to the script. "The trouble is," he says, "I am an old man — you do not think it worth your while to love me." And Bill, for the first time, looks credibly old. Stricken by failure.

Across the stage, Yolanda replies, confesses, and begs in the playwright's vocabulary, but with a face lit by forgiveness. Her eyes are clear. Her words, this time, are not accusatory, but elegiac. And I see how readily, all these years, I've underestimated her.

I exit the theater in tears. Thinking: Love is real. It was up there on stage, palpable, just out of reach. And it is impossible in this world.

· · ·

Entering my apartment, Yolanda sets her coat and scarf on the arm of the sofa but does not sit. She's kinetic: pacing the length of my narrow living room, bending to ply her calves, high-kicking into another stretch, hugging knee to forehead. Restless as a caged acrobat. Two days after the closing of her show, and Yolanda has energy to burn.

"A walk would be good for you," she insists. "The sun is out."

"I've had it with what's good for me." Dumb retort. But Yolanda backs off. "*That*"— I continue in a high, childish tone, indicating the package lying askew on my windowsill where I let it fall last night— "*that* is not good for me."

In the window's clear light she picks up the Priority Mail wrapper, pulls out the copy of *Gravity's Rainbow*, and studies it. "From George?" she says.

Gone is Yolanda's habitual mask of makeup. Belatedly I realize that it's been absent for weeks, rendering my oldest friend visible, laugh lines and all: this fellow traveler whom— I'm grateful for this single thought rising above the morning's litany of self-pity— I love.

Slowly I nod. "It's a book I lent him. There wasn't even a note. As if this was an ordinary breakup, instead of . . . it's not like . . ." Words fail. "He's just turned his back."

Yolanda sounds weary. "I think," she says, "that if it was an ordinary breakup he would call to say goodbye. I think he's doing it this way because he's devastated by what you did."

It feels pointless to explain myself once more. But I do. "It was *his* choice, Yolanda. I know you think it's illegal to return an engagement ring, but I swear I never broke up with him. I just said he couldn't press-gang me into marriage— we needed to sort out each step together. I was telling him the whole time that I wanted to be with him. But he was suffocating us." As I speak I'm visited by a stern image of George's father.

"I hear you, Tracy. I've been listening these last two weeks. Honestly, I have." She checks some minute detail of her manicure by the light of the window. "I just think . . . you know what I think."

I shake my head blindly. I'm as tired of this conversation as all my friends are. I've trodden this ground with either Yolanda or Hannah on a daily basis; at least twice this week, Adam lowered the volume on his television to provide gruff support. "It would have been marrying under false pretenses," I repeat. "I couldn't live with that."

She sets the book on the sill. "You won't have to."

It takes a second for the gentleness of her voice to register. Then I know with a thump in my gut that Yolanda sees me as a tragic figure.

I watch her lace her fingers, turn her palms out, and crack her back in a graceful yogic twist. "What's up?"

"Nothing much." She huffs and bends double, pressing palms to my floor.

"You're a crappy liar."

She straightens, rubbing the dust off her palms. It takes a moment for her to look at me. "Remember the delivery guy?"

"The pizza guy? From last week?"

"No, the one who got knocked over on Eighth Avenue. Whose food got stolen by that skateboarder."

It takes me a minute. "The *not English* guy?"

"Did you think he was cute?"

"I don't remember. All I remember was you were spectacular. And he was in awe."

She can't hold back her smile. "Well, he found me."

"What do you mean *found* you?" I didn't intend the indignant tone. I rise and step to the window.

She speaks carefully. "He was hanging around by my health-food shop. I think he's been doing it for a while, and a couple weeks ago he found me."

"A couple *weeks* ago?" I turn to face her.

"I didn't want to tell you then, Tracy. You were —"

I wave this off. "And?"

"He's sweet." Yolanda looks unaccountably embarrassed. I don't quite understand; I don't believe I've ever seen Yolanda embarrassed.

"You two have been dating?" I probe.

"Sort of. Not exactly. I mean, we've gone out a few times. But he's a gentleman. He hasn't made too many moves yet. I kissed him first, last night, because I was getting sick of waiting."

"What's his name?"

Again the embarrassed look. "I call him Chad."

"But that's not his name?"

"I can't pronounce his name. Chad is where he's from."

"When did he come to the U.S.?"

"Last summer, I think."

"Did he come alone?"

"I think."

"You think?"

"I think." Yolanda twists her torso into a deep left-leaning stretch and holds the pose: shot-putting champion of Twenty-third Street.

"How old is Chad?"

"Maybe thirty," she says to the ceiling.

"What do you mean, maybe?" My voice, despite my efforts, is sharp. "Didn't you ask?"

"Well" — she grunts as she releases her stretch — "his English isn't very good."

"How not good?"

She sets her hands on her hips and looks at me square. "I'm teaching him words. We've gone to two movies together and talked about them, but I speak English and he speaks mostly . . . Chad. What language do they speak there?"

"French. I think."

"Okay. And you remember how I was in Spanish class."

"Or he might speak Arabic. Or something else."

"Well, whatever it is, I don't understand it. We can't talk on the phone. I have his phone number, but that's only when we want to say hello and then just kind of listen to each other breathe, you know? We have to arrange our meetings before we part. I write the time and place on a piece of paper."

"So this is about sex?"

She shrugs, extending her palms in wonderment. "That's the funny thing. I haven't even gotten him in *bed* yet, he's so courtly. And he's had the chance, I mean he's been in my apartment. He's just . . . sweet. And he has this great smile."

On the street below my window, cars and cabs jostle — a Manhattan shell game. I tell myself: under one of these shells is George.

"Yolanda . . ." I begin.

She composes a serious face, but the corners of her mouth look ticklish.

"You know," I say, "I love you like a sister."

She waits.

"And I've seen you get your heart broken before, Yolanda."

Her face sours, and I'm sorry. I check myself. Happiness has been too fleeting for Yolanda, and I want to be a good friend.

"It's just. Yol, I'm sure he's a sweet guy. All I'm saying is, maybe try not to put too much weight on this Chad until you know him better. He doesn't speak English, so he can't say all he thinks. And for all we know, what he thinks — about sex, about life, about yoga — might horrify you."

She undoes her ponytail and wraps her hair into a knot, which she fastens with one defiant jab of a clip. "Don't you believe you can know a person without words?"

I want to answer yes. I want to believe it's possible — with or without language — to truly know another human being. To lie on his chest, rise and fall warm on a skiff that will bear you safely, steadily, who cares where.

"Just try to make sure," I say as gently as I can, "that you're not loading too many hopes and meanings onto him. You —"

Her jaw juts.

I shut my eyes momentarily, then open them to beg Yolanda's understanding. "Please forgive me if I'm being clumsy about it, Yolanda, I don't mean to lecture you." Only to save you. From him? From yourself? From love?

Yolanda lifts her coat from the sofa, her mouth curling once more into that unconscious half smile. "He likes the seeded parts of cucumbers," she says. She buttons her coat, her hands proceeding from her knees to her throat as though each match of button and loop were a promise fulfilled.

I'm riding the D line uptown, returning from a visit with Hannah, when the fair hair and doughy features of a man across the car resolve into a face I've met before: Joel, George's boss, to whom George introduced me two months and a hundred years ago.

As I rise in the jolting train, I can see George sitting at his desk. Shoulders steady, hand turning a page. Roy Hargrove playing softly, rebounding in my gut. I walk, swaying, and grab the nearest pole. "Joel?"

He looks up, blinks. An expression of discomfort crosses his face. "Hi, Tracy."

"Awkward?" I say.

He gives a chagrined smile. "It's good to see you."

"He won't answer my calls."

Joel hesitates, choosing his words. "George has pride. That's for sure." A slight, wry grimace plays on his mouth. "He said you ended things."

"That's not what I think. Not at all. I didn't want to end it. Please, if you can, tell him—" I turn my palm up, at a loss to continue.

"I'm sorry, Tracy." His face is grave. "I don't seem to have his confidence anymore myself. I'm not sure why. And he's out of town now. I haven't seen him much anyway lately. You know— or maybe you don't? He's job-hunting."

"You're serious?"

"Oh, yes." Joel's commentary—sharp and unspoken—is written on his face. "He's moving back to the finance world. He told me he sees a *clear path* for himself there. Says he can always do volunteer work in education on the side." The train slows. Joel picks up his briefcase and stands. He looks tired. "I'm interviewing to replace him. It's not easy. As you know." Black-on-white lettering scrolls outside the window of the train: WEST FOURTH STREET. Joel speaks quickly. "For what it's worth, he's in Toronto."

"He is?"

"His father had a minor heart attack. George went a few days ago. Bought a used car and took off. I haven't heard from him." With a gentle squeeze of my shoulder, Joel gets off the train.

At home, I rack my brain for Paula's last name. It takes ten minutes of variant spellings to get her number. I dial, my heart thudding.

"Hello?" In the background I hear her children.

"Paula?"

"Yes?"

"It's Tracy. Farber."

Silence.

"George's Tracy."

Silence.

"I heard," I say, "about your father."

"He's all right," she says slowly. "Thank God."

"Thank God," I echo.

Silence.

"I'm so sorry," I tell Paula. "For the hurt I've caused. But I think it's a misunderstanding. I truly do. I just wish George would talk to me. But he won't answer my phone messages."

Paula sighs. Then she says, in a neutral voice, "Whatever my disagreements with George's lifestyle, Tracy, I'll say this. He's honest. And he's not willing to dignify what he considers a lie. He's told me you're leaving him messages. But he's not calling you because there's nothing to say after what you did. He says honesty was the best thing you two had, but now you just want to ease the shock, make the parting more comfortable."

"That's not what I'm trying to do."

Her voice rises. "Tracy, with all respect, you're ripping him up. Stop leaving him messages. It may ease your conscience, but it's the wrong thing to do. You rejected him. Why should he have to demean himself by negotiating that fact?"

"I didn't reject him."

She sounds impatient. "You didn't give your whole heart to him."

Terrified she'll get off the phone, I back down. "What else does he say?"

"He's heartsick, Tracy. I mean . . ." Her words slow. "He went to our father in the recovery room. And he said, *I failed.* Tracy, I don't know if you understand what it took for George to say that. He and Dad have had some battles that defy description. He said to Dad, *My love wasn't what I thought. My life wasn't what I thought.*" Paula lets this sink in. "I'm not saying George is coming back to the church, that's not mine to predict. But he's bent his neck."

"Paula," I say. "Is George in your house? Right now?"

A moment's hesitation. "I don't know if that's a good idea."

"Please," I say. "Paula. I just . . . I need to speak with him."

Another silence. Then she says, in a low voice, "Meg, go tell Uncle George that Tracy is on the telephone."

I hold my breath.

"Tell him," Paula calls hurriedly after her daughter, her voice rising with what I know to be an argument for me. "Tell him Tracy called to see how Grandpa was."

"Thank you," I whisper.

Nothing. Then, in the background, the barely audible voice of a girl.

"He's not coming," Paula says quietly. "He thanks you for asking after our father."

She waits on the phone. I imagine her sitting patiently with me, holding my hand until I'm ready to depart.

"I love him," I say at length.

Her farewell is gentle. "I'll pray for you."

I set down the phone. I microwave dinner. Then sit with the plate in front of me, unable to swallow.

Pulling up my shade, I turn off my light, and face it squarely: the white flush of the city, its strangling refusal to assume any shape I recognize. My choice — my one slender protest against the armies and acolytes of marriage — has become the organizing principle of my life: isolating me, reshaping my perception of the world, demanding a stubborn, pointless faith that what I saw and felt was real. That I knew when love was being choked; that I knew when I had to upend everything to save it. That I had any idea at all what love was.

Far below my window a slow crawl of humanity make its way from work to home. Cabs sail down narrow tributaries, marquees twinkle, elevators rush unseen in dark shafts, children's nightlights flicker. With a twist in my gut I think of Elizabeth in her hospital bed, settling down to blank dreams beneath the buzz of the corridor's fluorescent bulb and the radio murmurs washing from the nurses' station.

Yolanda rises when I enter the Chinese restaurant and leads me back to the table with an expression I can think of only as goopy.

"*This,*" she says, "is Chad."

Chad, whose skin is so dark it shines under the restaurant's unsubtle lighting, stands at my approach and beams at me. He extends a warm, dry hand and folds mine into his palms. His eyes, as brown and deep as his smile is white, are lovely. I can't help softening. He touches his forehead, miming appreciation. Then he invites me to sit and asks me — I'm not certain how he accomplishes this, no words are involved — how I am. He seems to know my story and his deep nod acknowledges the complexity behind my truthful answer: "Managing."

I ignore the significant look Yolanda gives me; I'm not ready to sign on completely. But I'm impressed.

Next to Chad, wearing a worn *Mad* magazine T-shirt, sits Adam. Next to him Worms, his roommate, leans back against the restaurant's taupe wall, lids at half-mast under the rim of the ever present baseball cap. Hannah is home getting a last good night's sleep; she's past due, and her OB is inducing labor tomorrow. This dinner was Yolanda's idea, a nearly intolerable generosity: get Tracy's friends together, cheer her up, get her to leave the books and shake off her mourning for an hour. I wouldn't have accepted the invitation except that Yolanda is so patently right: I need to get out.

The food is delicious, the platters piled high. Chad serves himself only after everyone else has taken from each dish. He refills Yolanda's water glass from his own. When Yolanda drops a piece of tofu he picks it off her breastbone with the deft tips of his chopsticks and pops it into her mouth, where she incises it delicately with her white teeth. As the two pieces melt on her tongue Chad watches: patient, gratified. Yolanda has, it's obvious, lured her man to bed.

The conversation hops among work, sitcoms, and what it means when gay men kiss women friends on the lips. Worms remains unaccounted for, rocking Buddha-like on the two rear legs of his chair.

Chad watches the proceedings with such bright attention that I expect him to open his mouth at any second and speak eloquent English.

"Saw *Great Expectations* on TV last night," says Yolanda. "Do you teach that, Tracy?"

"Dickens was British. I'm an Americanist."

"Yeah, but isn't that practically the same thing by now? I mean, with *Masterpiece Theatre* and everything?" Yolanda serves herself a spoonful of bright purple eggplant. "I felt sorry for Pip, but especially for Estella."

I poke at my lo mein.

"Though I guess they all come out better than Miss Havisham," Yolanda continues.

"The spider lady?" says Adam.

"Yeah," says Yolanda. "It's lousy to be left."

"I didn't *leave* him." Only after the words are out of my mouth do I realize Yolanda wasn't referring to George, but to her own pained romantic history. No one came here tonight to chide me about George . . . but I've been too enmeshed in my own grief to recognize that. I blink Yolanda an apology, and finish haltingly: "I was trying to *save* something between us." I picture the books awaiting me in my quiet apartment and wonder how soon I can leave. The air in the restaurant feels thick, the ceiling low. I am becoming Miss Havisham. I am becoming a Dickens character, smoldering with my grievance, burnishing my arguments. Shrinking instead of growing. "Sorry," I say.

"No offense meant, Tracy," says Yolanda. Chad is watching me, his eyes bright with such overflowing empathy that I have to look away. When I turn back he is squeezing Yolanda's plump turquoise-laden hand.

"The heart is a muscle," Worms says.

The table is silent.

Worms teeters peaceably on his chair, intent on a plastic hanging plant above the corner radiator.

But of course, I think, that's right. The heart is a laborer. It's built for this. Love is meant to be work. The notion is, in some small way, fortifying.

"Ew," says Adam, smacking the side of Worms's head. "Don't get all deep."

Worms picks up his fork and continues eating.

After dessert Yolanda walks me to the door. "You sure you're okay?"

I shrug my coat onto my shoulders and give her a grim smile. "Thanks a lot for doing this. I really appreciate it."

She hesitates, then digs in the rear pocket of her jeans for a piece of paper, which she hands to me.

"He's in my yoga class," Yolanda says. "He's a little stiff in the upper back — most businessmen are — but he's pretty limber for a guy with a stable job. He's cute, and he's looking for someone. I gave him your number."

In a neat blue script, orderly but masculine, is the name "Dan Cooper." And a phone number. The paper floats on my open palm, neither accepted nor rejected. The slightest breeze from a fan could blow it away, but there is no breeze. The paper rests on my palm, and I know George isn't coming back.

Dan Cooper sits opposite me, buttering a roll. He is a thoughtful, good-looking, perfectly nice man.

"I graduated from Harvard in eighty-seven," he answers. "But I didn't go straight to law school. Before that I took a year off to bike."

"That must have been interesting," I say automatically — then, with a surge of restless energy, I preempt his response. "*Not really. Actually it was a stationary bike.*"

He holds the roll in midair for a full second. Then he laughs politely. "Oh, no. I biked all over the Pacific Northwest. I'm very passionate about the environment."

He bites into his roll, and chews.

Elizabeth's voice is so wan I strain to hear. "Thank you for coming." Dressed in a pale blue button-down shirt and baggy sweatpants, her wet hair smelling like baby shampoo, she seems more like an undergraduate on study break than a recent discharge from a locked psychiatric unit.

As I hang my coat and set down my briefcase in the apartment's narrow entryway, Mary appears with a steaming mug. She passes me the tea with both hands and the sotto voce greeting "Hot."

I blow on my tea. The moist heat reflects upward to my brow and cools there, leaving me lightheaded. I don't know why I'm here. I could have taken Jeff's advice and refused Mary's request, but I didn't, didn't even consider refusing. It would be a lie to say I'm here on a mission of mercy. It's more selfish·than that. I need Elizabeth, for some urgent unarticulated reason, to snap out of it.

"Thanks," says Elizabeth for the third time. "For coming." She turns and walks ahead of us into the living room.   ·

"There haven't been other visitors," Mary explains.

"The grad students are probably spooked," I say to Mary. "People get superstitious. Which is no excuse."

She seems unperturbed by the absence of Elizabeth's fellow students. Without another word she turns to follow her daughter. She reminds me, I think with yet another flash of anger, of my own mother. Too passive to shout, storm, question. My mother, whose primary response to my breakup, other than a few phrases of puzzled sympathy that sounded like reproach, was *Your father will be so disappointed.*

Another insomniac night has left me frazzled. Balancing my tea with care, I follow Mary down the narrow corridor and into Elizabeth's apartment.

I'd pictured Elizabeth breaking down in a florid jumble, tearing wallpaper from her Fort Greene walls like the Charlotte Perkins Gilman heroine. Instead her apartment is impeccably neat, decorated with Shaker-like austerity. White sheets shroud two floor-to-ceiling bookcases. Mary's hand is evident, too, in the bare desktop, all evidence of literary striving presumably sealed into the cardboard box in the corner, marked PAPERS. The apartment is a literary crime scene. My eyes wander repeatedly to the box. I find myself thinking of the gems of observation trapped there, attained at such cost to Elizabeth.

Seated on the sofa, Elizabeth is utterly still. Her lips are pale and her blinks so slow and infrequent that I find myself anticipating each with mounting disquiet.

I sit in the chair Mary indicates.

"I need your help," Elizabeth murmurs. "That's why I asked my mother to call you. Joanne will let me off the hook if I write a letter of apology." She unfolds herself: a protracted process, as though her limbs were steeped in regret. On the side table sits her mother's handbag. Opening it, she produces a pen, which she cradles with a moment's longing. Then she hands it to me. "Joanne says she won't involve any committees. She says the whole thing will be between the two of us. It will be settled, I won't get forced out of the program. But it's hard" — she stares at the pen, which lies in my open palm — "to write. And my mother says she doesn't want me doing it alone."

"You know the politics, Tracy," injects Mary firmly from the sofa.

"You want *me* to write the letter to Joanne?"

Mary and Elizabeth nod.

I set the pen on the coffee table and address myself to Mary. "You do realize, don't you, that this won't end the problem? A letter of apology, which constitutes a confession, will sit in Joanne's desk. Any time she feels like bringing Elizabeth down, all she has to do is hand it to a dean. That could be a year from now. It will prevent Elizabeth from having any real security in the department, so long as Joanne is around."

Mary hesitates only a second, then answers decisively. "We still think it's generous of Joanne to offer this option."

"Have you *met* Joanne?"

Mary looks at me sharply. "No. Why?"

"Come *on,*" whispers Elizabeth with sudden passion.

Mary reaches for a small gray answering machine positioned beside the phone, and presses Play.

This is Joanne. It's four o'clock in the afternoon. A long, forbearing sigh blows from the machine's microphone. *Elizabeth, while I don't at all understand what happened, I am willing to accept a written apology. I could take that letter you sent me to the faculty senate, you know. I could take it to them for next week's meeting.* A long pause. *But I won't. If I receive a letter from you.* Joanne's voice drops; she seems to pull the receiver closer, and when she speaks next, enunciating clearly from inside the small gray box of the answering machine, she sounds like she's right here in Elizabeth's spare living room. *I forgive you.*

Elizabeth's light touch on my hand makes me jump. Undeterred, she puts the pen between my fingers. I shake her away, but don't drop the pen. I have to agree with Mary: Elizabeth doesn't have a choice.

With the slightly awed demeanor of a child embarking on an art project, Elizabeth brings a notepad. "If you write," she says, "my mother can type it later."

Determined to get this over with as swiftly as possible, I settle at the bare desk and set pen to paper. "To Joanne Miller," I say.

"Dear," says Elizabeth. "*Dear Joanne.* No last name."

I write the words, then turn back to Elizabeth. "*I would like to apologize for—*"

"*I beg your apology,*" she says.

"*—for the offense I caused you?*" I suggest.

"And my poor judgment in doing so," adds Elizabeth.

"It wasn't poor judgment," I say testily. "It was a breakdown. How about *I was not well?*"

"My poor judgment," insists Elizabeth. "I should have known better than to let them make me do things people wouldn't understand."

"Why did you ask me to do this if you're going to write it yourself?" My voice quivers with unexpected anger.

Elizabeth takes a step backward. "Thank you for doing this, Tracy." She looks so meek I want to shake her.

"When I have regained my strength," I say, penning the words, *"I hope to make this apology in person. For now —"*

"It will be in person. I mean . . . I'm going in to the department to give this to her," says Elizabeth.

"That's crazy."

Mary flinches. Elizabeth looks out the window.

With a sigh I strike the line and continue. *"I would like to assure you that I am aware my actions were deeply inappropriate. I intended no harm to you, and hold you in great respect."*

"Greatest," says Elizabeth, who has crept back to peer over my shoulder. When I don't respond she repeats, quietly: *"Greatest."*

I write the word, then add what's necessary in a rush of irritation. *"I hope this incident, inappropriate and upsetting as it has been, will not overshadow my years of work and devotion to the department. I am committed to completing my dissertation just as soon as I am well, and I hope to have the opportunity to demonstrate my dedication to academia and to this department. Whatever I can do to make up for my behavior, I will do."*

"Thanks a lot," says Elizabeth, when I've set down the pen. "I think that's my best chance at getting back."

I hand her the letter. She stands reading it: pale, beautiful, young. She could tear up this letter and go on to a different profession, one that wouldn't commandeer her sanity so powerfully. One that doesn't prize, above all, solitary fever-pitch thinking. "Are you sure you want to go back?" I say.

Elizabeth presses the page to her chest, uncomprehending. "It's my life. It's . . ." A powerful grief crosses her face, a grief I feel in my gut. "Literature is the most beautiful thing in the world."

Her speech is reflexive, a blind plea for understanding. "It will be hard to go slow, when I'm better. You don't know what it's like. Being *lightning*. Being able to hear them directly, to write down what they tell me. On the medicine, I have to figure it all out for myself." Elizabeth offers a strange smile. "Don't worry. I'll stay on my medicine. If I don't, I burn up. No one can be lightning without burning up, right? Not for more than a millisecond. Or something." She giggles miserably. Then, soberly: "I'm going to ask Joanne to be my adviser. When I go back."

"That's *insane*," I say before I can censor myself.

"She emphasizes the evolution of prosody," blurts Elizabeth. "So do I."

"She emphasizes the evolution of *sixteenth-century* prosody," I fire back.

Elizabeth says nothing.

I stare at her. There is a taste of acid in my throat.

Mary sips her tea.

"What makes you think Joanne would even accept that?" I say.

"I just — know her. You know what I mean?"

Slowly I shake my head. I imagine Joanne: the iron gray noticeably taking over her hair, the moon-round face, the thickness in her voice. The slight limp she seemed to develop out of nowhere this week. Then I look at Elizabeth's wan features. I don't understand the symbiosis at work here. Elizabeth and Joanne, and whatever bargain of despair, punishment, or reward they might transact, have stepped beyond my reach. Only when Elizabeth turns her head toward me do I see her request for forgiveness.

When Elizabeth trudges off to the bathroom, Mary turns to me. "She says she needs to show her face and let everyone know she's still devoted to the program. Is that true?"

"Mary," I say, "I don't know whether she'll be able to recover from this politically, no matter what she does."

Mary takes this in. Her face is stolid. She motions toward the bathroom. "She wakes up in the morning thinking of books. I won't take that away. Is there a way for Elizabeth to do this dissertation without being driven day and night?"

"That depends whether she chooses to wear Joanne's choke collar."

Mary looks annoyed. Then she continues as though she hadn't heard me. "Her outpatient treatment is going well. But the doctor says Elizabeth can't go back to work for two months. The department has already had to find a replacement for the section she was teaching. Elizabeth says she needs to show up to prove she hasn't just vanished. You know she can't go in there alone. She needs you to go with her."

"That's—"

"I'm afraid for her," Mary interrupts. This is not a confession; Mary neither seeks nor expects sympathy. Nor, it's suddenly evident, does she like me.

I struggle to contain my hurt. Why should I care if Mary thinks me condescending? She has no understanding of the pressures I face. "My tenure committee meets a week from today," I say. "I hope you'll understand why I can't be involved in this. I've extended myself more than—"

"You're the only one who knows the whole situation," Mary continues. "In a week that faculty senate could already have kicked her out."

"They wouldn't kick her out," I counter testily. "They'd force her to take a temporary leave of absence."

"Which would turn permanent. Wouldn't it? Probably?"

I sigh a long sigh, then nod.

I'm being asked to hold Elizabeth's hand while she delivers an apology I've ghostwritten—even as she spurns me as her adviser. If there is something too raw about Joanne's forgiveness of Elizabeth, the same might be said for my deepening involvement in this mess. By all logic, I should walk away. Yet I, too, have been seduced by something about Elizabeth, hooked in until her well-being feels essential to my own. I run my fingers through my hair, digging into my scalp, and take momentary refuge in well-trodden indignation: that Elizabeth has lost her grip is tragic enough; why did it have to be a goddamn tabloid scenario, the kind Eileen lives for?

My thoughts drift longingly toward George; I wrest them away. Shutting my eyes, I ask myself: Why—honestly—am I so angry?

Here is my answer: If the world stopped making sense—if I heard voices in the midnight library stacks—I would have a choice. I could believe there were aliens who also happened to be literary giants—a belief that would be at once glorious and harrowing, upending my understanding of all I've ever known.

Or I could believe there were no aliens, and I was losing my mind.

Which would be less terrifying?

Head in hands, I listen to the flush of the toilet and Elizabeth's soft tread, and it occurs to me that there are two kinds of people: Those who, told they're crazy, turn their opinions over to surer hands. And those who will pay any price, no matter how steep, to remain true to their own vision, without which the world is a sickening void.

I'd choose aliens.

I would not have been any more willing than Elizabeth to step back from the verge, to alert a friend, to turn myself in for treatment and shut my eyes to revelation. Recalling the Dickinson poem, I can hear it now only in Elizabeth's low whisper: *Most— I love the Cause that slew Me / Often as I die / Its beloved Recognition / Holds a Sun on Me.* Up close, devotion and folly grow indistinguishable. Elizabeth's courage, her choice to trust her mind in the face of all evidence to the contrary, is the sort of bravery that might under different circumstances have made her a Romantic heroine. Instead it's made her tragic. I'm not furious at Elizabeth for clinging to outlandish visions, but for being wrong.

I've read enough about bipolar disorder to know that her visions may yet kill her, that in such extreme, psychosis-inducing cases, the suicide rate is fearfully high. Elizabeth's prospects terrify me. But my fear goes deeper than altruism. My own fate seems to rest obscurely on making sure she's not burned at the stake for her beliefs. I can no longer deny how powerfully I see myself in her. How I've hated her vulnerability because I understand it; how I can imagine all too well the scald of her loss; the dizzying fear that she can no longer trust her judgment, that her choices were madness, that the vision that lit her world is gone forever.

And I, like her, refuse to believe I was wrong. Contrary to every sensible friend urging me to declare my love for George dead and look to new horizons, I refuse to turn my back on the truth of what I saw.

Nothing but luck separates Elizabeth from me. To suppose otherwise is hubris. The tenderness I feel, as I understand this, is pow-

erful enough to make me break stride. I think: We are all just crea-
tures swimming toward the light.

Sometimes life is like this. Sometimes all the scrims drop at once:
theory, professionalism, politeness. We stand, totter with loneliness. Brace ourselves. Fling fingertips to the sky.

"What time?" I say to Mary.

This is what happens when Elizabeth steps off the elevator: The
air in the department ionizes. A heightened quiet settles over the
corridor as I greet her with a squeeze of her shoulder and lead her
to my office. We pause here inside my fortress of books, its floor-
to-ceiling shelves dwarfing Elizabeth, who scans the spines with a
darting glance. She is breathing shallowly.

"Thank you," she whispers. "I owe you big-time."

We walk to the faculty lounge, Elizabeth with a boxy, stretch-
marked backpack riding high and empty on one shoulder. Inside
the lounge she pours coffee, then warms her hands on the cup
without drinking. We don't have to wait long. Footsteps approach,
the door swings wide. Victoria and Joanne enter, Joanne with a
startled glare in my direction. It's obvious Elizabeth didn't tell her
I'd be present.

Victoria's forehead furrows. She looks at Elizabeth with strained
concentration. As I expected, the sight of her has wakened Victoria's sympathy.

Victoria's voice is kind. "You didn't have to do this in person."

"I wanted to," says Elizabeth. Her voice catches on the words.
Then, more steadily: "It's important to express how sincere I am in
my apology, and how dedicated to this department."

Victoria settles, with a watchful nod, onto the sofa.

Elizabeth swings her backpack from her shoulder, fishes in its
roomy cavity, and produces a single folded sheet of paper. She
hands it to Joanne, who takes it with a rough gesture and leaves.

During the ten minutes that Elizabeth, Victoria, and I wait in
the lounge, a half dozen faculty members show for coffee breaks.
One by one they enter, linger over the electric kettle or coffee
machine, peruse the shelves in vain for an unaccountably absent
volume. They murmur to Elizabeth — *Good to see you, How's it
going.* Empty queries, excuses for a few seconds' searching gaze,
enough to take in the fiercely ironed blouse and slacks, the peaked

face and clenched hands. They leave tucking their impressions into their pockets, tender for barter at a later and livelier gathering.

The door opens. Joanne is winded. Her grip bends the letter's slim profile. She holds it, chest-level, like a trophy.

Elizabeth's struggle to lift her eyes is monumental.

"The apology," says Joanne, "is clearly sincere." She swirls the air with Elizabeth's letter. Her face is flushed. "I'll grant you the right to continue in this program."

Elizabeth's lids close in thanksgiving.

"But forgiveness isn't everything," Joanne cuts in. "There's the matter of your dissertation."

"I—"

Silently I counsel: *Don't let her ruffle you.*

"I'll get it done as soon as I'm able," Elizabeth breathes.

Good girl.

"That's not enough. You've already got one gap in your résumé. Just how long do you plan to delay before going on the job market? It won't look good."

"Joanne, I've been meaning to ask you—" Elizabeth glances guiltily at me: we'd agreed she wouldn't suggest this today, but like an affection-starved child she's unable to refrain from giving all. "Will you be my adviser?" In her quavering voice the question sounds like a proposal of startling intimacy.

Joanne lifts her chin. Without turning from Elizabeth or altering the substance of her words, she addresses herself directly to me, and her message is one of unalloyed triumph. "Inefficiency," she says, "is a luxury you can no longer afford."

"I think what Joanne means," Victoria interjects, a distinct note of warning in her voice—to Joanne? to Elizabeth?—"is that this event has damaged your reputation. The more promptly—within reason—you can demonstrate that you're capable of getting your work done, the better."

"I understand," says Elizabeth.

"Do you?" presses Joanne.

In my thirty-three years I have never felt so strong an urge to punch another human. I catch Victoria's eye. Her mouth is pursed.

"We're running out of time," warns Joanne, as though she expects Elizabeth to start typing right here. "I'll work with you. But if you don't give us your final draft soon we'll have to take it out of your hands."

No one can bring a dissertation draft before a committee without the author's permission. Surely Elizabeth sees through this bluff?

Joanne steps heavily toward Elizabeth, close enough for a private conversation. Under Joanne's stare Elizabeth seems to lose her ability to focus. Her eyes widen but find no purchase.

"I don't understand what's been taking you so long," Joanne confides.

And something in me turns to stone.

Elizabeth's speech is thick. "I'll reset my defense-date as soon as I can. I'll let you know. I want to tell you how grateful . . ." She cannot finish the sentence. Her face is saturated with abasement, and with an emotion I recognize even if she cannot: hate. Her eyes drop to the floor. After a long silence her head drifts up and, with a quick, admiring glance at Joanne, she leaves the room.

Victoria turns to Joanne. "She'll need time to recuperate."

Joanne shrugs. She folds Elizabeth's letter neatly in two, and slides it into the pocket of her slacks.

"You were hard on her," Victoria persists. "Understandable, but —"

"I see myself in her," Joanne says evenly. "I know what she's capable of."

"It's a real gift to a student," says Victoria, "when a professor takes a personal interest in her abilities. But let's remember that for the moment Elizabeth is not as capable at *living* as she is at literature."

In the pause that follows, both women seem to become aware of my presence. I don't budge. To move would be to jar a fragile new understanding: I've been wrong. Joanne does not want Elizabeth driven out of the department.

"You need her here, don't you?" I say.

Joanne laughs aloud.

"Like a house," I say, "needs a lightning rod." The words are spoken. There is no stepping back now, between us.

She turns to me: face set, fists curling at her sides, stance defiant. Solid limbs chaining her to a crippled future. The statuesque body, the athletic grace and physical power Joanne has exerted all her life like a magnetic field, have betrayed her. In another universe she and Elizabeth and I would console one another — each in our own way bereft. But Joanne, heedless, hurtles toward vengeance. It's to silence her own grief that she's flagellated the department. And it's for this that she'll exact punishment of the department's brightest star.

I've read miles of gothic literature, in which demons embody the power of human malice. But I've never understood — have never even bothered to wonder — what draws the demon to its victim. Now I see it. Joanne's relationship with Elizabeth, I understand, is the truest intimacy she's got.

In the stifling room, the ponderous bulk of Joanne's isolation is all but overwhelming.

With my eyes I condemn her to it.

"Too bad about losing your advisee, Tracy," she says. "And too bad about your engagement. I hear it was quite precipitous. Rash entry, rash exit. Next time maybe you'll be more judicious."

Victoria stands. "Joanne Miller, that was cruel."

With a deliberate, luxurious motion, Joanne removes her glasses, blows a speck of dust off one lens, and puts them back on. "Terribly sorry to hurt you, Tracy," she says. Then she gives a smile that chills me. She starts for the door.

My voice, to my shock, is steady. "Elizabeth needs to recuperate before she can take on a shred of academic work. The doctor was adamant. Nothing less than six months' complete rest."

Halfway to the door, Joanne stops. Without turning she says, "I'll give her two."

They leave, Victoria with an uneasy nod to me.

Alone in the lounge, I reach shakily for a volume of Arnold. I read.

Listen! you hear the grating roar
Of pebbles which the waves draw back, and fling . . .
With tremulous cadence slow, and bring
The eternal note of sadness in.

"Hey," says Joseph Yee. He sticks his head in the door and scans the room with a disappointed expression. "How's it going?"

In answer I lift the book and read. *"We mortal millions . . . in the sea of life enisled."*

Five minutes later I'm walking Elizabeth out of the department.

Within ten steps of leaving my office her composure crumbles and she sobs violently in the deserted elevator.

On the sidewalk Mary waits, cradling a steaming cup of coffee; judging by her stained mittens, it's not her first.

Elizabeth opens her arms and takes her mother in a fierce hug, which Mary returns guardedly, swaying with the force of her daughter's sudden, giddy laughter. "Joanne accepted the apology!" Elizabeth sobs into her mother's neck. "I can't believe it. She says I can stay if I turn in my dissertation soon."

I watch Mary's face. Uncertainty solidifies into a grim anger that heartens me.

"I told Joanne that Elizabeth needed six months off," I tell Mary.

Elizabeth lets go of her mother. "But you know the doctor said I only need —"

"Don't you think I know my colleague?" I snap. To Mary I say, "Joanne agreed to two months."

"That's until *February*," says Elizabeth, as though Joanne's counteroffer were the height of kindness.

"That's still enough pressure to bring you down, and don't forget it."

Elizabeth's tear-streaked face goes blank. But, to my surprise, I've earned a forceful nod from Mary: a first, spare gesture of appreciation.

The two retreat along the avenue of gray stone buildings: the mute pollution-tinged bones of the city that appear, in this failing light, to embody stoicism.

I slip inside the coffee shop. There, I buy an espresso as though the act were a religious devotion, and drink it George's way — without sugar. Is there no bottom to missing him? No point at which I give up wishing for his return? Weeks have passed. I no longer call. The days of his absence stack one upon the other, throwing an ever more damning shadow against the count of our days together. Yet he can still walk into my thoughts without warning, order my coffee, decline sugar.

In the crowded coffee shop I recall a time when I observed in safety, content to know all and risk nothing, cagey about what role love might play in my life. From this distance, my former musings about love seem like fatally flawed equations, physics problems calculated without factoring in a basic condition. Love has mass and volume. Put it into your life; it must displace something. As it has displaced my notion of what was good and important in the world, and substituted this: The knowledge that there is nothing more important than people willing to stand up for the truth of each other. The understanding of what it is to protect another fragile being. The understanding that I, too, will grow old.

I could have done no different with George. But nothing prepared me for how much love would hurt.

Is that it? Is that where my love story ends?

Tragedy! says the dying father to his daughter in the Grace Paley tale. *You too. When will you look it in the face?*

The daughter, gutsy and inventive, has a different idea. *Everyone,* she insists, *real or invented, deserves the open destiny of life.*

The shop is bright and noisy and I want to rivet it with a cry. I try instead to summon some vestige of postmodernism. The object, I counsel myself numbly, is fungible. "Love" passes on, and in its place come new and equally powerful "Loves."

Like a wave.

I drink the espresso and burn my throat: a small act of truth.

Hannah's baby looks like a radiant, bright-eyed Winston Churchill.

"She's the make-out queen." Hannah's voice is suffused with unspoken delight. The air is thick with a sweet, waxy, new-baby smell. Hannah, propped in bed against a bank of white pillows, wears a girlish ponytail and the white granny nightgown that robes her like a maternal angel. "She gets this twinkle in her eye, then she just opens her mouth and sucks on my face. Ed's too. When she's older she's going to get herself in trouble."

Ariel may weigh only seven pounds, the motions of her limbs may be confined to flailing and involuntary startles, her vocabulary may consist of mews. But every crinkle of her pinched face implies mischief. She's going to keep her mother good company.

Hannah wolfs a chocolate scone. "I can't believe you traveled an hour and a half on the subway just to buy me these."

"Eat." Yawning, I fluff the quilt around Hannah's legs. I was awake until one A.M., reading. The restoration of my solitary, meditative evenings has indeed brought its pleasures. Only when I lie down to sleep does my body turn inarticulate, its recently learned language torn away — my hands so cold my belly flinches from them and I swathe myself in a cocoon of blankets and curl, immobile.

Nonetheless.

I woke this morning, dressed, and made the admittedly absurd trip uptown to Hannah's favorite pastry shop. Hannah neither demands nor expects extravagant generosity. It's what makes surprising her such an uncomplicated pleasure. I'm trying. No more Miss Havisham.

Ariel's head rests on Hannah's knee, and I caress its oval top. The startlingly rapid pulse in the silky skull tattoos my palm in reward. I shut my eyes and relax into my place at this tableau. Babies have always made me the tiniest bit claustrophobic. But this one, for some reason, feels different. I could sit here forever, paying homage to the miracle of this tiny breathing body.

From the living room Elijah shrieks and Adam gives an answering banshee wail. The smell of waffles comes from the kitchen: Ed is making a rare cameo as chef.

"Did I mention that I get a full week off from house duties?" Hannah grins as contentedly as though nursing day and night, with a toddler barging in to demand boo-boo kisses, were a holiday.

Then her smile fades. "Still no word from George?"

"And I don't expect it. But my problems are the last thing you need to worry about. Look at her."

Ariel is taking in the red-and-blue-patterned quilt, blinking at the stitches millimeters from her glistening eyes.

"I'm really sorry, Tracy."

I keep my eyes on Ariel. "Anyway," I say softly, "I'm trying to concentrate on other things." I glance at Hannah, who is patently relieved. "Like work," I say. "And my tenure review. The politics with one of my colleagues have been horrendous lately. More than I've had time to tell you. More than anybody this minuscule" — I indicate Ariel — "should have to hear. Also" — I make a face — "I've got to get a dress for this faculty club affair. It's a big deal. You know how much I hate shopping."

"I'd go with you if I could."

From down the hall there's a thump, a howl from Adam, and a storm of giggles from Elijah.

"Adam!" Hannah calls sharply.

There's a delay, then a recalcitrant *"What?"*

"Come here."

There is a heavy dragging sound, and a moment later Adam slide-steps into the room, Elijah clinging to his leg.

Hannah pats my knee with her free hand. "I know who owes you a personal-shopping favor."

Adam eyes his sister, then turns to me. "I told you she's a moron," he says.

I push open the door of the boutique. The air smells of some complicated plum sachet, and orderly classical music plays from concealed speakers.

"The saleswomen are a bit intense," Hannah warned. "But the selection is great." She gave Adam fierce instructions: I'm to treat myself to something nice this time. No frugality allowed.

"I can't believe I'm here," says Adam.

With trepidation I approach a rack of black fabric. The blouse I touch is silky and slips away from my hands.

Adam looks miserable. He pulls a Game Boy out of his coat pocket and settles cross-legged, his sneakers leaving gritty smudges on the immaculate carpet.

Continuing my tentative browsing, I take a dress from the rack. It weighs less than the upholstered hanger it's suspended from.

"May I help you?" Everything about the saleswoman is sharp: her figure, her plucked brows, her eyes; crimson fingernails, stiletto heels, serrated French accent.

Demurring, I drop my handbag next to Adam and retreat with the dress and three other shimmering dusky outfits into a changing room. A moment later I'm parading in front of Adam in my white socks, wearing a black pantsuit that's cut with more daring than I'd realized. "Is this one decent?"

Adam is urgently involved with the Game Boy.

"One of those trying-too-hard outfits?" I prod. "A little too revealing?"

He thumbs a button fiercely, then gives me a quick glance. "Nope. I don't see a single breast."

"Thanks." Before I can swing back into the room, the saleswoman spike-heels her way from across the mirrored showroom, giving Adam wide berth.

"Any luck, dear?" she glitters at me in her English that would rather be French.

"Not yet. I'm just getting started. Thanks." I match her smile tooth for tooth, and she leaves me be.

Inside the dressing room I shed the pantsuit and pull on a silvery sheath that makes me feel like a cosseted absurdity. "My aunt is phoning me daily at the office," I tell Adam through the slatted door. "She says she just wants to check in. Then she keeps me on the line for twenty minutes, interrogating me about why George and I called it off and going on about how disappointed the whole family is . . . except for *her,* because *she* understands these things happen. In other words, she's relieved, because George wasn't Jewish. I tell Rona the same story every time, but she doesn't believe the truth. She thinks if she keeps prying she'll get the *real* reason for the breakup." I shed the silver sheath and slip on the black dress. It's perfect: sophisticated, festive, a tiny bit sexy.

Looking in the mirror, it occurs to me that my life might not in fact be over. I might get tenure. I might even some day feel excited about the future. I put on a pair of too big black heels I find in a corner of the dressing room, and step out the door.

Adam is frantically pushing buttons. After a round of cursing, he stops abruptly and leans his head against the wall. "Stupid boulder traps," he says with genuine pain. Opening his eyes, he stares at me for a long moment. "Hey," he says brightly.

I can't help smiling. "Not bad?" I say. With Adam watching me, I look in the mirror. Then, before I can stopper it, I start to well up.

"You know," the saleswoman's tight accent cuts in. In the mirrored wall, her bright red suit and patterned scarf stand out behind my black figure, and it takes only a second to trace my déjà vu: a portrait from a traveling exhibit I once saw of Medieval Dutch art, a picture of a devil giving counsel over a vulnerable maiden's shoulder.

I wipe my eyes and glare at her.

With an expression of barely masked distaste, she indicates Adam. "I don't see why you need a friend to tell you how it looks. It looks *fabulous.*" Oblivious or impervious to the tears that continue to fill my eyes, the woman lowers her voice and confides. "But you're very smart to come with a man. It's better than coming with a single girlfriend. A single girlfriend may not tell you what looks nice."

"Why in the world not?" I snap.

"Jealousy," she sings, her lips puckering at my naiveté. "Also, for the same reason, a friend who is a mother and has lost her own figure is not the best adviser."

"I think," I say, "that I have different friends than you do."

She waves a bone-thin finger, the gesture friendly and menacing. "You cannot trust."

"I'd like to try on the last dress," I say, sniffing.

Her face freezes. "Darling, if you come here you take my advice. Believe me, you'll waste your time. What you want is the dress you're wearing."

True, but I've never hated anyone as much as I hate this woman right now. "I'm going to try on the last dress I've got in the changing room."

"All right," she says, in a way that gives the impression these syllables mean something entirely different in French.

"Darling," says Adam. Rising, he tucks his Game Boy into the back pocket of his jeans and dimples at the saleswoman. "Allow me to explain what's going on here, and put an end to this silly charade. The dress isn't for *her*." He chucks me under the chin; tottering backward, I barely avoid falling off the borrowed shoes.

The saleswoman turns to me for his dismissal. Regaining my balance, I nod confirmation. Her smile hardens.

"It's for me," says Adam. "My friend here is trying on dresses for me, because she's my future size. After the operation I'll be a six." Adam's face goes dreamy. "I've told the doctors I want my body to stay weedy. Weeeeeedy." He gives her a saucy smile.

That does in the saleswoman. She disappears and leaves me to gather my belongings while Adam, who has strung a $300 purple satin bustier across his chest, gives me a double thumbs-up.

Leaving the store, tissue-paper-wrapped dress stowed in perfumed shopping bag, I fall into step with Adam. Neither of us speaks. We walk down the avenue in silence. Only after several blocks do I look at him: rangy blue-jean stride, backward baseball cap, cowlick sticking out the gap over his forehead. Blue eyes.

"You know," he says, "you're a real hottie in that dress."

We pass half a block of heavily bundled passersby and belching traffic before I answer. The notion that Adam would think me attractive feels so absurd it makes me smile. I realize it's the first real smile I've had in weeks.

And in truth, Adam's presence acts on me like helium. Not to mention that he's the only person who thinks following my gut with George was sane; the only friend who sticks up for me in a way that doesn't feel complicated. And — humor is rare.

But like a plant seeking light I turn endlessly toward who George was: Toward gentleness and force, solemnity and curiosity. Toward a man who composed theories of the universe, knew when to laugh, cared for something outside himself, knew how to jump with both feet. Jeff was right: There is something nineteenth-century about me. Back then they thought love was like an element, like the most fundamental particle. Unsplittable. Irreducible. The modern mind, in contrast, is supposed to believe anything can be split — its components reshuffled, recycled, explained away. *Nothing,* according to the modern mind, is irreplaceable. Nothing is immune to reason.

The love I felt for George is immune to reason. I will not logic him away, or rationalize what I saw. But neither will I polish my grief for the rest of my life.

Among the narrow choices that remain to me (walking past glistening bakeries, chic boutiques), I choose this: I won't close my eyes to what I know, now, about love.

My heart may be, at least, softer for seeing it.

"You're not bad yourself," I tell Adam.

We continue along the sidewalk, content in our confirmation that we'll never get together.

"No offense," says Adam after another minute. "It would be like kissing Worms."

I crow, and smack Adam on the back of the neck, and, drawing cold, fresh air into my lungs, walk beside Adam to the subway, bag banging freely against my leg.

Steven greets me at the door of the Howard Perry Room. With a gallant sweep of his arm, he presents the velvet-bedecked, tuxedoed gathering. It's a smaller crowd than I'd expected. "You look lovely," he says. Without pausing for a reply he takes my elbow and leads me into the room. Deans — men and women whose new-lecture-hall dedication speeches I've endured, from whose left hands I've received my diplomas while shaking the right—now greet me from close range. Some smile true, nonmandatory smiles. I smile back, tentatively at first, then with genuine ease. The dress fits right in. I feel so glamorous I halfheartedly wonder whether Steven is single, though reality quickly reasserts: he may be good-looking, but he's got an ambitious gleam I don't trust. Not that I'm not grateful. He introduces me to the silver-haired wife of Dean Frederick before repairing to the appetizer table.

"I understand you're shaking things up," Susan Frederick says to me. Dean Frederick, the senior member of the Coordinating Committee, was the force behind the pioneering New Century Curriculum initiative. His wife, who is wearing a dark green velvet dress that's both tasteful and royal, nods curt approval. "Good girl," she says. "Steven was just talking about some of the goings-on in English. A turbulent time for the department I'm certain. As it is for everyone in this university who cares about academic culture. This curriculum review is going to set our course for some years."

Her husband appears, wrapping an arm around her thick waist. "We like to know our young faculty," he says, in a tone that all but pats me on the head. I select a small piece of cheese from the glistening plate of appetizers he offers, and thank him. "This isn't Harvard, you see," he says, offering the plate to his wife. "We like to *set* the trends." He gives a slow, exaggerated wink. "Then Harvard will adopt them in eight or nine years and take credit."

I follow his wife in a hearty laugh.

"No matter," he says. "People know who the real groundbreakers are."

Dinner is called. Steven sits between the Fredericks. At Susan Frederick's direction, I sit between her husband and Dean Ralph Phillips, a heavyset man whose blue irises look small in their roomy whites, and who gives off the impression of someone about to come down with a cold. "He acts like the living dead," Susan whispers, "but he's a good man to know. And if you're going to join the band trying to keep the intellectual sparks flying here, you may as well be on friendly terms with the forces of inertia."

The napkins are a heavy cream-colored linen. The beaded chandeliers throw necklaces of light against cream-colored walls. When the administrators lift their utensils I follow suit, eating with my left hand firmly in my lap. I comment to Dean Phillips about the room; he responds that it used to be more elegant before the renovation. I ask him when that occurred; he says twelve years ago. I ask him how the room used to look, and his spooky eyes light up. "It seemed . . ." He pauses. ". . . a rather larger space. Due to the décor." He takes a bite and chews slowly, shaping his next thought, comfortable in the knowledge he won't be interrupted. He swallows, pats his lips with his napkin. "The décor was somewhat . . . continental . . . in those days," he continues.

Between courses Steven comes over to my chair. Bending, he speaks softly into my ear. "For your information, Frederick just said he looks forward to confirming your tenure after your departmental approval is out of the way. That sort of comment travels down the channels, you know. Word will spread before your tenure meeting that the deans are impatient to green-light you. It's terrific for you."

I blush. "That's certainly good to hear. I've been a bit concerned about" — I gesture — "politics, lately."

His laugh, at close range, startles me. "Joanne?" It's clear from his tone how little he thinks of her.

I hesitate.

"You don't have to worry about her," he says in my ear. "All bark and no bite. Trust me."

I give Steven a flustered thank-you. I'm not certain why he's taking such interest in my tenure prospects. If he's romantically interested, he seems rather restless; already he's turned away and is greeting a newly tenured History professor with a high-wattage smile.

The university president, who has been making rounds, stops by our table, assistant in tow. President Talman circles the table, greeting each faculty member in turn, asking after children, spouses, the quality of the wine. When he reaches me the assistant whispers discreetly in his ear, and President Talman shakes my hand and calls me heartily by name. His grip is firm. "Welcome," he says. He cocks his grizzled head at the candlelit room. "Make yourself at home."

Talman passes. I settle slowly into my seat.

"It was a style even then out of favor on the continent, of

course," says Phillips, setting down his water glass. "But timeless all the same."

Behold the undisturbed gustation of a dean.

And finally, despite all my efforts to ignore the countdown of days, it arrives.

Swirling his glass, feet propped on my desk, Jeff smiles at the music of the ice cubes. "The zero hour," he says.

"Are you trying to make me feel worse?"

Jeff takes another gulp from his iced tea. "You sure you don't want some? I can spike yours if you'd like. I'm holding off in case I need my wits in there."

"Look at you, sipping iced tea in December. A real Southern gent." I wave the offer away. "Maybe later. Thanks again for coming."

"Hell, I've got nothing to do in Atlanta this week."

"Liar."

He concedes.

"I should have listened to you. I shouldn't have let Elizabeth drag me in. You should have seen the showdown Joanne and I had. She's going to be on the warpath."

Jeff doesn't answer. He surveys my office. He indicates the poster of Zora. "She looks exhausted."

"I expected I wouldn't want to come in today," I say. "Thought I'd take a conspicuous day off."

"Then you woke up and couldn't stay away."

"I figured I'd come in to do some writing, assert normalcy. In retrospect a hideous idea."

Jeff shrugs. "It would be torture either way." He tilts his glass toward my desk lamp and studies the thin slice of lemon resting at the bottom of the drink. "By the way, any news from Elizabeth?"

"I haven't heard from her. I'm assuming that's a good sign."

He nods. "Well, if she starts channeling British writers, let me know. Maybe I can learn something." He drinks, draining half the glass in a gulp. We lean back in our chairs. I believe both of us are considering the eight-year arc of our friendship, its recent strains, the many hundred miles that will soon separate us. After all this time there seems to be some sort of debt we owe each other, though I'd be pressed to articulate it. Opposite me Jeff reclines, pensive. Wondering whether his wry humor will find a welcome in Atlanta, I feel a small stab of protectiveness.

He glances at his wristwatch. "It's time." He stands.

"Eileen says they can't afford not to tenure me. But that's crap. They can always hire someone. This city is teeming with Ph.D.s."

"Not Americanists with your strengths. Buck up." He squeezes my shoulder.

"Will you come as soon as people turn in their votes?"

"I'll wait for the tally. Then I'll come back."

"No, just come back after the votes are collected. You'll know which way it went."

There's a knock on the doorframe. Steven Hilliard greets me with a salute. "Shall we?" he says to Jeff.

When Jeff doesn't speak, Steven gestures toward the conference room down the hall.

"Since when," says Jeff, "do they let visiting Oxford men attend tenure meetings?"

"I'm not planning to attend. I'm just going to pop my head in." He examines his fingernails. "And ask to say a few words on Tracy's behalf before the meeting starts." He looks up with a puckish smile. "They can just consider me one of the external reviewers."

"They're not going to consider you anything." Jeff's voice is uncharacteristically brusque.

"All I plan to do" — Steven's smile turns ironic — "is say a few words before proceedings begin. Then I'll hie my *visiting Oxford man* self away." He levels a gaze at Jeff. Then he turns to me, his face unreadable despite its pleasant expression. He says, "It's a simple matter of supporting a deserving candidate."

Jeff is silent. He looks as though he's recalibrating something. Without another word to me, he follows Steven down the hall.

I stare at the wall. I tell myself to get busy with work. I am still staring at the wall minutes later when there is a rap on my doorframe. Turning, I'm greeted by Steven's jaunty salute as he strides past. He doesn't stop.

I take out a file labeled "Syllabi — Spring" and survey my plans for week one of my Literature of the American City seminar. Slowly I scratch notes onto a pad — the outline of a lecture.

Forty minutes pass. An hour.

An hour and a half.

Some tenure meetings, I tell myself, take a long time. Surely some must take more than an hour. It doesn't necessarily mean something's wrong.

A door swings open down the long corridor, and thuds shut. Footsteps approach. Victoria appears at the door.

"How are you?" Her voice is tense.

I don't answer.

"May I sit?"

I nod, a dreadful constriction in my throat. She settles heavily into the chair.

"Tracy, your committee is in the midst of deliberation." She meets my eyes. "You know that, of course."

I don't answer.

"There is a question," she says, "that has come up." She purses her lips, choosing her words. "Due to the length of the discussion, the committee decided to take a ten-minute recess. And knowing that you are in the building, one of the committee members suggested that we ask for your input on a particular matter that some are finding puzzling." She sighs; for an instant her posture softens and she looks at me frankly, as though she'd like to tell me, for real, what's going on. Then she straightens. "As the moderator of this meeting, I've been dispatched to speak with you."

"Elizabeth." My voice, loosed from its moorings, wanders high and low over the name.

Victoria nods. "Specifically, the strife between you and Joanne over Elizabeth's work and well-being. Whatever motivates you two, it's created a difficult situation in the department."

"Whatever motivates us *two?*" I say.

She's silent.

"Victoria." My voice rises. "You've seen me try to get along with Joanne. The only thing I couldn't do was sell my own advisee down the river. Do people truly think this is just competition between Joanne and me?"

Again, silence.

"Because . . . and please forgive me for speaking plainly, Victoria, but" — I lean into her eyes, placing my trust — "everyone knows Joanne's at the root of the problem. But no one wants to blame her because she's sick."

"Because she's sick," Victoria echoes, her expression guarded.

"Yes. But also because Joanne takes on a Herculean load of committee work. Even in the midst of her illness, she breaks her back for this department. Without Joanne . . ." Victoria stops. She lines up her hands and slides them against each other, moving so slowly it's more meditation than motion. Slide. Slide. Slide. She stops. "No," she says. "I don't feel you're ultimately at fault in the conflict with Joanne, Tracy. And no one who truly thinks about it will blame you for the tension. But everyone wants this" — her eyes rise warily to the clock — "unpleasantness to end."

I feel nauseated. "Has the committee taken note of the fact that I made sure one of our graduate students got help? While she was facing her own potentially fatal illness? Victoria, you never saw Elizabeth at her worst, but I need you to trust me that it was bad. If I hadn't . . ." I stop myself. Victoria is watching me. "I could have walked away," I say.

"I appreciate your intervention. And others do as well. But Elizabeth's fate is her own responsibility. This is an English department, not a counseling service. You chose to help a graduate student, and that's kind. But your championing of a student who was teetering on the brink of an unsavory dismissal, and whose behavior was directly harmful to a faculty member with whom you'd clashed, has raised questions among some of your colleagues" — her face clouds with disapprobation, directed at some unspecified constellation of faculty members assembled down the hall — "about whether they can count on you."

"I'm a team player, Victoria. I always have been. Maybe I haven't been the savviest political player, but that's just because I'm not *playing* here. I'm teaching and studying and living and breathing American literature." I force myself to pause until my voice is under control. "Since the day I came here I've done everything this department asked."

"I appreciate that," says Victoria slowly. "Perhaps more, Tracy, than you credit me for. You've been steady and unselfish and smart, and it hasn't gone unnoticed." She hesitates. Then, her eyes fastened on mine, she crosses the line: a breach of academic protocol that would mean little coming from anyone else. "As I'm sure you can guess, Tracy, I've recommended your tenure."

The door opens. Jeff enters. His lips are compressed, and he gives no response to the silent question I send his way.

Victoria frowns and ignores him. "I should get back in there, Tracy. But if there's anything you can say that will strengthen your position, I'll go back in there and report it."

I face Victoria. What words, to persuade a collection of people I've known without knowing them — people who have in turn labored alongside me without the slightest real notion of who I am — of my worthiness?

"If I've erred," I begin, "it's been with the best of intent." The words drain hope. "I've worked, and would like to continue to work, to build —"

"Don't waste your breath," says Jeff. "Victoria wasn't sent to talk to you during everyone else's smoke break because the committee wanted to give you a shot at defending yourself. She was sent so that if your tenure is denied, committee members can tell themselves they were fair-minded and can sleep well tonight. The gesture isn't generous, it's despicable." He shakes his head crisply. "Nothing you can say is going to sway the vote one way or another. You have plenty of support, Tracy. Don't think you don't. God knows, if a certain Oxford professor were a member of this faculty, you'd not only be tenured, you'd be chairwoman."

"Jeff —" Victoria cautions sharply.

"Hell with confidentiality," Jeff says, turning sharply to face her. "Victoria, you know how this works. You know that despite the criticism Joanne is taking in there, people are going to hesitate before voting against her, because she pushes this department and makes sure we have a place at the table for major university decisions, and nobody else wants to have to do that work. And you know what Tracy gets from the straight world for breaking off an engagement. She's bad luck. Open game for wicked speculation." He doesn't so much as glance my way. "The effect will take about a year to fade, and even then it won't fully disappear unless she marries. Tracy needs other voices defending her right now. She needs members of this faculty to speak out. Regardless of *tone*."

Victoria's jowls dimple with concentration. I expect her to contradict Jeff's statements as absurd. Instead she rises and, with a curt nod to me, follows him out the door.

Voices rise periodically from down the hall, a muted surf. There is a long silence, then a distant rise in tempo like a washing machine

going into spin cycle in the basement. I shut my door. I pick up
Welty: A Companion and read a long segment on the author's uses
of metaphor, taking meticulous notes.

When Jeff opens the door his expression is grim.

"What?"

He enters, and leans against the wall, flexes his shoulders. "I
don't know," he says.

I can't speak.

"I just don't know," he says, "which way this one is going to
go."

"Tell me," I manage.

"You're sure you want details?"

I hesitate, then nod.

"If these people are your colleagues for the next twenty years,
you may find it easier not to know." He looks at me. Then folds
his arms. "All right," he says. "As you're aware, your record is
fantastic. There was absolute agreement on that. In fact people
agreed on that so quickly they had to move on to a more controversial subject. Tracy, I don't know what possessed you to leak
word of that half-conceived project you're working on, but —"

"Who —"

"Steven made a speech about it at the start of the meeting. He
very Britishly begged everyone's pardon, and asked to offer a comment before the meeting was called to order. He discussed your
new project as an example of your groundbreaking ambition, and
mentioned parenthetically what a strong impression you were
making on higher-ups." Jeff grimaces. "Joanne was ashen. But not
for long. Clearly Steven's plug was the first she'd heard about your
project, but she knows good grist when she sees it. She could barely
wait until he'd left the room to start taking you apart. She said this
project was just the latest example of a tendency to be lightweight.
She said your projects are too broad, too ambitious, too focused
on primary sources at the expense of critical literature. She said
now you're getting lost in sweeping generalities about happy endings. She called your book idea grandiose, tilting at windmills,
lacking a sense of scholarly rigor. Which of course she used to
bring the conversation to the topic she'd obviously prepared to
discuss: your selfish obsession — that's her phrasing — with controlling your advisee's work. She made out like she was Elizabeth's

protector, and you were unreasonably interfering with that collaboration, obstructing her efforts to deepen Elizabeth's dissertation so that it considers the whole critical literature. *Tracy must not be encouraged to take shortcuts with the honest academic travail to which this assembly devotes its hours. I've been working all my professional life to defend academic standards.* She was developing stigmata up there.

"Victoria tutted at her, but only a bit. You know Victoria." He sighs. "I think the response to that was divided — some people fell for it, others didn't. Your record of achievement, after all, speaks for itself. But nobody was sure what to make of your new project, or whether it enhanced or undermined your record. For once, though, there was plenty of back talk to Joanne. And also plenty of pointed comments about competition between you two . . . *women at each other's throats.*"

"That's a sexist —"

"Of course it is." He shrugs irritably. "The more Joanne hammered away, the more people sank their teeth into the question of your defense of Elizabeth. That conversation went on forever, and kept getting more tangled — as Victoria let on. You should know that several people spoke strongly in your defense. But then it got really interesting."

I don't think I want to hear more.

"Paleozoic stood up."

"He *stood up?* In a tenure meeting?"

"*And* his eyes were open. He made a speech that was just incredible. I'll confess it took me entirely by surprise. I didn't know he had it in him. Made me think maybe he was once more than a figurehead. He said academics were bolder in his day. He said they used to take on the big questions, the sweeping questions, the questions at the heart of our culture, things that helped us understand where we come from and where we're going. He said academia today has nitpicked its way into nonsense. He went on a couple tangents there about everything after formalism being a wrong turn, and sex obsession in American culture — not sure why that was relevant — but the whole arc of the speech was actually pretty glorious. He said it's rare to find someone bold enough to take on more than a tiny corner of literature, and you ought to be commended."

"I'm flabbergasted."

"You ought to be. He was goddamn regal there for a moment, in a dusty kind of way. It was the professorial version of Rockwell's *Freedom of Speech*. When he sat down people were affected, you could tell. The conversation limped along while everyone absorbed the way he'd challenged them. People were uncomfortable. You could tell they were thinking about their own academic ambitions, wondering how they measured up." Slowly Jeff shakes his head. "And then he goddamn threw it all away.

"I picked that moment to make my big speech. I'd saved it up." He makes a wry face. "Everyone knows I'm now irrelevant. There's a limit to how long I can hold the floor before they tune me out — as Shakespeare understood, a ghost gets only one good monologue before the living take over. I said, before I leave this faculty, I need to make a stand for its future. Joanne immediately jumped in, of course, to say that was hard to believe, given my campaign to undermine the department's grading standards." Jeff sighs, and raises a finger. "Which is a move I would not have made, Tracy, had I known Elizabeth was going to throw political bombs in your path. But no one supported Joanne, to her obvious shock. I talked about your publications and your invitations to conferences, and the interest your approach to departmental issues has aroused among the deans. I talked about what an uncomplaining kick-ass colleague you are, and I very respectfully submitted that Joanne was dead wrong about your stewardship of Elizabeth's academic inquiry. And I went for the heartstrings — I talked about how you defended Elizabeth, which is the most unselfish thing you could have done, given that you acted in full knowledge that you were about to be judged by this assembly.

"And when I said that, Paleozoic, who'd looked like he was asleep, gave this little chuckle. No one would have made anything of it, but Joanne pounced. She demanded to know — you know how she *demands* to know — what he was laughing about. I figured Joanne had just put the nail in her own coffin. She's always been too smart to bully the old man, especially right now when people actually were looking at him with respect. Paleozoic went a bit purple, and you could just feel the room turning on Joanne. Then he wheezed something apologetic about how he'd had to smile at my indignation, because after all I've been courting both Elizabeth *and* you."

"You're joking."

Jeff doesn't answer.

"He must have been laughed out of the room."

"That would have been better. Nobody laughed — not out loud. They just traded smirks. You could watch the whole room relax back into dismissing him."

"Did you contradict him?"

"Of course not. Everyone knows it's nonsense. Paleozoic didn't undermine my testimony, he undermined his own." With a frown Jeff considers me. "I went on the offensive," he says. "I invoked my years in this department, said I hoped they all knew me to be an honest and fair-minded colleague. And I told them it was my firm and studied belief that Joanne was persecuting you out of her own psychological issues."

"You didn't."

"At this point, Tracy, there's nothing to be gained by holding back. I know a pile-on when I see it, and if your opponents play dirty you'd better be prepared to do it too. Whatever happens from here forward, Joanne's not coming out of this unscathed. I brought up her illness. I did it respectfully, but I said she wasn't acting in a rational manner. She countered that accusing women of irrationality was a time-honored sexist tactic, and I said be that as it may, the faculty can judge based on their own experience of her over the past four months. I was courteous, Tracy, I was bend-over-backward compassionate about her illness, I was deferential about contradicting a colleague at such a difficult moment in her life, but I did have my observations to report. I talked about your integrity."

I wait for Jeff to subvert the compliment with a tongue-in-cheek aside, but he doesn't. He regards me soberly as he speaks.

"I talked about what a good role model you are for the under-grads and grad students. And how you've held your tongue despite poor treatment. I also said some Emory higher-ups had asked about you and had mentioned a salary that would raise pulses among our august assembly. I said I'd tried to lure you to Atlanta but you'd refused, expressing loyalty to this department."

"They believed it?"

"I do have a reputation for honesty. But it made Joanne go for the jugular. Not mine. Yours. She'd been saving this for a last resort. She pulled out a report she'd typed up in November. Then she just passed the single page around the room." Jeff rubs his brow. "It was a brilliant move, not making copies. You couldn't beat it for dramatic tension. You could have heard a pin drop while every single solitary person in the room read the page and passed it.

"It was a report paraphrasing a statement from one of your TA's, who apparently complained that you threw a book at a student who was misbehaving during class."

I open my mouth. Then shut it. After a few seconds I try again. "Who would have said that? All three of my TA's know me."

"And all three have a lot at stake in proving themselves to the tenured faculty. Besides, who knows how Joanne twisted the TA's original comment?"

"It was a joke," I say weakly.

"I told them so. I pointed out that the *student* didn't complain, which corroborates that you didn't throw the book in anger, and in fact you intended for him to catch it. Joanne countered that the absence of student complaints doesn't matter, the point is you engaged in dangerous classroom behavior."

"I threw it right *to* him. That's different from throwing something at a person. He *caught* it."

"Joanne emphasized that he might not have. That hardcover book might have struck him or another student on the head. It might have caused injury."

"Carole Highsmith said you weren't the type to act out, and she was sure the TA's words had been taken out of context and you probably dropped your book by accident. Joseph Yee said he wasn't sure, he'd gotten the impression you were a little off lately."

"*Off?*"

"He said you quoted poetry to him."

"This is an English Department."

"He said he finds you dark." Jeff curls and flexes his hand restively. "I said even if you *had* shown poor judgment with the misbehaving student, you'd had a lot on your mind this year and ought to be forgiven a single thoughtless action. Joanne's response was, and I quote, 'Plenty of people get engaged. Tracy's not special.'

"At which point every single person in that room was past his limit. No one could sit still. Carole made a motion for a show of hands to conclude discussion, Victoria seconded it, and everybody filled out their paper ballots in utterly rancorous silence. And here I am."

Behind Jeff, the corridor is still.

"What about Victoria?" I say.

Jeff's expression darkens. "This is Victoria," he says curtly. "In other words, she didn't cross lines of propriety. She stated your case firmly, but in respectful terms. A few times she commented about being *distressed at the nature of this dialogue*. She cautioned Joanne when Joanne got egregious — but she cautioned me too at several points. She performed her function as moderator with *admirable* evenhandedness." The word, as Jeff pronounces it, could cut diamond. "She thinks highly of you, Tracy, and told everyone so. But she made equal time for Joanne's tirades. Fairness is Victoria's religion. She's too bloody well-bred to take sides. She could have — she's one of the few people who knows the whole story and is senior enough not to be intimidated by Joanne. But she was appropriate. Meaning her voice never rose above the indignant. Not even when it might have been the only damn thing to wake people up. She worked at protecting our *collegial tone*. She made a final statement about you being a solid scholar and good colleague, and told the group she trusted this would be taken into account."

I splay my fingers on my desktop.

"I tried, Tracy. So did Jesse Faden. And Jim Lakes, which was a surprise. But I've never seen so many guilty-looking mutes. If it's any comfort, I don't think half the department's going to be speaking to each other after this."

"I'm going to lose my job." I loft the sentence in the air, expecting it to dispel. Instead it gains weight. "Because of politics."

Jeff stays mum, though his answer is right there in his pained expression: What do you think I've been trying to teach you all these years?

"Do you think you swayed them at all? Maybe?"

Jeff shrugs.

I consider closing my office door, but don't. If my tenure is refused, I want every faculty member who chose the path of least resistance — every one too timid to stand up to Joanne — to have to walk past me.

A door bangs open down the hall. Footsteps follow as the conference room drains of occupants. No voices accompany the footfalls. At the sound of someone nearing the office, I swivel bravely to face the corridor. Joseph Yee, I think blankly. Or Henry Shillman. Or Jim Lakes.

Just before they reach my office, the footsteps stop short, then softly about-face.

"Jesus," says Jeff.

I don't look at him.

"I'm sorry," he says.

He leaves my office. A moment later he's back. "You lost it by one vote. And Grub abstained."

"Grub never abstains," I whisper.

A brisk, determined tread approaches, its owner unmistakable. I stand and, turning my back on Jeff, step into the corridor. Joanne nears, her face turbulent. She does not slow as she nears me. Only at the last minute do I understand that she is planning to pass without acknowledging my presence. A victory fly-by.

Blindly I step into her path.

She stops. The brisk walk I interrupted has left her grabbing for breath, her chest rising shallowly, sweat dampening the neckline of her blouse. Her thickened features are flushed. "Get out of my way," she says.

"You've won."

Joanne's mouth twists.

"Now admit it," I say. "What you just did in that conference room was a crime."

"You," she says, "have an astonishing sense of entitlement. Who promised you tenure?"

"I never assumed I'd get tenure. I assumed I'd get a fair hearing."

"I believe you just had one."

"I had nothing of the kind."

Joanne breathes. "Sour grapes." Her voice is husky.

"Admit what you did to Elizabeth."

At the mention of Elizabeth, Joanne smiles. Her face is frightening, nearly erotic in its intensity. "What precisely would you like to hear me say?"

Carefully I pronounce each word. "This thing of darkness I acknowledge mine."

Joanne's pale lashes bat her cheeks.

"Don't give me that shit," she says after a moment. "I'm the one who's going to see Elizabeth through."

Too late, I see that this is the truth — and I recognize the role I've played in this drama. Joanne never meant to destroy Elizabeth, only to bring her low enough to be forever indebted; only to make of her gratitude a monument to Joanne, defying mortality. I've misunderstood. Elizabeth was never the canary in the coal mine. It was me.

"Well?" says Joanne. There is a flicker on her face — a moment of choice. Then her eyes, rock-steady, fasten on mine, and decline to see a fellow human.

I start shaking. I can't stop. The trembling of my limbs is undisguisable. I've never been so cold in my life. Pivoting, I let Joanne pass.

A second later Jeff is standing beside me with my briefcase and my coat. He sets a hand on my shoulder. "I give you an A for outstanding use of Shakespeare."

I wrap my arms around myself. "You give everyone an A."

He seats the coat on my quaking shoulders. "I'll give you an A-plus. Come on, valiant warrior. Let's get out of here."

I don't budge.

"Haven't you had enough? I know I have."

I pull the coat tighter and, leaving Jeff without another word, set off down the hallway.

"You've heard?" Victoria says when I step into her office. Studying my face, she sighs, then motions me to sit.

I don't move.

"You know," she says. "This is one of those rare occasions when I could really use a drink." For a moment her gaze rises and settles on the wall behind my head. Then, with an expression of forbearance, she turns to me. "The incident with the book was what clinched it. People didn't know what to think. I believe there was a record number of abstentions. And while I respect people's decision not to vote, it didn't help the —"

296 ⁓ Rachel Kadish

"Why?"

She tilts her head.

"*Why* do you respect it?" I charge.

She's silent. Then she shutters her eyelids and opens them slowly, indicating her fatigue, and by extension implying mine: a pantomime choreographed to excuse my behavior. "I'm sorry, Tracy." The words are an offer. She's handing me a good soldier's death, a restrained and noble farewell.

I turn to leave. At the door I stop. I know I should not say this, and know I'll regret it if I don't. "Victoria." The shaking has quieted; my voice is surprisingly steady as I face her. "I used to respect impartiality. I now see it as cowardice."

She shuts her eyes and does not open them.

Jeff is waiting outside my office. He drapes my scarf across my shoulders and buttons me into my coat. Carrying my briefcase, he ushers me toward the elevator.

"My God," I murmur. As the elevator descends, bubbles of dread swim through me. "Don't they know —"

"In the back closets of their minds they do."

"We could find that kid. He'd say I threw the book *to* him. For him to catch."

The elevator quivers to a halt.

"I didn't throw it at him," I say.

On the sidewalk, the frigid air stings. Jeff knots my scarf.

"Throwing the book," I repeat, "wasn't assault. It was a celebration. Of literature. Of postmodernism."

"Of *love*," corrects Jeff. "You were high on love, and you shared it with the world." He straightens. "I'd like the world better if more people acted that way. I'd be a different person." He stares darkly up the avenue. "Let's get you a cab."

This is how the world likes to believe in courage: there is a gene for it.

People who lack the courage gene? Their frailties are understandable and deserving of consolation. People who have the courage gene? They are laudable, and need no support. They are, after all, courageous: constitutionally resilient.

Besides, haven't they, through their own stubborn behavior, brought their problems on themselves?

Hannah and Yolanda try. But there is only so much they can say. I drift from their thin phrases of comfort. Thoughts of my career fill me with dismay — I flee them. Reading is intolerable. I light on books with a greedy hope that is, with the abrupt turn of a page, snuffed. There is no refuge in the house of words, the delicate latticework of references and the pretty patterns it used to cast. The corridor of my thoughts, which always augured a destination, now opens onto a void.

I am not in this room, I think, sitting in my apartment at night. I am not here. This is only my body. And I find it hard to care what happens to that.

Now and then my thoughts lean in vain toward the extinguished sun of George. What I remember has grown totemic. In his absence I recycle longings. For his eyes. For the warmth of his broad hands. For my own body, revealed to me. This is what it means to have lost someone: to turn him into a fetish.

Seated on my sofa I open Adrienne Rich's *Dream of a Common Language* and read the words aloud to the quiet apartment. *I choose to love this time for once / with all my intelligence.* I shut the book, then fling it onto the table and watch it slide to the far side and drop out of sight. Fuck intelligence. I'm here on the rooftop, having cannily avoided the floodwaters of dishonest relationships and hypocrisy. No one comes. I could feel betrayed by feminism for setting my expectations so high. But feminism isn't any more to blame than the golden rule, or any other principle that coaxes a person toward a more exacting standard of behavior. I used to quote that old movie line to Yolanda without really believing it: where love is concerned, the only way to win the game is not to play at all. I've never known a lonelier postulate. If I had the energy I'd call Washington and suggest some edits to that hypocritical Declaration of Independence our civics teachers love to quote. *Life?* Yes. *Liberty?* Sure. *The pursuit of happiness?* Ha. Double ha. Happiness draws enemies. In fact I'd underestimated the virulence of the problem: We don't just have cultural *fear* of happiness. It's outright hostility. The joy that lofted a book through the air is held against me; academia takes its mortar and pestle and grinds. *O true apothecary! Thy drugs are quick.*

Thus with a kiss I die.

The bell of my soul—is there anything bleaker, amid depression's inertia, than to be conscious of one's own melodrama?—has stopped ringing.

Lying motionless on the sofa, I weigh the urge to upend my tidy apartment. Make life look like it is. Instead I telephone Adam.

"I thought being independent-minded was the point," I say. "I thought I'd be *seen*. They acted like they could substitute a bunch of rumors for what they knew of me."

"Yeah, Trace," says Adam, "but you should have seen some of the petty bureaucrats in Russia. That's how people act when they know they don't matter. I mean, nobody cares about literary criticism except the people who do it, and every single English department knows that . . . no offense."

So now I'm culturally irrelevant, on top of everything? My thoughts scatter. Then, at length, regroup: Literary criticism matters. It's like the computer code behind a program everybody uses. Only a few people care enough to work on the code, but it keeps the program of cultural transmission on course. Thinking this ignites a brief flare of resolve—until I consider the daunting prospect of job searching so late in the season. "Shit," I say. "How am I going to get top-notch recommendations after that tenure debate? Forget those fellowships I applied for—the committees ask for rec letters. Forget finding another good job, let alone anything local. I'm going to have to leave New York. Or, I'll stay. I'll work as a tattoo artist. I can tattoo lines of Poe onto people's chests. I can tattoo Plath."

"You're going to get a job," Adam says. "I keep telling you. It'll be a few sucky months, and then you'll be appointed emperor of Workaholic U."

"Everyone said I *had* tenure, there was no question. Until I fucked it up. I fucked it up, just like I fucked up with George."

Through the phone I hear the long scrape of a wooden window opening. Adam says, "Anyone who thinks that's the dumbest thing they ever heard, honk your horn."

Boerum Hill's rush hour floats through my telephone, a sustained surge of automotive indignation. Adam holds me out over the street for a long time.

The window rattles shut.

"Okay?" he says.

He waits as I settle.

Quietly, elegiacally, I say, "I must be the stupidest Ph.D. in the world."

"Statistically speaking, Tracy, there's got to be a stupider one."

The relief of not being addressed in hushed tones sustains me until late that afternoon when I leave my apartment to pick up my rental car. Mary's phone message was dispassionate. Elizabeth is back in the hospital, this time one north of the city. It's more expensive, but Mary's been told good things about the medical staff. Elizabeth tried to kill herself. Two weeks ago. The same day she brought the letter to Joanne. Mary turned to check the time on the subway platform's wall clock. And then a man was grabbing Elizabeth, just as she was about to dive.

Now, said Mary's voice on my answering machine, she's on a new medication. She seems improved.

A train, a blasting horn, the tunnel's shuddering air. I don't know which is more unbearable — this image, or Mary's matter-of-fact tone.

The Manhattan I find outside my door is transformed. Or, perhaps, only stripped at last of a foolish veneer. I pick my way through the landscape that was rushing all along beneath the familiar one — every subway platform a ledge I could step over and be broken, every snow-dusted car a vehicle I might die beneath.

I am too practical.

At the rent-a-car bay I take off my boots, settle with dread into a gray sedan, spread the map on the passenger seat, and stiffly pilot my way north, the pedal a living thing beneath my socked foot.

I reach the hospital. Elizabeth looks smaller, like a child clinging to the enormous blue raft of the sofa. Her black eyes are lifeless. She says little to me and avoids direct contact.

"I'm so sorry," I whisper to Mary while Elizabeth is occupied with a nurse. "I wish I'd known earlier. I would have come."

Mary's look says it all: I'd made it abundantly clear I needed to focus on my tenure.

"She told me," Mary says after a moment, "that it was because she couldn't hear the voices. She said the world was too dark without them. She told the nurse she was a dazzled soul. Maybe you know what she meant by that?"

I close my eyes and sigh. "*A Grant of the Divine — That Certain as it comes — Withdraws — and leaves the dazzled Soul — In her unfurnished Rooms*. Emily Dickinson."

Mary purses her lips and nods.

"How long will she be here?" I ask.

"The doctors say there's no telling how long this time. I've rented my place in Chicago, and signed a month-by-month lease on an apartment just a few blocks from here. I've lined up some library work as well."

I study Mary's expression. She has just uprooted her entire life to undertake a long siege outside the gates of her daughter's mind. Yet again she's as straightforward as if it were a grade-school outing she'd been asked to chaperone.

The nurse finishes her conversation with Elizabeth and retreats.

"Did you get tenure?" Mary says, glancing at me.

I rub my neck. "No."

She's silent. "I'm sorry."

We listen to the nurse's hushed tread fade down the hall. Mary watches me gravely. Then something shifts in her face. "I didn't think," she says, "that you'd stick by my daughter."

"Then you underestimated me." The words are bitter.

"Yes," says Mary without rancor. "It's usually the right judgment."

"I can't figure you out," I blurt. "Don't you get angry?"

There is a long, serious silence. Mary's face flickers with the effort of memory. "Not anymore," she says. "I ran out of things to do with it."

We stand together, neither of us speaking. Then, after a moment, she smiles: a rueful, gentle welcome.

Before leaving I approach Elizabeth. She's retreated to a wicker rocking chair, where she sits motionless: legs blanket-draped, weightless as a moth. For just a moment she lifts her chin. The smile she offers me, small and lovely, is the greatest act of determination I have ever seen.

I will pick myself up, move on, carve a new life. But I let myself stop insisting she will.

I set my palm on her bony shoulder. The chair sways. She looks up once more. "It's okay," I say. "We just . . . trusted the world too much."

Very slowly, she nods.

Weeks pass. Classes begin. I prepare lectures with grim attention; watch undergraduates tramp slush into the auditorium; stand at the lectern and loft them silent warnings against the afflictions of a life in books. After they leave the floor is dark with grime. I avoid faculty meetings. Infrequently, I visit the faculty lounge. My colleagues, who it turns out were just about to leave, greet me with tight nods. Only Victoria lingers, asking after my work and prospects without mention of our last conversation — a denial I privately deride only to discover, as days pass barren of other conversation, that I welcome it.

The semester chugs along with its onslaught of midterm labor, but without the adrenaline that normally fuels the uphill jog into spring. I finish out my evenings marking student papers with my office door shut, in a froth over humankind's cowardice. My red-penned commentary has grown keener: I am generous with praise for originality, incisive at the slightest hint of intellectual slavishness. My lazier students grow increasingly anxious about grades. The best seem increasingly devoted, as though my sharpened bull-shit-detector has uncovered a craving more powerful than the desire for A's.

Late at night I e-mail everyone I've ever been on a conference panel with. I dig through files for addresses of colleagues who teach in Chicago. In Denver, in Iowa City, in Seattle. Santa Barbara, Los Angeles, Austin, Houston, Philadelphia, Pittsburgh, Ithaca, Syracuse, Toronto, Middlebury, New Haven, both Cambridges. New York City. This is the first round.

On a Friday morning in mid-March, Jeff flies in from Atlanta to tie up loose ends at his old apartment. He comes into the department in the afternoon to collect mail and turn in his key to Eileen. I meet him at his office, as planned; we'll get a drink before he heads to the airport.

His empty bookshelves rattle as he closes his door for the last time and flips the key into his palm. It's three-fifteen P.M. Grub and Paleozoic occupy the lounge; the pipe smoke seeps from under the door as we pass. At the spot where we'd normally cut past Eileen's desk toward the exit, Jeff flashes me his cat-ate-the-canary grin. Without explanation he leads me to the right, the long way to the elevator. In front of Paleozoic's closed office door, Jeff slows. "I gave him a farewell gift," he says.

Taped to the door are three index cards. They read, in black marker, from top to bottom:

I

AM

GAY

Lower on the door there is a smaller white card, with the single word LOOK and an arrow. The arrow points to a color photograph of Jeff and a sandy-haired, athletic-looking man, kissing.

We settle into a corner at the Switchboard Pub. Jeff orders gin and tonic, I sip a beer. Jeff is already mocking Atlanta — the accents, the attitudes, the fashion choices and undergraduate social rituals. He has nicknames for half a dozen new colleagues. He's happy, shedding his wry observations like sunshine. I've never seen Jeff happy before. His cracked smile is almost goofy. We leave the bar, exchange a powerful and brief hug and the economical goodbye of people who know they will be in touch. I am released into the raw late afternoon. Faintly woozy from the beer, but dreading a too early return home and an endless evening's fretting, I go back to the department, past Eileen's bright inquiring "There you are!" and to my office. For a long while I bow my forehead to my cool desktop.

I dial Yolanda, and begin speaking before she's had a chance to say a word.

"Yol, it's me. Can you take hearing about my shitty prospects again? About how this is the worst time of year to go on the market? I've got to sort out whether to try for adjunct positions, which you know is an idea I hate, but what if I don't find anything?"

There's a long silence. Then a deep, thrumming *Yes*.

Chad.

"God, I'm so sorry. I thought I was talking to —"

"Yes," he says. It's a reassurance. And an invitation.

"It's just . . ." I stop. Then hear myself continue. "I'm worried."

"Yes," he says.

I don't speak for several seconds. "I'm more than worried."

He hums his assent.

"I don't want everything I've done to be for nothing."

He breathes. And slowly, as the minutes pass, I begin to understand what Yolanda meant when she said she and Chad like to get on the phone and just listen to each other breathe. In the silence on the line there's some living presence, some palpable, substantial exchange. An inaudible conversation, like something turning deep under the water.

I sit back in my office chair and close my eyes. In Chad's company my anxiety slows. Drizzles. Settles.

When we get off the phone, I'm calmer.

I leave, locking my office for the night. I pass through the nearly deserted corridor, resisting the notion that the scattering of colleagues still at work have shut their office doors so they won't have to see me. I greet Eileen with a nod, aware that despite her faults she's one of the few people in this place with whom I have no bone to pick. Eileen, at least, rarely pretends to be other than she is. Dazedly I scan the departmental calendar with its highlighted meeting reminders, then pull my stack of mail from its cubbyhole. One envelope stands out, and I open it with my face half-averted, as though to protect myself from its slap. I read.

Dear Professor Farber,

We beg to inform you that you have been selected as a Fielding Fellow for the upcoming academic year. You receive this honor in the company of a small number of innovative scholars and artists around the country.

Please contact us at your earliest convenience to confirm your acceptance of the award and for further details.

Congratulations.

Sincerely,

Frederick Daley

Chairman, Fielding Foundation

I read the lines again, then fold the paper and stand still, licking my chapped lips.

A near hysterical giggle rouses me.

"Took you long enough to check today's mail," Eileen says. "This is the latest I've stayed in this office in fifteen years."

Obediently my eyes find the clock: five-forty P.M.

"But I decided you should find the letter on your own. Without my hinting."

She waits for thanks.

"The fellowship . . ." I begin. I hold up the envelope.

". . . is *fantastic,*" Eileen sings. "Great for your résumé. But, even better, it bails you out, doesn't it? It lets you sit out your mess for a year, doesn't it? And do your work that you do. This changes everything, doesn't it?"

When I don't respond, Eileen answers for me. "It changes everything. Well, I'm glad I played a teeny little part in making it happen." Her lip-gloss-bright smile broadens in a way that says she's got a story to tell; but this time beneath the usual avarice for credit there's genuine pride. "They called two months ago," Eileen says. "They'd narrowed it down to finalists, and they needed references for the final cut. They wanted a letter from him, of course." She nods toward Grub's shuttered office. "You'd listed him on your application. I passed him the message. The letter he wrote was" — she gives me a significant look — "less than his usual."

Still numb, I count weeks. This would have been just after my tenure was denied.

"It didn't have *zing,*" Eileen says.

I picture, for a moment, a private sun-filled office. Shelves full of files. Time to write without teaching responsibilities. Time supported by a Fielding Foundation that believes what I'm trying to say matters.

"It was the kind of recommendation letter that would make you lose to another one of those finalists. Not that he said anything direct. Just those little hints he uses to say what he means. No wonder his wife died of throat cancer."

I look up. "When did she —"

"Oh, years ago." Eileen waves airily. "Also, I wasn't sure he understood your new project. In all its *significance.*"

This last comment sounds so little like Eileen that I finally give what she's been angling for: my full attention.

"So I wrote a new letter." She inspects her polished nails. "He doesn't even know what he signs."

"You —"

"Want to see?" Brightly she opens a folder on her desk, shuffles pages, and hands me a sheet of paper.

To the Fielding Committee,

Professor Tracy Farber is the most estimable scholar to grace this department in the memory of this scholarly assembly. She successfully interrogates the catechistic corners of the literary canon, positing theoretical slippages of meaning and loosing the moorings of the prosody tradition with groundbreaking paradigmatic idiom.

Eileen meets my gaze with a defensive smirk. "Don't you think I know how you people talk?"

She is a paragon of pedagogical prowess. She is also an autodidact, having grown up on a farm.

"A farm?"
"You grew up out west, didn't you?"
"In Seattle."
"See?" Eileen nods ferociously. "Local color."

Catch this rising literary star while you can. Her voice is critical to the critical cantabile.

To call her work a radical departure doesn't do it justice.
Sincerely,
James Manning
Chairman

I set the page gently on her desktop.

Eileen waits — for once, with patience — for me to speak. She wears the astonished half smile of someone who has, to her own surprise, proven herself.

"I'm stunned."

"It figures," Eileen says. Then, before I understand what she's doing, she stands, leans across her desk, and plants a lipsticky kiss on my cheek. "Now go do something good."

Along the Hudson, cars whizzing by, I blink into the gusts. I veer east, walk up Broadway, turn west and north in an ever expanding circuit. Manhattan sheds yet another disguise, revealing itself to be a medieval labyrinth: its streets full of mendicants, penitents, and the dazed and footsore newly blessed. To walk is to meditate. I change direction to pay tribute to the museums, monuments to long-past eras and cultures that I haven't visited in months because I've been saturating my senses with books. The museums invite me to march up their broad steps and take possession. I raise my head and laugh aloud. Then, crying, divert course to a favorite park, which I circle humming a tuneless and quizzical riff. It's well past dark before I've completed a long enough circuit to befriend my ballooning thoughts, hear them out, and corral them sufficiently to carry them home to my narrow apartment.

Sitting on the stoop of my building, a monument to an era and culture long past, is George.

PART IV

CAREFULLY HE SETS a paper coffee cup on the concrete. He stands.

And I think: George.

He's different from the George of my imagination. He's taller. Handsomer than I'd remembered. And dangerous. Though I've imagined his return endlessly, I always saw it in sweeping, sensuous generalities. Not like this. Not with George so serious he looks as if he can hardly stand. Not with me wrapping my arms protectively around my chest.

Neither of us speaks.

A stern-faced police officer passes on foot, eyeing us: two more potential miscreants on his beat. He strolls to the end of the block and disappears.

"When you called Paula's house," he says, "I didn't come to the phone." His voice is low, emphatic. His expression seeks nothing from me other than that I listen. "Because I couldn't. I couldn't speak one word to you."

I set down my briefcase.

His voice, his face, his generous mouth. His hands, loose at his sides.

He speaks slowly, as though it is imperative that I understand the meaning of each word. "I let myself be bewildered in that house." He's silent for a moment. "I said to Paula: I made a new life, but it didn't hold the weight I rested on it."

We look at each other. A breeze picks up, but we don't move.

George says, "I let Paula tell me how to dress for the weather. I let my father tell me what work needed doing around his house. Which relatives to call to give updates on his health. Every call I made, Tracy, was penitence. An apology for the life I'd tried to live." The wind flops his hair across his forehead. He doesn't brush it away.

"My father tried, with me," he says. "His health shocked him into trying."

His hands rise as though to explain something to me; then drop. And I see it as I never saw it before: his solitude.

He says, "All I could think was: I lost my delight."

"I know," I say. "George, I—"

"With you I had this *dream*. That everything could be the way it was supposed to be. Then you threw it in my face. And after that, it was just . . . I could hardly . . ." He stops. His face is empty. "One morning, when my father was back on his feet and Paula and I were sitting in the kitchen, she said to me, 'Why would any woman give back a ring?'

"And I answered her, without thinking I just said, 'It's because she wants me to finish tearing myself in half.'"

He watches me.

"My mother used to like the hymn 'Abide with Me.' I never believed it, never believed Jesus offered that kind of"—in his voice the word has dignity and heft—"*guaranteed* love." A few cars float past; George is an island. "But I believed it," he adds quietly, "of her." He stands motionless, as though allowing the vision to take form, then dissipate. I watch it go. "It wasn't enough to give up that dream once," he says. "You made me do it all over again." Slowly he wags his head. "Tracy." The syllables of my name carry crushing freight. His expression falters. "I'm here because the truth is more important than whether I can stand the ache. And you were telling the truth about me."

He stops, drained. Then he looks directly at me. "The world has its rules," he says. It's a statement of grief.

I set my hand lightly on his chest. Under my fingertips his heartbeat declares itself. At its steady, quiet message, humility suffuses me so thoroughly I can hold his gaze only with difficulty. I had only love to lose—no more, no less. He risked everything.

"George," I say. Something breaks the surface of my voice.

I was wrong on that first date with George: Love isn't rest. Love requires you, from time to time, to rip up your soul and replant it. To dare your lover to do the same. To muster sympathy where it seemed impossible. To be, perpetually, two kids joining hands, drawing breath, and deep-diving.

I can't foresee what hurdles or negotiations might lie ahead. All I know is this: love takes faith. And there it is — the first faith my mind hasn't been able to wrestle to the ground. It's a faith at which I'm only a beginner. But I'm willing to labor, imperfections and all, for its sake. I think: let love be my religion, its intricacies, its euphorias, its trials. I think: I want to learn from this man for the rest of my life.

I take a solitary moment to feel it: the silent, improbable blooming of awe. Then I give the answer that's mine to give.

"That doesn't mean," I say, "that we have to live by them."

He nods the brief, pained nod of a survivor.

The street is still. The police officer makes his way back toward us, stick swinging. I watch him, momentarily paralyzed by the notion that he might charge at us. Then I find my key and unlock the door to my building, only daring to look up into George's face when I've heard the door latch safely behind us.

The dark sets us loose, the hulking sofa and woolly carpet exert gravity. A blue spark from my fingertip anoints his shoulder as we shed a thick rope of clothing and emerge: The rope of our two bodies. What I've starved for.

Every angel, according to kabbalist literary tradition, has a single purpose. There is an angel to foretell each war, an angel to foretell each birth. There is one angel to open heaven's windows, another to shut them. George and I reunite as simply as though we had no other purpose in life than to teach each other this: this touch.

Don't think it's easy. We stumble, clash, retreat. Laughter resurfaces slowly. Anger surges and has to be pried loose. Love may be my religion, but I am (he was right) irretrievably Jewish. And skepticism is part of the believer's duty.

We meet at the reception hall. It's deserted. With another thank-you to the blank-faced custodian, George leads me to a spot near the center of the room. "Here," he says, tracing an invisible circle on the beige carpet. "Ground zero." He opens the bottle of wine. We sit.

At the Italian restaurant I draw faces on the steamed windows and refuse to utter so much as a monosyllable about my work. "Okay," I say at last. "Here's the question that's been burning in me for four months. If we're all doing the wave in the stadium, who are we cheering on?"

We see Yolanda in *Downhearted Revue,* in which she's been cast (by an admirer of her H.D.) as the aging, ruined proprietress of a failing cabaret. The play is passable, Yolanda's performance unconvincing because she looks too damn happy. We walk Yolanda to the subway, paying our compliments. ("You were radiant," George tells her.) Later, in my kitchen, George falls silent, then laughs until he has to set down his ice cream spoon. "You know I respect you, Tracy. But can you please explain to me again why you insist that other play wasn't as bad as we thought?"

A weeknight; both of us with morning meetings; who cares. Near midnight we smother the clock under a pillow. We face each other on his sofa, beers in hand. "Don't stop to think," he says. "Tell me," he says, "about the worst anybody ever broke your heart."

The work of repair is not interesting. It's hours when you expected to be finishing the roof tiles but you're stuck laying foundation — miles of it. There is, of course, a CIA directive against discussing this part. Love — this is what they don't want you to know — isn't for the faint of heart; it requires modern skepticism as well as an anachronistic gameness for hard labor. The film industry, being in cahoots with the CIA, collaborates by fading to sunset as soon as the heroes are horizontal. Hollywood shows sex because it's easier than showing love. Love — real love — is not cinematic. The entire film industry runs shrieking from the part where George convinces me in a lengthy kitchenette soliloquy that he knew enough about me to propose. Where I realize this is a man who truly prizes honesty; who won't let either of us get away with what he thinks is bullshit; a man with whom I can't, so long as I speak my mind, get lost. It's the stuff no one talks about: How trust grows rootlets. How two people who start as lovers become custodians of each other's well-being.

At the hospital George settles opposite Mary and addresses her as though he sees, immediately, what it took me months to see: that her seemingly static vigil over her daughter — the silent, shock-absorbing acceptance that so ticked me off — was never apathy, but strength. And a form of maternal love I'd never seen. As Mary talks about Elizabeth's condition, George reaches for Mary's hand. Mary lets out a surprised huff but doesn't pull away. Half an hour later she's cackling as she tells him an anecdote from Elizabeth's childhood.

Never, in all those months, did it occur to me to hold Mary's hand.

We walk Central Park, the new grass a lovely pale green in the cordoned-off fields. Children funnel down the paths toward the carousel, trailed by stunned-looking parents. Neither of us speaks until we reach Sheep Meadow. "Okay," George says. "I get the part about timing. I see that I pushed. But what was the problem with the whole world getting in your face about engagement? I mean, isn't that supposed to be part of the fun? When everybody gets excited for you?"

"People congratulating me," I say, "would have been fine. But not when I knew you and I weren't working. That was unbearable. And, George, you don't know what the wedding buzz is like for women. People all but yelling at you to drown your worries in floral arrangements. Wedding vendors vending kitsch as if it has a thing to do with love. Bridal magazines blaring: *Weddings are romantic. Roses are romantic.*"

As George listens, a corner of his mouth twitches, and I see he's about to laugh at my distress. I finish, an extra edge in my mimicry: "*Moons are romantic.*"

With a settled expression he reaches for his belt buckle, turns around, and, in the middle of a trafficked path, in the center of Central Park, moons me.

The smell of simmering onions warms Yolanda's apartment. In the living room she addresses me in a hurried whisper. "Would you believe it?" she says. "He's an electrician. Or maybe an electrical engineer. One or the other."

I set the coffee table with plasticware. "I'd believe anything. I've decided he's one of the smartest people I've ever met."

"He fixed my oven this afternoon, just took it apart and rewired it. Then he made this little diagram of what he'd done for me, and he looked up the words in the dictionary, and explained he'd been at school a long time studying it." Yolanda's glowing. "He has a six-year-old boy back home, and an ex-girlfriend who broke his heart — until he met me. He showed me his son's picture. He says he'll introduce us one day, maybe we can visit him."

From the kitchen George laughs aloud; through the door I see him pass a beer to Chad. George says something in a broad, Canadian French, which prompts a roar of laughter from Chad — then a long, mellower-accented, bemused-sounding reply. They clink bottles.

"*Santé,*" says Chad.

"*Santé,*" George replies.

Yolanda is still whispering. "Chad says — he looked the word up and he swears this really is what he means — he says I'm *vivid*. And he loves it. But he thinks I work too hard at being vivid. He thinks I need to *float*."

Yolanda looks so sated I think she's going to pass out.

"He's perfect." She shakes her head, trying to disbelieve herself and failing. "Okay, he does have this one thing he does. I guess it's a cultural thing. He comes to my yoga class, and during silent meditation he sings. Loud. It's kind of beautiful, I think. But some of the other students complained that it interfered with their solitude. So the instructor — who I guess tried saying something to Chad, but she was probably so polite and Buddhist about it that the message got lost — just left me a voicemail telling me, in a polite Buddhist way, that we've been kicked out. I haven't told him. I just said I'd outgrown the class and we're going to a new studio."

"Don't you need to say something, in case he gets the same reaction in the new class?"

She shakes her head firmly. "No way. I made a promise to myself. I promised I'll never tell him. I'll make myself live with the embarrassment. This is a big city. There are plenty of yoga studios." Beneath the light of the side-table lamp she splays the fingers of one hand, examining her manicure. "It's good to be reminded there are things about each other we have to just accept. Isn't it?"

• • •

I move into his place and sublet mine. There is no talk of weddings. We're too busy learning how to argue.

I flex my fingers once more at George's head. "I'm changing your mind," I say, "using magic brain waves."

He lowers his magazine. "I still think the sofa looks better on this side."

"Maybe I willed you to say those exact words just now."

Dropping the magazine, he springs out of his seat, hoists me on one shoulder, and lands us on the sofa. "Try it my way," he whispers, as I stretch beneath him, lacing my fingers into his.

I shut myself in the bathroom and cry. George thinks it's self-indulgent that I'd rather eat takeout or canned soup seven days a week than give up work time in order to trade off cooking dinner with him. But how can it be self-indulgent if I'm willing to eat cardboard pizza slices so as to have one hand free to hold a pen? If I'm not asking him to cook for me, either? I'm certain Shakespeare's depressed stifled sister cooked gourmet meals every night. Me, I've read Virginia Woolf. I harbor murderous intentions toward the angel of the house.

Between the claustrophobic bathroom walls, cracked tiles swimming before me, I wipe tears and turn on the shower. As I shampoo I continue the quarrel under my breath. Winning. And shut off the water with the unsteady hope that George will be waiting for me in our bedroom; that he will not have closed himself off from me with a change of subject, a faraway expression; that he will feel it, too: that happiness can be built up, brick by brick, out of argument.

Which is — I confess it to myself in the steamed bathroom — the most Jewish idea in the history of Jewish ideas.

I wrap myself in a towel (in our bedroom he stares at the ceiling, meditating his way to a compromise) and I take a moment (he inhales steam from my shower, sighs) to let my breathing settle. With my finger I write it on the mirror: *Love [sic]*.

The labor of becoming a couple is bewildering. But this time I choose it. And I discover this advantage to commitment: arguments get solved. You can storm out onto the fire escape if you like. But it's a long shaky climb down, and an awkward drop to the sidewalk. And then what? Where will you sleep? At a certain point you begin to feel ridiculous out there. At a certain point you

lower your head, climb back in through the window, and negotiate.

"You hardly ever let go, do you?" he says, turning to me as the
cab bounces down the avenue. "You wear your mind like armor.
Like you're afraid if you're unintellectual for too long, you might
actually enjoy yourself." And before I can respond he's calling to
the driver for a change of destination.

"I thought we were going home."

Wrapping his arms around me, George murmurs in my ear.
"We're going to a karaoke bar. I'm not letting you back into the
apartment until you've made an ass out of yourself in front of
strangers."

And, two beers later, I do.

Before I met this man I was perfect: I had no faults I was aware
of. Now all I can do is absorb the pleasures and stings that come
with being known. And conduct myself with humble, patient ob-
stinacy — knowing that while a woman's independence may be a
hothouse flower, I am not. I will survive the jousting. So we stake
out positions, compromise, draw and redraw lines. I trust George.
But I don't trust the world. And I can't forget the first thing I
learned from the month I wore an engagement ring: if you're not
careful, it represents engagement not only with the man you love,
but with the world — with its propriety obsessions, its taboos, its
hysterias. A step not to be taken lightly.

But then there's the second thing I learned: that that ring repre-
sented an extraordinary invitation — to stop watching the mess of
human desire from the shoreline.

"Halt!" shout the feminist police. The squadron crests the hill
and stops, horses chafing. "Do you have a permit for that compromise?"

"It's just a small concession," I explain, "about how often I
cook dinner."

"No woman should ever feel obligated to be domestic," calls
the lead officer, her cheeks glowing from the wind. "Just say no."
She wheels her horse and, bright standard fluttering, squadron following, gallops off.

Feminism taught me how to critique the world, but not how
to live in it. *Relationships are sacrifice,* my aunt Rona mentions

casually at the end of a phone conversation; and I set down the receiver and glare at my office bookcase, outraged: no one in years of women's studies colloquia ever mentioned this. You cannot mention feminism and voluntary personal sacrifice in the same sentence. It's against the law. Feminism has been too busy rebounding from millennia of oppression and establishing our right to be all we can be to acknowledge that every human being — every human being who wants to live in relationship to others — gives up some portion of her wide-open vista.

Which may not be feminism's fault. But it's time to update the model.

On lunch break at the American Women Writers' symposium I overhear two senior English majors discussing Frances Newman. "She was amazing," says one of them, dipping a piece of celery into creamy dressing. "Did you know that she never gave herself to anyone? She just lived for herself — for her writing. She made a feminist choice."

Reaching for the vegetable platter, I chide the two gently. "There's no such thing as a *feminist choice*," I say. "That's redundant. Feminism *means* having a choice. And feminism doesn't care which choices you make, either. Just that you have them. The point has never been to establish some principled refusal to give yourself to another human being. The point is to make sure you can give yourself — or *not* give yourself — of your free will." The two listen warily, their faces set in that impassive expression students use to rebuff overenthusiastic professors. "Feminism has nothing against relationships," I persist, "even those with actual men." I dunk a slice of pepper into the dressing. "We get to talk about love too, you know."

One of the students looks indignant. The other relieved.

Weeks pass. Two walls have dropped from between us: pride and justice. It no longer matters who was right. The Hippocratic oath has no place here — *do no harm* is the wrong standard for love. Everyone does harm. Now George and I have new problems to face together. George's search for a well-paying, conscience-satisfying job. Elizabeth's troubled progress. George's father's continuing uneven health. My own parents' awkwardness as they re-

318 ～ Rachel Kadish

embrace George: awkwardness fueled, I understand, by their love for their only child—a love I know is real, though inaccessible to me.

"Don't take the SchoolNet job if it's not right," I say to George as I pull a Mrs. Hale's Presto Chicken Pie out of the oven. "I can swing us for a few months. Find the job you want."

"How will I pay you back?"

I shut the oven. "We'll put it on our thirty-year to-do list. Let's make a thirty-year to-do list."

George nods. Then he nods again. He leaves the kitchen for a moment, then returns. He stands opposite me. "We'll work through our differences," he says. "But while we're working through them—because I expect that may take thirty years, or fifty, if we're lucky—will you?"

The ring glimmers from his palm. I slip it onto my finger.

"I always loved this ring," I say.

George folds my hand in both of his. His voice is deliberate; his eyes are a bright brown, and wonderfully still. "Please," he enunciates. "This time, keep it on."

Slowly I nod. We look, together, at the ring on my finger. It's the sign of a beginning.

As is the courthouse wedding we plan. Thirty guests. Dinner at our favorite Italian restaurant. Tulips. George will convert because it's important to him. We'll go to synagogue for holidays, listen to the sermons, hash them over at home. The prospect of marriage, to my surprise, has transformed while my back was turned. It's no longer a threat. Marriage is a tool for our protection. An arrangement designed for the express purpose of making sure we hang in there while doing the necessary work. And this time it's for the two of us—nobody else. No gifts, thank you kindly.

"The important thing," says the hawk-eyed matron pairing socks at the Laundromat, "isn't whether two people can find each other. That's hormones, and the thrill of the unknown. Got nothing to do with nothing. The important thing is whether, after you lose each other, which you *will*"—she shakes a menacing finger—"you can find each other again."

I set my hands on her shoulders and look straight into her piercing eyes. "Thank you," I say.

• • •

My last lecture concludes with an overview of contemporary literary trends and a meditation on their influences on journalism, Hollywood, Hallmark cards, and the White House's PR machinery. When I've finished, there is a surge of applause. I don't take it to heart. I haven't yet issued final grades, and there are several students in the hall who wouldn't be past hoping such an expression of good will might be reciprocated. I organize my papers at the podium, wave curt thanks to the students, and wait for the hall to empty. The applause goes on, long enough to make me uncomfortable. I look at my hands, at the clock, and finally back up at the clapping students. I imagine their life goals flittering in the air like newly hatched moths.

I pack my office, rejecting the temptation to wait until evening to haul the book boxes to the elevator. I've got nothing to be ashamed of. I work with the windows open, admitting a spring breeze that makes everything — even the stale departmental air — smell newly woken.

Eileen has settled on the edge of her desk to survey my progress. She nods approvingly each time I huff past her with a large book box. "I've seen them come and go here, love," she says. "And now, now you're leaving."

I carry my box toward the elevator.

With a wicked lilt, Eileen continues. "And some people don't deserve to have their secrets kept anyway."

I kneel stiffly, tipping the box onto my thigh and from there onto the carpet beside two identical boxes. When George arrives at six we'll load his car. Together we'll bear my academic life along trafficked side streets to my new office: a bright airy Hudson Street room with a view of brownstone rooftops. "I don't think I want to know," I tell Eileen. "No offense."

"As if I believe that. Now" — she glances exaggeratedly around to confirm that we're alone in the reception area — "why do you think Steven took a year off from Oxford to come here?"

I have no patience for riddles of a faculty that's ejected me. But before I can turn away I know the answer.

"He and Joanne met at the MLA conference two years ago," says Eileen. She giggles. "He said her passion *rocked his world.* Can you imagine it? I guess some people think arrogance is attractive."

Brushing away the distaste that's since overlaid the image, I recall Joanne at her lectern in the shadowy light shedding from the screen. The soaring vaults of an anonymous sixteenth-century architect behind her. The ocean of uncertain faces before. In a ringing voice she revealed it to them: earth and firmament, error and luster. Vanity, death, mighty love. She was, in her conviction, stunning. As Steven doubtless saw. Their meeting must have felt like gravity.

Eileen stage-whispers from the edge of her desk. "After a year of visits they decided to try living on the same side of the ocean. They made the plan last March, but by summer they were through — just before her diagnosis." Eileen shakes her head with an expression that falls short of sorrowful. "Steven decided to stick it out here and be civil, and help Joanne if he could. Of course she didn't let him — she barely spoke to him all year, even though he went to all those horrible meetings for her. Wounded pride. God knows why she never cut the cord and took him off her little faculty-meeting e-mail list. The sicker she got the nastier things got. I don't know which one hates the other more now."

Looking back, it's so obvious I'm shocked: how Steven's participation in faculty meetings evolved from steady conspiratorial support of Joanne in September, to thin-lipped demurral by Thanksgiving, to pitched battle by December. As Steven's solicitous encouragements replay in my head, I see the dozen ways he used my tenure candidacy as grist, provoking Joanne in a language no one else understood.

"She's a horrid person, Joanne," Eileen says brightly.

"Who knew about this?" I ask.

"Not a one of you," Eileen pronounces, the enormity of her burden stilling her. It's a moment before she nods herself back to duty. "Except Victoria. And *him*." She points toward Grub's office. "When Steven interviewed. And we can all be sure *he* forgot the minute Steven told him." Eileen crosses her arms against her bosom.

I used to think love was an extra — a spice that made life more fulfilling for some. It occurs to me now that it's dangerous, that who has it and who loses it decides the course of the world.

I know better than to believe Eileen kept a departmental romance to herself all year. Probably she learned of it only now, from a departing Steven, who left this week for England. Probably he debriefed Eileen, after his year's forbearance, in a burst of bitterness.

Or perhaps Joanne spilled the beans herself. I realize I don't care. I can set Steven and Joanne's tale down beside so many others, turn my back, and walk out of this building.

I am in my office, girding to lift the last box of books, when Joanne appears in my doorway. Scanning my emptied shelves, she speaks with studied neutrality. "Packing?"

Let Joanne flaunt triumph. My eyes belong on a bigger prize. I work the tape over the box's top flaps.

Joanne watches in silence. When I'm finished she says, "Let me." Brushing past me, she kneels and, with a slight stagger, lifts the solidly packed box. "Where to?" she breathes. There's something plaintive about her expression. Yes, she's showboating, but her gloating can't harm me any further, and she knows it. Rather she needs to prove something, to me and to herself: that she can stare down illness.

I let her hold the box for a moment. Her arms tremble noticeably.

"There," I say in a low voice. I point to the desktop not two feet from where she's standing. She sets the box there with an expression of regret.

"All's fair?" She extends her broad hand.

As she waits, her hand wavering slightly, her pale brown eyes telegraph an urgent request. It's a request not for forgiveness but for something more: confirmation that I can see in her a colleague I recognize; that my seductive, magnanimous adversary is still alive; that Joanne Miller is something other than what illness has made her.

She never intended to be this way. No one does. That's the definition of tragedy.

I hoist the box. "*Did not we meet,*" I say, "*to Truthe enthrall'd, our Soules enlarg'd in this Hallow'd Hall.*"

Her hand is still extended. I leave her in the emptied office.

In the faculty lounge I find Paleozoic withdrawing his saucer from the cabinet. Three o'clock. He acknowledges my presence with a world-weary smile, then fills his infuser with tea leaves and lowers it delicately into his steaming cup. In his gray V-neck and slacks, white-dotted navy socks and bedroom slippers, he bends carefully over a side table, where he sets his tea to brew.

I find my mug in the cabinet and wedge it into my briefcase. From behind me comes the rasp of a match, then a surge of blue pipe smoke. The sofa's springs creak, taking Paleozoic's weight. He lets out a contented gasp.

"Something you ought to know, Tracy." He waits for me to turn. His lined face is furrowed with the delicate work of breaking difficult news. "It's come to my attention that Jeffrey Thomas was, all this time, a closet homosexual."

The smoke thickens the air. If there is any activity in the department outside this room, its sound does not penetrate.

"Really?" I say.

Paleozoic replies with a grave nod. Slowly the small, Churchillian smile reasserts itself. "Our friend hid it well," he says. "Anyone might have been fooled. But at the end of the day, secrets will out." He sucks on his pipe.

"How did you know?" I say.

"Ah." He lets the syllable trail off in a ripe puff of smoke: it may take some time, but a man of discernment can tell.

"Aha," says Grub from the doorway.

I glance at the clock: 3:05 P.M.

"Aha indeed," rumbles Paleozoic.

Noticing me, Grub gives a vague, apologetic wave. "Beautiful afternoon, isn't it?" He doesn't wait for a response but crosses to the cabinet, whence he withdraws a saucer and cup along with a small French press. From the freezer he extracts a bag of his own coffee — no bitter departmental brew for the chairman. He mixes coffee and hot water noisily, then, leaving the used spoon on the counter, settles on the armchair, one palm hovering atop the French press.

Searching the cabinet for traces of my career in this room, I find few. My sugar packets I bequeath to the department. My honey bear I reclaim, unwilling to leave its pudgy belly to my former colleagues' grasping hands. The petty logic of the rejected. I turn to find Paleozoic scrutinizing me from the sofa.

"You know, Tracy." Paleozoic pulls on his pipe: a small wet sound like a feeding fish. Slowly he exhales. "You can't always get what you want." He fishes a small metal object from his pocket; tamps his pipe gently; examines the tamper minutely, replaces it in his pocket. "But, if you try sometimes, you just might find . . ." He trails off. A few seconds pass; he begins to look alarmed.

"You just might find . . . ?" prompts Grub, slowly pushing the plunger on his coffee.

Paleozoic bobs his eyebrows in thanks, then finishes his advice with an ash-scattering flourish. "You get what you *need*." Sucking on his pipe once more, Paleozoic turns to his longtime colleague and, with an expression of gratitude, claps him on the back.

This is what the state of New York provides to a couple upon issuing a marriage license.

> Newlywed Kit.
> Distributed by First Moments.
> Congratulations on your upcoming nuptials.
> The valuable coupons, samples and literature contained in this package have been carefully selected to help give you both a great start.
> Contents:
> - Coupons for Proactiv® Acne Solution
> - Secret® Sheer Dry Gel Solid antiperspirant deodorant.
>   Goes on Clear
> - Oil of Olay®—lipstick and moisturizer samples
> - 1 roll Bounty® paper towels
> - 1 free sample Mr. Clean®
> - 1 free sample Tide® with bleach alternative
> - 2 free samples Bounce® (It doesn't.)
> - 1 small roll Charmin® Ultra

I am not making this up.

We visit. Elizabeth, wan but alert, greets us with a lovely, heart-turning smile. The doctors believe she will soon be ready for a limited resumption of her work. Mary isn't taking chances. Elizabeth's dream has always been a life in academia; Mary is selling her home back in Evanston and will stay with her daughter until she finishes her dissertation.

In the noisy restaurant where we take her for dinner, Mary watches a family seated nearby: a toddler girl and two older boys, parents issuing orders across a crumb-strewn table. Midway through the meal the younger boy cries, is comforted, and clambers onto his father's lap, from which safe perch he will eat the remainder of his dinner. Mary's face is inscrutable as she watches. When the family has gone she says, "You turn your life upside down for the people you love." She folds her napkin and sets it on the table. "It's what love is for."

It's late when we drop her back at the hospital. She thanks us once more for dinner and stands in the poorly lit parking lot until our car rounds the corner. I imagine she remains there: a compact woman in a jean jacket, colossus of endurance. Watching our rented car's progress down the long slope toward the highway. Then she turns and steps back to the ward where her daughter, with the humility of a child, awaits permission to read and write once more.

We zoom down I-87. This stretch of highway has no lamps, and the red taillights of the sweeping traffic are a pageant of human focus: the couples and the families, the late-evening commuters, the long-haul truckers. Driver after driver flaunts his immunity to the speed limit and the laws of physics. George's foot plies the accelerator, mine taps a phantom brake. A fleet of motorcyclists on bikes half the girth of our car weave dangerously between lanes. Swooping around us at an impossible angle, a biker somehow straightens from a dip that — as it plays on in my mind — flips him onto the pavement, snaps him, sends us spinning. I hardly catch my breath before another roars past in similar style.

People courting death left and right. George drives with one hand on the steering wheel. His face is lit faintly by the dashboard. The resilience of his skin, the expanding width of his shoulders as he draws breath, the flushed warmth just beneath his collar: all are palpable to me from this distance.

There's not much point in trying. No description in a book or movie or song has ever come close to what it is to be in the presence of the man I love. Lying next to George at night; coming across him unexpectedly as I unlock the door to our apartment; sitting beside him as we drive the reckless highway; he is breath and heat and welcome; he is the steady thread of a pulse, a path laid out to the horizon, the part of life that says *forward*. No one has ever made me as loving, angry, sexy, forgiving. I've lost my map, and navigate by feel. We settle into each other with a warmth so perfect I can mention it only with awe.

I rest my palm on his thigh. Without taking his eyes off the road, he lifts it to his chest and holds it there.

People misunderstand happiness. They think it's the absence of trouble. That's not happiness, that's luck. Happiness is the ability to live well alongside trouble. No two people have the same trouble, or the same way of metabolizing it. Q.E.D.: No two happy people are happy in the same way. Even Tolstoy was afraid to admit this, and I don't blame him. Every day brilliant people, people smarter than I, wallow in safe tragedy and pessimism, shying from what really takes guts: recognizing how much courage and labor happiness demands.

George and I hurtle down the highway, having breached that boundary where logic evaporates and all that remains is a single instinct, that love is simply this — this monumental and elementary thing: the willingness to be changed by someone.

A driver invisible to me unrolls a car window and, from the dark interior, taps a cigarette on the sill. A shower of tiny red lights bounce and split on the road, skidding in the rush of wind and dark wheels, then extinguish without a sound.

The short happy life of a spark. Leaning heavily against the back of my seat, I will myself to stop scanning the traffic for potential accidents. *If our car crashes,* I say to myself. *If our car crashes and I am snuffed out,* let me be unprepared. Let me have failed to anticipate it. Let me go through life the way we are, after all is said and done, meant to: shocked.

For Discussion

1. Tracy Farber is a young, educated, professional single woman living in a big city. How is she similar to and different from other heroines in contemporary literature?

2. Tracy's ex-boyfriend describes her as "the world's most unlikely romantic" (p. 9). What does he mean by that? How is this description apt? In what way does George challenge Tracy's outlook on romance?

3. Tracy states, "For people who claim to want happiness, we Americans spend a lot of time spinning yarns about its opposite" (p. 4). Do you agree that American literature has a fixation on doom and gloom? What lies behind this cultural mixed message? Do you agree with Tracy — does the happiness that we have an inalienable right to pursue deserve our serious consideration as well?

4. On her first date with George, Tracy explains the many reasons for her deep love of literature (p. 42). Do you agree or disagree with her list of the attractions of literature? What motivates you to read? Would you add any reasons of your own to the list of literary pleasures?

5. Tracy goes on to describe her choice of twentieth century interwar literature — Zora Neale Hurston, Ernest Hemingway, William Faulkner — as her specialty, after very nearly succumbing to the seductions of Herman Melville and his contemporaries in nineteenth-century American literature. What does her choice say about her as a person? When Jeff says to Tracy, "There's something very nineteenth-century about you," what does he mean by this? In general, how do your own reading choices reflect your personality?

6. How does Tracy's vacillation between the romantic and modern/post-modern literary periods parallel her shifting thoughts on love?

Tracy later reflects on the difference between nineteenth- and twentieth-century views of love (p. 280). Which view do you think is healthier?

7. In the course of dating George, Tracy solicits advice from friends and relatives — Hannah, Adam, Yolanda, Jeff, her cousin Gabby, Aunt Rona — each of whom offers different counsel. How do each person's own romantic views color how he or she reads Tracy's situation? What would your advice to Tracy have been?

8. Kadish threads a great deal of humor throughout the novel. Which incidents and observations did you find most entertaining?

9. Aunt Rona and Tracy's mother, in encouraging an otherwise perfectly content Tracy to find a husband, subscribe to a very limited definition of happiness. How do their opinions on love and marriage reflect larger societal trends? Is Tracy's reaction to the pressure typical of professional women of her generation?

10. As it turns out, George, too, has a very narrowly defined idea of what constitutes happiness. How does his revelation of his future plans affect his relationship with Tracy? Do you think Tracy is justified in responding the way that she does?

11. George and Tracy come from different cultural backgrounds — George still grapples with the fundamentalist Christian upbringing he's left behind, while Tracy comes from a Jewish family. In what ways are their situations more alike than it would appear on the surface? How do their religious differences play into the relationship?

12. Consider some of the other couples in the novel — Jeff and Richard, Hannah and Ed, Yolanda and Chad. How do Tracy's observations of these very different relationships influence her thinking about her relationship with George? What does each of these couples offer as evidence for Tracy's larger theory of happiness?

13. How does the literary correspondence between Nathaniel Hawthorne and Herman Melville factor into the intradepartmental tension among the English faculty? What ironies are inherent in the episode involving the letter? What comment does it make about the relevance of literature?

14. Tracy speculates at various points in the novel that Joanne might be jealous of her, jealous of love, jealous of life. What, in your opinion, is the truest source of Joanne's animosity? Do you think her actions are justified?

15. Tracy's professional life is marked by conflict and betrayal, yet she tries to stay above the political fray whenever possible. What are some examples of actions that could have damaged her career? Do you think she made the right decision in helping Elizabeth?

16. Who, in your opinion, is ultimately correct about happiness — Tolstoy or Tracy Farber? How does the novel *Tolstoy Lied* itself support Tracy's claim that the opening line from *Anna Karenina* is misguided?

For information about other Mariner Reader's Guides, please visit our website, www.marinerreadersguides.com.

From a Sealed Room

"A gifted writer, astonishingly adept at nuance, narration, and the politics of passion."
—**Toni Morrison**

"I hope it reaches many homes and many hearts."
—**Elie Wiesel**

I N HER POIGNANT and perceptive debut novel, Rachel Kadish reflects on the ghosts of the past, the difficult bonds of family, and the tensions of war. *From a Sealed Room* entwines the lives of three women—an adventurous young New Yorker, an Israeli housewife, and a fragile Holocaust survivor—in a tale that moves between New York and Jerusalem. The *New York Times Book Review* lauded this novel as "an intense, ambitious story that explores the chasms between truth and falsehood, past and present."

ISBN 978-0-618-56241-1

Visit our website: www.marinerbooks.com